THE BUILDING

Richard Snodgrass

Book One of the Furnass Towers Trilogy

Calling Crow Press

Pittsburgh

Also by Richard Snodgrass

There's Something in the Back Yard

An Uncommon Field: The Flight 93
Temporary Memorial

Kitchen Things: An Album of Vintage Utensils
and Farm-Kitchen Recipes

Published by Calling Crow Press
Pittsburgh, Pennsylvania

Book design by Book Design Templates, LLC
Cover Design by Jack Ritchie

Printed in the United States of America
ISBN 978-0-9997249-4-1
Library of Congress catalog control number: 2018901243

*This book is for Carol
and the memory of Jack Martin
and, as with everything,
for Marty.*

The Building

... it is the mid-1980s, in early spring, a time in southwestern Pennsylvania, the town of Furnass, that is barely distinguishable from late winter, just a hint of green on the otherwise bare trees and bushes with the first buds of the season, a dusting of green on the valley's hills still too undefined to be considered anything more than a hope, a promise of warm days to come, but as yet the sunny days surprisingly and disappointingly chill, the possibility still of waking in the morning to find a covering of light snow or at the least frost, enough to make the sidewalks and bricked streets slippy as they say in this part of the country, the windows of the cars parked along the narrow streets needing scraped before the cars can be driven, though on this night, sometime in the darkness after midnight a breeze starts deep in the woods in the hills beyond the town, nothing you can see but is present nonetheless, persistent as desire, a stirring in a patch of gooseberry vines and fallen leaves that stops a deer dead in its tracks, freezes a groundhog in its burrow ... but it is only a gust of air, and the deer flicks its tail and continues to pick its way between the dark trees, the groundhog continues to dig further into the hillside after waking from its hibernation and prepares for the coming summer ... it is only the wind, little more than an added chill to the night air that sweeps along a dry creek bed and up a ravine, over some sandstone boulders to the top of the hill and along the ridgeline, being drawn by natural forces or its own momentum down the slope of the valley on the other side, cascading through the just-budding branches of the hickory and oak and maple trees and over the town at the base of the hills along the river ... the gust of air plays among the narrow peaked roofs of the houses and whistles in the chimneys, dips down into the playground next to a grade school and rides the teeter-totter and gives a push to the swings before tumbling down the dark deserted streets under the streetlights, heading toward the abandoned mills and factories along the river now in the pre-dawn

hours, then detours and climbs into the black open tower, the tall building under construction on the main street . . . it whisks through the stack of empty floors and swirls up the unfinished stairwell, setting a string of bare bulbs swinging, creates a small dust devil from a pile of debris and sawdust in a corner, rattles a stack of electrical conduit and sets a loose two-by-four clapping against a wood form, up across the top deck of the building high above the little town . . . it dances in and out among the rows of unfinished columns sticking up for the floors above, it tests the guy wires supporting the columns' cages of reinforcing steel and sets them waving gently as if they were little more than clusters of tall grass . . . the gust of wind sings through the cages of steel, it curls around inside the hollow shafts, playing with itself, dallies there longer than it should and loses focus and becomes scattered and spends itself and dies there among the spirals and spacers and ties, and the construction site becomes still again . . . soon the black sky will lighten above the hills on the other side of the valley with the first hint of dawn, soon the workers will arrive on the empty floors of the building under construction and there will be different currents at play, different forces at work, but for now the construction site is quiet and the town is quiet, no one is about, nothing stirs, except . . . there, do you see it? . . . a solitary pickup truck is parked at the end of the wood fence that fronts the jobsite along the main street . . . a man sits at the wheel, the jobsite superintendent, drinking a cup of coffee, waiting, thinking about something . . .

PART ONE

The Building

1

Jack set his coffee on the dashboard of the truck, making sure that it stayed where he put it on the sloping surface before removing his hand. Steam from the paper cup clouded the windshield, spreading up the dark glass; traces of green then yellow then red from the stoplight at the corner flared with the workings of heat and cold, shifting and wavering in the clouded glass, obscuring his view along the main street. All the windows were beginning to fog over. Jack started the engine again, turned on the defroster. That's all I need, a cracked windshield. Can steam do that? I suppose that's another one of those things I'm supposed to know about. Well, I don't so forget it. Add it to the list. She said Why do you always think you have to know everything, no, that wasn't it, she said Why do you always think everything depends on you? Because it does, that's why. He wanted to see what was going on.

Along the sidewalks an occasional figure appeared in the predawn darkness, a cluster of dark figures was beginning to gather in front of the locked gate in the fence. Jack rested his left arm on the bottom of the steering wheel, rubbing absently at the soreness in his elbow. It was usually his favorite time of day. Sitting in his truck alone, the half hour or so before the job started, waiting for the others to get there. A time to get his thoughts together, go over in his mind what they had to do during the day. A few quiet moments to himself, before the noise and the shouting and the confusion started again. Before he had to be *Jack* again.

But he knew already what he was supposed to do today. He was supposed to wait for the concrete crew to get there, and then send them home again. Rotten way to run a job. How were they ever going to get anything built that way?

When Mac called a half hour earlier, Jack was just leaving his hotel room.

"What took you so long? I didn't wake you, did I?"

"Yeah, sure thing, Mac."

"Or maybe you've got somebody there with you. I didn't interrupt you and a lady friend, did I?"

"Don't you wish."

"You and me used to have some good times when we worked out of town." Mac chuckled but there was weariness in the Old Man's voice too. "Remember that redhead up in Erie, her and her sister? We called them the Daily Double. I doubt if your health has slowed you down very much."

Jack shifted the receiver to the other ear to ease the crick in his arm. "Sorry to disappoint you, but I was halfway out the door. I've got the concrete crew coming early this morning. You wanted those columns on seven poured today, remember?"

"Yeah," Mac said. "Well, now I'm telling you to hold off on them."

"Hold off?"

"That's what I said."

"You've been chewing on me all week to get those columns done. We'll have the last two welded up by this afternoon and then we can—"

"Now I'm chewing on you not to get them done."

"The concrete pump will be here any time now, the first ready-mix truck is probably batched already and on its way from Pittsburgh, I've got men coming for a six o'clock start, I've even got an inspector coming today to look at the rebar—"

"And I'm telling you forget about those columns. Send the trucks and the men home, send 'em all to hell for all I care, especially the goddamn inspector. What the hell is an inspector coming out for now anyway, there hasn't been an inspector on that job for months, we can get along fine without some candyass getting in the way. Just do what I tell you." Mac's voice had grown loud, his anger starting to run away with him, though Jack could tell he was trying to keep it in check; the Old Man obviously wasn't any happier about the situation than Jack was. After a moment's silence, Mac said, "Look, I'll be down this morning to fill you in about what's going on. For now I'm telling you don't worry about pouring those columns today. Look at it this way, you're getting a little breather."

"Yeah, I'll be standing around breathing when you get here."

The phone call put him off his good mood. Now that Mac was field superintendent for Drake Construction and Jack the jobsite superintendent—for years it had been Mac who was the jobsite superintendent and Jack the foreman—Jack was supposed to have control of his own project. He didn't like being told which columns to pour in the first place—Jack knew better than Mac which columns needed to be poured; before, when they worked together on projects, Jack always told Mac the schedule for the pours because Mac couldn't keep such things straight—and he especially didn't like being told which columns *not* to pour now. Jack took a sip of coffee. And what the hell was that talk about his health all of a sudden? Look at it this way, you're getting a little breather. Did Mac think Jack wasn't pulling his own weight? You old bastard, I had to carry you even when I was the one in a wheelchair. Even his coffee didn't taste as good as it usually did this morning, the more he thought about the phone call. It was Friday, for shit's sake, you were supposed to be in a good mood on a Friday.

A pair of headlights came down the street behind him; Jack caught a glimpse of them in the sideview mirror as they turned at the corner, turned up the hill and out of sight. Her Corvette? He listened for the roar of an engine but couldn't hear anything over his own defroster. Maybe she was just coming in after a late night. Or maybe it wasn't a Corvette at all, maybe it was some-body else, bringing her home. At one time, at the start of the project, he could have seen her windows across the alley from here, could have watched to see if the lights came on in her apartment—that is, if he cared whether she was just getting in or not—but the building was too tall now and blocked the view from the street. Why do you think everything always depends on you? Why do you always think you're responsible for everybody else? Because that's my job. But you're ill, you've been ill. Why can't you let somebody else help you? Probably wasn't Pamela at all. Somebody else entirely. Maybe it was Bill swinging by for a quickie before work. Last night he said I want to talk to you about something. I'm thinking about leaving my wife for Pamela. One of the figures in front of the gate broke away from the others and came toward him in the darkness. Jack rolled down his window.

"Nippy this morning," George, the labor foreman, said, grinning.

"Your kind of weather."

"Yep. Good hunting weather. Good working weather." He looked up at the dark framework of the building rising above the fence, then back at Jack. "I forgot. You probably need to be careful you don't catch a chill."

Jack ignored the remark. "All your men here?"

George Slovodnik was nearly as old as Mac, somewhere in his sixties, with a knobby, weathered face and prickly white hair showing under the rim of his old-fashioned rigger's hardhat. Mac had hired him away from the mills thirty years earlier; once George had a taste of working outdoors, he had stayed with Mac, going with him from company to company, project to project, though the two men rarely spoke and didn't care that much for each other personally. As he looked off toward his crew at the gate, George swept back the tails of his long denim jacket as if it were a frock coat and stuck his hands in the side pockets of his bib overalls.

"Well sir, I'd hazard a guess and say they're all present and accounted for. 'Cept, of course, for those that haven't made it yet."

"Wonderful, George."

"Always count on a few stragglers. That way you're never disappointed. Nature sees to it that you always have some who straggle."

"I'm never disappointed, George, in anything."

"I like a man with blind faith in himself."

Jack grunted. Sometimes George was easier to take than others. "The pump should be here any minute."

George stood with his legs spread, one foot aimed east-west and the other north-south, as if braced for any eventuality. "You know, the rumor is that the company's going to pull off this job today. Going to shut her down completely."

"Where'd you hear that?"

"Eddie the truck driver was in the main office last night picking up some stuff and heard Mac and some others talking about it. Yep, going to send us all home to play with mama."

"I don't know anything about shutting down the job. But Mac decided he doesn't want those columns poured today so I'll have to knock off most of your crew. I was waiting till they all got here before I said anything."

"Any reason why Mac doesn't want to pour the columns?"

"Because Mac said."

"Reason enough. Must be that's what Eddie heard them talking about. You know how rumors are." George thought a moment. "We still have to pay the men two hours for showing up."

"Thank you, George, I'm aware of that. I may have trouble getting around sometimes but my mind hasn't gone. Yet."

"Just thought I'd mention it," George said. He gave a gentlemanly nod of his head; all that was missing was for him to tip his hardhat. "I guess I better go count noses."

Jack was surprised; at the mention that the company was thinking of shutting down the job—his job—something gave way inside him. For a moment he felt lost, then it quickly turned to anger. What the hell do they mean, shutting down my job without telling me? What the hell for? It wasn't that he might be out of work himself; he knew there were other jobs he could go to, Mac had talked about moving him to another project for months. And he didn't blame Mac, the Old Man was just doing his job. It was the idea that something like this could happen without his having a say in it. If they shut down the job, what were his men supposed to do? Were there other jobs for them? And what about all the work they had put into this building, were they supposed to just walk away from it?

The concrete pump had arrived, rumbling toward him through the dogleg in the main street several blocks away; the front of the truck was lit with running lights, glowing like a mechanical dragon in the empty street. Jack got stiffly out of his truck, easing his weight first onto one leg and then the other, easing into the pain like a man stepping into water. And a thought occurred to him. He smiled to himself, then grinned openly. Why not? You've got to be crazy. Old Mac would shit a brick. You really going to do this? He angled his hardhat on his head, lit a cigarette, and headed toward the gate. In his mind a tiny toggle switch flipped to *On.*

"What the hell you guys standing around for?" he bellowed in a voice that both meant what it said and made fun of the way he said it. "We've got all those columns to pour today. Why the hell don't you get to work?"

Among the half-hearted grumbles somebody said, "You heard the man." Another voice, deep and melodious—Jack was sure it was Marshall, one of the laborers—replied just loud enough to carry, "A man'd have to be deaf not to hear Jack Crawford."

The Building

As Jack waded through the men and unlocked the gate, George said to him, "I thought you weren't going to pour those columns today."

"I changed my mind. We're pouring them after all. I've got the men, I've got the pump, I'm going to have the mud and I've got a place to put it when it gets here. Sounds like a concrete pour to my way of thinking."

"Fine with me. You know what you're doing."

No, I don't. For a second Jack marveled at himself. This is crazy. Whooee. Jacky-Boy, what are you getting yourself into this time? But as he pulled the chain through the links in the gate and pushed it open, the men brushing past him on their way to get to work, he felt his good mood returning. Besides, if we're walking off this project we have to pour those columns today, wouldn't be safe just to leave them standing there. End of discussion. Around him the bustle and activity of the job started up again—the voices of the men calling to one another, the slam of the gang boxes being opened and the engine of the manhoist coughing into life, the *Bla-a-a-at!* of the air horn from the concrete pump waiting in the street. He stuck his hands in his jacket pockets and lifted his face in satisfaction to the dark morning sky, feeling more like his old self than he had in months. Years.

2

As he sped along Ohio River Boulevard north from Pittsburgh, Gregg Przybysz checked his watch: 6:01. It was bad enough that he was going to a project that he'd never been to before; it was worse that he was going to be late. A six o'clock start. What idiot starts a concrete pour at six o'clock in the morning at this time of year? It's still pitch-dark. He was convinced that the only reason he was assigned to the project was because Emory, the dispatcher, didn't like him.

"Here you go, Professor," Emory said last evening in the office. He threw a slip of paper at Gregg, then spun around in his swivel chair, rolled away to the opposite leg of his desk and busied himself with some paperwork. "Just try to stay out of trouble on this one. For once."

All it said on the slip of paper was *Furnass Towers, Drake Construction Co., on the main street,* along with some hastily scribbled directions.

"What am I supposed to do when I get there? Assuming I can get there from these directions."

"See a guy named Jack." Emory kept his back turned, working at the back side of his U-shaped desk, his shoulders hunched beneath his stiff white shirt; his scalp showed through his gray crew cut as if he had scraped the top of his head. "He'll tell you what they want you to do. I think they have some welding and reinforcing steel to be inspected, along with the concrete."

"But I've never done any welding inspection, and I've hardly done any rebar. You usually send me out for just concrete. . . ."

"Old Clarence was out there a couple months ago and he didn't have any trouble."

"Old Clarence never gives anybody any trouble. That's why all the contractors like him."

Emory spun back around in his chair and walked it forward to the front leg of the U. He was angry, but instead of becoming flushed his face turned pallid; he looked at a point on the wall above Gregg's right shoulder.

"That's the trouble with guys like you, Przybysz. You go to college and you think you know everything. Here's a chance for you to get some experience in something new, and you're giving me trouble about it. Do you want the job or don't you? Because if you don't you can stay home tomorrow and I'll get somebody else. There's plenty of guys out there who would jump at the chance, who would be grateful for the chance. Plenty of guys out there who wouldn't give me static all the time."

Down along the dark river to his left, he passed the mills and refineries on Neville Island. The towers and smokestacks were dotted with lights like the superstructure of a battleship; clouds of steam vented in the darkness like silent salvos aimed across the water. The bastard. Why didn't I stand up to him and tell him to get somebody else? Why did I let him send me out on a job that I don't know anything about? Beyond Edgeworth he crossed a tall concrete viaduct over the mouth of the Allehela River and came to the turnoff marked FURNASS. It figured: according to Emory's directions he should have come to it five miles back. The bastard. Gregg spiraled down the access road toward the dark town below, his old Toyota shuddering through the curves, totally dreading this day.

On his radio the Pittsburgh rock station was playing a favorite song by the Police. Gregg clicked it off. In the lower end of town near an abandoned railroad station, lights glowed dully in the dirty windows of a block of row houses. Men and women getting ready for work, Gregg supposed, children getting ready for school. Much of this part of town seemed deserted. Along the dark streets a few isolated houses and small factory buildings stood amid vacant lots where other houses and factories had been. Frost paled the bare patches of earth, the few parked cars, the surface of the side streets toward the river. It's like it's been bombed out. A wasteland. Who would live in a place like this? Gregg was in unfamiliar territory; most of the projects he had worked on were in the city or suburbs. He grew up in the southern part of the state, farm country except for an occasional mine tucked back between the hills; he knew these mill towns along the Monongahela and Ohio River valleys only by their reputations for being tough, he didn't know what to expect, didn't know which sections to avoid because there could be trouble. This end of Furnass looked poor and dangerous. He scratched uneasily at his mountain-climber's beard and sped up.

At a juncture of angled streets and railroad sidings, across some flattened blocks, the Triangle Tavern was busy at this hour of the morning, half a dozen cars and trucks parked in the lot beside the building; above the café curtains in the windows, figures moved in the neon glow of beer signs, the bright eye of a television set glared down from a dark corner. Yeah, I'd start my day plastered out of my mind too if I had to live here. Matter of fact . . . no, I better not. . . . Gregg followed the double yellow line up a short hill into the main part of town. The first gray smudge of dawn outlined the saddle of the scruffy hills across the river from the town. Some of the stores at this end of the main street were boarded over, others were abandoned. In the main part of town the decorations in the store windows couldn't make up their minds, some still had hearts and lace left over from Valentine's Day, others had rabbits and eggs looking forward to Easter; the lights of Gregg's Toyota passed in the dark glass as if he traveled under water. Down the steep side streets he caught glimpses of a large mill but the buildings were without lights; it appeared as a blanked-out space along the river the exact size and shape of a mill. A banner over the main street said YOU'RE IN STOKER COUNTRY.

What do you suppose that means? What's a stoker? Do I really want to know? It should read WELCOME TO THE ENDS OF THE EARTH. I went to four years of college, I worked to maintain a 3.8 grade point average, my mom and dad gave up vacations for ten years to pay for my education, I gave up my high school sweetheart, all so I could be bossed around by a cretin who can't look anyone in the eye and work as a concrete inspector in the original black hole of the universe. I can hardly wait till my first class reunion. Oh, and what have you done with your life? Let me tell you.

The Building

Beyond a dogleg in the street, the lights of the Furnass Grill on the corner washed out through the large front windows over the sidewalk; inside, a waitress worked her way down a row of booths, holding a coffeepot. *A cinnamon roll, my kingdom for a cinnamon roll. At this point I'd even settle for a glazed doughnut. Evidently my kingdom can be easily had.* In the next block the black skeleton of a building under construction loomed above the two- and three-story buildings around it. *That has to be Furnass Towers. Holy shit, it's huge. What are they doing putting up a high-rise in the middle of a little town like this? This is a major project, I think I'm in trouble.* In front of the project, a ready-mix truck maneuvered in the narrow street, getting into position to back in through the gate. Gregg parked his car in the empty spaces in front of Woolworth's, grabbed his hardhat and clipboard, and hurried down the sidewalk.

The concrete pump was parked inside the fence, cab first, in the narrow lot between the fence and the building. On the back of the pump, the operator scrambled about the platform assembling the boom. The concrete mixer waited outside the gate in the street; its drum revolved slowly, the mix inside sifting and clacking over the blades. Gregg took up a position along the fence at the rear of the mixer, trying to look official or at least as if he belonged there. On the fence was a mural obviously done by local schoolchildren, crude paintings of *Peanuts* characters celebrating Easter, the paint gleaming in the streetlights and the running lights of the truck; Gregg found himself standing under an image of Snoopy pushing a wheelbarrow full of decorated eggs. Next to that was some spray-paint graffiti—DONZI LOVES MARCIA; GO STOKERS; EAT ME; he moved several paces away. After a few minutes, a burly guy smoking a cigarette, his jacket open and his shirt collar up in the manner of a street-corner tough, came out of the gate. His battered hardhat bore the label JACK.

"You the driver? No," Jack answered his own question and walked on to the cab of the truck. The driver was slouched down in his seat, one knee up against the rim of the steering wheel, his Steelers cap pulled down over his eyes. Jack took off his hardhat and banged it a couple times against the door.

"Wake up, Guido. You going to back this thing up to the pump or do you need a private invitation?"

The driver slowly straightened up and gazed down at Jack, blinking lazily. "Anything you say, Jack. Seeing as how you ask so nice."

"Isn't that wonderful? I think that's wonderful," Jack said, looking at Gregg. From Jack's tone of voice it didn't sound as if he thought it was wonderful at all; Gregg didn't know what to say. "Come on, come on! Back it up!" Jack said, clapping his hardhat back on his head.

As the driver ground the transmission into gear and angled the truck backwards toward the gate, Jack stood in the street to act as flagman. A car was coming a block away, speeding through town; it blinked its lights to warn Jack out of the way. Jack turned to face the car, his hands in his pockets, cigarette stuck in the corner of his mouth, apparently unconcerned about the headlights bearing down on him. The car swerved to miss him, clunking into a pothole as it passed and almost hitting Gregg's parked car farther along the street. The driver complained with his horn as the car continued through town. Jack took the cigarette from his mouth, pursed his lips in the imitation of a duck, and blew a puff of smoke after it.

The ready-mix truck stopped halfway through the gate. It gave a short blast of its air horn; the driver held his hands palms up and pumped his shoulders a couple of times. Jack looked at Gregg as if to say Well, what are you going to do about it? Gregg stood there with his clipboard in one hand and his hardhat in the other. What's he looking at me for? What am I supposed to do?

Jack tossed the cigarette away disgustedly and came back to the
rear of the mixer, motioning Gregg out of his way with a nod.
When Jack could see the driver in the rearview mirror, he sig-
naled the truck to come back. The truck lurched backwards as
Jack fluttered his hand, coming faster than it should, then
slammed to a stop when Jack snapped his hand into a fist. The
chute of the mixer came to rest inches above the hopper of the
pump, exactly where it needed to be. Guido swung down from
the cab and sauntered back to the mixer controls. Overhead, the
pump's articulated boom rose in the air, hydraulics whining. The
operator, a young man Gregg's age dressed in a cowboy hat and
boots, worked the controls from the platform above the hopper,
a few feet from where the ready-mix truck almost crashed into
him. He glared down at Guido.

"Someday somebody's going to kill me doing that," he
drawled.

"You're okay as long as he pays attention to my signals," Jack
said.

"Did I tell you I ain't got no brakes on this rig?" Guido said.

Jack took a pack of cigarettes from his shirt pocket, flipped it
a couple of times until a cigarette stuck out, and grabbed it with
his teeth. Then he turned abruptly to Gregg. "So, what do you
do? Or are you here on vacation?"

"I'm the inspector," Gregg said uneasily.

"Same difference, right, Jack?" Guido said.

As Jack turned away to holler instructions to the operator,
Gregg realized he wasn't wearing his hardhat and quickly put it
on. The hat was cold, the plastic liner brittle and crimped, and
the hat tottered ludicrously on his head. I don't have to be afraid
of these guys. I'm the inspector, they're supposed to treat me
with respect. They're the ones who should be afraid of me. He
was about to ask Jack what needed to be inspected when an old
man walked through the gate. He was dressed all in khaki, with

an antiquated metal hardhat shaped like a pith helmet perched on the back of his head. His face was a mass of wrinkles and folds of skin. He slouched along, hands deep in his pants pockets, shoulders rolled as if he carried a backpack, scuffling his shoes in the dust and loose gravel as he came through the half-light toward them. Gregg thought maybe he was some local character who had wandered in off the street.

"Who the hell's this?" the old man said to Jack.

"Inspector," Jack said and turned away, taking a sudden interest in the side of the building. Gregg thought he caught the trace of a grin on Jack's face—just before the old man exploded.

"Then what in the hell is he doing down here on the ground— Holy Mother of God, why isn't he up there on the deck checking the goddamn rebar, where he's supposed to be—Jesus H. Christ, I've run work from the Snake River to New York City and I've never seen an inspector yet who knew his ass from a hot rock or which end of his dick to piss out of—I'm telling you right here and now that no goddamned mother-sucking pig-sticking dog-humping pussy-licking dumb jacking-off son-of-a-bitch inspector is going to tell me what to do on one of my projects—the only reason he's out here in the first place is because that candy-livered architect said we had to have somebody look at this shit—we'll pour those goddamn fucking columns and any other goddamn fucking thing I goddamn fucking feel like whether some mother-jumping, dog-sucking, pig-diddling hippie asshole inspector approves it or not." The old man, who had been addressing the world at large, turned and glowered at Gregg to make sure there was no question whom he was talking about.

Gregg stood spellbound, entranced at the tirade itself and astonished that it was aimed at him.

"Gotcha, Mac," Jack said, lighting his cigarette, still looking up at the side of the building. "I'll take care of it."

Mac nodded once for emphasis, then slouched on, his hands still in his pants pockets, shoulders humped, over to the job trailer and up the steps.

When the old man was gone, Jack turned around, took the cigarette from his mouth, and gave Gregg an appraising look. "If I was you, I think I'd get up there on that deck. He might decide to come back."

"If I was you," Guido said, leaning casually against the back of the mixer, "I'd give some serious consideration to *flying* up on that deck."

Confused, embarrassed, Gregg clutched his clipboard and hurried inside the wall-less building. He heard somebody laugh in the darkness and was sure it was at him.

3

The trailer was tucked into a corner against the inside of the fence and the brick wall of the building next door; the windows of Jack's office glowed in the ashen morning light. Mac was waiting for him, leaning on his elbows at the far end of the plan table made of two-by-fours and rough plywood. This is where I get chewed out for going ahead and pouring those columns today, this is where Mac reams me a new asshole. Well, I've been here before. Have at it, you old fart, have yourself a good time. Jack leaned on the near end of the plan table, in the same position as the older man except that Jack rested the sole of his left work boot on the toe of his right. Neither man looked at the other. They looked out the windows at the activity going on in the narrow lot between the fence and the building, at the concrete pump and the mixer and the men going about their work.

"You remember the inspector we had on that insurance building up in Pittsburgh?" Mac said after a few minutes.

"That goofy bastard."

"Walked by a concrete truck one day, listened to the drum spinning, and told the driver the mix sounded too dry, told him to add ten gallons of water to it."

"Yeah, and the truck had just finished unloading, there wasn't any concrete in it. I remember. Walter something or other. Or whenever he said a load was too wet and rejected it, the driver would drive it around the block and bring it right back again. Walter never knew the difference, didn't recognize that it was the same driver or anything. He'd look at the load and say, 'Yeah, this is a better load.' Goofy bastard."

Mac rocked his hardhat back and forth on his head a couple of times to scratch his scalp, then reset it at a different angle. "Wonder whatever happened to ol' Walter?"

"He's probably still wandering around looking for his head, after the last time you bit it off. He tried to stop us from making a pour because he said the rebar was all wrong, and it turned out he had the drawings for a different floor. He never did come back to the job after that."

"You mean, I never let him come back to the job after that," Mac said, shifting his weight onto one elbow so he could look at Jack.

"Same difference." Jack continued to look out the window, watching one of the laborers trying to unravel the kinks from an electrical cord. The cord flopped around him like a live thing; as soon as he straightened out one section, another section kinked even worse, and the coils wrapped around his legs and threatened to trip him. What's the old bastard getting at? What's he waiting for? Get on with it, get it over with, let's go, I've got things to do. "What made you think of him?"

"I don't know. Thinking about inspectors, I guess—what with this cherry you've got out here now."

"Yeah, just what I need. A kid who can't tell which end of the building is up."

"On the other hand, he shouldn't give you any trouble. He doesn't know what he's doing, so he probably won't say very much."

"Since when did I ever listen to anything an inspector said?"

Mac grinned slightly.

"That's the way you taught me, isn't it?"

"How's Bill doing? Is his rebar ready for inspection?"

"Yeah, if he ever gets his head out of his asshole."

"Thought you got along with Bill. Thought you two were buddies."

"I get along with him all right: I tell him to get along and get to work. I don't have buddies, you know that."

Mac didn't say anything for a moment, thinking about something. "So. You're going to pour those columns today after all. After I told you not to."

Here we go. Now we're getting into it. Jack straightened up, hitched his baggy pants around his middle, and looked at Mac. "Yeah. I decided I might as well. Seeing as how they were ready, and I had the men and equipment all set to go."

"And you couldn't stand to leave something unfinished."

"That's what you pay me for. Besides, if we're walking off this project, I didn't think it was safe to leave those columns sticking up in the air without being tied into the rest of the building. I want to get that first lift poured. I was the one who convinced the architect to let us fabricate the steel in three-floor lifts, remember? If something happens to them, I don't want it on my head."

"Where did you hear we were walking off the building?"

"Word gets around."

Mac fingered the dog-eared corners of the stack of drawings he was leaning on; he tried straightening the bent corners but they were too badly creased and he folded them back the way they were. He seemed regretful, almost sad. "I probably should have told you more on the phone this morning."

He's trying to be nice, why the hell is he trying to be nice? I think I liked it better when he was going to chew my ass. "Any particular reason why we're pulling off? Or is it some kind of secret and nobody wants me to know?"

"I knew you wouldn't be happy about it. That's why I came to tell you in person."

Jack could feel himself getting blustery but he couldn't help it. "Happy? What's there to be happy or unhappy about? Why would I care? It all pays the same, doesn't it? One building's the same as another in my book. Sure, let's just walk away from it. Leave it sticking up here in the middle of town like a hard-on. That makes a lot of sense. Wonderful." He puttered his lips, a kind of raspberry, and went and stood in the doorway, looking out.

"It's like this, son. We haven't been paid for a couple of months."

"What do you mean we haven't been paid?"

"Just what I said. We haven't received a cent for two months. And only partial payments for a couple months before that. Architect says he's approved the invoices for payment, but we don't see anything coming from the owner."

"And what does the owner say?"

"The owner says check with the savings and loan."

"And what does the savings and loan say?"

"They say they're working on it."

"What do you think the problem is?"

Mac shrugged. "We don't really care at this point. We've been lenient to keep working as long as we have."

"If they paid us, we'd come back on it, wouldn't we?"

"I'm not so sure. This project has been more trouble than it's worth from the beginning. We're not in this for the fun of it, you know."

"Shit, and here all this time I thought we were." Jack left the doorway and sat at his desk. This'll get the old bastard, he hates it when people slouch in front of him. He pulled out the top left drawer and draped his leg over it, leaning back in the old wooden swivel chair. "So I fucked up royally, going ahead and pouring those columns today. We could end up eating them."

Mac looked at him, washed his hand down his saggy face, and looked out the window again. "That's why I told you to hold off."

"I got to say you don't seem very upset about it. Usually you'd be hooting and hollering by now."

"I'm just not going to tell anybody in the office what you're doing, that's all. As far as they're concerned, you didn't pour today. And when it comes out later, I'll already have you on another project. We'll get our money eventually, I suppose, through the courts. Most of it, anyway." The old man brushed the back of his hand disdainfully across the drawings, as if to make the building disappear. "I never wanted Drake to do this one in the first place. I thought it was a bad project when we bid it. Too many loose ends. Look at the stack of change orders we've had already. But nobody listened to me."

"So how the hell did I end up with it?"

"It's small compared to most of the projects you and I have built. I figured it wouldn't take much effort on your part. Hell, you could build a project this size with your left hand, while your right hand plays with one of your dollies. I figured it would give you a chance to take it easy, get rested up. Get your health back."

"Well, I've got my health back, and I don't like the idea of walking away from a job. It's not my style. I brought her to the party, it's up to me to take her home."

"I knew you'd feel that way. But as far as I'm concerned, we'd be better off to walk away from it, rather than have to deal with all the construction claims once it's built. This project will be tied up in litigation for years, whatever we stand to make we'd lose to the lawyers. I'd much rather take what we can get now and have you available to go someplace where you can make some real money for us."

"Wait a minute, now I get it. I'll bet you're in trouble on another project, aren't you? That's why you're not more upset about losing this one, because you need me to bail you out somewhere else."

"It's that high-rise we're doing in downtown Pittsburgh. Forty-three stories, that's more your speed anyway. The boy I've got on it just can't handle it. He's really got my tit in a wringer."

Mac leaned into the plan table, his forearms flat against the slant of the table as if he were afraid he might slide off. This was a different Mac than the one Jack was used to; Jack didn't see him as much since Mac became field superintendent for the company, maybe the Old Man was changing. Jack took his leg down from the desk drawer and sat up, it wasn't any fun if he couldn't get a rise out of Mac. Besides, his leg stuck up in the air like that was killing him. He leaned over and rubbed his ankle gingerly, feeling for swelling, lumps.

Mac watched him rubbing his ankle, then went on, staring out the window again. "You remember that medical building we did out in Oakland? They came in with all their critical-path schedules and fancy computer printouts and said there was no way we'd be able to get that building done before summer. But I poured concrete every single day right through the winter and we beat all their fancy figuring by a month and a half and were still under budget."

"Because I figured out a way to build the forms for the walls in sections so we could use them over and not have to make new ones for each floor. I remember, all right."

"We sure showed 'em that time, didn't we? Mac and Jack, everybody knew Mac and Jack in those days. We built the biggest buildings in the city, and we built 'em better than anybody else."

"Yeah, that was us." Jack got up and stood in the open doorway again. He was pleased in spite of himself: pleased that Mac still thought of them as a team, pleased that the Old Man needed him on another building. He didn't like to think of giving up on this one, but it was a good feeling to think that Mac still counted on Jack to get him out of trouble. From force of habit he reached for his cigarettes, but told himself to hold off for a while, to prove to himself that he still could. He cradled his left arm in his right, absently massaging his elbow, the spot where the golf ball-sized lump had been.

"You okay, son?" Mac said.

"Yeah, why shouldn't I be?"

"Dunno. Just wondering." Mac studied him a moment before coming to the door. Jack moved out of his way. "Guess I better get going."

"I was wondering if *you* were okay."

Mac studied him. "Why's that?"

"All this talk about the old days, buildings we built. I don't usually think of you as the sentimental type."

"Don't you like to think about the old days sometimes? Reminisce a little?"

"No way." As Mac went on down the steps, hobbling a little, Jack took up his position in the doorway again, spread-legged, hands in his pockets, as if to block anyone from coming in, or to keep something inside from getting out. "I don't look down when I'm up in the air, either."

Mac eyed him as if he wanted to say something, then thought better of it and slouched off toward the gate. As he passed the pump and mixer, the operator and truck driver watched him warily, as if a bear in a hardhat were in the neighborhood.

That's all there was to it, I'm going ahead and pouring those columns, I could be costing this company six or eight thousand dollars, and that's all he had to say about it. That's sad. He was the toughest, meanest, loudest, most ornery son-of-a-bitch you ever worked for, and what is he now, a tired old man thinking about the old days. Lord, I hope I never get like that. What did she say to me? What are you ashamed of? Don't you think people ever get sick? I'm not sick. Don't you think people ever get older? I'm not going to get old, I'm going to break before I wear out. What's the matter, Jack, afraid you're getting older? Or are you just afraid? Shit. What are those assholes doing?

"Hey, you jack-offs!" Jack bellowed from the doorway at two laborers on the second floor. "I told you to sweep that deck, not make a career out of it. Get your asses in gear!"

The two laborers ducked their heads and bent over their brooms. That was more like it. Jack was aware that when he hollered, every workman in sight looked at him, wondering if he was yelling at him; Jack loved it. He worked his shoulders to get the kinks out, reset his hardhat, and lit a cigarette. Jack was Jack. His good mood was *On* and running smooth. Last night Bill said I want to talk to you about something. I'm thinking of leaving my wife for Pamela. No, I'm not going to think about that now, that has nothing to do with me now.

PART TWO

The Building

. . . it is a town in the bend of a river, two bends actually, an S-curve, to be exact . . . the main part of town filling the space within the lower crescent of the S, the buildings of Buchanan Steel covering most of the flatland adjacent to the Allehela River with the town of Furnass stacked up on the steep slope of the hillside above it . . . the Allehela here winds slowly through the valley on its way to join the Ohio just beyond the town, the bluffs on the other side of the valley fronting the town like a tree-covered wall, the river in its final undulations delineating what the town is and what it isn't, what it can and cannot be . . . though the people who live here pay little attention to the river, no more than they pay attention to the hills, for them the hills are only something in the way, something that must be climbed over to get from here to there, the river something that must be crossed . . . it is the mill that has dominated and in effect defined the town for generations . . . the mill like a great castle on the bank of the river with the little town huddled at its gates . . . the flames of the furnaces coloring the town night and day and leaving the stores and little houses and even the trees along the streets and in the backyards blackened with soot, the smoke and steam from the mill providing the town's smells though the flames of the furnaces and the smoke and the steam are gone now . . . for generations the town woke each morning to the sounds of the machinery at the mill and the ringing of metal on metal and the screech and bump of railcars being switched along the sidings, but those sounds are gone now too . . . for the past year or so the town has wakened to the sounds of keening power saws and men calling to one another and hammering hammering hammering . . . the sounds of the new building under construction on the main street, the men and women working on it for the most part strangers to the town, coming here from someplace else and going on to someplace else once the building is done . . . because the mills are gone now, or at least closed, the soot-black husks of the buildings along the river

all that's left now of that way of life . . . though life finds ways of getting on in the little town, adapting . . . as for example on this morning, in her apartment across the alley from the jobsite, Pamela DiCello stirs in bed as a generator sputters into life on the top deck of the building that's grown now above the height of her windows, clears a wisp of her thick black hair from her face, turns over on her tummy, smiles as she thinks of something or someone and goes back to sleep . . . and the river flows on and the life of the town flows on . . . and as later, after the column continues to lean against the top of the wood form for another second or two, before the two men clinging to the cage of reinforcing steel, one at the top and the other halfway up the opposite side, can do anything to prevent what is happening or climb down to safety, the cement dobies inside the form crack and crumble and the two-by-four braces snap and the square of scaffolding begins to tip and the wood form splinters and breaks open as the column keeps on going in the direction it has started, only faster now, the tons of top-heavy steel leaning farther and farther . . . but not yet, that comes later, lifetimes away. . . .

4

I can't put it off any longer. Can I? Oh God, what am I going to do, they're waiting for me up there, I have to do it. What kind of an inspector am I, I can't even climb the ladder to get up to the work. Everybody else does it, it must be safe enough, the ladder is probably stronger than the rest of the building, now there's a comforting thought. I can't stall any longer, I have to I have to I don't want to have to. . . .

The ladder was made of two-by-fours, nailed together on the jobsite and wide enough for several people to climb at one time. It stood in the darkness of a stairwell at a rear corner of the building; except for the ladder, the stairwell was empty, the rebar sticking out from the block walls the only indication of where the treads and stringers would eventually be. What's the matter with these people, why can't they ever build the stairs along with the rest of the building? No, they always put the stairs in last, they must like these ladders. Nothing like a little shot of primal fear to start off your morning, right? Hey Charlie, let's go see if we can fall down the stairwell. Sure sounds like fun to me. Before taking this job as an inspector Gregg had never climbed a ladder in his life; it was as if he had been raised with some middle-class notion that nice people didn't do such things, at least not in public. Oh God, I have to. The ladder was still quivering from the last man to go up. Gregg grabbed a rung at shoulder height and looked up into the well; overhead, he could just make out a pair of ankles and shoes disappearing into the gloom. Gregg started to turn away—No way get me out of here I'm not doing this for anybody—and came face-to-face with an electrician who was draped with coils of wire over his shoulder.

"You going up or what?"

"No, that's okay, you go ahead," Gregg said and stepped aside. The guy gave him a dirty look and scampered up the ladder, hand over hand, oblivious to the bouncing swaying ladder or the coils of wire that threatened to trip him at every step. Gregg sighed. There was no way out of it.

The first problem was his clipboard: what to do with it. He tried holding it in his hand as he climbed but it prevented him from getting a grip on the rungs with that hand and the clipboard threatened to slip from his grasp. He settled for tucking it under his arm as he hugged the ladder closely. With every step he could hear the ends of the ladder poles working against the concrete, hear the two-by-fours creak under his weight. How did the Crusaders ever scale those castle walls? Onward Christian soldiers! For Harry and Saint George! If it was up to me we'd all be heathens. Then you get to the top and somebody on the parapet tips the ladder backwards on you. Timber! Oh God. The ladder began to shake violently; something fell from overhead, a chunk of concrete—it was more like a pebble—dinged him on the hardhat. Earthquake! The building's falling down! I knew it! As Gregg pressed himself against the ladder, a pair of work boots descended inches from his face; a plumber rattled down the ladder without so much as looking at him. Gregg slithered on. At the top, the ladder should have extended several feet above the level of the floor so there was something to hold on to when the climber stepped off, but it didn't and there wasn't; the ladder ended only a few inches above the slab so that Gregg had to go down on his hands and knees to keep from toppling backwards into the well. He didn't dare stand up until he was several feet away from the gaping hole. I did it!

The trouble was, that was only the first ladder. There were still six more ladders to go.

He leaned forward, very carefully, and looked up the shaft: the remaining ladders crisscrossed the darkness above him, leading up toward a small rectangle of murky morning sky. As the stairwell got higher, the ladders became more dangerous, the next ladder slanting up from the opening for the elevator in the block wall on the second floor to the opening on the third, a wooden framework suspended over a two-story drop, and the ladder after that was suspended over three stories, then four, five . . . he tried not to think about the accepted wisdom concerning falls—it doesn't matter how far you fall after two floors, it might as well be twenty or two hundred, your odds of survival are the same, Splat City—tried to remember the correct method for climbing a ladder, let your body hang loose, lean away from the ladder—not on your life, sucker—repeated to himself the cardinal rule for climbing or walking heights on a building—never look down or up, don't even look at the next place you're going to put your foot, focus your attention on a point a little ways ahead of you— tried to take his mind off the immediate realities of the

The Building

situation—Oh sure—tried to have faith in his body—Come on, body!—faith that his instincts wouldn't let him fall—Please, body, please—and continued the climb.

When he finally scrambled from the last ladder onto the top deck, he was exhilarated. He straightened up when he thought he was a safe distance from the opening, brushed himself off, and looked around. The concrete deck, the seventh floor of the building, seemed to float above the rooftops of the town tiered down the hill toward the railroad tracks and the mill and the river. Above the hills on the other side of the valley the sky had lightened; a thin layer of clouds like a band of luminous orange filaments traced the ridgelines, though above him the sky was still blue-black. The dark panorama of the town and the valley opened in front of him as if he were on a great tabletop or stage.

He took a few hesitant steps, getting used to the feel of being up here in the air, when he heard a clanking behind him as if from a small leaden bell—*clank, clank, clank.* A tall rawboned man, with a red beard and ponytail, horn-rimmed glasses and stack-heeled lineman's boots, ambled up to him out of the morning gloom. The clanking came from a pry bar and hammer dangling from his ironworker's belt; a long curl of tie wire stuck out from the coiler on his belt as if it were a thin black monkey's tail. Written with a Magic Marker on his dented hardhat were the words CRAZY LEVON.

"This your first time up here?" Crazy Levon said as he moved something to the other side of his mouth with his tongue. The curl of tie wire projected dangerously close to Gregg's crotch.

"Yes," Gregg said. "How did you know?"

"Most of us don't crawl," the ironworker said without expression and clanked off again.

Embarrassed, Gregg looked around to see if anyone was watching him. At the far end of the deck, Jack stood beside the guardrail. Gregg was startled. How did the superintendent get up here ahead of him? Jack spotted him and came across the deck; he walked like a man ready to bowl over anything or anyone who got in his way.

"That old man's a pistol, isn't he?" Jack said, breaking into a grin. He stuck his face close to Gregg's. "Old Mac looks like Death warmed over, but he can still swear better than any man I ever knew. If he gets a rhythm going he can go for several minutes and never repeat himself. He's got a real talent for it."

Just as quickly as he had come up to Gregg, Jack backed off and looked around. Gregg was confused. How did he get up here so fast? Is he trying to be friendly? Downstairs I thought he was going to hit me, what's going on here?

"One time up in Pittsburgh," Jack went on as if continuing an earlier conversation, "we had a labor crew that was scared to death of that old bastard. I mean, they were scared shitless. All Mac had to do was look at them and they acted like they had just heard the voice of God. So, when Good Friday came along, I told them that Mac was going to give an Easter sermon in his office during lunch. I'll be damned if the whole crew didn't troop into Mac's office at lunchtime and gather around his desk with their hats in their hands, waiting for Mac to give them a benediction. You should've seen the look on the Old Man's face. He couldn't figure out what they were doing there, all standing around looking at him."

Jack looked off toward the river, chuckling to himself at the memory. Then he was back in Gregg's face, serious again. "What the hell took you so long to get up here? What'd you do, climb the ladders? Why didn't you take the manhoist?"

Beyond the edge of the slab, the cage of the temporary elevator was just ascending into view.

"I needed the exercise," Gregg said. Why didn't I see that before?

The Building

"Well, I need the inspection," Jack said. He squinted to read the label on Gregg's hardhat. "What the hell does that say? Is that a real name?"

Gregg laughed uneasily.

Jack leaned closer. "P-r-z-y-b . . . whatever."

"Przybysz."

"I'll just call you Alphabet."

"You can call me Gregg. With two *g*'s." Why on earth did I say that?

Jack looked at him as if to say Oh yeah? and looked away.

"What are you going to pour?" asked Gregg.

"These columns, obviously, what the hell does it look like? We've already started. Are they okay?"

Each column on the floor was encased in a wood form to the height of eight or ten feet, with the rebar for the next two floors above sticking out of the top; each wood form in turn was surrounded by a square of scaffolding. At the front of the building, the boom of the concrete pump angled high in the air over the slab. The thick hose at the end of the boom hung down toward a column; the concrete crew, standing on top of the scaffold around the column, grappled with the hose to aim it inside the formwork.

"I don't know if they're okay or not, I haven't had time to look at them yet. . . ."

Jack didn't seem to be listening. He went over to the nearest column and leaned against the scaffolding, his hands tucked in his jacket pockets, appearing very proud of himself. "I left the forms open at the bottom so you can see the welds. Isn't that wonderful? I designed the formwork that way myself, after the architect said it was okay to have the column steel fabricated for three floors at a time. That saves us plenty of time all the way around. And having them open that way is also handy for cleaning out the bottom of the forms so the concrete gets a good bond. See? I was already thinking of you. All you have to do is go around and look at the welds and tell me they're okay, then I drop the forms back into place and button them up and they're ready to pour. Isn't that wonderful? I think that's wonderful."

"What about the one you're already starting to pour?"

"Well, naturally, you're not going to be able to look at that one. I already buttoned it up so we could get started. But you can look at the other ones. They're all the same. And there's two down at the end the welder's still working on."

"I'll need a drawing to look at. . . ."

"Christ, now he needs a drawing to look at," Jack said to a black laborer who happened to be walking past.

The laborer was apparently used to having such comments addressed to him; he nodded and said, "That's right, Jack," and kept on walking. Gregg couldn't tell if the superintendent was angry or only kidding about his request for a drawing. Without saying anything further, Jack clomped over to a makeshift plan table and began riffling through the drawings, tossing the sheets of paper this way and that as he muttered to himself.

"Nope, that's not it, what the hell's this? Maybe we threw it away. Nobody on this job uses drawings anyway. . . ."

He puffed out his cheeks comically, the parody of a man looking through a pile of drawings; Gregg decided it was a joke after all. Then Jack wheeled abruptly at the laborer who walked by again.

"Goddamn it, Marshall, don't just walk around up here. You're not here to sightsee, you know?"

"The guy I was looking for wasn't where I looked for him, Jack."

"Then pick up a board or something and carry it with you. I don't care, just look like you're doing something. . . ."

Jack went back to tossing the drawings around. Gregg stayed a respectful distance away, afraid to get too close. Finally the superintendent pulled one out of the stack and thrust it at him.

"Next I suppose you'll want me to read it for you too."

"No, I can read it. . . ." Gregg opened the drawing and tried to study it. Don't let him boss you around, you're the inspector, he's supposed to answer to you.

"Start with the columns toward the front because those are the ones I'll pour first. Check the welding and the number of bars and whatever the hell else you inspectors get paid to do."

"You don't have to tell me, I know what to look for," Gregg said. Then he realized, apparently at the same time Jack did, that he was holding the drawing upside down. Gregg laughed nervously and righted the drawing.

"Hoo-boy," Jack said and wedged his hands deep in his pants pockets. Marshall came back again, this time with a scrap of two-by-four leaning on his shoulder like a soldier on parade.

"Mr. Crawford," Marshall said, not looking at him as he passed, "I just want to say that you are without a doubt the most outspoken man I ever worked for."

Jack looked at Gregg. "Isn't that wonderful?" he growled.

This guy's worse than that crazy old man downstairs, this guy belongs in a cage. Gregg, the drawing open and right-side up, hurried off in the opposite direction to look at the columns.

5

There were five rows of six columns each spaced across the deck, thirty columns in all. The bars for the columns were three stories high, though the concrete for the columns was only poured one story at a time. Above the squares of scaffolding and the form-work surrounding each column on this floor, the continuation of the reinforcing bars for the next floors towered thirty feet overhead—tall narrow cages of black steel, like skeletons of columns, almost delicate except that each bar weighed hundreds of pounds, each column weighed tons. As Jack said, the square wooden forms that would hold the concrete were lifted on each column to expose the welds at the base, the jointure of these bars with the bars from the columns below.

Gregg started to ease himself sidesaddle over the diagonal bracing of one of the squares of metal scaffolding until he realized that wouldn't work; he withdrew his leg and tried to step through, riding the brace momentarily like a broomstick horse. That got him inside the narrow space between the scaffolding and the formwork. But when he tried to straighten up he hit his head on a corner brace; his hardhat pinballed down between the bracing, noisy as an empty pot. He found that he could hardly move; he squatted down to retrieve his hat and take a look under the formwork at the base of the column. Though it was getting lighter by the minute on the deck, he could scarcely make out the bars inside the shadows of the formwork. I need a flashlight. I wonder if Jack, no, better forget that. But he could see well enough to know he had a problem. He climbed back out of the scaffolding again and looked at the drawing one more time.

In this situation he didn't have to know very much about welds or welding inspection, the notes at the bottom of the drawing told him all he needed to know: the specifications called for full-penetration welds—welds that extended through the entire thickness of the bars to be joined together. And because they were to be full-penetration welds, the welding code called for continuous inspection—continuous inspection while the bars were being welded. All these welds were already done.

Gregg's spirits sank, his bowels turned to water. That meant that whether the welds looked okay or not, they were unacceptable. Every weld completed on the floor failed to meet the requirements of the welding code because an inspector hadn't been present while the work was going on. Now it was his job to reject the welds. Every weld completed on the floor, which was most of them.

What'll I do? How can I get out of this?

The Building

He looked around, trying to fight the panic that threatened to overwhelm him. Jack had returned to the front of the deck; he was leaning on the guardrail, his back turned, watching something down on the street. None of the other workmen seemed to be paying any attention to Gregg. From the rear of the deck came the sound of the generator for the welding machine, revving up each time the welder struck an arc. Gregg tucked the drawing and his clipboard under his arm, stuck his hands in the pockets of his army surplus field coat, and tried to appear casual as he walked down the row of columns. He whistled a little tune to himself until he realized it was *I'll be watching you.*

The welder was working on the last column in the row; Gregg stopped at the other unfinished column in front of it and climbed in through the scaffolding. As far as he could tell, the fit-up for the welds looked more or less the same as on the drawing. At each joint, the bars were beveled, the gap between the narrow ends of the bars backed up by a steel angle; temporary tack welds on the backup angles held the bars in place until the full-penetration welds filled in the bevels. Gregg took out his tape and measured the gap between the bars, the way he had seen welding inspectors do, but it was too dark at the base of the column to see the lines of his rule. He didn't know what the gap was supposed to measure anyway. He let the tape recoil back into its housing with an authoritative *Snap!* and nodded knowingly.

What am I going to do? How am I going to tell them? Tell Jack. He'll kill me on the spot. He looked up through the cage-like scaffolding; the tower of black steel bars loomed above him against the blue of the morning sky. They say it has to be this or that but how much do they really mean it, how much of the codes and specifications are arbitrary? The notes on the drawing call for full-penetration welds, there's no getting around that. But the truth is the engineers themselves probably don't know what it's supposed to be, they try a set of calculations for one project and if the numbers work and the building doesn't fall down they say that's the way it's always supposed to be. These small tack welds are obviously strong enough to hold the rebar in place, the bars are standing here aren't they? Like that project out at the airport, I found all the joists were wrong and the engineer said don't worry about it, the joists were overdesigned anyway. How are you supposed to know what's right, which rules to follow? It's like everything else in the world. He climbed back out of the scaffolding. They make rules because they don't know what else to do, because they're afraid to live without them—society lives by its rules, Rousseau said that didn't he? if he didn't he should have. The generator for the welding machine revved up again, engulfing him momentarily in a cloud of thick black smoke; he turned away. Societies die by their rules too, I said that or should have. They told me I should get a job and contribute to society and look at me, counting steel bars and trying to reason with a pack of jackals, that's contributing to the social fabric, all right. When the cloud of smoke passed he turned back. Maybe the punks and the hippies are right after all, slam-dancing in the mosh pit at the Decade, tear it down whatever it is, because it won't do you any good anyway, but what does that leave you with? He went on to the last column to have a look at the welder. The condemned man marches to his doom.

A low wall encircled the welder, a barrier of four-by-eight sheets of plywood turned on edge, to protect the other workmen from the flash of the arc and to protect the arc itself in case of wind. The welder sat hunched on an upside-down bucket at the base of the column. Gregg peered over the makeshift barricade for several minutes; he was waiting for the man to stop welding and lift his hood so he could ask him some questions. But the welder kept at it, long past the time when Gregg thought he should stop.

The Building

One of the things that Gregg had picked up from listening to welding inspectors was that it was critical for a welder to stop after every pass and clean the slag from the weld. It was one of the principal reasons why continuous inspection was required on full-penetration welds, to make sure the welder was following the correct procedure. If the welder didn't stop and chip the slag from the weld and brush it clean, the slag could be trapped inside the next layer; there would be pockets of slag inside the joint instead of solid metal, which could cause the joint to fail under stress. But this welder, he kept on welding . . . and welding . . . and welding. . . . Gregg's anxiety increased as half a minute went by, then one minute, one and a half. When he couldn't stand it any longer, he slipped inside a narrow opening in the barricade and stood close behind the workman, protecting his eyes from the flash with his clipboard.

Finally the welder stopped. The generator for the welding machine settled into a steady *putt-putt-putt-putt* idle; this end of the deck became curiously still without the constant revving of the machine. For a moment, the workman continued to sit hunched over, resting his forearms on his thighs, the nozzle of the welding gun between his knees, apparently staring into the darkness inside the welding hood that covered his face. Then he raised the hood with a jerk of his head; the smooth fiberglass mask flipped up, sticking out from his forehead like a shelf. After staring straight ahead for a few seconds longer, the welder began sniffing the air, making a production out of it; he tilted up his head and sniffed again.

"Somebody in this here pen smells real purty," said the welder, "and it sure as hell ain't the workingman." He sniffed a couple more times, still looking away from Gregg. "I'll bet the only person in the world who'd wear a purty aftershave like that would be an in-spec-tor."

The welder turned his head slowly to look over his shoulder at Gregg. The plastic label on his hardhat read ANDY YURICK. Andy Yurick grinned.

"My, my. The young gentleman in-spec-tor wears purty after-shave, but he doesn't shave. Must be he just likes to smell purty."

Gregg scratched his beard uneasily. "Er . . . hi. What're you doing?" *I can't believe I said that.*

"What am I doing?" Andy Yurick contemplated. He had silver hair and a flushed leathery face; his nose and chin angled toward each other as if trying to meet, his mouth a slit in the narrow space between them. He looked off thoughtfully for a moment in the direction of the alley, at the buildings farther up the hillside.

"What I am doing? Well, actually I'm working on a new the-ory of quantum physics in here, but I have to be a little careful." Andy Yurick leaned toward Gregg as if to share a confidence and lowered his voice. "This is a construction site, you know? I don't want the other guys to think I'm a pansy or something." He looked around to make sure no one else was listening, then winked at Gregg. "So, I've cleverly disguised myself with this hood and all this gear and everybody thinks I'm welding these bars to-gether. Nifty, huh? All I have to do is flash this light every once in a while and make a lot of smoke and keep this hood down over my face, and everybody leaves me alone and I can go on thinking about my quantum physics theory. That is, until some smart young in-spec-tor comes along and finds me out. You won't tell nobody, will you?"

Gregg laughed nervously. "I mean, how's it going?"

"The quantum theory or the welding?" Andy Yurick shifted himself on the upturned bucket, as if he decided he had taken the joke far enough. "Actually, the work's going purty good. Only got these two columns left to do. This here welding gun knocks 'em out in no time."

The Building

The welder took a pair of clippers and snipped off a bead of metal from the end of the wire sticking out of the welding gun. Gregg had never seen anyone use an automatic welding machine before, the only welding he had seen was done with individual welding rods, but as far as he knew the same rules applied. He folded his arms, pressing his clipboard to his chest.

"I noticed you aren't cleaning your welds after you make a pass."

"Don't have to. This here is short arc."

"The code still says you're supposed to brush after every pass."

"You're talking about toothpaste and you mean you're supposed to brush after every meal." Andy Yurick grinned. When he saw that Gregg wasn't grinning in return, he held up the gun. "I told you. This is short arc. You don't have to do all that with short arc."

Gregg stiffened. Jack was coming toward them across the deck; he looked happy about something but his shoulders were hunched and squared, as if ready for a confrontation.

"Hey Andy, you done with that other column already?"

"Nope, haven't even started it yet."

Jack frowned. He stood outside the plywood barricade, not leaning on it, his hands in his pants pockets, watching the two of them inside. "Then what the hell you doing this last one for?"

"Oh, I just wanted a little variety. A little break in the routine, a random happening in an ordered world, a touch of chaos in—"

"Go to hell," Jack said. "Where's Bill? He's the rebar foreman, it's his job to keep tabs on these things."

"Haven't seen him," Andy Yurick said. "Nobody here but us chickens. And the in-spec-tor, of course."

Jack focused on Gregg. "So. What'd I tell you? The welding looks great, right? I can go on ahead and pour the columns, right?"

Richard Snodgrass

"If they looked any better you'd have to charge admission," Andy Yurick said, gazing up at Jack and Gregg from his bucket.

"Well, I don't know. . . ," Gregg said. He looked at the drawing again.

"What do you mean, you don't know?" Jack said. "If you don't know, who does? You're the inspector, aren't you?"

"Yeah, yes. I mean—"

"Then they're okay to pour, aren't they?" Jack walked around the barricade so he was beside Gregg.

Within arm's length so he's just a punch away. You're the inspector, aren't you? How did I ever get into this? I've got to have the right tone of voice, the right amount of authority and reason, animals can smell fear.

"You see, the drawing here calls for full-penetration welds."

"And that's what you've got, full-penetration welds," Jack said.

"But, you see, I don't know that."

"What do you mean you don't know that? I just told you they're full-penetration welds. You can see for yourself, they've got backup bars and everything, just like they're supposed to. Right, Andy? Everything's copacetic." Jack looked at Andy Yurick and worked his eyebrows up and down, clowning as if to try to smooth things over, as if to cover the anger that had begun to come into his voice.

Gregg's mind raced as he tried to remember the wording of the code; he wanted to explain it to Jack the way it had been explained to him, he wanted to make the superintendent understand. Don't you see it's not my fault, I'm only doing what I'm supposed to. "The code says that the inspector is supposed to be on the job while the welding is in progress—"

"So here you are. Andy's progressing with the welding and you're standing here."

"I ain't nothing if I ain't progressing," Andy Yurick said.

• 44 •

"But the code means the whole time the welding is—"

"Don't give me that shit," Jack said, leaning close to Gregg's face, no longer clowning. "No inspector stays with a welder the whole time. The other inspector we had out here spent most of his time over at the coffee shop. What do you think you're going to do, stand there and bird-dog Andy all day long? Don't make me laugh."

Jack turned away and looked across the deck. The concrete crew was finished pouring the first column and was moving on to the second. Above the slab, the boom of the concrete pump maneuvered jerkily toward the new position; the thick rubber hose dangling from the end of the boom swung back and forth like a giant black worm dancing down from the sky. Several laborers stood over the portable generator for the concrete vibrator, taking turns pulling on the starter rope. The vibrator, lying nearby on the deck, was a six-foot-long flexible shaft with a penis-shaped end; when the generator finally caught, the vibrator clattered off on its own across the deck until the crew captured it and turned it off. Jack turned back to Gregg. The man was obviously trying to keep himself under control, but he still looked ready to reach over the barricade and pick up Gregg and pitch him off the side of the building.

"So what are you telling me? Is the welding okay or not?"

. . . Look at how fast it's getting light now, the sun is almost up, the sky is no longer pink above the hills across the river, it's sort of peach-colored, and the sky overhead is baby-blanket blue. I just want to get away from here, I wish I were walking in those hills, kicking the leaves, what am I going to tell him? If I say the welds are rejected I can tell him about the welder not brushing after every pass but the welder says they don't need it and I don't know enough to know the difference and Jack will call my company and Emory will be all over me for causing trouble and what if I'm wrong, they're watching everybody's watching me. . . .

"Well, I don't hear you telling me that I *can't* pour the columns," Jack said finally. He squinted against the growing sunlight to get a better look at Gregg's face, as if giving him a chance to say something else. "Matter of fact, I don't hear you telling me anything at all. So fuck it. I'm going on ahead and pour them."

As he looked from Gregg to Andy to Gregg again, Jack clamped his mouth shut and puffed out his cheeks in a mock-grumpy face, but his eyes defied either one of them to say anything. Then he stomped off toward the front of the deck again, one pants leg riding up on the back of his boot, waving his arms and yelling at the concrete crew.

"What the hell you guys standing there looking at me for, pour the mother!"

Gregg looked down at Andy Yurick sitting on his bucket. Andy Yurick shrugged. "I wouldn't worry, young fellow. For all his hot air, Jack's one of the best in the business. You're in good hands. Now, if you'll excuse me, I'm going back to my quantum physics."

Andy Yurick aimed the welding gun at the joint he had been working on, nodded sharply once to flip the welding hood down over his face, and struck an arc. Gregg looked away.

That's all I did, I just stood there with a stupid grin on my face and it's all over now, I don't have to worry anymore, it's all taken care of, just like that, it was that easy, but that's not right, is it? No, I know the answer to that, I copped out, but it's over now.

He turned to leave the barricade but his knees were quivery and he found he could barely walk.

6

At the front of the deck, Jack leaned on the saggy guardrail as he watched the goings-on below. The next ready-mix truck had arrived and was waiting outside the fence, causing a minor traffic jam on the narrow main street. The drum of the mixer unloading at the pump was starting to rattle, the telltale sign that it was almost empty. The driver, an ex-wrestler named Bert who liked to strut around as if he were still in the ring, climbed up slowly onto the rear fender of the truck and worked the mixer controls with his foot; he spun the drum at high speed as he used the truck's water hose to wash the dregs of stone and sand and cement down the chute into the hopper of the pump. Then he began to casually hose off the rear blades inside the mixer.

Sloopy, the small hunchbacked laborer whom Jack had assigned to work at the concrete pump, turned around and looked up at Jack. Jack motioned with his hand: Get that guy out of here, get the next truck into position. Sloopy went over to the truck and said something up at Bert. The driver ignored him. Sloopy took the shovel in his hands and banged it a couple of times against the side of the fender to get Bert's attention. Way to go, Sloopy, you're learning. Bert stopped his spraying and, looking down from the fender of the truck, his boots approximately at the level of Sloopy's nose, said something to the laborer on the order of "Go to hell." Don't talk that way to my laborer, I'll take you apart. Sloopy didn't say anything; he pointed up at Jack. Bert looked to see where Sloopy was pointing—Yeah, asshole, I'm watching you—put the hose away and climbed down from the fender; as he started to get into the cab, Bert glanced up once more to see if Jack was still watching—Yeah I'm still watching—before he drove the truck out the gate.

Next time Bert comes back me and him are going to have us a little chat about how he treats Sloopy, whether I'm standing up here or not that fat-assed bastard.

As the next truck backed in the gate, Marshall came out of the first floor of the building and stood close to the fence so Jack could see him. He pantomimed to ask if he should take Jack's pickup and go to get some snap-ties. Jack shook his head: No. Marshall began to gesture something more about the snap-ties, then apparently thought better of it; he broke off his signals and headed toward the trailer to get something else, scuffling his feet in the dust, unconcerned one way or the other. Shit, Marshall was probably right, it would be a good idea to get the snap-ties now before lunch, no, wait a minute, we might be pulling off this job after today so we won't need the snap-ties anyway, three cheers for me, I just made another brilliant decision and didn't even know it, aren't I wonderful? Jack took the occasion to reward himself with another cigarette.

The next concrete truck backed up to the pump and its chute positioned over the hopper. Sloopy looked up at Jack to see if it was okay to start, his hands folded on top of the handle of his shovel as if in prayer. Jack nodded. Sloopy in turn nodded to Cowboy, the pump operator, and to the truck driver. The driver, standing at the rear of the mixer beside the controls, set the drum to spinning clockwise at high speed for a minute or so to make sure the concrete was thoroughly mixed, the truck rocking violently as the eight cubic yards inside were tossed about; then he reversed the direction of the drum until the first of the concrete spilled over the back fins and down the chute. As the hopper filled with concrete, Cowboy revved up the pump, sending up clouds of exhaust and diesel fumes like smoke signals; the twin pistons slammed back and forth, forcing the concrete up through the boom that towered a hundred feet in the air. When Jack was satisfied that everything was okay at the pump, he turned his attention to the work going on around the deck.

Holy shit, what is that kid doing now?

Across the deck, the young inspector was down on his hands and knees at the edge of the stairwell; he was backing over the edge, one leg floundering around through empty space as he tried to find a toehold on the ladder without looking. When he finally got himself onto the ladder, he hugged the rungs and oozed down out of sight. Jack was embarrassed to watch. The dumb jacking-off son-of-a-bitch, fooling around like that is a good way to get hurt. God, to let yourself be that scared of a little shitty-ass thing like a ladder. The poor dumb jacking-off son-of-a-bitch. Jack would have to keep an eye on him; he didn't want him to hurt himself or someone else in the process. But Jack had no intention of letting the inspector—any inspector, much less a green kid—interfere with the work going on today. Regardless what Mac or the pencil-pushers in the main office had in mind, as long as Jack was here it was his building, and things were done Jack's way.

Now, if my ankles would stop feeling like I've got red-hot pokers in my socks and my knees would stop trying to freeze up every time I'm in one position for more than two minutes and my elbow would stop feeling like it's about to drop off I'd be in good shape. Hell of a man. Hell of a condition for a man to be in. Take it easy old son, the doc said it'd take a while, no reason to think you won't keep getting better, you're lucky to be able to get around at all. What was it the doc said, We've never seen anyone like you before. Take a good look, I said, 'cause you're not going to see me again.

*

He had been the first workman for Drake Construction on the project, at a time when there was only a hole in the ground filled with rubble from the demolition of the existing buildings. While the demolition contractor finished hauling away the debris and leveling the site, Jack called in George, the labor foreman, and Marshall and several other laborers to help with the cleanup. Then he added carpenters to build the wood fence across the front of the project, and the carpenter foreman, Frank the German. Working with the transit, he and Frank the German transferred the benchmarks to the site and established the control points; then they laid out the walls of the building itself, making sure everything was square and true. It was Jack's favorite time on a building, any building. It was the time on a project when he could still do something with his own hands, when all he had to worry about was his own workmanship; it was the time when he got the most personal satisfaction from a building, before all the other trades were involved and he had to deal with their mistakes.

There was also time to play around. One afternoon he took the transit and aimed it at the rear of the buildings across the alley; he wondered if the rumble of heavy machinery during the demolition or cleanup had damaged the nearby structures. As he panned slowly across an orange brick surface, a window draped in lacy white sheers appeared in the small circle of magnification. Standing at the window was a black-haired young woman in a nurse's uniform. She was giving him the finger.

"See ya later," Jack said to Frank the German. He climbed out of the hole and took a walk up the hill to the other side of the block.

It was a three-story apartment building, on a street of three-story apartment buildings and large houses converted into doctors' and dentists' offices. In the entryway, the only label on the mailboxes that wasn't old and illegible was for apartment 3B: DiCello. The front door was broken so it wouldn't lock. Jack went up the stairs to the third floor and knocked on the door. The young woman in the nurse's uniform opened the door but kept the safety chain fastened.

"Hi," Jack said.

"Hi yourself. I see you got my message."

"Yeah. I was wondering if you have something against construction workers, or are you generally unfriendly?"

"I don't like being spied on," she said, not unfriendly, just matter-of-fact. "I figured if you were spying, you'd get my message."

"I wasn't spying, I was checking out the wall. Your window happened to get in the way."

"Hmm. Well, I still don't like someone peering in my windows without me knowing about it. To me that's spying."

"But you did know about it, because I was standing right out there in plain sight. So I couldn't have been spying. Maybe you were the one spying on me."

She started to smile but caught herself, as if she wanted to think that one over before she conceded too much. "Another thing," she went on. "Your generator or whatever it is that makes all the noise wakes me up in the mornings."

"If I'd known that, I would've put it around in front of the lot."

"You still can."

"Yeah, I guess you're right." Jack leaned on the door frame, still wearing his hardhat, one foot crossed over the other. "Anything else you want us to do for you? While we're at it?"

"Well, seeing as how you asked. . . ," she laughed. "Don't make your building so tall that it blocks my windows. I'm just getting used to having a view, I didn't have one until the old buildings that used to be there were leveled."

"That's going to be tough. They've already got the plans and everything saying how tall they want it. Tell you what though, suppose I leave a big hole in it right across from your apartment. That way you can see through it."

"Somehow I don't think it'll be the same. Wait a minute."

She closed the door to unfasten the chain and opened it again, wider this time though not all the way. Jack guessed she was in her early thirties, an attractive girl without being flashy, with dark eyes set wide apart and a mouth that she probably thought was too wide; her thick black hair and olive skin contrasted with her white uniform. She stood with one hand on the doorknob, the other fisted into her waist, studying him, a pleasant, slightly bemused smile on her face, as if he were a new patient with an ailment she had heard about but had never seen before. Jack pushed off from the door frame to stand upright; he filled the doorway, feet planted and squared, his hands in his jacket pockets.

"You going to work or just coming in? Or do you wear that uniform around because you know it makes you look good?"

"Every man loves a girl in a nurse's uniform, don't they?" She modeled it by swinging her shoulders back and forth. "It combines all the male fantasies of the Good Mother and the Virgin."

Jack grinned and cocked his head. "Offhand, I wouldn't say either one about you."

She laughed. Her voice was throaty, almost hoarse. "So, why aren't you down there playing in your big mud puddle? Or did you come over here to hassle me about giving you the finger?"

"Nope. I thought I should come over here and do a little inspecting."

"Oh. Are you the inspector?"

"Nah. I wouldn't stoop that low. 'Inspector' is sort of a dirty word to a workingman. But in special cases I do some inspecting on my own."

"And what's so special now that you think you need to inspect?"

"I was wondering if the work across the alley had opened up any cracks over here."

"I'll just bet you did," she said, appraising him.

"I told you. That's what I was doing with the transit when you gave me the finger: I was checking for cracks."

"And did you find any?"

As he said it about cracks opening up he realized how it might sound, that it sounded sexual when he didn't mean it that way—that would be pushy even for him; but there was something in the tilt of her head, the slight almost mischievous smile, the sureness in her eyes, that prompted him to go on with it.

"I'm still looking," he said, resetting his hardhat. "But it's getting promising. I guess it all depends on you."

"Do you want to explain that?"

"Well, the only way to see if there are any cracks here is in your apartment. So, it depends on whether or not you invite me inside."

"That remains to be seen, doesn't it?"

What the hell, I'm into it this far. . . . "I thought it was your cracks that remained to be seen. In your apartment, I mean."

"Suppose I let you in and you still don't see my cracks. Suppose they're the kind of cracks that you can't see right away?"

Jack was surprised; she could not only play this kind of game, she could turn it back on him. It was a relief: this young woman had strengths enough to match him. "I guess to do it right, I'd have to keep coming back until I did see them." He shrugged. "It's a dirty job but somebody has to do it."

She looked at him and shook her head as if he were hopeless. Then she opened the door the rest of the way and stood back. "All right, you can come in. I have to hand it to you, that's the most direct approach I ever heard."

"It worked, too," he said, brushing past her.

But once he was inside her apartment he began to have second thoughts as to what he was doing there. He felt out of place, out of scale even, among her things—the glimpse from the hall of her frilly pink-and-white bedroom; the living room tastefully decorated in earth tones, greens and browns; the small collection of china bells on the mantelpiece; the hutch of formal dinnerware in a dining room that looked never used—he who had worked out ways to feel comfortable almost anywhere. But after pushing it this far, he only knew to push it as far as it would go. In the living room he sank down on the brown plaid couch, took off his hardhat and set it upside down on the green shag carpet, and carefully rested his leg on the side of the spindly-legged coffee table. As she watched him get settled from the doorway, he said the first thing that came into his mind.

"Got a beer?"

Her name was Pamela. He didn't sleep with her that day—it would be more accurate to say that they didn't sleep together, to reflect their mutual states of mind—but the point was that he didn't even try. Nor did he sleep with her the first half dozen times he took her out. Which was something of a first for Jack; usually by that time, Jack had not only slept with a girl, he was already thinking of how to get away from her. But things with Pamela were different from the start. That first afternoon when he got back to the jobsite, he had George and Marshall help him hook up the generator to the back of his truck. Then, despite the fact that it meant laying out several hundred extra feet of hose once it was relocated, he towed the generator from the alley underneath her window around to the front of the project. When they were finished he looked up across the lot to where she watched from her window. Jack tipped his hardhat; Pamela curtsied in return.

"Mmm-mmm," said Marshall.

"Oh brother," said George.

He would meet her when she got off work, often close to midnight depending on her shift at the hospital, and they would go for drinks or a late snack. Sometimes she wore her nurse's uniform when they went out, sometimes they stopped at her apartment so she could change. She delighted in wearing something other than what was expected of her when they went somewhere— among the salesmen and businessmen who frequented the bar at the local Holiday Inn, she liked to wear jeans and her torn denim jacket; one night when they went for scrambled eggs and Jack Daniel's at the Reo Grill, she wore a little black cocktail dress and spike heels. She told Jack that it was something she had always wanted to do, to say to hell with what other people thought and wear whatever she felt like whenever she went someplace around town, to flout the small town's small-mindedness in its face; she said she had never had the nerve to do it before—which meant, before she was with Jack. Jack, who wore work clothes no matter where he went—a hickory shirt and black Frisco jeans, work boots and a zippered yoke-shouldered jacket; a clean set, of course, for going out—said only, "Isn't that wonderful?"

Late at night, they would ride through the dark, silent streets of the mill town in his pickup. She never sat close to him, all lovey-dovey in the middle of the seat, but stayed close to the opposite window, which was a good thing; either she understood how Jack felt about such matters—Hey, you've got your half of the seat and I've got mine—or she felt that way herself. Nor did they ever take Pamela's white Corvette whenever they went out. She liked riding in the truck, the new, tall perspective on her everyday world; she liked the wide bench seat that let her spread out as they drove along talking about this and that. Jack figured she just liked to be seen riding around in a pickup truck. She also seemed to realize that the matter was never really open for discussion. If the question had ever come up as to which vehicle they took, Jack would have settled it on the spot: "We'll take my truck."

The first time they slept together was one evening after he had taken her to Pittsburgh to show her some of his favorite haunts. They had dinner at the 1902 Landmark Tavern in Market Square, then went across the river and up to the heights of Mount Washington to the Georgetowne Inn for drinks and dessert. They sat for a long time looking out the picture windows without saying anything. Spread below them were the lights of downtown Pittsburgh in the Golden Triangle, the fountain at the Point where the Allegheny and Monongahela Rivers meet to form the Ohio, the lights of the Duquesne Incline slicing down the dark hillside. Finally, Jack said to her, "You want to go to a show or something, as long as we're here in the 'Burgh?"

She leaned across the table and cupped her two hands over one of his. "No. You've accomplished what you set out to do."

"And what's that?"

"You've treated me like a lady."

"Yeah, right," he sniggered and looked out the window. The cars of the incline were approaching each other along the lighted tracks, one sliding down, the other climbing up to meet it; they passed in the middle of the dark slope and each traveled on.

"You've showed me how much you think of me and that I don't have to be afraid of you."

He looked at her again, but before he could say anything she went on. "Now it's time to go back to my place and fuck."

*

Even that first night it was like we had been making love together all our lives, it was always like that with her—no, it got even better as time went on, usually if you fuck as much as we did it gets boring after a while but it was always exciting with her. Exciting and comfortable, old and new. So what happened to us, how did it go wrong? The same way it always goes wrong. They always want to get too close, she started to act like she wanted to be part of me or something. That's what always happens, that's just the way things are, what can you do? It's the same with everybody you have to deal with in this world, you give 'em a little bit and they want everything you've got. . . .

The outdoor buzzer on his telephone in the trailer was ringing. Jack turned around and leaned over the guardrail so he could see the trailer below. The ringing stopped; Marshall came out of the trailer, looked up, held an imaginary receiver to his ear, and pointed to Jack. Jack shrugged his shoulders: Who is it? Marshall thought a moment, then held up his left hand, slipped an imaginary ring on the fourth finger, and pointed again to Jack. My wife. Speaking of things that always go wrong. What the hell would she be calling about at this hour of the morning? Must be another one of her emergencies: a light bulb burned out that she can't reach, or one of the characters on her favorite soap opera died. Oh boo-hoo. Jack cupped his hands around his mouth and, over the noise of the concrete mixer and the pump and several generators and the welding machine and the vibrator and the crane and two electric saws plus the noise of traffic along the main street, shouted down to Marshall:

"Find out what she wants!"

Along the sidewalks on either side of the main street, nine different people, each engaged in separate activities such as waiting for the drugstore to open, coming home from morning mass, or going to the grocery store, stopped whatever they were doing and looked up toward the voice from on high as if to say Find out what who wants?

Marshall nodded and went back inside; when he came out a minute later, he tried to yell something to Jack. Jack cupped his hand to his ear: What? Marshall looked around as he considered the problem; then he held up his hands in front of him as if they were puppets and mimicked them talking back and forth at each other. He grinned broadly, proud of himself, knowing how Jack felt about talking to his wife. Jack gave him the finger; Marshall doubled over laughing and did a little dance. She'd never call me at this hour just to talk, something must have happened. He held up his wrist so Marshall could see it and tapped his watch: Tell her I'll call her later. Marshall nodded and went inside again. When he came back out, carrying an electrical cord, which was the reason he was in the trailer to begin with, he nodded up at Jack. Can't be too serious if that's okay with Ellie, otherwise Marshall would be lacking an ear right about now from her chewing it off. Marshall laughed again at him, exposing his teeth to the gum line, but Jack ignored him and turned back to the deck.

A few minutes later he glanced down again and saw Gregg walk out of the building. Wonderful, the kid's just getting down to the ground, he must have hugged the ladders the whole way down, that's all the Old Man would need to see, an inspector farting around like that, there'd be no more inspector. But I guess it's better this kid than some guy with a hard-on. Gregg stood ill at ease beside the mixer, trying to get the driver's attention. When the driver finally turned his head, Gregg said something but the driver only shrugged and went back to watching the concrete as it slid down the chute. As Gregg walked away, the driver and Cowboy grinned at each other and shook their heads. Wonder what the kid said, no, I don't want to know.

Jack was about to turn away when Bill and his crew of ironworkers came out of the building and headed out the gate and across the street.

"Hey George, where the hell is Bill going?"

George came to the railing beside him. He folded his hands meditatively inside the bib of his overalls as he looked over the edge of the building. "Well sir, I'd hazard a guess and say he's going across the street."

"I can see that, goddamn it."

"And, from the looks of it, I'd say he's heading for the Furnass Grill and taking his crew for their coffee break."

"It's not even nine o'clock. What the hell is he taking his coffee break now for?"

George took a pocket watch from inside his overalls and flipped open the cover. "According to my chronometer, it is exactly nine-oh-eight. So he's jumping the gun by twenty minutes or so."

"Where the hell has he been all morning? I haven't seen him."

The Building

"He was down on three for a while, straightening the dowels for the block man," George said, putting his watch away. He took off his rigger's hat and rubbed his hand over his stiff white brush cut and reset the hat on his head. "And he's been watching for his truck in the alley. He's got a load coming in this morning. You had me move the crane around there, remember?"

"Yeah, I remember." *You old bastard, are you making fun of me? I never can tell. I'm surrounded by smart-asses and know-it-alls.* "Nice of him to tell me he's taking his coffee break early."

"What would you have said if he told you?" George asked.

"I would have told him to take his break at nine-thirty like everybody else."

"That's probably why he didn't tell you."

Jack looked at him. George was gazing across the rooftops of the town at the hills across the river, a faraway look in his eye. *You old bastard, you don't even care, do you, you're out there walking the hills chasing after a deer or something. Why can't I be more like that, what the hell am I doing killing myself over this shit all the time?* George turned toward him, chomped once on empty air, and went back to his labor crew.

What did Bill say to me last night? Let's go out and get a drink, what do you say? I want to talk to you about something. I'm thinking of leaving my wife for Pamela. What's the matter, you too good to drink with me now? Asshole, it's probably a good thing I haven't seen him this morning. This here is Bill, I brought him over to take a look at your cracks. You son-of-a-bitch Jack I know what you're doing. I should never have. But hey, you make your own party.

Below, close to the mixer and the pump, Gregg wandered over toward the fence; he kicked at a small mound of dried concrete, the dregs that some driver had washed down his chute, then tried to stand on top of it. *I wouldn't do that if I was you. . . .* The young man's weight broke loose some of the dried aggregate that became like marbles under his feet; he slid off the mound, his arms and legs going like a skater's trying to keep his balance, catching himself on one outstretched arm so he didn't fall completely on the ground. Cowboy and the driver exchanged more grins.

Poor dumb jacking-off son-of-a-bitch, though he did look funny there, maybe I can fix him up in the trailer, give him my desk to sit at and get him some magazines to read or something, he could stay in there all day and keep out of trouble, I'd be doing him a favor.

It was time to take another tour of the building, move the hat around; it was time to make sure everybody knew he was there and keeping an eye on things. Jack pushed off from the railing, corkscrewed his pants back up into position around his waist, and sauntered across the deck. Look out, you pussies, here I come. Don't nobody mess with me today. I should never have introduced Bill to her.

7

Bill van Hayden could feel the color rising to his cheeks as he entered the Furnass Grill. Look at everybody turn around and look, I hate this, just mind your own business. There were empty seats at the back on one side of the long U-shaped counter. He thought it best to sit away from everyone else, aware that he and his crew were in their work clothes and dirty and out of place; the problem was that it meant calling more attention to themselves by trooping past everyone to get there. He led the way down the long counter, past the businessmen and secretaries, the early shoppers and the mental patients from the local community houses, the patrons who filled the coffee shop at this hour, assuming Crazy Levon and Tony were right behind him. Halfway down the row he remembered his manners and took off his chromed hardhat. He had almost made it to the empty stools when there was a loud *Bonk!* behind him: he looked back just in time to see Crazy Levon's dented orange hardhat come skating down the floor toward him. The hat ricocheted off Bill's boot and clattered like a fiberglass pot among the stools along the counter.

Everyone in the restaurant froze, wondering what was going on. Bill's face was blotchy with embarrassment. At the front of the long aisle, Crazy Levon crouched like a bowler who had just completed his follow-through; he straightened up, pumped his arm once, and called "Stee-rike!"

How could he do that to me? Everybody's watching me.

Tony Serrabella, the old man of the crew, gave Crazy Levon a shove from behind. "Come on, you crazy sonamabitch, you disturbing everybody in the place. Sorry, everybody, you go back to eating. I try but I can't do nothing with him."

Levon careened off-balance into the wall and doubled over laughing. Bill pretended to ignore him and sat down. They're watching me. Levon caused more of a stir along the aisle by getting down on his hands and knees to retrieve his hardhat from among the feet along the counter, keeping up a steady monologue as he hunted around for it.

". . . 'Scuse me, folks, 'scuse me . . . nice shoes you got there ma'am . . . wonder if they ever sweep down here . . . c'mere, damn you hat. . . ." Tony took the opportunity to kick him in the ass. "Thank you, thank you," Levon said, backing out. "I don't know who you are but you've done me a world of good."

Jo came down the counter to Bill and waited, coffeepot in hand. "Can't you put a leash on him?"

"Both of them," Bill said.

"Bof of 'em," Jo said, echoing one of the local quirks of pronunciation. She grinned with one side of her mouth as she turned the three cups right-side up and poured their coffees.

Bill was handsome, with movie-star good looks, a stirrup chin and high cheekbones; in contrast to his angled features, he had a baby-smooth peaches-and-cream complexion and tended to blush easily. The other two ironworkers straddled the stools on either side of their foreman. Levon, his horsey bearded face twisted with laughter, reset his glasses and collapsed against Bill, put his arm around his shoulders.

"I'm sorry, Billy. I didn't mean to embarrass you, but you looked like a lone tenpin there. I don't know what comes over me . . . Lord, if you could've seen your face. . . ."

"You know, guys, we're trying to run a nice quiet respectable place here," Jo said, doing her best to appear stern.

Bill looked around for someplace to put his shiny hardhat; and, as he did every morning, ended up holding it between his knees. Levon and Tony put theirs on the floor at their feet.

Jo shook her head in mock exasperation and got them three glasses of water. She was the same age as Bill and Levon, in her late thirties, maybe a little older, with a full fleshy body, easy smile, and collie eyes. When she bent over to get something from under the counter, Levon pretended to leer down her blouse. Jo gave him a look that sat him upright again. She looked down the counter to check on her other customers, then wet her thumb and rustled through her order pad to find her place.

"You're something else, brother, I'll tell you that," she said to no one in particular.

"That ain't nothing," Tony said. He was a small wiry man with gray sideburns arced across his cheeks and a heavily waxed spiked mustache. "You shoulda seen him the time he beat up a car."

"You beat up a car?" Jo said. "What do you guys want?"

"Sweet roll," Bill said.

"Sweet roll," Levon said.

"Sweet roll," Tony said.

"I don't know why I bother to ask," Jo said as she stuck her pad back in her apron pocket. She took three sweet rolls from under the plastic cover of the pastry tray and put them in the microwave. Then she cocked her hip at the trio, waiting. "So, you going to tell me? What did he do to the car?"

"We was stuck in traffic one night, up there near the West End circle, it was a couple of years ago, and this crazy sonama-bitch—ah, you tell her, Bill." Tony put his head in his hands.

"Somebody tell me," Jo said.

"This guy behind me kept honking about something," Bill said. "I guess he wanted me to stop letting cars in ahead of me."

"Gentleman Bill always lets cars in ahead of him," Crazy Levon said as he flipped his long red ponytail off the back of his neck. "Drives me crazy."

Jo smiled. "That sounds like Bill."

"You didn't help matters any," Bill said to Levon, "giving the guy the finger."

"And that sounds like Levon," Jo said.

"The guy was har-assing my man Bill," Levon said. "Nobody har-asses my man Bill."

Bill was embarrassed at being the center of attention as he proceeded with the story; the red patches grew on his cheeks. He shifted his hat between his knees, touched his water glass as if to take a drink then decided not to. "Anyway, the guy finally bumped my truck a little. Not hard, just a tap, I still say he didn't mean to."

"Nobody taps my man Bill. Nobody," Levon said without humor. He stared straight ahead.

The microwave buzzed. Jo hot-fingered the rolls onto plates and served them. Then she leaned on the counter, hunkered down on both elbows, to hear the rest of the story.

Bill laughed a little. "Well, Levon, after the guy taps us, he gets out of the truck real calm and goes back and leans over the bed and gets his hammer out of his tool belt—"

"It was my hammer," Tony piped up. "Sonamabitch gets my hammer!"

"I got the first hammer I found," Levon said proudly.

". . . takes the hammer—traffic's beginning to move ahead by this time, of course, we're holding up the whole line of cars behind us—and goes back to the other guy's car and beats the hood in."

"You're kidding," Jo said, merry-eyed.

Bill shook his head.

"Wham! Wham! Wham!" Crazy Levon said, demonstrating with his fork. "Beat that sucker to a pulp."

"Damn near. Put a half dozen good-size dents all over the front of the guy's Cutlass." Bill laughed again.

"Oh the look on that guy's face," Tony said, holding his head. He took his hands away and mimicked a look of bug-eyed terror and then held his head again.

"You're lucky the guy didn't have a gun and shoot you," Jo said.

"He's lucky I didn't beat his head in instead," Levon said. "Nobody har-asses my Billy-Boy and gets away with it. 'Cept me, of course."

"Levon jumps back in the truck and I get us the hell out of there, I took the first side street I came to."

"It took us five hours to get home that night," Tony said between bites of sweet roll. "I bet we hid from that guy in every bar in the West End, didn't we, Bill?"

"We sure as hell gave it our best shot," Levon remembered fondly.

"You're all crazy," Jo grinned.

"That's when I stopped riding with these guys, they get me into too much trouble," Bill said. "After that, I don't care how far away the job, I ride by myself."

"You never did hear from that guy, did you?" Crazy Levon said. "He musta been too scared to write down the license plate number."

"Or afraid if you found out who he was, you'd go after him again."

The three men laughed. Jo straightened up, shaking her head but obviously amused, and took the coffeepot down the counter, looking for half-filled cups.

Levon and Tony continued to snigger as they ate their rolls and drank their coffee, breaking up whenever one or the other remembered something else about the incident. On the other side of the U-shaped counter, two men were watching Levon, insurance agents from a local company, large soft men in ill-fitting polyester suits; they looked at Levon as if they were observing a lower form of life. Bill stared back at them. You got a problem with him? Huh? Don't look at him that way, he's my best friend, my partner, I'll come over there and. . . . When they noticed Bill watching them, the men quickly looked away and became interested in their own conversation.

. . . but you can't blame them for looking, the way these two carry on, making a spectacle of themselves, they're like children, giggling back and forth at each other across me, all I am is in the way between them. Why can't I be more like that, like Levon, he never worries about what people think of him, he just enjoys himself and to hell with other people, screw 'em. And look at all these people along the counter, in the booths, sitting here enjoying themselves, coming in here was no big deal for them, they're just here to have a nice time, what's wrong with me, why does going somewhere anywhere always have to be such an effort for me, why can't I just enjoy myself like other people, why can't I turn off my mind. . . ?

He hoped Jo would come back, he wanted to talk to her some more; but every time she returned to refill their cups she was busy and didn't stay. The lethargy, the heaviness that seemed his constant companion lately, was coming over him again. He sat tapping the uneaten half of his sweet roll with his fork.

"If you're done beating that thing to death, I'll eat it for you," Levon said, reaching across him and spearing the roll with his fork.

"C'mon, it's time to get back," Bill said, getting up quickly and heading down the aisle. Levon and Tony shrugged to each other and hurried to finish.

As Bill stopped to pay at the front counter, Jo came over and told the waitress who was already at the register that she'd take care of him.

"They stick you with the check again?" Jo said, ringing it up.

"Yeah. My lucky day."

Jo smiled. After she gave him his change, she stepped out beside the counter to be closer to him. "Do you know if Jack's coming over this morning?"

"Careful of your vitals there, Billy-Boy," Levon said as he passed on his way toward the door. "I think she's got her eyes on 'em." Jo flicked her hand under her chin at him. Tony pushed the giggling taller man out the door.

Jo was looking at him, waiting for an answer to her question about Jack.

"I don't know if he'll be over or not. They're pretty busy, they've got a big pour today."

"I thought maybe he said something."

"Nope." Bill looked out the front windows at the traffic going past. I said I want to talk to you about something and Jack said You and me don't have nothing to talk about.

"Something wrong between you and Jack?"

"Why? Did he say something?"

"No, you know Jack. He talks a lot but he only tells you what he wants to."

"Big-mouth Jack."

She studied his face, looking for something. "You two don't seem to get along like you used to. When that job started, I thought you two went out drinking all the time."

"We went out a few times," Bill said with a shrug. What does she want from me? Why is she looking at me like that? I said I thought you and me were friends and Jack said Well you thought wrong. "What's all this talk about Jack for, anyway? Here I come over to see you, and all you want to do is talk about some other guy. That's no way to be."

She smiled tight-lipped and rubbed the flat of her hand up and down his arm. "How's Pamela?"

"What's that supposed to mean?"

"Nothing. Boy, you sure are touchy today."

"First you have all those questions about Jack, and now you want to know about me and Pamela. Do you know something I don't?"

Jo closed her eyes, shook her head. "No, I don't know something you don't. You're not hearing me."

Didn't you see Jack last night? I thought maybe you were the reason why he was busy last night. You thought wrong. We're not friends, we're coworkers. That's all we are and I said What's the matter, you too good to drink with me now?

"I'll tell you, Bill, you're a real nice fellow. But you sure could use an attitude adjustment."

"Thanks. Anytime I need straightened out I'll remember that you have all the answers."

"Don't go away mad."

"Yeah, I know, just go away."

She started to touch his arm again, but decided not to; she shook her head and went back down the counter to clear dishes. Bill watched her go, watched her pillowy ass in the tight waitress uniform. What was she getting at? Is there something she's not

telling me? Jack said Only your friends will screw you. What was
he telling me last night? Or trying not to tell me. Jesus, why
can't I leave it alone? He stuck a toothpick in his mouth, angled
his chromed hardhat on his head, and pushed out the door after
his crew.

8

When Gregg came down from the top of the building, he stood
for a while close to the inside of the fence out of everyone's way,
pretending to watch the concrete truck unloading at the pump.
He was mortified about what had happened with the welding; he
was ashamed of the way he had acted, or failed to act, in his
confrontation with Jack. Gregg was sure that everyone on the job
knew he had made a fool of himself and was talking about it
among themselves. Did you hear what happened up on the deck?
That kid just stood there with a stupid grin on his face and let
Jack do whatever he wanted. What a pussy. He had even risked
climbing down the ladders rather than take the manhoist; the
fear of falling down the stairwell seemed nothing compared to the
fear of having to talk to Jack again. I'm still shaking, did the guy
scare me that much? You better believe it. Like trying to reason
with a runaway truck. He looked like he was going to hit me.
Gregg was furious with himself for letting the man rattle him; at
the very least, he should have admitted that he wasn't sure about
the welding procedure and told Jack that they needed to clear it
with the engineer or architect. He was furious with Jack for bullying him into accepting it.

Gradually, however, some of his confidence began to return.
Of course he didn't know about welding, how could he know
about welding, he had never inspected it before, he was a concrete
inspector. He decided to get his equipment from his car and do
the tests on the concrete that he was supposed to do. Concrete
was something that he did know about.

The Building

There were a number of tests required by the building codes. The most important one was to take test cylinders; that consisted of filling three or four six-by-twelve-inch metal cans with fresh concrete, then storing them carefully on the jobsite until they were taken to the laboratory for compression tests. Another test involved filling a tall-necked bronze container with concrete and swinging it about like an Indian club, the purpose being to measure the amount of air in the mix. But Gregg's favorite, if only for its name, was the slump test. For that, he took a twelve-inch-tall cone, open at both ends, and filled it with concrete, then carefully lifted the mold; the concrete would stay in place for a second or two, quiver a bit, maybe give a slight shudder, then, from its own weight and consistency, the cone-shaped glob would—how else to describe it?—slump. When he told people about his job, old friends he knew at Pitt or the girls he met at his apartment complex, he pantomimed the action of the concrete during a slump test, slouching all the way to his knees if the laughs were good enough; he always ended with the line, "And for this I got a college degree?"

When he returned to the job with his equipment—bucket, scoop, bullet-shaped rod, slump cone, test cans, thermometer, air meter—he was disappointed; he had hoped the sight of all his test gear might make an impression on Cowboy and the truck driver—Watch out, here he comes, now we're in trouble—but they barely acknowledged his return. His heart sank when Jack, coming out of the manhoist, saw what Gregg was getting ready to do and came over.

"Hey, why don't you let him take those cylinders for you?" Jack's hands were in his jacket pockets, his arms winged out at his sides; whenever he moved the water-repellent material of his jacket hissed slightly. The "him" Jack referred to was the hump-backed laborer, Sloopy.

"No, that's okay, I'll get them myself," Gregg said.

"I'm serious," Jack said. "That's what I did for the other guy."

"What other guy?"

"The other inspector who was out here. The old man, Clarence. I felt sorry for him messing around with all that stuff, so I had Sloopy take the cylinders for him. Right, Sloopy?"

Sloopy looked at Jack, to make sure that it was all right to agree, then nodded at Gregg. His face was calico-colored with large birthmarks, his head misshapen as if at some time it had been badly squeezed; his lips were permanently puckered so that when he spoke the words seemed to dribble from his mouth. "I can sure enough fill those cans for you, good as anybody."

He's making fun of me now, that's what he's doing, he's saying a laborer can do my job. "No thanks. It's my responsibility."

"Suit yourself." Jack shrugged to Sloopy and lit a cigarette. He obviously intended to stay close by to watch what went on.

Gregg found a clean sheet of plywood and laid it on the ground as a work surface a few feet from the pump; he made a production out of checking to see that the sheet was level, using scraps of wood as wedges to brace up one end. The son-of-a-bitch wants to make it tough for me, he doesn't think taking cylinders is serious business, I'll show him, I'm doing this strictly by the book.

When Gregg was almost finished setting up his equipment, Jack hollered to him over the noise of the truck spinning its drum at high speed, "You want some of this load? It looks pretty good."

Gregg took his time answering; he went over to take a look at the concrete coming down the chute as the mixer started to unload again. Of course he'd want me to sample it if it looks good, it would serve him right if I took it from the worst-looking load I can find but I guess this will do. "Yes, but I'll need a wheelbarrow."

Jack squinted at him for a moment, gauging whether Gregg was serious or not, then moved closer so he wouldn't have to shout so loud. "What do you need a wheelbarrow for? The other inspectors just use a bucket or something."

"Because I've got a lot of tests to run and I need a representative sample."

"'A representative sample.' Oh Jeez." Jack laughed, puffed out his cheeks, and looked around at Cowboy and Guido, the driver. The machinery had settled down to a steady din; the pistons of the pump snapped back and forth, the mixer revved occasionally as Guido worked to keep a steady flow of concrete coming down the chute. Jack's normal voice was loud enough to carry above the noise. "I had an inspector once who used to get 'a representative sample,' all right. He brought a set of flagstone molds with him every time he came to the job to take a set of test cylinders. Some for you, some for me. He had himself a nice little business making patios on the weekends."

Cowboy leaned down over the controls of the pump to listen; he sputtered and laughed and reset his cowboy hat on his head, he could believe it. Guido, sucking on a section of an orange, nodded. Jack looked at Gregg to see his reaction to the story. Is he trying to be friendly? Don't be ridiculous, you can't trust him, he's only trying to intimidate you some more.

"Okay, okay," Jack said. "I'll get you a wheelbarrow. Sloopy!"

Jack barely had the name out of his mouth before the laborer appeared in front of him. Jack sent him inside the building. In a few minutes Sloopy returned, bouncing an empty wheelbarrow over the ruts of hardened mud and concrete in front of the building.

"Here it is, I found it, Jack. It was right where you said, I got it." Sloopy turned the wheelbarrow up on its nose to present it to Gregg, as proud as if he had made it himself.

"Isn't that wonderful?" Jack said.

Gregg looked at the wheelbarrow, looked at Jack. "I'm afraid it has to be a clean wheelbarrow."

Jack eyed him, the smoke from the cigarette in his mouth creating a small gray curtain in front of his face. Sloopy leaned over and peered inside the wheelbarrow.

"It sure enough looks clean to me," Sloopy said wistfully.

Gregg took his finger and flaked off a piece of the dried mud, sawdust, mortar, and what have you that lined the inside of the wheelbarrow. "You see? It'll flip right off like that and get into the test samples."

"Then don't flip it off like that," Jack smiled.

How can I explain this? Don't trust him. "The book says—"

"Oh Jeez, they sent me a book jockey," Jack said, more like a groan. "Okay, okay. Sloopy, go hose it out for the book jockey."

Sloopy bounced the wheelbarrow over to the water hose near the fence and began to wash it out, muttering dejectedly to himself, "I thought it was sure enough clean, it looked sure enough clean to me. . . ." In the process he sprayed everything and everybody within fifteen feet. Cowboy and Guido got very busy with their respective machines. Gregg turned his back to the occasional shower that drifted his way, but Jack stood there as if it didn't exist.

"It's really for your own benefit," Gregg said. I'll try a little basic psychology on him. "We want all the tests to come up to specifications, don't we?" He thought the "we" was a nice touch.

"You know what happens to a book-jockey lieutenant in the army, don't you? He gets himself fragged. Somebody rolls a fragmentation grenade under his cot while he's asleep."

Jack looked at him sideways, a kind of grin on his face. So much for basic psychology. Gregg's stomach sank a couple of notches; he had heard stories of inspectors who were met after work by laborers wielding two-by-fours, stories of something heavy that happened to fall from a floor above as an uncooperative inspector walked below. As far as Gregg was concerned, he had just been threatened with bodily harm. Gregg and Jack stood side by side as they waited, neither one saying anything to the other.

In a few minutes, the calico-faced laborer brought the wheel-barrow back again. This time Sloopy didn't turn it upright for Gregg's inspection. "It's sure enough clean this time, Jack. 'Less'n he wants me to take the paint off it too." Sloopy smiled, his lips folded over each other like a llama's, proud of his attempt to make a joke.

Is he laughing at me too? Is everybody in the whole world?

"That's clean enough, Sloopy," Jack said, leaving no room for discussion. "Take it over to the truck and get your shovel."

It wasn't clean enough, of course, it wasn't even close; the crust of old material on the inside of the wheelbarrow was still there, only it was wet now. But Gregg decided that he'd better not push the issue any further, he'd just have to remember not to scrape the sides. That was the least of his worries at the moment. Sloopy had scrambled up onto the back of the pump and stood straddling the grate over the hopper, ready to shovel the concrete flowing down the chute into the wheelbarrow.

"Now what the hell's the matter?" Jack said, reading the pained expression on Gregg's face.

"The chute needs to be swung over so I can get a sample of the entire flow. . . ." Is my voice shaky? How'd I ever get myself into this?

"But I'd have to the stop the pour to do that."

"See, otherwise the concrete might separate as it comes down the—"

"Stop the pour!" Jack bellowed, loud enough that it startled Sloopy—Cowboy had to grab the laborer's arm to keep him from falling off the pump. Guido stopped the drum of the mixer; the section of orange he was sucking on covered his mouth like an orange grin. Jack continued to bellow as he tossed his cigarette away and went over to the mixer, looking in turn at Guido, Cowboy, Sloopy.

"Everybody knows it's more important to take test cylinders than it is to pour columns, doesn't everybody know that? That's the only reason we're all out here today, isn't it? We're only pouring those columns up there to have something to do until the inspector's ready to take his goddamn tests. Isn't that wonderful? Get down from there, Sloopy, I'll take care of this."

Jack waited until Sloopy had climbed down, then he swung the chute away from the hopper and unfolded the double section; the two sections of the chute snapped together with a resounding *Kerchunk!* like the sound of a guillotine. With the chute positioned over the wheelbarrow, Jack nodded to the driver.

"Okay, Guido. Give him what he wants."

Jack stood back, hitching up his pants around his middle, then pushing them down again as he jammed his hands in his pockets.

Guido looked at Gregg, speaking through his orange-peel grin. "You ready?"

"Let 'er rip," Gregg said, trying to be jocular.

Guido let 'er rip; he gunned the mixer and sent a glob of concrete splashing down the chute that completely filled the wheelbarrow, several hundred pounds' worth. Guido spit out the rind, the orange grin replaced with his own. "Oops. Looks like I gave you a little too much."

"That there is sure enough a rep'sentative sample," Sloopy said.

Gregg stared at the wheelbarrow for a moment. Now what am I going to do? How'd I ever get myself into this? I've got to go through with it now. Without saying a word or looking at any of them—I'm not going to let these guys get the better of me, I can do this—he took his place between the handles of the wheelbarrow—I can do this, I'm in pretty good shape . . . I better be able to do this—and lifted, getting a feel of the weight—Oof!

The Building

Christ it's heavy. . . . He waited until the sloshing mass settled down—Just take it easy, take your time, you can do this—then took a step—There, that wasn't so bad—and a second—I'm rolling!—and tried to turn the wheelbarrow toward the sheet of plywood and his equipment—I've got it now!—when the weight shifted and the wheelbarrow tipped over—No! Please!—spilling the concrete on the ground and over his boots.

"Hoo-ee!" Cowboy hooted from on top of the pump.

"Oh, oh, oh, oh, oh, oh, oh, oh, oh, oh," Sloopy said, genuinely dismayed.

Gregg looked at the concrete on the ground, then turned around and started to walk away. Just get out of here as fast as you can just leave it just go—

"Where the fuck do you think you're going?"

Jack's voice stopped him in his tracks. Gregg turned around slowly. Jack was bearing down on him as if ready to hit him. Here it comes, here it finally comes. But he brushed by Gregg and pulled the wheelbarrow from the lake of concrete and dragged it back under the end of the chute.

"Pour me half a wheelbarrow," he said quietly to Guido, "and you'll eat every bit that's over that."

Guido filled the wheelbarrow exactly half full. Jack picked up the handles and wheeled it over beside Gregg's equipment, then came back to Gregg, his face within inches of Gregg's face, and spoke in an undertone that no one else could hear.

"You take your fucking cylinders and you stop your fucking around and then you get the fuck back upstairs with that fucking pour and those fucking columns where you might be able to do some fucking good, you fucking hear me? And don't you ever fucking let me see you turn your fucking back and try to fucking walk away from some fucking mess you've made. Ever."

Jack glared at him, staring him in the eyes, his round pudgy face glowing with rage. Then he walked to his trailer and slammed the door behind him. For a moment nobody said anything. Finally, Sloopy said to no one in particular, "Jack sure enough gets mad sometimes, don't he?" The laborer took his shovel and began to skim the concrete off the ground and put it into the hopper.

It was decidedly against the code to mix the contaminated material with the good. But as soon as he could get his legs to function again—Here I am again shaking like a goddamn kid because of Jack or maybe it's something else—Gregg picked up his scoop and went over to help.

9

What was Jo getting at? How's Pamela? What's that supposed to mean? Boy, you sure are touchy today. Who wouldn't be? Nah, think I'll pass. I said What's the matter, you too good to drink with me now? I thought we were friends and Jack said What, just because we went out and had a couple of drinks once in a while? No way. We're only guys that work together, that's all, we're coworkers on a job. I don't want any friends because it's your friends that'll screw you. Your enemies never screw you because you never let 'em close enough. Ah just forget about it, no I won't.

The glint from Bill's chromed hardhat, a spidery crescent of reflected light, preceded him as he walked along the sidewalk; it scuttled across the storefronts at eye level a few feet in front of him, dipping in and out of doorways and the murky pools of the display windows—across the plaster smiles of mannequins in the latest spring fashions; a display of shoes as if all that remained after a small crowd was vaporized; signs for a sale of Valentine cards and decorative hearts—a constant companion now that the sun was out, though Bill was unaware of it. Farther down the street, Levon and Tony ambled along, taking their time as they waited for him to join them, but Bill was in no hurry to catch up. The patches that appeared whenever he was angry or embarrassed burned on his cheeks—clown patches, he thought of them, as red as if he had used his wife's blusher. He rolled the toothpick in his mouth from one side to the other and turned away from his reflection in a dark window.

Ahead, on the other side of the narrow main street, the building under construction looked down upon the smaller buildings around it. He was glad that their part of the project was coming to an end in a month or so, it would be a relief to get away from here. At least maybe it would make Mary happy; maybe then she would stop bugging him about all the time he spent driving back and forth to Furnass. As if he had a choice of where the jobs were and where the company sent him. As if he had a choice regarding most things in his life. As if I didn't have a wife to worry about too. As if Mary wasn't a part of my life, as if I didn't leave her each morning and return to her each night, as if she wasn't the mother of my child and we didn't share the same bed. How can I even think of another woman when I love Mary, at least I think I love Mary, it's as if during the main hours of the day five days a week Mary doesn't exist, as if our life together doesn't count for a thing, what makes a person do something like that? His head snapped to the side involuntarily; he wouldn't think about such things. He took the toothpick from his mouth. Broken already; he hated when they did that. He considered going back to the coffee shop to get another but it meant that he might have to talk to Jo again. He tossed the toothpick in the gutter.

Levon pulled Tony into the doorway of one of the storefronts. Bill continued to poke along behind them at his own pace.

It would be a relief about Pamela too. At times he couldn't stand the thought of the job coming to an end, of not being able to see her every day during the week; as he thought of it now his breath caught in his lungs, he felt as though his chest would collapse from within. I want to talk to you about something. I'm

thinking about leaving my wife for Pamela. But when this job
finished up, his relationship with Pamela would be out of his
hands in many ways; it would be a relief not to have to worry
because so much would be determined for him. It would depend
on where the next job was, where the company sent him; it would
depend on how close the new job was to Furnass, how often he
could get away to see her. It would depend on how much she still
wanted to see him when he wasn't just across the alley. Can I
help it if you got yourself mixed up with a girl that's popular
with a lot of guys? Who could say what would happen? Maybe
on the next job he'd find another girl that would make him forget
all about Pamela. That was the way Jack did it. You make your
own party. Jack had trouble with Pamela so he started to see Jo.
Simple as that. That was the way Jack did it. But he wasn't
Jack.

Levon and Tony had stopped to look in the windows of the
Five Animals Kung Fu Studio. It was originally a jeweler's shop;
on either side of the deep entryway, the art deco display windows
zigzagged in and out across from each other like interlocking
pieces of a puzzle. In the windows, arranged haphazardly on faded
velvet steps, were trophies from martial arts tournaments, Asian
statues, curved swords; photographs showed men and women
dressed in white or black pajama-like outfits going through various exercises. Several large photos showed a man with Asian features and sleek black hair down to his shoulders demonstrating
fighting styles: Lion Dancing, White Crane, Drunken Praying
Mantis. As Bill joined them, Levon stood on one leg and stuck
out his arms in a crude parody of one of the pictures.

"Look, Billy. Drunken Ironworker."

Bill shook his head as if Levon were hopeless.

"I can't help it, Will-yum," Crazy Levon said. He collapsed
with laughter, wrapping his arm around Bill's shoulders. "I was
made for this kind of stuff."

"Yeah," Tony said. "All you weirdos have long hair."

Bill extricated himself from Levon's grasp. "Well, next time don't scare all the nice civilians in the coffee shop. Jesus, I can't take you anywhere."

"See how they talk to me?" Levon looked to the heavens for understanding. Then he grabbed his long red ponytail dangling from under his hardhat and flicked it a couple times at Bill. Bill looked at him blankly.

"An ironworker goes into a bar," Tony said, "and sits down next to this other guy who's mouthing off at everybody. 'You don't want to mess with me, I'm a trained killer,' the other guy tells the ironworker. The ironworker, he ain't impressed, so the other guy jumps up and goes into one of these here crazy poses and yells, 'Ha-ee! Karate!' The ironworker takes one look at the other guy, picks up the stool beside him, cracks it over the other guy's head, and yells, 'Ha-ee! Barstool!'"

Tony twisted one point of his mustache, proud of his joke. Levon chuckled appreciatively, but Bill wandered out of the entryway back to the sidewalk.

"My brother-in-law told me that one," Tony said. "Only funny story that sonamabitch ever tell me, you know?"

"He still living with you? I thought you said you were going to run him out," Levon said.

"I tried but he won't go. That sonamabitch, he says . . ."

Bill tuned them out. Usually being with his men cheered him up, but today they were getting on his nerves. What was the matter with him? He felt like he wanted to pop someone, anyone. He stood on the curb across from the entrance to the job and waited for the other two to stop their messing around.

First she had all those questions about Jack, and then she wanted to know how things are between me and Pamela. What was Jo getting at? She talked like she hadn't seen Jack for a while, I thought maybe that's why Jack didn't want to go out for a drink last night, I thought maybe he was going to see Jo, but if he didn't see Jo where was he? Pamela said she had to work last night, that she couldn't see me last night, you don't suppose, no he wouldn't do that, he wouldn't see her now, he knows she's my girl now, he didn't want her but I know she still thinks about him or at least I think she does, he said You only screw your friends, you don't suppose he, no. . . .

Levon and Tony had joined him on the curb, still chattering about something. Bill started between the parked cars but Levon grabbed his arm and pulled him back.

"Whoa, hoss!" Crazy Levon said as a car went past. "I know you're anxious to get to work, Billy-Boy, but there's no sense getting run over to do it. Here we go."

Levon and Tony ran across the street between the moving cars but when Bill tried to follow he pulled up lame; pain shot up his leg from his ankle, the result of an old injury. Goddamn it, I know better than to try to run, what's wrong with me? Now this son-of-a-bitch will hurt all day. He hobbled on through the gate behind his men so they wouldn't see him limping.

Inside the fence, the trio stopped at their gang box where they had left their toolbelts. As soon as Bill strapped on his belt again he felt better; it held the tools of his trade—his snub-nose wire clippers in the holster ready near his right hand; his coiler, the flat metal canister holding a roll of tie wire, close to his left; the holder with his keel and his rule and the clip for his hammer—he always felt more like himself when he was wearing the belt. He settled it low around his hips like a gunslinger. He was ready to get back to work.

In front of the building, the concrete pump stood idle. Two toots from an air horn came from outside the fence; the next ready-mix truck had arrived and needed a flagman to help direct it into the gate. When no one responded, the horn sounded again, this time with an ear-shattering blast. Sloopy came tumbling out of the portable toilet, trying to hitch up his overalls and run at the same time, but Jack came from his trailer and beat him to the gate.

"Hold it hold it hold it hold it hold it hold it!" he bellowed as he waded into traffic on the main street and held up his arms. A car nose-dived to a stop a few inches from his leg. Jack petted the hood ornament, grinned at the startled driver, and mouthed, "Thank you."

The truck pulled diagonally across the street. Jack waited until the driver could see him in the sideview mirror, then led the way toward the gate as he propellered his hand in the air: "Come on, come on, come on. . . ." The truck had barely begun to creep backwards when Jack clenched his fist and hollered, "Stop!"

The driver stood on his brake pedal and looked panic-stricken in his sideview mirror, afraid he'd run over someone. Bill and his crew wandered over to the gate to see what the problem was. Waiting to cross the sidewalk in front of the gate was an attractive young woman dressed in a tailored maroon suit and high-heeled boots carrying a briefcase. The noise from the jobsite and the warning bell on the truck had apparently confused her: she didn't know if she was supposed to hurry across before the truck got there or wait until it passed. Before she could decide what to do, Jack came over, tipped his hardhat to her, and smiled.

"Here you are, young lady," he said, offering his arm. "Let me help you."

The young woman looked at him as if confronted with a talking bear. Then she softened and smiled a little, as if she decided that she rather liked talking bears. She took Jack's arm and allowed him to escort her around the puddles and loose gravel in front of the gate and on down the makeshift sidewalk to the end of the fence. When she released his arm, Jack tipped his hat again. The young woman nodded once in acknowledgment, smiled in spite of herself, and hurried on down the street.

Jack watched her go for a moment, sighed, then stormed back to the gate.

"What the hell you waiting for, Christmas?" he yelled at the driver. "Come on, get this truck in here, you're holding up traffic!"

Crazy Levon walked over beside Jack, looking down the street after the young woman. "You're too much, Jackson. How'd you like to have that sit on your face?"

"Mind your manners, son," Jack said, not looking at him as he continued to direct the truck back through the gate. "How do you know she's not a friend of mine?"

"No pretty girl like that would want a fat old fuck like you," Levon laughed. "Don't give me that shit, man."

"I'll give you any shit I want to. Man." Jack still hadn't looked at him.

"Hoo-ee!" Cowboy said, standing on the back of the pump. He took a couple practice jabs in the empty air. "Sounds like a rumble in the jungle to me."

"What makes you think I'd take any shit from you?" Levon said.

Jack finished signaling the truck into position at the pump. He lit a cigarette and looked around to make sure everything else was taken care of. Then he turned to Levon, squared off in front of the other man, a deadly little grin on his face.

"You'll take any shit I give you because I'm the one man on this job who can take you apart and give you a new asshole."

"What do you think of that, Billy?" Levon said. With one swift practiced motion he took off his horn-rimmed glasses and put them in his pocket.

For a moment Bill was repulsed by the sight of them; he hated their stupidity, the stupidity of the situation. Tony had dropped his toolbelt on the ground and moved closer to Levon, but Bill stayed where he was.

"You're on your own," Bill shrugged, "if you're going to say things like that about Jack's girl."

"That was your girl?" Levon was no longer sure of himself. He looked from Jack to Bill and back to Jack again. "You're serious? Hey man, I didn't know that. That's different."

"Don't worry about it," Jack said. "And she's not my girl."

Now Levon was totally confused. Jack grinned and patted Levon's upper arm good-naturedly; but he looked at Bill. "I was only funning you. I never saw her before in my life. But if it'll make you feel better, I'll try to get a date with her next time I see her."

Levon looked at Jack and Bill again, trying to puzzle out what was going on between the two of them. Then he shambled off, shaking his head, his toolbelt clanking as he headed toward the manhoist. Tony picked up his toolbelt and followed. Jack continued to study Bill, the grin gone from his face. Bill felt his cheeks color. What's the matter, I thought I was going along with the joke.

"Levon's not too smart," he said.

"He's smart enough," Jack said, still watching him. "He's a good worker. A good man."

"Yeah, he is that."

"And he's your partner."

Is he mad at me? We used to joke all the time. Let's go out and get a drink, what do you say? I want to talk to you about something. Jack looked as if he wanted to say something else but decided against it; he turned away and headed for the trailer.

"Jo was asking about you," Bill said.

Jack stopped but didn't turn around, didn't say anything.

"She said to say hello."

"Good for her," Jack said, looking back at him. "Say hello to her for me."

"So. What'd you do last night?"

Jack only cocked his head. He took another drag on his cigarette and flicked it away. "Something eating you, Bill?"

"I was just wondering what you did last night, after we talked
about going out for a drink. I thought maybe you had a date with
Jo, but she talked like she hadn't seen you."

"Maybe the lady doesn't kiss and tell."

"Yeah, maybe that's it." Yeah, maybe that was it. Maybe that
was why she wanted to see him today, because she had seen him
last night, the way I always want to see Pamela the next day, I
read it wrong.

"Now, if I was you, I'd get up on that deck and take a look at
your rebar in those columns. Make sure everything's okay before
they're all poured. Like you're supposed to." Jack turned to go,
then looked back at him again. "Besides, it's about time for your
little floor show, isn't it?"

"What? Oh, yeah. My floor show." Bill grinned. He's joking
with me, it's like when we were friends. "Those poor bastards up
there eat their hearts out, don't they?"

"Whatever turns you on," Jack said without expression.

"Whatever's right," Bill said and headed toward the manhoist.
He ran to catch up with Levon and Tony, trying not to limp with
his bad ankle, trying not to show the pain, before the operator
closed the door.

10

Below, in the space between the front of the building and the
fence along the sidewalk, workmen moved about in truncated
form, reduced at times to only a pair of shoulders or a foreshort-
ened torso under the disk of a hardhat, legs flicking out as they
walked. Seen from the top of the building, the ordinary was trans-
formed into abstractions and new perspectives. Cars and trucks
moved through the geometry of narrow streets. Toward the river,
the rooftops converged into a crazy quilt of angles and planes.

The Building

Slanting morning sunlight created a chiaroscuro that blanked out much of the town in shadow, reducing the two- and three-story buildings along the main street, the narrow pitched-roof houses, and the abandoned mill and factories along the river into simple patterns of light and dark.

It was one of the things that Gregg enjoyed most about the job of being an inspector: it gave him the opportunity to be on the upper floors of buildings where he could look down on the normally unseen tops of things—it was a kick. He had discovered that heights themselves didn't bother him, in fact he found that he liked being up in the air; heights only bothered him when his safety depended upon his ability to hold on or to keep his balance, when it was up to him to keep from falling off. Such as climbing a ladder. At the moment, he felt a whole lot safer on top of the building than down on the ground. He was still shaky from the fiasco of taking his test cylinders; he had made a total fool of himself in front of Jack and the other men. He was glad to be as far away from the ready-mix trucks and the pump—and Jack— as possible.

The truck that had been unloading was finished and pulled out of the gate; another waited in the street for a flagman to help direct it into position at the pump. From this height, the goings-on had the appearance of a dumb show, a pantomime. Gregg leaned over the edge for a better look. Easy. Careful. He had learned that there was a correct way to lean over a guardrail and he was mindful of it; he used the railing as a balance bar, keeping one foot behind him, his weight evenly distributed, so he could jump back quickly if something gave way. Please don't give way. He was looking to see if the test cylinders were safe where he left them—What am I going to do if they're not, go down and move them, not on your life, let somebody kick them over for all I care, that way the tests would be sure to fail, that would teach them a lesson—when he noticed a young woman in a maroon suit and high-heeled boots coming down the sidewalk. Hello, Puss-in-Boots. She hesitated at the gate as the concrete truck started to back up, confused about what to do. Then Jack went over to her, offered his arm, and escorted her down the temporary sidewalk, tipping his hardhat to her as he sent her on her way. A carpenter named Clyde came over to the railing to see what Gregg was watching.

"That Jack," Clyde said. He laughed, shook his head, and went back to his work. "All the women love him. I used to think it was because of that big belly of his. Women could rest their head on it and feel secure, women need that. But then Jack got sick and lost all that weight, so I don't know what it is. Animal magnetism or something."

Clyde was a stocky, sallow-cheeked man in his fifties; his shoulders were permanently scrunched up against his neck as if someone from above were trying to lift him by the straps of his overalls. With his power saw he went back to cutting a sheet of plywood that lay across a couple of sawhorses. The blade keened into the wood, sending clouds of sawdust into the air. There was the smell of burning wood; motes of dust drifted about Gregg like snow, threatening to get under his contact lenses; his beard was already dusted. Clyde looked up and grinned amiably.

Down in front of the building, Jack was joking around with Crazy Levon and the other ironworkers. It was probably about the girl in the maroon suit; Gregg could imagine the kind of obscene comments they would make about her, the posturing and boasting about what they wanted to do with her in bed. Like sea lion bulls whumping around the beach to divide up the females. There's your animal magnetism. Scattered around the edge of the deck, close to Gregg's foot, were six-inch sections of angle iron. Jack stood directly below him, in line with the end of Gregg's boot. It would be so easy. All he would have to do is move one of the angles over to the edge of the slab with his toe and give it a little kick; at this height a piece of metal that size would go clear through a man, probably cut him in half, no one would ever know how it happened, it would be an accident. . . .

How could I even think of doing such a thing to another human being, even to that bastard Jack, but I did, that's exactly what I thought to do, it seemed so close, so easy, one little kick and all this trouble would be over, *Bonk*. . . .

Gregg shuddered and looked away, over the maze of rooftops to the hills on the other side of the river. The hills were a thin wash of green with the first budding—a frosting like a confectioners' glaze. When he looked back down in front of the building, Crazy Levon and the other ironworkers were heading toward the manhoist to come up on the deck. Gregg moved away from the railing.

Across the deck, everyone had stopped work. The concrete crew was climbing down from the scaffold where they had been pouring a column; carpenters and plumbers and electricians were busy gathering up planks and sawhorses and anything else handy and carrying them to the opposite end of the floor.

"What's going on?" Gregg said to Clyde, wondering if someone had called a sudden strike.

Clyde turned off his power saw and looked at his watch. "That time already?" He dumped the plywood he was cutting onto the deck, picked up one of the sawhorses, and hoisted it onto his shoulder. "This must be your first time on this project if you don't know about it. Come on."

With his free hand Clyde grabbed his lunch pail and hotfooted it after the others. Gregg, having no idea what was going on, trailed behind.

The men arranged makeshift bleachers for themselves close to the edge of the deck so they could look down on the building across the alley. It was an old orange brick apartment building, three stories tall; its roof was a few feet below the height of the deck. Andy Yurick, the welder, came out of his plywood pen carrying his bucket and took up a position directly in front of everyone else; he ignored the comments as to his possible sexual preferences and the breeding practices of his mother. Gregg couldn't figure out what he was supposed to be looking at. Clyde waved him over to an empty space beside him on the sawhorse.

"What's going on?"

"Patience, patience," the carpenter said and dug a Twinkie from his lunch pail.

"She's late today," an electrician said, pouring himself a cup of coffee from his Thermos.

"Must've had a rough night," commented another.

"Where's Bill?" Some of the men chuckled.

"Here she comes."

"Yay!"

Across the alley a light switched on in one of the windows on the top floor of the building, a bathroom window. A shower window. When the shower was turned on, the water streaming down the hammer-patterned glass made the glass clearer. By the time the naked young woman stepped in front of it, the window was almost transparent.

"Nice, huh?" Clyde said, munching his Twinkie and taking Gregg's arm in his. "Does that every morning about this time. Every job has its little compensations."

Gregg was dumbfounded. He was also busy watching. As she splashed and turned and rubbed herself in the water, she looked like the torso of some ancient statue come to life, though there was no question that this was very much a flesh-and-blood creature.

"Doesn't she know everybody's watching her?" Gregg turned away, reluctantly, to look at Clyde, then turned right back again. "I mean, doesn't she know the glass gets clear like that when it's wet and everyone can see her?"

"What do you think?" Clyde said. A small peak of white cream stuck out from the end of his nose.

"Somebody should tell her. . . ."

"And I suppose you know just the person to go over there and let her know." The carpenter, his arm still locked in Gregg's, gave him a playful squeeze.

"No, I don't mean me, I mean, well, somebody. . . ."

Clyde looked cross-eyed at the cream on the end of his nose; he wiped it off with his sleeve and sniffed it to make sure that's what it was, then licked it off the material. "To these eyes she looks like the kind of girl who knows exactly what she's doing."

"Hey Bill, here's your girl," one of the men said.

The ironworkers came across the deck from the manhoist, Crazy Levon clanking along a few steps behind Bill and Tony. As Bill joined the audience, standing behind the other men, he grinned slightly. Crazy Levon and Tony got to work sorting a bundle of rebar.

"Hard night last night, huh Bill?" said one of the men, not really friendly. "She was late getting up this morning."

"Hard is right," said another.

"She sure looks like she'd be pretty good, Bill."

"Nah," said someone else. "I had her mother and she was nothing."

A few of the men laughed, the laugh of having heard the same joke a dozen times before. A plumber, a bearish man with a red bandanna tied around his head under a railroader's cap, stood up, spread an imaginary pair of thighs or maybe buttocks, and tongued the air. An apprentice carpenter took a two-handed grip and flailed away at an imaginary erection. Bill glanced at their antics but didn't say anything; he continued to watch the girl in the shower, the little grin still on his face, his cheeks blushing.

"Is that really his girl?" Gregg whispered to Clyde. What's going on here?

"If that's what you want to call it," Clyde laughed. He leaned back to get a good look at him. "Why, can't you tell, boy? That there's an immorata. Your basic Whore of Babylon. You pays your money and you takes your choice. Ain't you ever seen one before?"

"She is?" *Immorata*? He must mean *inamorata* but where the hell would he learn a word like that? Uh-oh, I'm afraid I can guess . . . but they said she's Bill's girl and he's just standing there, what's going on here?

"Well, sure. Why else would a girl do a thing like that every morning? Been doing it for the last three or four floors now. It pays to advertise, you know? I've heard tell of a couple guys around the job who's had her, but I guess Bill's the only regular." Clyde squeezed Gregg's arm tighter and leaned confidentially toward his ear. "I think he went and fell in love with her. Can you believe it? In love with an immorata." He leaned back to observe Gregg's reaction.

I don't get it, I don't understand. Gregg looked from Clyde to the window and back again. "But it doesn't seem to bother him that everybody can see her like that." If that was my girl I wouldn't want me watching her, I mean anybody. . . .

"You know, you look like a nice young man," Clyde said. He kept Gregg's arm locked in his while he dug one-handed in his lunch pail. "A little messy with that beard and all but I've got to remember the good Lord had a beard too. Funny how times change. Here they are." He pulled out a couple of pamphlets from the bottom of his lunch pail and handed them to Gregg. The one on top had an orange and white picture of Christ feeding the multitudes; the title was *Let Jesus Be Your Friend.* "Maybe you'd like to come over to the house some evening. My wife, Ruth, will fix you a real Christian supper, and I could fill you in on the workings of Satan."

"What?" If that's his girl why isn't he standing up for her honor, he's just standing there watching her with all the rest of them. . . .

"I can tell by the way you're watching that immorata that the devil himself is breathing down your neck. Can't take your eyes off'n her, can you? I'd like the opportunity to instruct you in ways to fend off the temptations of the world."

"But you were the one who came running over here as soon as you found out what time it was."

"Ah, but that's different. I'm watching with the eyes of the Lord. Somebody has to keep an eye on these things so we'll know just what the devil is up to. Tonight when I go home, I'll tell Ruth all about it and we'll go down on our knees and ask for this immorata's forgiveness in our prayers. It's the least we can do. Why don't you join us?"

"No, I don't think so. . . ."

"Suit yourself." Obviously, Gregg's response wasn't the one the carpenter was looking for. Clyde released Gregg's arm, returned the pamphlets to his lunch pail, and snapped the lid shut. He got up, ready to take his sawhorse and go back to work; when Gregg didn't get the message right away, Clyde lifted one end of the sawhorse and dropped it again. Gregg jumped up.

"See you on Judgment Day," Clyde said under his breath, shouldered his sawhorse, and stalked off. "You're no better than the rest of them."

What did I do to him? The guy's crazy.

The show was about over, the men were getting restless; the young woman had turned off the shower and was toweling herself off, her image starting to fade as the water stopped running down the glass and was replaced with steam. Gregg knew he should leave too; it wasn't a good idea for an inspector to let himself be included in something like this, an inspector had to keep his distance from the other men to maintain his objectivity. But he couldn't take his eyes from the window, he wanted to see more. Who is she? Does she really know that everyone can see her? Why would she do such a thing, God she's beautiful. . . .

"Hey inspector," one of the men called behind him. "The show's over for today."

A couple of the men laughed. Gregg glanced over at Bill and found the foreman looking at him. For a moment he was afraid Bill would be angry at him for watching his girl, but it wasn't anger that Gregg recognized in the other's look. Christ, it's like he's proud of it, it's like he wants us to like her, wants us to like him on account of it. How could anyone want to be liked that much? That's really sick. Gregg turned and started to walk away.

"Hey inspector, I didn't mean to scare you off," a workman called.

"Let him go," said another. "He's probably not old enough."

<h1 style="text-align:center">11</h1>

Vincent Nicholson, architect of record on the Furnass Towers, went from door to door to door, ten in all, in the outer lobby of the old theater, trying each one in turn, thinking each time that the next door must be the one that would open, but all were locked. Why would you leave the outside doors unlocked if you were trying to keep people out? Why wouldn't you lock the outside doors instead? Is he trying to give false hope that you might actually get inside, as if there was some reason to get inside? Doesn't make sense. Maybe that's Lyle's next project, make a homeless shelter, wonder this lobby isn't piled high with bedrolls and old mattresses like under the freeways, the daily detritus of the economic wounded. That's not a bad phrase, I should write that down. After giving the last door an extra push for good measure, Vince peered in through the diamond-shaped glass; it was dark inside, fathomless, all he could see was a murky image of himself. He hoped he hadn't come all this way for nothing.

The Building

He was a plumpish man in his late fifties, his thinning gray hair not really silver, more leaden, combed forward like a kind of shield to compensate for its deficiencies, with a round face and the perpetually surprised look of someone who has survived more than anyone expected, including himself. As he considered what to do next, he studied the crumbling stucco latticework, the chipped tile of the mosaics, the stalactite-fringed arches of the old foyer. Like a mosque of some sort. Of course, it was the Alhambra Theater. Pleasure palace of its day. More bizarre than Byzantine, Moorish boorish. Lord save us from bad architecture but I guess that's why He put me here, ha ha. In a frame that once held movie posters was a sign done with cheap paste-up letters and one of the renderings he had done of the proposed building:

COMING SOON!
FURNASS TOWERS
OFFICES AND APARTMENTS
INQUIRIES WELCOME

Welcome and needed and frantically sought, Vince said to himself. He pushed once more on the last door, then turned around and looked out the glass-paneled front doors at the passing scene under the marquee. Along the sidewalk, a man with the face of a mole, wearing three or four overcoats and a ruff of dozens of devotional scapulars around his neck, scurried along picking up cigarette butts and stray gum wrappers that he then carried like treasures to the nearest trash can. On the other side of the street half a dozen retired or laid-off steelworkers stood around a parking meter as if it were a microphone and they were about to sing. An old woman in a black dress carrying a net shopping bag, her face hidden by a black babushka, shuffled past looking like Mrs. Death. Welcome to Furnass. Home of the frayed. His hands in the pockets of his Aquascutum trench coat, lifting on the toes of his four-hundred-dollar shoes as if in a small way he might attempt flight, Vince pushed through the nearest pair of front doors and headed back to his car.

Look at them all. Even though I walk through the Valley of Dearth. It's the holding tank for the leftovers of the Industrial Revolution. Burial ground for the old who can't go anywhere else and the young who aren't old enough to go anywhere else and the damaged turned loose from the asylums with nowhere else to go. God, I could have ended up here if . . . and this is where they want me to put up a significant building. For Julian Lyle, Esquire, and his vanity I might add. Well, I'm giving him a significant building, and he doesn't even know how significant. There's an idea for a book there but it needs elaboration. Architects came into being because of man's vanity. That's pretty good. Architects as we know them only came about in the eighteenth century and the Industrial Revolution, before that there were only builders, masons and carpenters with big ideas. But as the new classes gathered wealth and the people who prospered began to look for ways to show off their newfound status, they hired other people, architects, to decorate their buildings so they—the buildings and the people who owned them—would stand out. Architects were only for those who could afford them, architects were like courtesans. Expensive whores. And I didn't think I had a sex life anymore, ha ha. I guess it all depends on your definition of getting screwed.

He unlocked the trunk of his BMW and took out a pair of rubbers, leaning against the hood of the parked car behind him for balance as he slipped them on over his shoes. He dug his hardhat out from behind his roadside emergency kit and tucked it under his arm; he always waited as long as possible to put it on, he hated the way the damn thing made him look. Like a pea balanced on a melon. Down the block on the other side of the street, the building under construction lifted up from the confines of the little town, monumentally out of scale; on the top deck, the columns of rebar—the few he could see from this angle along the front and side—reached higher against the chill blue morning sky. Whose vanity were you serving on this one, Mr. Nicholson, Julian Lyle's or your own? Don't be ridiculous. As Mies would say The greater the ego the greater the talent. I wonder if he really did say that, oh well it doesn't matter, if he didn't he did now as far as I'm concerned. He closed the trunk and waited for traffic to clear before continuing, somewhat reluctantly, toward the jobsite.

The history of modern architecture proceeds from the notion that ornamentation symbolizes social prestige and by inference moral standing. People no more care about the structural or aesthetic integrity of their buildings than they do about the development of their own character, they care only about the pretty surface, the bright gewgaws of the soul. It is the cross the architect has to bear. Hey, that's pretty good, I should be writing these down, collect them together into a book, maybe that's where my real talent lies. Maybe I wasn't supposed to be an architect at all, I guess I'll never do the International Hotel or the Seagram Building of my generation, but maybe I could become a critic, an author, an arbiter and decider of taste, did you read the latest book by Vincent Nicholson, he says such-and-such. What was it Rita said this morning in the kitchen, You've always been good at putting a spin on what you say, but she didn't mean it that way of course, didn't mean it kind, oh Rita.

At the gate, Vince sucked in his stomach and tucked in his elbows as he edged through the narrow space between the fence and the ready-mix truck, being careful not to touch anything; despite the rubbers on his shoes, he stepped gingerly around the puddles of water and spilled concrete in front of the building, giving the concrete pump a wide berth so he didn't get splattered.

I hate coming out to these jobs, a man could ruin a suit of clothes or a good coat without even trying. Dirt in all forms is the enemy. He had almost made it to the comparative safety (meaning to him the relative cleanliness) of the inside of the building when a voice somewhere overhead yelled "Headache!" He hesitated a split second—Headache? Wait! Doesn't that mean. . . ?—when a length of four-by-four slammed into the ground a foot or so in front of him, exactly where he would have been if he hadn't stopped. The piece of wood hit on its corner, gave a dull *Sproing!* and somersaulted away. Vince looked up to see where the wood came from; a head popped out from the edge of an upper floor, looked down at Vince looking up at him, and popped back in again. Holy Mother. That could have—he could have—I could have—. He realized that his hardhat was still tucked under his arm; he quickly put it on and, with his shoulders buttressed up against the back of his head, hurried inside the first floor of the building. He rested for several minutes beside one of the thick concrete columns, standing close to it as if it were a tall friend, until his heart stopped fluttering in his chest and he felt sure enough of himself to continue.

I could have been wearing that chunk of wood. Sticking out of my head like I was a unicorn. What would Mies have said about that? Form follows function but that was Sullivan. Fat Mies wouldn't have known a unicorn if it stuck him. Didn't know me either. Doesn't matter now. Life goes on and I guess I have to too.

The masons had begun the exterior brickwork at the rear and sides of the building; at this level they worked from the inside of the floor because the side walls butted against the existing buildings and the rear was buried in the slope of the hillside. A string of lights hung from the ceiling along the perimeter to illuminate the work going on, but the area was still cheerless and bleak; the lights showed only how dark the surrounding area was, how deep within the structure the men were, how closed off they were from everything else. Like being buried alive. Bricking in your own mausoleum. "The Cask of Amontillado." Building a wall around yourself, closing off the world in front of you. How do they survive? I could have let that happen to me. If I hadn't gotten out but I did. Poor people. At the moment, the low scaffolds—planks set on sawhorses—were empty; the mortar sat solidifying on the mortar boards, the hawks and trowels lay where they had been thrown down. The crew of bricklayers and hodcarriers sat in a row against the side of a nearby toolshed taking their coffee break; they had been talking loudly in a mixture of Italian and broken English but they fell silent as soon as they saw Vince. He nodded to them and walked along behind the scaffold for several bays—being careful not to brush up against anything—giving a once-over to the half-finished wall.

So they recognize me, That's him, that's the son-of-a-bitch who gives us trouble all the time about the color of the brick. Yes, it's me. Well, I'm not in this business to be liked, only to get the best building possible. It's their responsibility to do the job they're paid to do, however poorly they do it. Architecture would be an art form if it weren't for the fact that the architect is dependent upon others to build his creations, architects need imperfect people to make their perfect dreams come true. I've really got to start writing this stuff down.

One of the things he wanted to look at when he came to the job today actually was the color of the brick. The manufacturer claimed to be able to supply any color of brick Vince wanted; but despite the many color swatches and samples the company had sent, none of the bricks came anywhere close to the color— almond—that he had chosen. There were pallets of the bricks stacked around; the wall itself was up to a height of four feet; but in this light Vince still couldn't tell the bricks' true color—they looked more pink to him than almond. One thing he did not want was a pink building. It would look like a giant phallus sticking up out of nowhere. Vince's Penis they could call it. That's quite an erection. He decided the only way to know for sure would be to take one of the bricks and compare it in the sunlight with the approved sample that was kept in Jack's trailer. As he took a brick from one of the pallets and carried it away—carefully, holding it away from his body so he didn't get brick dust on him—the masons began talking again, except now in hushed and furtive tones.

Now I've got them more nervous than ever. What's he want a brick for? Keep them on their toes if nothing else. Since the art of building has developed to the point that it takes someone with special knowledge to design a structure—namely an architect—the average person doesn't want to see what's responsible for making a building stand up. People want the bones of a structure hidden from view, they don't want to know about all the tremendous stress a building goes through simply to keep from collapsing under its own weight. They want to think a building just happens, they want to keep how it is put together a mystery, that's the reason for the whole concept of the curtain wall. And it's probably a good thing too, because the art of building has developed beyond the ability of today's workman to construct a building without an architect to tell him how to do it. If the average person walking down the street knew how little actually holds together the world around him it would drive him mad. Amazing how heavy a brick can be. Got to be careful not to drop it on my toe, scuff up these good shoes even with my rubbers. This should be the last thing I have to worry about out here today, the color of the brick. I told Rita I've got to tell a man today why he doesn't have enough money to finish his building. She said That shouldn't bother you, you've always been good at putting a spin on what you say. A hard woman at times for all her weepiness. Hard as a brick, ha ha. Heavy as a . . . That's enough.

The Building

As Vince approached the trailer, Jack came to the door and stood with his legs spread, his hands in his pockets, filling the doorway. His hardhat was cocked at an angle above his pudgy face; he swayed from side to side, door frame to door frame, like a man riding a windy sea.

"You fixing to throw that at somebody?" Jack said, indicating the brick in Vince's hand. "Or are you just carrying it around for balance?"

"No, I always bring my own paperweight with me."

"With all the papers you push around I can see how that would come in handy." Jack gave him a wry look as if to say Gotcha and stepped back to let him through the door. Vince put the brick on the plan table. The approved brick sample was currently being used as a bookend on the shelf next to the window; Vince took it from its place and the half dozen books of specifications it had been holding slid down into a pile along the shelf.

"That's okay, wreck the place, see if I care," Jack said.

"They're only the specifications. You don't look at them anyway."

"You're right. Maybe it's the specifications I should be using as bookends. At least they'd be good for something. Now what in the hell are you worried about?"

Vince carried both bricks to the door and stood in the muted sunlight looking at them. "I'm not worried, Jack. I'm appreciating the fine details of the job you're doing on this building. Such as making sure that the brick they're using is the same color that I approved."

"Jeez, are you still going on about the color of the brick?"

"Just making sure we get what we pay for." Vince stared at the two bricks for a moment; he couldn't tell if they were the same color or not. Christ, now I'm not even sure which one is the sample and which is the one I brought with me. The sample has to be the one on the right, right? Has to be. Or is it? He frowned and carried the bricks back to the plan table. Just leave them here, let Jack figure out which is which. "I guess it's close enough."

"'I guess it's close enough,'" Jack mimicked and sat down at his desk. He lifted his hardhat and rubbed his forehead, then reset it at a new angle and leaned back in his chair, one foot up on the corner of the desk. "We're not making a watch, you know."

"I know, we're making a building. But I still want to hear it tick."

He liked Jack in spite of himself, or rather, he was amused by him. Jack was certainly not your average workman; for one thing, he knew more than most contractors about what he was doing, he had even come up with a few good suggestions as the project had progressed, ideas to make the building better, such as erecting the reinforcing steel for the columns three floors at a time; and for another thing, he was fun to spar with. All Sturm und Drang, signifying nothing. What Jack lacked in intelligence he made up for in verbal reflexes. That and he had no qualms about saying whatever crossed his mind. Vince didn't necessarily admire that quality about Jack—to him it was the same outspokenness found in children or those who don't know better; an example of the rough wit of the working class—but at times it could be entertaining.

"Must be nice to be able to toss other people's money around like that," Jack said, rocking back in his chair.

Vince took a couple of paper towels from a stack on the windowsill and wiped the brick dust from his hands. He's like a tough Broderick Crawford, or tries to be. *Highway Patrol.* Same last name. How many people today know who Broderick Crawford is? Or was. The fleetness of fame. Of course he can bully his men, no real opponent. He smiled and tossed the paper towels in the wastebasket beside Jack's desk.

The Building

"That's funny, Jack. If I didn't know you better, I'd think you actually cared about other people's money."

Jack puttered his lips in a strawberry and pulled his leg down from the desk; as he stood up his pants threatened to fall down, and he worked them back into position. He stood in the doorway of the trailer again, looking out at the jobsite.

"Spending other people's money is one thing, but you're ridiculous. I've never seen anybody so anxious to spend money on a project. All this fuss about the color of the brick: what difference does it make what color the brick is for the walls they're working on now? Those walls are hidden against the buildings next door, nobody's ever going to see them. And later on, the brick is going to be fifty or sixty feet in the air, no one's going to notice little differences in the color way up there. The birds sure as hell won't give a damn. The only brick that people will ever really see is on the first couple of floors along the street. The way it's going so far, it'd be cheaper to hand-color those bricks so we could get the exact shade you want, instead of having to deal with all this other shit you're putting us through."

An edge had come into Jack's voice, as if what started out as kidding had grown into something else. What's bothering him? Vince decided it was best to humor him, to try to keep the conversation light. He's like an overgrown child in a fit of pique.

"Suppose someday one of those existing buildings comes down and the walls are exposed. Don't you want people to admire your craftsmanship? The fact that the bricks are the same color as the rest of the building?"

"Bullshit. Don't give me that," Jack said. He turned from the door, looking at Vince from under the brim of his hardhat. "If those existing buildings ever come down, the brick on these walls will be discolored anyway. I think you just got a bug up your ass about something."

"And why would I have, as you so colorfully put it, a bug up my ass?"

"I couldn't tell you. But I will tell you this: because of your fooling around with one thing or another, the brick walls on this job are going to cost about eight dollars more a square foot than was originally estimated. I'll bet the owner doesn't know you're spending his money like that."

Wait a minute. What is he getting at? Does he know? Before Vince could answer, Jack began talking to somebody outside the trailer. Vince looked out the window. At the foot of the steps was a stocky workman with Asian features, rheumy eyes, and a small goatee, dressed in dirty white coveralls; strapped to his legs were heavy black knee guards, hanging from his webbed belt was a collection of trowels and floats—the tools of a concrete finisher.

"I'm telling you, Jack, I need me a new hose."

"And I'm telling you I already got you a new hose."

"Heh heh, that was down there on the fifth floor."

"And one on the third floor, and one on the first floor, besides all the hose I got you when we started this project."

"Well sir, that's true, heh heh."

"So what happened to all those other hoses?"

"They don't reach no more, Jack. We're up there on seven now. . . ."

"What are you doing, Chalmers, eating all that hose or something?"

"Heh heh—"

No, he couldn't know anything, he's just talking. Forget about it. There's a phone, I'd like to call Rita but not with him right here. I was sitting in the kitchen watching *Good Morning America*, the dark-haired girl, the one I like, was doing the weather, I was watching them track a tropical storm off Bermuda and Rita was padding around in her slippers and housecoat fixing French toast and I said I've got to tell a man today why he doesn't have enough money to finish his building and she said That shouldn't bother you and I laughed thinking she was kidding and I said What do you mean and she said You've always been good at putting a spin on what you say and then dumped the whole pan of French toast into the garbage and left the room. Menopause. Pause, O men, and get used to the idea of living by yourself with a strange woman in the house, that the woman you married is no more. I just wanted to talk to her but she never listens to me anymore, never hears me. She said I don't see things anymore. Take another look at your estimate, are you sure you can build this building for what you say?

"Everybody wants something," Jack said, turning away from the door again, the conversation with the workman over. "That goes for you, too. What the hell are you doing out here today?"

That won't work with me, bully-boy. "That's not a very diplomatic way to talk to the architect on your building."

"What difference does it make whether I'm diplomatic or not? Every time I see you, you cost me more money."

"I'm just making sure you live up to your responsibilities, that's all."

"Responsibilities," Jack laughed, though it was more like a puff of air. "From what they tell me, there aren't going to be any more responsibilities on this project, for me or anybody else, unless somebody comes up with some money real fast."

"I heard there was a little problem about the payment. . . ."

"Little problem. Oh, sure. If you call the contractor not getting paid a little problem."

"I know that we're exceeding our original estimates. . . ."

"I'll say we're exceeding our estimates. Thanks to you and your money-spending program."

Watch out. He does know something about—no, he couldn't. Just talking. Stay calm. "That's why I'm out here today, actually. I'm going to talk with the owner and find out what the problem is."

"I told you what the problem is. We haven't been paid for several months. At least that's what they tell me."

"Several months? I think you're mistaken—"

"That's what they tell me. They tell you something different? What kind of architect are you, anyhow? You don't even know what's going on with your own building? Jeez."

Stay calm. Magisterial. "I heard from the owner yesterday afternoon that there was a problem regarding the payments—"

"Won't be any problem after today. We're taking a hike. Poof. Gone. Bye-bye."

Vince looked at him a moment, considering what he just said, before continuing. "So that's why I'm here today, to see what the problem is and get things straightened out."

"You don't seem very worried about it. You must think you're some kind of magician."

"I've got a few tricks up my sleeve," Vince smiled. Are you sure of these numbers because something here doesn't add up. We're taking a hike? Don't worry. It's just talk.

"Yeah, I've seen some of those tricks already," Jack said. He lifted a stack of change orders from his desk, gave Vince a sideways look, and dropped them again.

You have nothing to be afraid of from this man. Put a face on it. "So, are you going to show me around?"

"Sure, why not? I need some more pain in my life."

"Jack, I'm the best friend you have on this project. I'm the only one looking out for your best interests." That was good.

"If that's true, I'm in more trouble than I thought."

Jack looked around the trailer as if to make sure he hadn't forgotten something, patted his shirt pockets as if to make sure he was all there, then led the way out of the trailer. As they walked toward the manhoist, Vince trailing a few steps behind, they passed Marshall the laborer headed in the other direction.

"Don't forget Chalmers needs a new hose," Marshall said as he passed Jack.

Jack stopped in his tracks, wheeled around, and started shouting after Marshall. "What the fuck is it with all this talk about Chalmers new hose?"

"Just thought I'd remind you," Marshall called without turning around. He continued on his way toward the trailer.

"Yes, I'll get Chalmers a new hose," Jack bellowed. "I'll get you a new hose too if that's what you want, I'll get the whole fucking world a new hose." He looked at Vince. "I suppose you want a new hose along with everybody else."

"Depends on if it's the right color," Vince said. Got you.

"You're a real comedian, you are," Jack said. He shoved his hands in his jacket pockets and clomped on toward the manhoist.

. . . it is an assemblage of parts, a building is, it is a piecing together of diverse elements into a completed whole, it is a juxtaposition of a scattering of ideas into a unified thought, it is a massing, a coupling of fragments into a considered totality, it is an interlocking of seemingly contradictory components into a reasoned sum, it is a culmination of efforts, it is a convergence of opposing wills, it is a rising up where there was nothing before, changing inexorably not only those who build it but also those who watch it become a presence in their lives . . . as in her apartment across from the jobsite, Pamela DiCello, having finished her shower, sits in her bathrobe at her kitchen table drinking a cup of coffee when she suddenly jumps as a loud Bla-a-a-at! *comes from the alley below and she peeks through the break in her red-and-white checked café curtains, thinking It's gone too far now, I've gone too far, now that the building is this high, now that the top deck is above my windows, and it didn't do any good anyway,*

sorry guys but from now on the show's over and lets the curtains fall into place again, afraid that someone might see her . . . as at the Furnass Grill, Jo Schramm walks along behind the counter holding the coffeepot high, watching for those who flag her or point to their coffee cups as she passes, wondering what was eating Bill this morning, stops and looks past her customers through the large plate-glass windows at the building under construction down the street and decides that Jack must not be coming to see her this morning after all, thinks Oh well and goes on down to the end of the counter to talk to a tall skinny guy with a screwy mustache who has been asking her out for several weeks now . . . as a local businessman named Dickie Sutcliff, a developer and builder of sorts in his own right, owner of Sutcliff Realty, on his way back and still wound up from his meeting earlier this morning with the owners of Buchanan Steel about his firm becoming the sole agent for converting the closed steel mill along the river into an industrial park, leaves his white Lincoln Continental on the steep side street down the hill from Seventh Avenue, the town's main street, and heads for the Blue Boar in the Colonel Berry Hotel, thinking This is early even for me but Lord I need a drink, I want to celebrate, I want to tell somebody, pauses as he crosses the street to take a look at the Furnass Towers under construction a block and a half away, its upper floors floating above the rooflines of the town's old brick buildings and thinks Look at them, the poor bastards, working like busy little ants on Julian Lyle's Tower of Babble, as if the whole thing couldn't come crashing down around their ears, and probably will . . . as on another street in town, one block up the hill from the main street, J. Howard Griffith stands on the curb in front of the J. Howard Griffith Funeral Home looking down the hill, killing time as it were by checking out the progress on the building under construction, from this point of view the building rising up from the center of town like a monolith, thinking It sticks up there like a giant

The Building

gravestone, I wonder what we should do for the inscription,
watches until the deliveryman from the Shadyhill Casket Company
has finished unloading another new coffin from the back of his
truck onto the gurney and begins wheeling it down the ramp into
the basement, Griffith then following along behind and instructing
that it be taken directly into the display room where he removes
the protective paper and stands back to admire his new piece of
inventory, thinking They're certainly doing nice things with bur-
nished gold and silver these days . . . and on the building itself,
on this Friday in early spring, it has warmed up a little though
not much, the low, angled sunlight reflecting off the concrete slab
has helped take some of the chill from the air, in response to
which—perhaps as much from generating their own heat as they
go about their work as from anything else, or the fact that they
think it's bright enough that it should be warmer—most of the
men working on the top deck have taken off one or two of their
multiple layers of jackets and heavy shirts, presented as they are
on top of the building—seemingly on top of the world—to the
nuances of weather and atmosphere like offerings on a plate . . .
an easy morning so far for Bill and his crew of ironworkers, only
a few odds and ends to take care of now that the columns are
formed up and ready for the first lift of the concrete until the
Bla-a-a-at! of an air horn sounds from the alley announcing the
arrival of the truck from the fabrication shop, the truck Bill has
been waiting for all morning, the first load of steel for the next
floor . . . the truck crane is already in position in the alley, having
moved around from the front of the building late yesterday after-
noon, ready to hoist the steel to the deck, and Bill sends Tony
down on the manhoist to take care of the unloading from the
truck, Tony's absolutely least favorite job: setting the chokers
around each bundle of steel bars to be off-loaded and then attach-
ing the chokers to the hook of the crane, tying a tag line around
the end of the bundle and then standing there underneath it as

the crane lifts the load praying to God that something doesn't go wrong and the load doesn't fall on him as he tries to guide it and keep it from spinning . . . as at the controls of the crane, Laurie Popovich, her mass of dishwater-blond curls tied back with a pink bow cascading down below the back of her hardhat, puts out of her thoughts the question of how on earth she's going to pay for her little boy's eye operation and her little girl's braces and still have money for the new sofa that she wants desperately to dress up her living room and concentrates on the business at hand, that being Tony, the short wiry middle-aged rodbuster with the pointy-tipped handlebar mustache who is currently grousing around on top of the load of reinforcing steel on the flatbed truck, kicking at the different bundles of steel bars (and who, if he isn't careful, is going to kick himself right off the truck) trying to find an opening between the dunnage where the chokers will fit around one of the bundles, who then gets down on his hands and knees, poking the looped end of the wire-rope choker here and there, swearing the whole time, "Sonamabitch, focking sonamabitch," until he finally manages to get both chokers wrapped around a single bundle of bars and gets the eyes attached to the hook of the crane and gives Laurie the signal to raise it, which she does just high enough to put tension on the chokers and she can see what she suspected and was afraid of, and she taps on the horn a couple of times to get his attention and points through the window of the cab at the chokers but all Tony does is look back at her (glare at her, would be more like it) and shrugs and goes back to tying the tag line on the end of the bundle, and she honks again and points again and Tony only looks at her again though this time it's as if he wants to throw something at her and probably would if she wasn't a woman (a girl to him) and still doesn't know what's wrong and finally Laurie sighs and slides out from behind the controls and has to do what she knows Tony is absolutely going to hate, opens the door of the cab and steps out onto the platform and yells at

him, *"The loops are threaded in opposite directions,"* and steps
back into the cab and climbs back into her seat behind the controls, not wanting to look at him, knowing that he's calling her
every name in the book under his breath but also knowing that
he's also aware of why she called his attention to the problem
(and knowing that he's all the angrier because he knows she's
right and that he should have caught it himself), both of them
aware that if the chokers are looped from opposite directions, the
bundle might twist or corkscrew while it is hoisted and make it
difficult to remove the bars from the bundle when they go to sort
it out later, and she lowers the hook again so the tension is off
the chokers and he can remove one and reset it (for some reason,
probably because he's so angry, he takes both chokers off the hook,
and now she's concerned that he'll end up reversing both of them
and they'll be right back where they started) and he gets down on
his hands and knees again, *"Sonamabitch, focking sonamabitch,"*
and tries to pull the short end of one of the chokers on through
so he can loop it from the other direction but it keeps hanging up
underneath the bundle, which is why he gave up and looped it
from this direction to begin with, his ass in the air, aimed right
at her, and Laurie can't resist, she gently, oh so gently, feathers
the controls and lowers the hook another foot or so and nudges
the boom over slowly, very very slowly, because a wrong move
now could turn a prank into an accident (the only reason she
even attempts the maneuver is because of her skill, because she
knows what she can do with the machine), just a little closer and
inches the hook carefully, carefully behind the kneeling, cursing
ironworker and . . . gooses him with it, as Tony gives a *"Yip!"*
and spins around and sits down quickly and looks to see who did
that to him and finds the hook dangling there staring him in the
face and he starts to scream, *"You focking sonama—"* and looks
at Laurie and she thinks *He's going to come over here and beat
the shit out of me* but then Tony's face breaks into a grin (because

he catches himself and remembers she is a woman, to him a girl which, now that he thinks about it puts a whole new slant on it) and he waves his fist good-naturedly at her, shakes his head and starts to laugh . . . as on the top deck Bill and Crazy Levon stand at the railing watching and Bill says, "What the fuck is going on down there?" and Levon says, "Hey Billy, she got Tony to laugh while setting chokers, I'd call that a major accomplishment," and Bill says, "I don't give a shit— Come on, goddamn it, what's the holdup?" Bill yells down at Tony (who ignores him and tells him under his breath, "Go fock yourself") and then says to Levon, "And you get your ass over there and get ready to land it, we haven't got time to stand around here all day," and Levon looks at him a moment and grins in a way that with anyone else but Bill would mean the start of trouble, would mean his taking off his horn-rimmed glasses in that one swift practiced motion, but doesn't say anything, goes off to do as he is told . . . and Bill, when Tony finally gets the chokers set and the crane slowly begins to lift the load from the bed of the truck, catches the attention of the crane operator and begins the hand signals to guide it, absently giving the signal to raise the load (which is actually unnecessary at this point because the operator can still see the load for herself, Bill's gesture more a description of what is already happening rather than what should) while he looks down across the alley at the windows of Pamela's apartment, wondering what she's doing right this instant and if by any chance she's watching him (she isn't; she's left the kitchen and is in the bedroom combing out her thick black hair) until the load is lifted above the level of the deck by twenty feet or so, much higher than it actually needs to be (because the load is this high in the air, Laurie doesn't have a good view of it and is dependent on whoever is giving her the hand signals to tell her what to do with it; for all she knows Bill needs the load that high above the deck in order to clear some obstruction that she can't see from the cab), and Bill remembers what he's doing and signals her to stop and then to swing the boom over the deck where Levon has placed a couple of four-by-fours on the concrete slab as dunnage and is waiting to land the steel, and as Bill continues the hand signals he thinks about Pamela dancing in the shower window this morning—it has been a while since he actually saw her dancing there though he knew she still did so because of the comments from the other guys; that she danced in the window each morning is the reason he started taking his crew across the street early to the Furnass Grill for their coffee break each morning, because seeing her that way only made him more confused about her than he already was; he had never told her about the window, that they could see her in her shower, hadn't told her because when she first started appearing in the window several months earlier he was proud of it, proud to be known as the guy who slept with her while all the other guys could only drool (he thought it was sick to feel that way about it, but he found he couldn't help it; he also found as time went on that he liked the other guys drooling over her less and less), and he hadn't told her later because she undoubtedly would want to know why he hadn't told her sooner—thinking all this on some level of his mind as he continues to signal the boom right on past where Levon is standing waiting for it and Bill finally realizes it and gives a quick hard signal to dog everything, which the operator does (Laurie can't see the load at all now from where she is in the cab, she can only see the boom stretching beyond the edge of the deck, and she's concerned from Bill's almost panicked signal that the load is in trouble or that she almost hit something) so that the load, from the sudden stop of the boom, continues to travel a little ways, swings forward, and then, of course, swings back (if there was a wind or if the operator didn't know what she was doing at this point, the load could pendulum and begin a cycle that could prove disastrous, the load swinging one direction so that the operator swings the boom in the opposite direction to compensate, but then swings the boom too far, which only makes the load swing out even farther, and then swing back even farther than that, which makes the operator swing the boom even farther in the opposite direction, which swings the load even farther still, the boom and the load starting to swing in opposite directions back and forth, back and forth in increasingly longer arcs until it's impossible to say whether the crane is swinging the load or the load is swinging the crane though it really doesn't matter because it's only a matter of time until the boom can't take the strain and snaps or the crane topples over and the load falls—but none of that happens this time, Laurie catches the swing, feels the swing of the load against the boom and rides with it a little ways and then brings the load back under control again) (Levon looks over at Bill, thinking *Where do you think you're taking this load, Billy, quit thinking about all that other shit and pay attention to what you're doing here*) as Bill, after the load settles down, reaches into thin air again over the guardrail and signals Laurie to bring the load back the other way and then to boom down farther and at the same time raise the load so that it will reach closer to where Levon is waiting for it, thinking *Maybe I'll go over and tell her about the shower today, this morning, that would give me a reason to go see her, maybe I could have lunch over there and we could knock off a quickie, it's been a while since we've done that, God I want her today but I guess I always want her don't I?* that's not the problem but he lets the load travel too far again, it sails right overhead where Levon is waiting for it a second time, Levon trying to grab the tag line dangling down as it drifts past (thinking *Jesus, Billy, where you taking it now, come here, rope . . .*) and Bill gives another signal without telling the operator to stop, signals for her to raise the boom again and hold the load where it is and when the bundle of steel bars is finally over the spot where Levon is waiting for it, signals for her to lower the load as he looks across the alley again at Pamela's *windows, looking for some sign of her, What was Jo getting at at the coffee shop this morning, first she had all those questions about Jack and then she wanted to know how things are between me and Pamela, maybe she wasn't asking about last night at all, maybe she knows something about Jack going over to see Pamela today . . . still signaling for the load to come down as Levon stands under it and grabs the tag line and starts to swing the bundle of steel bars around so it will rest on the four-by-fours he put on the slab (thinking That's it, Billy-Boy, now slow her down, nice and easy . . .), Bill looking in Levon's direction but apparently not paying attention to what he's doing because he's still signaling to lower the load at the same rate of speed but the load is coming too fast now and threatens to slam into the deck with Levon underneath it and Levon yells and drops the tag line and jumps back out of the way as Bill realizes that it's coming too fast and starts to signal to stop or maybe to boom up but then doesn't signal anything at all because it seems too late to do anything and he's frozen with the horror and fascination at the prospect of the tons of steel crashing into the slab (in the cab of the crane Laurie doesn't like it, Bill looks confused even as he continues to signal for her to lower it and she knows damn well the load isn't that high above the deck and stops the load on her own) as the load stops a few feet above the slab and Bill comes to himself and looks down over the railing at Laurie in the cab and gives the signal to lower the load slowly but the load doesn't move (everyone on the deck has stopped work now, everyone is watching what's going on, what will happen next) and Bill signals again but the load still doesn't move and he looks over the railing and screams down at her, "What the fuck's the matter with you, can't you follow signals?" but Laurie just sits at the controls of the crane looking back at him (thinking Signal all you want to, fucker, I'm not moving that load an inch, I'm not going to kill someone for you or anybody else) . . . as Levon, after he pats himself in a couple of places, chest, stomach, upper thighs, not so much to make sure that he's all there but in a kind of prayer of thanks and an acknowledgement that he's all in one piece, pulls the tag line away from the dangling load so it won't get caught underneath it when the load finally sets down and makes sure that the load isn't going to start to twist or turn while it's hanging there, then takes a couple of deep breaths to calm the shaking and the fury and walks over, the tools on his tool belt clanking with each step, to where Bill is now leaning halfway over the railing screaming at the top of his lungs, ". . . you goddamn stupid fucking bitch . . ." and puts his hand on Bill's shoulder and straightens him up and turns him around to look him in the eyes, saying in a voice that's controlled and dangerous, "Bud, why don't you go over and land that load where you're going to want it and let me take care of this," and Bill shakes his head and says, "Jesus fucking H. Christ," and shrugs off Levon's hand and starts to say something else to him but Levon is just standing there staring him in the eyes and Bill knows that look and turns away and grabs his hardhat from his head and is about to throw it down on the concrete in his frustration but remembers the last time he did that he really messed up the chrome and had to have the hat replated to make it look right, thinking Was she watching from the window, did she see what almost happened, she probably wouldn't even care, she'd be too busy if somebody was over there with her, maybe that's why Jack wanted me to get up here on the deck right away after our coffee break so he could go over there himself this morning, maybe he's been going over there during the days the whole time oh please cut it out I'm so tired of thinking all this and walks over to grab the tag line and land the load as Levon told him to (Pamela did in fact hear the commotion on the job as she stood in front of the mirror in the bathroom, putting on her eyeliner without turning on the lights so no one could see that she was there, thinking This is ridiculous, I'm going to put my eye out just so Bill doesn't see me and get any ideas about coming over this morning, I'm a prisoner in my own place, well that's all going to change, heard the commotion and the loud voices and the swearing but there's nothing new in that, paid no attention as she continued to get ready to go out and do her errands for the day) as Levon looks down over the railing and gives a little wave to Laurie, Hi babe, it's me here now, everything's cool, and signals to lower the load slowly and Laurie gives a little wave in return and begins to slowly lower the load, Levon still signaling as he watches Bill guide the bundle of bars onto the dunnage, thinking that he's going to have to keep an eye on Bill today, thinking I'm going to have to watch myself around him today, this guy's dangerous and the rest of the men go back to whatever they were doing before the excitement, the work goes on. . . .*

12

Jimmy, the manhoist operator, slid the door home with a cage-rattling *Bang!* inches from Jack's nose. Jack eyed him suspiciously.

"All the way?" Jimmy said.

"What do you think?" Jack said.

"All the way," Jimmy said. He pushed the control lever forward and gazed at the ceiling as if willing the cage upward. For one second, two seconds, nothing happened; then the cage lurched, shuddered, and began to rattle slowly up the framework on the outside of the building.

Jack stood at the front of the cage, his legs planted wide apart, hands in his jacket pockets and his elbows flared, as if he formed a line of defense against some unseen invader. Behind him, Nicholson, the architect, faced the opposite direction, watching as the view of the town and the valley opened up as they lifted above the rooftops of the main street. Jack stared straight ahead through the wire mesh; the building slid down in front of him as if it were sinking into the ground right before his eyes. He wished he had a cigarette, and refused to let himself have one for that very reason.

"Heesh," Jack said out loud.

"What?" Jimmy said.

"Heesh. Just heesh."

"Oh."

"It's nothing. It's just a word. Like I sighed or something. Heesh."

Jimmy shrugged and made a face as if to say *I see* when he didn't at all.

"It doesn't mean anything. It's like something a comedian would say, Jackie Gleason or somebody. I could have said shit. Or damn. Or fuck. I didn't. I said Heesh. Okay?"

"Anything you say, Jack. Heesh."

"Oh for shit's sake." Jack looked back over his shoulder. Nicholson had turned around and was grinning as if he enjoyed Jack's attempts to explain himself. Jack took out a cigarette, stared at it for a moment, and stuck it behind his ear.

On the fifth floor they stopped for a plumber carrying an eight-foot ladder; Jack stepped back grudgingly out of the way.

They're coming at me this morning. Everybody in the world is coming at me. Chalmers and his goddamn hose. This architect going on about the color of the brick. Now he wants his own private tour. What's the matter, can't he find his way around his own project? That kid inspector, him and his goddamn concrete all over the ground. And what was with Levon coming at me down at the gate? Then Bill sold him out, left him dangling in the breeze, his own partner. A man should look out for his partner, if you're lucky enough to find one, your partner should be somebody you'd give your life for. And Bill turned him over, you never know but I guess I should have known that about Bill. How did Mac used to handle all this shit? I liked it better when the Old Man was around, I took care of all the problems but Mac took care of listening to all the yammering. Now my goddamn legs are starting to hurt again. What am I talking about, they always hurt. Must be a change in the weather. When I get too crippled up and can't do this anymore I can become a weatherman, Jack's ankles said it would. Been standing too long, the doc said I have to sit down once in a while. Or if I sit too long I have to stand. Christ. And then there's Ellie. Talk about pain.

On the sixth floor, they stopped while the plumber and his ladder got off and Jack took up his position again in front of the door. Thinking.

He knew he should probably call Ellie back again; she was very upset when he called her earlier, to find out why she had called him. Women, goddamn women, they'd cry about anything. But he didn't really blame her for being concerned this time. She had done the right thing to call him; he would have been really angry with her if she hadn't.

"I think Marcy's going to leave," she had told him on the phone.

"It's about time."

"Jack, how can you say things like that? You know you love the girl."

"No I don't, I'm stuck with her, she's my daughter."

"You know very well what I mean. And you'd miss Little Jack like crazy."

"I'd be able to sleep in for once when I come up there."

"You sleep out in the cabin when you come up here. You can't hear him out there in the cabin."

"Don't kid yourself. You can hear him for miles."

"Jack."

"You were having trouble with raccoons before Marcy and her kid moved back in, right? And now you don't have trouble with raccoons, right? It's because that kid's bawling scared 'em off, that's why. I'll bet even the bear population up there in the woods has declined since that kid's been around."

"You don't mean a word of that and you know it."

"So what the hell you calling me for?"

"I thought you'd want to know that Marcy's leaving. I thought you'd want to talk to her."

Jack puffed his cheeks and gave a strawberry into the receiver. "What the hell am I going to say to her? Good-bye and good riddance. See ya later. I'll send you a bill for what you owe us as soon as I can find a calculator that can count that high."

"Don't you even want to know where she's going?"

"I'm sure she'll tell us as soon as she gets there. In fact I'm sure that'll be the very first thing she does—call us—because she'll have run out of money and she'll want us to send her some more."

"Jack Crawford, how can you say things like that about your own flesh and blood?"

He could hear in her voice—or was afraid he heard—the first signs of her starting to tear up. "Oh boo-hoo-hoo," he said, holding the receiver in front of him and screwing up his face. Marshall walked past his desk and grinned. Jack covered the receiver. "What the hell you looking at?"

"Just you, Jack. Just you," Marshall said.

"Yeah, well, get an eyeful. You're married, I don't have to tell you." Into the receiver he said, "The girl's almost twenty-six years old, it's time she got a life of her own. So far all she's got is that kid. It's time she got out there and learned how to take care of herself. Christ, it's almost time for her to start thinking about taking care of us."

"Life hasn't been easy for Marcy. . . ."

"You tell me one goddamn person life has been easy for," Jack said, looking around the office trailer.

"She's had some bad breaks. . . ."

"Hey, you make your own party in this world, you know that. And let me tell you, that girl has made more parties than just about anybody else I know. You don't have to worry about her."

"I just thought you should know."

"So, you let me know."

"Are you coming up here this weekend?" Ellie said, her voice noticeably smaller.

Christ, here it comes, Jack thought, if they're not pushing at you, they're pulling. "I don't know, I'll have to see." Go on, he thought, let me have the rest of it: tell me in that hurt little voice you save for times like this about how much you want to see me or how much Little Jack misses his grandpa or some other shit. But she didn't, she didn't say anything; he couldn't tell if she was crying or not. There was no question she was upset, and Jack knew she had good reason to be. Marcy, for all her brashness and defiance, couldn't keep away from men, couldn't keep her hands off them; there was no telling whom or what she'd get herself mixed up with if she got into a bind away from home. But there was nothing he could do about it now, the time for that was long ago, if ever, she was probably born with it; she was as bad with men as he was with women, he couldn't imagine a girl more like himself. The only good thing was that when she got herself in trouble, she could generally get herself out of it too—if only to come running home to her dad. He waited a moment longer but Ellie didn't say anything.

Finally he said, "Look, I got to go. Don't worry about the girl. She'll be fine. And you know I wasn't coming up there again until next weekend. Good-bye." And hung up.

Forget about Ellie and Marcy and Little Jack and the whole goddamn mess. I've got a building to build. Crank up the *Jack* thing. Rev up the engine. Put yourself in high gear. No brakes. Pedal to the floor. Drive, drive. Nobody gets in the way of Jack.

Unless you want to get run over, *vroom, vroom.* I'm not going to get old, I'm going to break before I wear out. What's the matter, Jack, are you afraid? What's the matter you too good to drink with me now?

As soon as Jimmy slid open the door on the seventh floor, Jack was out of the cage and stomping across the deck, Nicholson trailing along behind. Jack had a feeling he'd find Gregg near the plan table and he was right. The plan table looked like a small plywood house mounted on stilts, one side open so you could lean in out of the weather to look at the drawings; Gregg was leaning into the opening so far that he appeared about to be swallowed.

"This here's your inspector," Jack said. At the sound of Jack's voice, Gregg jerked up and spun around. Jack grinned. "I don't know if he's any good at inspecting but he's got great reflexes. Say hello to your architect."

Gregg, smiling awkwardly, shook Nicholson's outstretched hand.

"Well, young man, are you finding anything interesting?" Nicholson said. "Tell me what all is going on."

Gregg appeared embarrassed as he looked around, momentarily lost for words. Christ now what's he so scared about? The guy just asked him a question. Bill said Let's go out and get a drink, what do you say? As Gregg began a halting description of the work in progress, George the labor foreman came over, looped his arm around Jack's arm, and walked him away from the plan table. The elderly labor foreman held his arm in such a way that his elbow felt as if it were being wrenched apart, but he didn't let on to George.

"Where are you taking me, George?"

"Just thought you and me might take a little walk. Maybe go dancing."

"No thanks, George. Not today."

"Too bad." George stopped and dropped his arm, evidently catching the tone of Jack's voice. "I was also told to tell you that Clyde wants the other Ramset."

"He's already got one Ramset."

"That's apparently true. But it seems Clyde says the Ramset he has is broken."

"If it's broke, it's because he broke it."

"That I wouldn't know about." George smiled enigmatically and folded his hands beneath the bib of his overalls. He looked out across the deck at the hills across the river. "I am only the messenger. As far as that goes, I personally don't care if Clyde has a Ramset or not, broken or otherwise."

They make it difficult for you. They have to make it difficult for you. This is the most conscientious, hardworking, devoted labor foreman I've ever worked with, and I have about as much control over him as I would a mudslide. I guess I'm just lucky that most of the time we're sliding in the same direction.

"Did you tell Marshall to get the other Ramset?"

George stood with one foot placed in front of the other; he bent over slightly at the waist, as if at any moment he would unfold his hands and give a wide sweeping bow. "Nope. Waited until I talked with you. Which I might add is always a pleasure."

"Don't fuck with me today, George. Okay?"

"I wouldn't think of it."

What made me ever think that I wanted to be a jobsite superintendent? How did that old bastard Mac handle situations like this? How did he ever handle me? Is George throwing back at me the same things I used to throw at Mac? Jack sighed. "As soon as Marshall comes back up on the manhoist, send him down again and tell him to get the other Ramset from the trailer. Or I'll tell him myself if I see him first."

George nodded and offered his arm. "Would you like me to escort you back to where you were?"

Jack shook his head. "Get out of here, you bastard."

The slightest trace of amusement flickered across the older man's face but he didn't say anything and went to check on his concrete crew. They just keep coming and coming. The way Bill came into the trailer last night and was hanging around after everyone else had left. I tried to ignore him, I just sat at my desk and continued to file that latest batch of change orders, concentrating on punching the holes at the top and sticking them onto the holder, busywork, hoping he'd take the hint and go away but of course he didn't.

Finally he said, "Let's go out and get a drink, what do you say?"

"I don't think so."

"Come on, it's been a long time since we've done that together. It'll be like old times. Besides, there's something I want to talk to you about."

"Unless it's about the job, I don't think you and me have anything to talk about. And if it is about the job, we can talk about it right here." I kept on punching the holes and filing the change orders, all of Nicholson's goddamn change orders. And that was that, I didn't have to say anything else but I guess I couldn't leave it alone either. "Besides, I thought you were tied up most of these evenings with Pamela." Asshole. Fool. Dumb.

"You're right," Bill laughed, mistaking an insult for a compliment. "But not tonight, she's working."

"Isn't that wonderful?"

"I'll say she is," he said, misunderstanding me again. Am I the only one in the world speaking English? "Can't have enough of a good thing, can you?"

"I wouldn't know," I said but I was thinking I wouldn't know, I've never had enough of any good thing I ever wanted, but I wouldn't tell him that.

The Building

"In fact, that's what I want to talk to you about. It's so good with Pamela, I just might have to do something to make it permanent."

And I could see it coming and see it coming and I was praying he wouldn't say it, praying he wouldn't even think such a thing but he did. "In fact I'm thinking of leaving my wife for Pamela."

And I didn't say anything, I couldn't. All I could feel was the anger boiling up from somewhere deep inside me that I didn't even know existed and all I could think was I should never have introduced Bill to her. And he kept coming and coming and wouldn't let it go.

"Well, what do you think? Come on, let me buy you that drink now. We'll celebrate."

And all I could do was shake my head and keep staring at those change orders, keep punching the holes and threading them on the holder and try not to look at him because if I did I was afraid I wouldn't be able to stop myself and he said finally in a whiny tone of voice, "What's the matter, you too good to drink with me now?"

Jack shook his head violently to clear it. He started back to the plan table where Nicholson and the kid were talking earnestly about something—Uh-oh, don't like the looks of that—when he was intercepted by Gary the electrician foreman.

"You still haven't told me what you want me to do with that junction box on four," Gary said. He was in his thirties, good-looking in a baby-faced sort of way; his work clothes were color-coordinated sport clothes—starched chinos, a plaid button-down shirt, an ironed Windbreaker to match.

"I told Frank the German to tell you."

"I haven't seen Frank the German."

"Then I'll tell you myself," Jack said, hands in his pockets, feet squared. "Make it twenty-seven inches off the center of the column."

"That's going to run it into Chucky's pipes."

They just won't make it easy, will they? "Then I'll get Chucky to move his pipes, won't I?" Jack said and grinned, an imitation of a grin, a shark's grin.

"But if Chucky moves his pipes, they're going to be too close to that wall—"

"Fuck the wall," Jack said, no trace of a grin now. "Just put the fucking junction box where I fucking tell you, we'll make it up with the wall later. Otherwise your box is going to be sitting in the middle of a doorway. Look at your drawings."

"I don't know. . . ."

They just won't make it easy for themselves. Jack moved closer until he was inches from Gary's face. "Either we can do it my way, or we can take it to the architect over there and get him involved with the whole question. Then he's going to want to know why you put your conduit in the wrong place on the floor below which is why that junction box is going to run into Chucky's pipes now. And that's going to mean a bunch of back charges and more change orders, not to mention the cost to your company of—"

Gary pulled a face and nodded. "You're right. Sounds good to me. Twenty-seven inches off the column line."

"Isn't that wonderful?" Jack said. Humorless.

As Gary wandered off, Jack looked across the deck to where Bill was landing a load of steel being lowered by the crane. Why the hell is Bill doing the landing and Levon doing the signaling, it should be the other way around, signaling is a foreman's job. Just let it go, it's his business to run his crew the way he wants to, it's his job not yours, just stay away from him, the jacking-off son-of-a-bitch. Besides I've got an architect to play footsie with.

Nicholson and Gregg were still discussing something as they looked at one of the drawings. When he saw Jack coming toward them, Gregg lowered his eyes.

"Our young friend here tells me you have a problem with the welding," Nicholson said.

"I've got problems in all shapes and sizes," Jack said. Now I'll have that cigarette. "What problem are you talking about?"

Nicholson looked at Gregg, waiting for him to explain it.

"Oh . . . well," Gregg said. He reached in the pocket of his army field coat but apparently didn't find what he was looking for; he scratched his beard, cradled his clipboard with both arms across his chest, and kept his head down. "I was telling . . . er, the architect here what I told you about earlier. About the full-penetration welds—"

"We talked about that," Jack said, blowing them all away for a brief second in a cloud of cigarette smoke. "I thought we got that all straightened out. Those *are* full-penetration welds."

"I told him that I talked to you about the code requirements for full-time inspection. . . ," Gregg said.

"He told me about it," Nicholson said loftily, "and I asked him if he was satisfied with the procedure. Apparently he still has some concerns about it. I suggest we all go over and have a look."

The ball-faced man raised his eyebrows to each of them and headed off toward the rear of the deck, swinging his arms and bouncing on his toes as if he were on a lark. Gregg didn't move. He stood with his head lowered, his eyes peering up at Jack from under the brim of his hardhat; his mouth was drawn into a bow as if he were trying to be super-serious, as if he were mocking him, daring him in some way.

"I thought you signed off on that welding," Jack stopped in front of him and said under his breath. The smoke from the cigarette between his fingers curled up into the young man's face. "I thought you said it was okay."

"No, I didn't say that," Gregg said, his eyes darting here and there. "You must've assumed because I didn't say for sure . . . I thought as long as the architect was here. . . ."

"Okay, little brother, you play it your way. You went looking for more trouble and now you've found it. But you keep this in mind: whatever happens you're going to have to live with it. From here on out you're on your own."

13

Why did I have to say anything? Why did I have to go and open my big mouth for? The problem with the welding was all taken care of, Jack asked me about it and I just stood there and didn't say anything so Jack figured it was okay and he kept on pouring the columns, the whole problem just went away, I didn't have to do a thing. Another couple hours and all the concrete would have been poured and all the welding would have been covered over and nobody would have been able to tell the difference anyway. Why did I have to mention it to Nicholson? Now there's going to be trouble. . . .

Gregg caught up with Nicholson at the rear of the deck. The architect stood looking over the barricade of plywood sheets around the base of the last column in the row; Gregg hurried over and stood beside him. Jack came along at his own speed and took a position a quarter of the way around the plywood circle from them. Inside the circle, Andy Yurick sat on his upturned bucket at the base of the column, drinking a cup of coffee from his Thermos, gazing back at them.

"My, my," Andy Yurick said, "ain't I the popular one all of a sudden? Or are you folks looking for the lion cage?"

"This is the architect, Andy," Jack said. "So be careful how you act."

Andy Yurick nodded and smiled. "I'm the one inside the fence, I thought I was the one who was supposed to be dangerous."

Gregg laughed a little too much; he looked in turn at Nicholson and Jack and Andy Yurick. There's nothing to worry about, everything's going to be all right, Nicholson seems like a nice guy, I'm getting along with him okay, oh please let everything be all right.

Nicholson stayed a foot or so back from the plywood, being careful not to touch it. He and the welder looked at each other. The lines around Andy Yurick's blue eyes were etched in black from the smoke; his welder's leathers, a short jacket of rough-side leather, covered his shoulders and top half of his arms; his welding hood in its raised position stuck out from his forehead like the misplaced beak of a bird. After a long moment of staring back and forth at each other, Andy Yurick drank the last of his coffee, shook out the metal top that he was drinking from, and screwed it back on his Thermos.

"I get the distinct feeling that you all didn't drop by to admire my sense of humor."

Nicholson seemed to come to himself again, as if he had momentarily lapsed into a reverie. "Is somebody going to explain the problem to me?"

"What problem?" Andy Yurick said.

"Go ahead, Mr. Inspector," Jack said, leaning one elbow on the edge of a sheet of plywood. "You brought him to the party, you dance with him."

"What problem?" Andy Yurick said.

Gregg tapped his clipboard against his leg, flipping it rapidly back and forth like the spring of a clock. Mr. Inspector. I don't know how good he is at inspecting but he has great reflexes. Help me. Nicholson seems like a nice guy. "Well, I guess the problem is, basically, that there was supposed to be continuous inspection on all the full-penetration welds. And there hasn't been."

"You *guess* the problem is. . . ," Jack started to say, then swallowed it.

"Were you planning to bring the matter to my attention?" Nicholson said to Gregg. "Or, if I hadn't happened to come out here today, were you just going to let it slide?"

Gregg smiled weakly, trying to think of what to say. What does he want me to say?

"I don't really expect you to answer that, incidentally." Nicholson looked at Jack as if they shared some joke. Jack wasn't smiling.

"I hate to sound like a broken record," Andy Yurick drawled, "but what problem?"

"Is there some way I can get inside this thing?" Nicholson said, pointing to the wooden barricade as if it somehow offended him. "That way I might be able to see for myself what we're talking about."

"I can stand it if you can," Andy Yurick said. "I haven't bitten an architect in two, maybe three years."

Jack came around the circle and slid one of the sheets of plywood back out of the way so Nicholson could step inside. Gregg didn't know if he was expected to go inside as well—How can the welder talk to Nicholson that way? Why is Jack looking at me? What am I supposed to do?—but he decided it would be too crowded. Nicholson took out a pair of half-frame glasses and perched them on the end of his nose; with one hand placed on the welder's shoulder for support, he leaned over and worked his head up and down until he had the connections at the base of the column in focus. Andy Yurick looked at him sideways, a bemused smile on his face; his raised welder's hood nearly brushed Nicholson's cheek.

"I think the young in-spec-tor there," Andy Yurick said, "was a little worried because he didn't see me brush the welds after every pass. Which in turn made him wonder about the fit-up and the rest of the whole procedure. Now, I grant you that's a legitimate concern, brushing after every pass, if this was stick welding, where you might end up with slag in the weld. But this isn't stick welding, this here's inert gas welding—short arc—and all you get after a pass is a tiny bead of silicone like that. The next pass always burns it right out of there again, or if it gets too big I pop it off."

Andy Yurick pointed to a small shiny bead, the size and thickness of a fingernail, sitting on top of the weld he had been working on; he took his chipping hammer, tapped the weld once with the long pointed end, and the bead of silicone popped off. Andy Yurick and Nicholson looked at each other under the raised welding hood as if they met under a small black table.

"And as for the fit-up, if the gap between the two bars to be welded isn't wide enough, I can't get my nozzle in there, the wire can't strike an arc, and the gas can't cover it to shield it. Which means I can't weld anyway." Andy Yurick tapped the bar again with the hammer—*Bink!*—and turned back to Nicholson: So there. Each gave a cursory nod to the other.

He's going to fool around and piss off Nicholson and Nicholson will say I was right. Someday I want to get a trench coat like his. All flaps and buckles. Secret agent. Someday when I make enough money. You did a good job young man, that'll show Jack.

"In other words," Nicholson said, straightening up and putting his glasses back in their case, "you're telling me that with this process, the welding is acceptable by definition. Because if the process is incorrect, there isn't any welding."

Andy Yurick looked at Jack. "I love the way this guy talks. Perfect example of less is more."

Nicholson looked at him quizzically, as if trying to decide if the man was making fun of him. "There are times, however, when less is only less."

"Which shouldn't be confused with more or less," Andy Yurick said.

"Or, that no matter what else you may say about it, more is always more."

"What the hell are you two guys talking about?" Jack said. "I just want to know if I got a problem here."

I don't know what they're talking about either, I don't know what he was saying about the welding, Nicholson seems like a nice guy, this'll show Jack, all that concrete all over the ground, they all laughed at me, oh please let me be right.

Nicholson patted the welder on the shoulder and stepped back outside the barricade. He looked down the front of his trench coat to make sure he hadn't gotten it dirty then gazed around the deck.

"Are all the other columns finished on this floor?"

"All except these two," Gregg said.

"What the fuck do you think I should do?" Jack said. "Chip out every fucking column on every fucking floor so you can have a fucking look at them?"

Nicholson smiled wryly to himself about something. He studied the toes of the rubbers on his shoes, first one then the other. He smiled a different smile as he looked at Jack again.

"No, I'm not suggesting that."

"Is the welding okay?" Gregg said.

Nicholson turned to him. "Oh no, that's not my job. That's your job to tell me. You're the inspector."

What does he mean? What? "But I can't say they're okay if I haven't seen them all. Can I?"

"No, you certainly can't say that you've seen them all. Unless you want to lie, that is. But you can say in your report if the work you saw in progress is satisfactory or not. It becomes a matter of phrasing, I suppose. The choice of words. Or you have the option to say in your report that you didn't in fact see all the welding, and call it to the attention of the city engineer. If you do that, of course, then the city engineer will probably do what

Jack said, he will probably require that all the columns on all the floors be chipped out and maybe X-rayed to make sure the welds are according to code. You'll give him no choice, with a report like that from you. But, as I say, it's up to you. You're the inspector, it's your job to look at things and report what you see. Whatever you say, we'll have to go along with it."

He's turned on me, what did I do wrong? What am I supposed to do? They're all looking at me.

And for a moment it was if the world had cracked open in front of Gregg, and everything he had tried to build up for himself, everything he had worked for since he graduated from college—his job, his apartment, his dream of a new Firebird, the chance to meet a really nice girl—was falling away from him into nothingness. That he was about to tumble into the same nothingness and his only hope to save himself was to leap in first on his own. He stammered a couple of times, looked from Nicholson to Jack and back again, tapped his clipboard nervously against his leg.

"Well, the columns I looked at seem to be okay . . . and I guess I can assume the same procedures must have been used for all of them. . . ."

"Are you saying that you accept them?" Nicholson said. "Are you saying that your company accepts them?"

What am I supposed to say? What does he want me to say? After another moment, Gregg said, "Yes. I accept them."

Nicholson turned to Jack. "Very well, then. There's your answer."

"Watch your eyes, guys," Andy Yurick said and, with a sharp nod of his head, flipped the hood down over his face. "The welder's got welding to do."

"Wonderful," Jack said. "All this bullshit just to get back to where we started."

Nicholson watched Jack walk away and then turned to Gregg. "Well, you can't please everybody, can you?"

Gregg didn't say anything. He stood looking around the deck, feeling emptier than he had before. *I did what he wanted me to, didn't I? Does he still like me?* The generator for the welding machine revved up again, engulfed momentarily in its own cloud of smoke; beyond the wood barricade, the arc crackled and flared. Brighter than the morning light.

14

"Let's step over here a moment, young man," Vince said. A look of desperation flitted across Gregg's face. Vince smiled to himself, not unsympathetically. *I know exactly how he feels.* Lifting on the soles of his feet as he walked, he led the way back across the deck to the plan table.

Mies would come into the classroom and you could feel the ripple of fear pass over the room as if God Himself had just stepped in the door and in many ways I guess He had, that old man crippled up with arthritis clattering along on his metal crutches, still clutching his lighted cigar between his fingers, the wisps of smoke issuing up around him as if he was not only his own celebrant but provided his own incense too. All his acolytes were there then, all his believers, his disciples and apostles, all the stars of his fourth-year studio critique, Mies's beloved though they didn't fare much better than the rest of us mere mortals whenever that quarrelsome old man turned his wrath upon them, whenever they dared question his sacred word, Mies making his way shakily from drafting table to drafting table, each one of us in glowing anticipation of a visit from the meister, *keeping our heads buried in our own work though listening hungrily for his comments to the others—Wherever technology reaches its real fulfillment, it transcends into architecture; Remember that every decision leads to a special kind of order; Architecture begins*

where one brick is placed carefully with another—the whole process of building a high-rise or the Barcelona Pavilion reduced to
just those two bricks though with Mies the operative word there
was "carefully"; and that day he stopped beside my table and
hung there on his crutches like an impeccably dressed scarecrow
in his tailored Knize suit, the pouches under his mean-spirited
uncompromising eyes sagging down his face like an old woman's
dugs, and he quoted Meister Eckhart: Your works are all dead
until some motive impels you to act; and even if God impels you
to act from without, all your works are still dead; if your works
are to have life, God must move you from within, from the depths
of your soul, and that is where your work must live: that is where
your life is, and it is only there that you truly are alive.

At the plan table, Vince leaned inside the enclosure, being
careful not to get too close so he wouldn't brush up against anything, and rummaged through the stacks of faded and weathered
drawings looking for something to write on.

"Which reminds me: have you heard anything about the contractor pulling off this project?"

"No," Gregg said, standing beside the shed, his knees locked
back as if he anticipated a gale.

"I haven't either. Jack said something about it downstairs, but
he must be mistaken, as Jack is wont to be." Vince fingered a
particularly grimy drawing with disgust. "When the drawings on
a job are kept in this bad a condition, it gives you an indication
of the job itself, don't you think? Here, let me see your clipboard
a minute."

Gregg hesitated, then handed him the clipboard. Vince took
out his half-frame glasses, perched them on the end of his nose,
and read the single notation on the yellow pad of paper:

> I am writing this to appear that I am writing this
> because writing this is the only thing I have to write.

"Hmm," Vince said, peering at him over the top of the glasses. Gregg looked as if he wished there were a hole he could crawl into. Got you. Embarrassing for him. Funny too. More effective if I don't say anything. He started to reach inside his suit coat for his pen, then thought better of it; he reached over and took the felt-tipped pen clipped to the pocket of the young man's field jacket. Then he assumed a classic draftsman's pose at the plan table—one leg cocked in front of the other, his weight propped on one outstretched arm as he leaned inside the protective shed— and began to draw.

"I have a little question for you. Suppose, in the words of the illustrious superintendent on this job, you have a 'fucking' wall here, and you have a 'fucking' slab extending out from the 'fucking' top of it here. Where does the—again in Jack's words—'fucking' rebar 'fucking' go? I'll make it easy for you and say it's a multiple choice: Does the rebar go in the bottom of the slab? The middle of the slab? Or the top of the slab?"

Vince tapped the pen repeatedly within the boundaries of his sketch, leaving marks to represent concrete. Then he tilted the clipboard so Gregg could see it.

Gregg smiled uncomfortably; his eyes darted about as if he hoped against hope that it was some kind of game and Vince would laugh and it would all go away.

"If you don't know, take a guess," Vince said encouragingly. He was having difficulty watching the young man's struggles with himself. And what does our Mr. Nicholson have to say about it? As always Mr. Nicholson's solution is rather extreme, but if we wade through the flotsam and jetsam perhaps we can find a kernel of something useful, Mies's smile like a flaw in granite to the others in the class.

"In the middle," Gregg said finally and shrugged.

"Wrong. It goes in the top. The reason is that steel is strong in tension but not in compression, in the same manner that concrete is strong in compression but not in tension. That's why reinforced concrete is such an ideal building material; together the concrete and the steel make up for each other's deficiencies, the way partners in a good marriage are supposed to. In a cantilevered slab—that's the type of slab this little drawing represents, in case you ever need to know—the slab will try to break or pull away from itself if it comes under load, because the unsupported end will want to go down, right? So, the steel, which is strong in tension, is placed in the top of the slab to hold the concrete together."

Vince tapped the pen on the drawing a couple of more times for good measure. Then he regarded Gregg over the top of his half-frame glasses, looking him squarely in the eyes. "You really have no idea what you're doing out here, do you?"

"No, sir."

Well, that was quick.

"How long have you been an inspector—let me rephrase that. How long have you been inspecting?"

"Several years." When Vince continued to study him, Gregg stretched his neck to the side and swallowed hard. "That's what I usually tell people if they ask me. Actually, I guess it's been about a year. A little under a year."

The interesting thing is he looks relieved that I found him out. Is that the way I looked to Mies? No, I was always just scared.

"Do you have a degree? Did you go to college?"

"Oh yes. Pitt. University of Pittsburgh."

"And your degree was in—let me guess—English."

"History."

"History. How on earth did you end up as a construction inspector?"

"I answered an ad in the paper."

"No experience necessary."

"They said they would train me."

"It figures, I suppose."

"Actually, they were pretty happy to get anybody with any kind of education."

"I'm sure that wasn't the only stipulation."

"No. Any kind of education and willing to work cheap."

I have eight years of advanced education in my chosen field, I studied with arguably the most important and influential of all modern architects at the finest school for the subject on the American continent, I spent years buried in the back rooms of architectural firms drafting other people's ideas so I could perfect my craft and earn my accreditation, and here I am standing here talking on equal terms to a child off the streets who holds the life of my single most important commission in the palms of his sweaty hands, and he got his job because he's willing to work cheap. It is indeed a very strange world we live in.

After a long moment, Vince asked him, "May I ask *why* you chose to become a construction inspector?"

"What else is a history major prepared to do?"

Fair enough. Out of the mouths of babes. When Vince didn't say anything, Gregg went on.

"There's not a lot of jobs out there right now. Especially with all the mills laying off and closing down. I guess I'm lucky those guys are all union and still holding out for the big bucks they used to make." The young man looked around as if trying to decide what else to say. "I'd sure hate to lose this job."

That's interesting. So he does care. But for what? As if he heard what Vince was thinking, Gregg added, "I really like working on buildings."

Mies said What I can't figure out, young man, is why you want to become an architect, you have the fire but so far you lack the heat and all I could think to say was Because I like buildings.

"How do you get by on other projects? Can you read drawings?"

"Fairly well." Vince looked at him dubiously, but on this point the young man stuck to his guns. "It takes me a little time, but I can usually figure them out."

Vince sighed. He put the cap back on the pen and put the pen back in Gregg's pocket. "You've got sawdust in your beard."

"Oh? Sorry." Gregg, taken aback, hurriedly combed his fingers through his beard.

"It's funny, in a way," Vince said, looking around the deck at the work going on.

"What? The sawdust in my beard?"

Is he mocking me? Or is he simply that obtuse? "I was thinking that Mies used to say that every building has its position in the stratum, that every building is not a cathedral. That certainly applies to this project, doesn't it?"

"Meese?"

Answer: he's that obtuse. "My point is that it's easy to get wrapped up in a project such as this and begin to lose your perspective of it. You devote so much time to it, and you put so much of yourself into it, that you begin to think of it as the end-all and be-all. When the truth is that it's a rather humble little project, all things considered. Despite the grandiose plans the owner has for it. At first it seems quite impressive, sticking up out of the middle of this retrograde little town but that says more about the town than the building. It's not Chartres, it won't define the age, chances are it won't even have that much of an effect on Furnass. Seen in another context, in another setting, it would probably be overlooked completely."

"It does seem rather pretentious," Gregg said, looking around.

Vince scrutinized him over the top of his glasses. I guess I asked for that, didn't I? And he's not smart enough not to give it to me. He sighed and put his glasses back in their case, the case back inside his suit coat.

"Enough of this idle musing. Back to the business at hand. Which is what are we going to do with you? In your favor, you at least had enough sense to tell me about the problem when you saw me today. My experience is that most inspectors who don't know what they're doing but think they have a problem would make for the nearest coffee shop. Or bar. And I am certainly aware that there are holes in every building. There isn't a building on earth, pretentious or not, that can be made exactly to the codes and specifications. No one could afford the price tag to build a building strictly by the book, there always have to be shortcuts and compromises. Like everything else in this world, I guess it comes down to what you want as opposed to what you can settle for."

Gregg just looked at him, the hopeful expectant smile still lingering on his face. He isn't even old enough to know there's a difference. He hasn't been around enough to find out that eventually they preclude each other.

"You know that on any other day, and probably under any other circumstances, I would run you off this building. By all rights I should run you off. I should be calling your company, raising all kinds of stink about sending unqualified people out to a project, threatening back charges, the whole bit—you know that, don't you?"

Gregg nodded solemnly.

"And it would certainly teach these people a lesson too," Vince said. At the front of the deck, Jack leaned over the guardrail bellowing about something to someone on the ground. Vince shook his head—Did I ever think that it would all come to this? That this is all it would come to?—and looked back to Gregg.

The Building

"I'll be here on the project for a while today, probably until the middle of the afternoon or so. What I want you to do is to keep your eyes open, question everything you see. And everything you see that doesn't look right, I want you to bring it to my attention. I already know how little you know about what's going on here, so the only wrong questions will be the ones you don't ask. If nothing else, maybe you'll learn something about the art of building out of all this."

Gregg started to thank him but Vince brushed it aside. "Don't thank me, I'm doing it for the building's benefit as much as yours. Sometimes it's the person who doesn't know the first thing about what he's looking at who sees the most. Mies used to say something similar in class. And I'll tell you something else Mies used to say. . . ." Vince cocked his head, about to recount another anecdote, then noticed the blank look on Gregg's face. "Another time. Just keep your eyes open." And headed back across the deck toward the manhoist.

*

Maybe I'll call Rita when I get down to the trailer. Tell her how I helped a young man today. I helped a young man today, a young inspector who didn't know his ass from a . . . no, that wouldn't work. It doesn't work to call her anymore. I used to call her all the time but now it's easier not to. She said I don't see things anymore. I see enough. I see her padding around the house all day long still dressed in her bathrobe and slippers. Cleaning the rooms for the kids even though they won't be home till the summer. If I told her about this young man she'd start thinking about our kids and how much she misses them now that they're at school and wondering how they're doing, how did she go from an attractive secretary with the greatest bottom I'd ever seen to a red-haired neurotic mess I'll never know. I laughed thinking she was kidding and said What do you mean, and she said You've always been good at putting a spin on what you say, and I said you make it sound like I'm good at hiding things. Take another look at your estimate, Mr. Nicholson, are you sure we can build this building for what you say?

He was hoping to make it to the manhoist without having to talk to Jack again, Vince had had enough of the overbearing superintendent for the time being; but the cage of the hoist disappeared below the edge of the slab before he could get to it. When Jack saw Vince coming in his direction, he stopped yelling down to the ground and turned around to face him; he leaned back against the railing, propped on his elbows as casually as if he were on a cruise ship. If that railing gives way. . . .

"You should be happy," Vince said.

"I'm ecstatic," Jack deadpanned. He leaned back even farther and looked down over his shoulder at whatever was going on in front of the building, the two-by-four guardrail creaked under his weight, the metal supporting posts tilted dangerously. Then he flashed a phony exaggerated grin in Vince's general direction, and just as quickly turned it off again. "Why do you think I should be happy?"

"Your problem with the welding is taken care of."

"I didn't have a problem. The kid just thought I had a problem. He was afraid there was a problem."

"Whatever about that. It has all been resolved at the hands of your young inspector."

Jack took one more look down over his shoulder; then straightened up and moved away from the railing, torqueing his pants into position around his middle.

"Yeah, I got to hand it to you. You really waltzed that kid around. I haven't seen footwork like that since I went with a girl who worked at Arthur Murray."

"I don't know what you mean," Vince said uneasily.

"You had that kid so turned around he didn't know if he was coming or going. He never had a chance with an old pro like you. You're good."

Mies once said it's better to be good than original. No, not the time to mention that now. "I'm only looking out for the best interests of the project."

"Come on, Nicholson, get off it. 'Best interests of the project.' In the trailer you were telling me that you're looking out for my best interests. Who do you think you're talking to here? Some kid who doesn't know any better?"

"Are you suggesting that I'm not looking out for the best interests of this project? Because if you are, I take that as a personal affront."

"'Affront,'" Jack said and scrunched up his face. "That's one of those fancy words I never did understand. Is that anything like an insult?"

"It's very much like an insult."

Jack shrugged, his hands in his pockets. "If you think you're affronted, then I guess you'll just have to think you're affronted. I calls 'em the ways I sees 'em. And the way it looks to me is the only 'best interests' you're looking out for are your own. Like everyone else in the world."

Vince was taken aback to be spoken to in such a manner. How dare he talk to me this way after I let that welding go. What is he getting at? What does he know? But he tried to keep his temper. "How would my best interests be different from the best interests of the project?"

Jack looked around to see what else was going on, then moved closer to him, peering at him as if he could see the inside of Vince's skull through an eye socket. "Making all that fuss about the color of the brick is one thing. And yeah, maybe you've got the right to do that. You designed the building to look a certain way, you're entitled to try to get it as close as you can. And the owner's entitled to get a building that looks like all the pretty pictures you drew for him. But how do you figure this: after all the contracts for this building were let, you came out with change orders for twelve different special shapes of brick? Most of them that have to be shaped and finished by hand. You can't tell me that you can't build this building with standard shape brick like everybody else."

"Of course you can, but then you'd end up with a building that looks like everybody else's."

"Maybe so. But it would also look like the building the owner thought he was paying for. The way it is now, you've sent him on an excursion without telling him where he's going to end up, and you're making up his ports of call as you go along. And you're charging him by the mile."

What does he know? How much has he figured out? "Even if what you say is true, and I'm not saying it is"—Why am I trying to justify myself to this, this—"what do you think I would get out of it? Why would it be in my interests and not the building's?"

Jack moved even closer as if he were about to kiss him. "I don't know. You tell me."

Not good enough, bully-boy. "And what difference does it make to you? You keep harping today about all the money that's being spent. You're getting paid for the work you do."

"Hey, you're right. What difference does it make to me? It all pays the same—that is, as long as it's paying at all. But if all these overruns and hidden expenses have something to do with why we're pulling off this building, then it's a different story, isn't it? You're fucking around with the livelihood of my men. Poppa's got a lot of mouths to feed besides this one," he said and patted his belly.

"That's the second time you've mentioned pulling off this building. I still don't know anything about that."

"Maybe not, but that doesn't mean it isn't so. You're not real good at paying attention, are you? It's like I told you, Drake Construction hasn't been paid for several months, so the powers that be are pulling us off this building. And from what Mac tells me, it's a permanent vacation. We're not only walking away from the building, we're walking away from our contract. We're history as far as this project's concerned."

Vince's knees went weak. "But you can't do that. You can't walk away from a project in the middle of a contract."

Jack took a puff on an imagery cigarette and blew an imaginary smoke ring. "Just watch us. If Mac says we walk, we walk. Offhand I would say Drake has more than enough evidence for a court to say that the original contract is null and void because of all the change orders."

"Then why are you going ahead and pouring these columns?"

"Mac wanted to know the same thing," Jack grinned. "Perversity, I guess. No, I'll tell you what it is. You're making a monument to yourself out here—there: you asked me what I thought you were getting out of this building and I just told you. I think you decided to make this into the Vincent J. Nicholson Architectural Memorial Tower or something of the sort. Me, I'm just making whatever I can. I'm a workingman, it's what I do. It's like when I see a good-looking woman: I can't leave her alone. I see some work to be done, and I got to do it. Call it perversity if you want to."

Vince tried to hold his voice steady. "Well, we're going to try to straighten out the problem with the payments today. That way you'll be able to keep working."

"Isn't that wonderful?" The cage of the manhoist had returned to the edge of the deck. Jack took Vince's arm in his and walked him over to the door. "Hey, you're not mad about anything I said, are you? I was just blowing off, you know me. I'm full of shit."

Vince was too unsettled to say anything; he let Jack guide him to the open door of the cage. Once Vince was inside, Jack pointed *Down* to the operator; without waiting for anyone else, the operator slammed the door closed. Vince walked to the rear of the empty cage, looking out over the town and the valley through the wire mesh; for an instant the floor gave out from under him as they started the descent.

What's going on here? Jack doesn't know anything, nobody knows anything for sure, it's only speculation. I've definitely got to see Lyle now and find out what's going on. Lyle sat there and paged through the presentation and I knew he didn't know what he was looking at, I knew beforehand that the only thing he'd care about was the model I had made up of the building, a stroke of genius that, and all the pretty drawings we did for him. But Sutcliff barely looked at the drawings or the model and kept his nose in the figures and then he looked at me and said Take a look at your estimate again, are you sure we can build this building for what you say? and Lyle said What's the matter, Dickie, don't you think the man knows what he's doing? and Sutcliff said I'm afraid he knows too much of what he's doing and the three of us laughed but I knew Sutcliff knew I was hiding something. I laughed thinking she was kidding and said What do you mean and she said You've always been good at putting a spin on what you say and I said You make it sound like I'm good at hiding things and she said You've been hiding things from yourself for a long time, husband o' mine. And I said How did we get on this, all I wanted to do was tell you that I had to tell a man today why he doesn't have enough money to finish his building and she said What kind of man wouldn't know that about his own building and thinking I could make a point I said A man who doesn't face up to his responsibilities and she said No, it's a man who doesn't face up to what's under his own nose and I said It's the same and she said No, it isn't, you can't take responsibility for what you don't see and you don't see if you don't open your eyes and you haven't seen what's going on for so long that you don't see things at all anymore and then dumped the whole pan of French toast into the garbage and left the room and all I did was sit there and stare at the television on the counter until the pretty dark-haired girl was through talking about the tropical storm off Bermuda and giving the forecast for the day and then I got my suit coat and raincoat and briefcase and left the house, I didn't even say good-bye to her this morning, the first time we ever left it that way.

The manhoist continued its slow rattly descent; as it passed the rooflines on the other side of the street, the sunlight and the panoramic view switched off as the cage sank into the shadows in front of the building. Vince steadied himself with one hand as the ground rushed up to meet him, his fingers stretched claw-like through the pattern of the mesh.

15

Jack took a pencil stub from his shirt pocket and began to figure on the two-by-four guardrail along the edge of the top deck; he pressed the numbers into the wood, trying to calculate if he had ordered enough concrete to finish pouring the columns. Salesmen from the ready-mix companies had tried over the years to give him concrete calculators, little plastic slide rules or calibrated wheels, to help him compute the number of cubic yards in a pour, but he always turned them down. "Nah, get those things away from me, I don't need any gadgets," he told them. "Those things are only for guys who can't do their own work." But here he was again, struggling to figure it out for himself, a man who hadn't even made it through high school. If I just wasn't so goddamn pigheaded . . . what the hell is 12 times 3½ times 4?

His figuring was interrupted when he noticed, below in front of the building, Nicholson standing near the concrete pump. Now what's he going to stick his nose into? How much is it going to cost me this time? But Nicholson didn't appear to be looking at anything in particular; he seemed undecided what to do next. He looked at his watch, started toward the front gate, then hesitated, looked around as if lost then headed back toward Jack's trailer, lifting on his toes as he walked. What's with that bouncy-bouncy shit? Walks like a fruitcake, like a high school kid who thinks he's cool except this guy ain't cool at all, not very dignified for somebody his age and his position but hey what do I know, what do I care how the guy walks, as long as he does his job. Which Nicholson doesn't. What a joke. Jack liked to work closely with the architect on a project; when a problem came up, he liked to have someone he could take it to and get it resolved quickly so he could move on to something else. But Nicholson? Not a chance. Mac was the one who spotted what they were up against, the first time they met Nicholson at a pre-construction meeting.

"He's a real lightweight, son," Mac said to Jack when they went for a drink afterward at the Blue Boar, sitting side by side at the bar. "Do what you have to do to keep him happy, make sure he has copies of everything, call him once in a while with little problems so he thinks he's involved. But try to stay clear of him as much as you can. If anything major comes along, call the structural engineer or the mechanical engineer or somebody else. Try to bypass Nicholson until it gets resolved and then let him know what happened. My sense is that he's the kind that will pick you to death about the small stuff, and never notice that the back end of his building is falling off."

"He seems agreeable to everything I've suggested so far, like putting in the rebar for the columns three floors at a time. . . ."

"That's probably because it's the easiest way to keep you out of his hair. He seems to have something else on his mind about this project, but I can't figure out what it is. It's almost like he drew one building on paper but is seeing another one in his head.

We're already starting to get change orders from him and we haven't even broke ground yet."

The Old Man's suspicions of Nicholson had certainly proved to be true. But the business today with the young inspector had shown another side of Nicholson, a side that Jack more or less knew was there, given Jack's view of human nature, but one Nicholson had never demonstrated before. It wasn't pretty to see someone get turned over that way—The kid got himself fucked and nobody bothered to get the Vaseline—but Gregg definitely had it coming. Why couldn't the kid see that Jack was trying to help him? Then to go behind Jack's back and dredge up the welding again—Jack shook his head. Poor dumb jacking-off son-of-a-bitch. It wasn't pretty but it sure was effective. Made a believer out of the kid. He'll be licking his own asshole the rest of the day. Won't have to worry about him anymore. Welcome to the real world, Greggory. With two *g*'s. Jack put the pencil stub back in his pocket and spit.

Beyond the edge of the deck, the boom of the concrete pump angled up toward the graying, late morning sky; the boom jerked with each pulse of the concrete through the system, the mix hissing through the metal pipe overhead. At least people had stopped coming at him; maybe things would settle down now, maybe everyone would stop trying to wreck his good mood. Maybe they could get through this day without any more hassles and get their work done and get out of here. Get off this project. The bell to summon the manhoist was ringing from one of the lower floors. He turned away from the view of the town and the river and looked across the length of the deck. To where he used to see Pamela's windows across the alley, before his building grew taller than her apartment building. It was strange to think that this might be his last day on the project. Strange to think that he wouldn't be here every day. That he wouldn't be across the alley from her. Even these times when he consciously tried to avoid her, he was always aware that she was close by. The bell for the manhoist was still ringing, insistent. And he thought about the doorbell at Pamela's apartment.

*

"I'm going to do something about your front door downstairs."

"What's wrong with my front door?"

"What isn't? The door doesn't lock, the doorbell doesn't ring, and the buzzer to let people in doesn't work."

"The buzzer to let people in doesn't have to work as long as the door doesn't lock."

"That doesn't make a whole lot of sense, now does it?" he said, leveling his eyes at her. It was the fourth time he had gone to see her, but it was the first time that she hadn't been standing in the window watching them before he left the job and walked around to the other side of the block and up the stairs to her apartment; they sat together at her kitchen table having a beer, watching out the window at the work going on below in the excavation. "What's the sense of having a door if it doesn't work like a door?"

The seriousness of his tone and the look he gave her sobered her a bit. "It's been that way as long as I've been here."

"Well, it's not going to be that way anymore. I'm going to fix it. Somebody could just walk in and come up the steps."

"Somebody did."

They were both surprised at how strongly he reacted. "You mean somebody tried to—"

"No, relax," she said, reaching across the table to pat his hand already gathered into a fist. They were both surprised, too, at the intimacy of her touch; she quickly withdrew her hand again. "I only meant that *you* did. You just walked in and came up the steps. As bold as you please."

"Yeah, right." Now they were both surprised that he seemed a little embarrassed. "And after that, I'm going to put up a curtain and shade in that window in your shower."

"What for?"

"There weren't any windows in the backs of the buildings that used to be across the alley, were there?"

"No. . . ." Then it dawned on her. "Can people see me when I'm in the shower?"

"You can see something, but you can't really make out what it is. You're probably okay as long as it's daytime and you don't turn on the light in there. But as soon as the building goes up a few floors you'll have guys right across from you. I don't want to take any chances."

"That's very nice. You're trying to watch out for me."

"Nah. I just don't want any of my guys falling off the building trying to get a better look. It's too hard to find good men these days."

"I'll say."

"If I happen to find one, I don't want to lose him."

"I'm beginning to think that way myself," she said.

Jack squinted at her sideways, as if trying to see if there was something behind the remark, but he didn't say anything.

I should never have introduced her to him. What the hell was I thinking? Self-preservation. No excuse. That's something I wouldn't do to my worst enemy, much less to the love of my . . . she said Why do you think everything always depends on you? Why do you always think you're responsible for everybody else? And I told her Because that's my job and she said But you're ill, you've been ill, why can't you let somebody else help you for a change? She said I looked up your records at the hospital and I said What records? and she said The time you came in for a cortisone shot, it must have been right after you started working on the building and I said Are you happy now? and she wanted to know what was wrong with me so I told her about the time I had the trouble a year or so ago but I made it into a funny story. We were on this building up at Pitt and all of a sudden these knots started coming up on my arms and legs and I had one here on my elbow the size of a golf ball, no lie, I had trouble getting my shirt on over it for a while and all my joints started freezing up on me, I thought I was going to become like one of those dummies in a department-store window all stiff and everything and that old bastard Mac thought he finally had me, he thought once and for all he was going to show me that he was stronger than I was and more of a man because he's got a dozen years on me and could get around when I couldn't, he kept telling me just to stay in the trailer and run things from there, he would have loved that, he was even talking about getting a bed for me in there and kept making jokes about rigging up a telescope so I could keep an eye on things but I foxed him that old bastard, I got myself a wheelchair and I had one of the laborers, Marshall, push me around everywhere, Marshall loved it, he used to wear a chauffeur's cap and we'd go all over that damned building and I brought it in two weeks early even as a cripple and that old bastard still can't get over it and she said What are you ashamed of? Don't you think people ever get sick? I'm not sick. Don't you think people ever get older? I'm not going to get old. I'm going to break before I wear out. What's the matter, Jack, afraid you're getting older? Or are you just afraid? Ellie said Are you coming up here this weekend? Oh boo-hoo. They're always coming at you, always pushing or pulling, you give a little bit and they want everything you got. I got to remember to get some money for Marcy, Ellie said Life's been hard for her and I said You tell me one goddamn person that life's not been hard on, life's got a hard-on for you whoever you are. Got to remember to tell Chucky to move his pipes on four. And find out what happened to the Ram-set Clyde was using. And tell Mac about Nicholson not knowing that we haven't been paid in months. And yeah, Chalmers's hose. Always something. Always coming at you. We were going to 1902 Tavern that time and it had been raining and the sidewalks were a little slippy or I was afraid they were and I started to take her elbow and Pamela said No, I'll take your arm and that was the first time she ever did that, it's like at times I can still feel her hand there on my arm and what it felt like to have her there beside me as we walked across Market Square and as we started toward the door she walked ahead of me and I reached out and put my hand on her waist to guide her and even through her sweater I could feel the movement of her body, it was like I could feel the softness of her skin through her clothes as if there was nothing that could separate us, just the touch of her—Oh Christ, Bill thinks I'm looking at him, he's coming over to talk.

*

Across the deck the rodbusters stood bent over, the three men stiff-legged as wading birds, folded at right angles at the waist as they broke open the new bundles of reinforcing steel and sorted out the bars; when he noticed Jack was looking his direction, Bill straightened up and sauntered over.

"That guy who was here a little while ago," Bill said. "Wasn't that the architect?"

"That's what they call him," Jack said, not really looking at Bill, looking past him as if he weren't there. Maybe if I don't encourage him. He stood with his fists jammed in his jacket pockets and his legs spread, leaning into the pain in his ankles.

"What did he want?"

"The inspector had a question about the welding on the columns. Why didn't you come over and find out what was going on when he was here? Those columns are your responsibility, you know."

"I figured if it was anything that concerned me, you'd tell me about it."

Shit. Then I went and started talking to him and got him in a conversation. Shit shit shit.

"The welding's okay, isn't it?" Bill said.

"It's wonderful."

Bill twisted around to get at the coiler on his belt; he removed the lid of the metal canister and undid a snag in the roll of tie wire inside. "That inspector's an asshole."

"What did he do to you?"

"He's a smart-ass. You can tell by looking at him," Bill said. "Hell of a time to start worrying about the welding now. Andy's on his last column."

You dumb shit, you're the rebar foreman and you don't even know what your own men are doing, it's the second-to-last column, Andy's got one more to go after this one. Well I'm not doing your work for you, it's your business to know what's going on. You'll have to find out for yourself.

After Bill put the cover back on his coiler, he took his wire clippers from their holster and pulled a two-foot length of wire from the opening to make sure it was feeding properly; he clipped off the wire and tossed it aside.

"Don't leave that lying around," Jack said. "Somebody'll trip over it."

Bill looked at him to see if he was serious—Yeah, I'm serious—retrieved the wire and wound it into a fist-size bundle. "I'll say this: your inspector sure got himself an eyeful of Pamela taking her shower this morning."

"He's not my inspector." That's a sorry mess, I suppose he is my inspector.

"Whatever. He enjoyed himself."

"I'll bet he was thrilled," Jack said, still not looking at him, only glancing at him from time to time, looking past him at the work going on. The thick black hose at the end of the boom from the concrete pump was plugged up; George and the concrete crew stretched it along the deck and stood over it, beating it with their hammers to break up the clogged concrete inside. Beating it and beating it *Whump! Whump! Whump!* as if trying to kill it.

"Why don't you ever watch her?"

"You seen one, you seen 'em all." She said Can people see me when I'm in the shower and I said You can see something, but you can't really make out what it is, I don't want to take any chances and she said That's very nice, you're taking care of me. Jack caught himself starting to rub his elbow and jammed his hands back in his pockets again.

Bill worked his wire clippers up and down the bundle of wire in his hand, idly squeezing the individual strands in upon themselves, twisting them cable-like into a tighter mass. "I've sure seen you watching Jo's ass enough times."

"You don't talk about Jo," Jack said, looking at him now.

"You don't talk about Pamela."

"I didn't, you brought her up—Oh for shit's sake." He wants trouble, doesn't he, it's like he wants me to hit him. If he's not careful I'm going to take him up on it—ah just leave him alone. Jack turned away and hunched over the guardrail; he tried to occupy his thoughts with whether there was enough concrete in the truck unloading at the pump to finish the column they had started to pour. Behind him, George and his crew must have unplugged the hose; the pump started again, the boom jerking again with each thrust of the concrete through the lines. He hoped Bill took the hint and went back to work—he didn't want to turn around to see—but Bill joined him at the guardrail, standing in the identical pose, forearms resting on the two-by-four, fingers loosely entwined, right foot pushed forward and tipped over the edge of the slab. Jack's shadow.

People. Goddamn people. Why do they always want something from you?

"Looks like you're having a busy day," Bill said.

"You could say that."

"I was wondering. I didn't see you around for a while there this morning. I thought maybe you went somewhere."

"I was here."

"I thought maybe you disappeared. For a while."

Now what in the hell is he getting at? It's a conspiracy today to keep me off my good mood. Goddamn people. He decided it was best to let it pass. But after a moment, Bill went on.

"I didn't think you'd gone over to see Jo because she said she hadn't seen you this morning."

"That's right."

"'That's right' what?—that you didn't go see her?"

They just keep coming. "Okay, Bill, what is it?" Jack said, straightening up and turning to face him. "What's on your mind?"

"Nothing," Bill laughed and straightened up as well. "I was just wondering. If you didn't go see Jo this morning, if . . . you know, if you went. . . ."

"Went to see somebody else? Is that what you're trying to say? Get a life, Bill. And get your ass back to work."

Jack started to walk past him. Bill reached out and touched his arm and Jack stopped and looked at him—Don't you touch me motherfucker nobody touches me—looked at Bill's hand on his arm, and Bill took his hand away.

"What the hell is it with you?" Jack said. "What the hell do you want from me?"

"Nothing. I don't want anything from you. I just want to talk, that's all."

"We don't have nothing to talk about. Nothing except what's going on on this job. And there won't be nothing going on if you don't get the hell back to work."

"You and me used to be buddies when this job started," Bill said, almost a whine. "Are you mad at me about something? Is it about Pamela? Do you think I'm wrong about leaving my wife—"

The Building

"Christ almighty, get away from me!" Jack shouted—I'll kill him—his hand slicing through the thin air in front of him. He stormed past Bill toward the manhoist. The cage had already started to descend, but Jimmy saw him and came back to get him.

PART THREE

The Building

. . . the bells of the Church of the Holy Innocents, the bells of the Angelus, ring out over the little town, ring out over the layers of rooftops to the hills on the other side of the river and back again, the sounds of the children running and playing in the schoolyard at Holy Innocents cut off abruptly as the first bell tolls as if time itself has stopped, 163 children suddenly frozen in their tracks and merriment as they begin silently but in unison the prayer "And the angel of the Lord said unto Mary, and she conceived of the Holy Spirit, Hail Mary, full of grace. . . ," the single tolling bell of Holy Innocents in the second verse of the prayer joined by the recorded bells from the PA system mounted on the tower of the First Methodist Church a few blocks away that start to play "Sweet Hour of Prayer" (to Pamela DiCello, hearing them as she enters the Blue Boar in the Colonel Berry Hotel, the song that the bells play is "Sweet Hour of Bears," a reference to a private joke between her and Jack when he used to visit her at this time for a quickie on her days off, the spelling of which to her mind could just as easily be "Sweet Hour of Bares") along with the steely ding of Saint Josaphat and the wavery chimes of Trinity Lutheran Church, the dull clink of the Reformed Congregational Presbyterian Church and the library clock at Covenant College on Orchard Hill, the bells of Furnass at one time accompanied by the noontime whistles from the mills and factories along the river, the Allehela Works of Buchanan Steel and Furnass Tool & Die and Allehela Erectors, though Buchanan Steel is shut down now and the corporation has started to demolish the buildings of the sprawling mill and Furnass Tool & Die is working only a skeleton crew and Allehela Erectors was bought out a couple of years ago and all its equipment crated up and moved someplace else, rumor has it to China; and as if in celebration of all the ringing bells (and the memory of the screaming whistles) that echo across the valley or perhaps a physical manifestation of them, the dozens of pigeons that roost on the eaves and ledges

and drainpipes of Holy Innocents, as well as smaller groups from above the doorway of First City Bank and the chimney of the G. E. Murphy Five & Ten and the minarets of the old Alhambra Theater, lift and join in one body with a great flurry of wings above the main street of the town, the birds wheeling en masse across the narrow strip of sky between the rooflines of the building facades before they head down the sloping hillside toward the river, banking sharply around the unused smokestack of the old Keystone Steam Works with a flash of their underbellies as they climb for altitude again and circle back, full of a kind of mock fear at this point, a ritualized frenzy, making the circuit above the town several times before whatever drives them seems to spend itself or the birds weary of the game and after gliding one more turn around the town they divide into their various groups again and flutter down to their respective perches, cooing softly among themselves as they get settled along the ledges and eaves and drainpipes as if nothing had ever happened . . . and life goes on in the little town, the day that started out sunny is clouding over, not so much that you would notice it at first but as something cumulative, the sky that at ten o'clock was acetylene blue has turned chalky by noontime, the sunlight that earlier was crystalline has become somewhat murky, it is still bright though there is a sense that the day will only become darker now that it has reached its zenith, a realization that it is as warm as it is going to get from a sun without heat . . . though it is nonetheless busy today in Furnass, the sidewalks are bustling and there is a steady stream of cars along Seventh Avenue, it is as busy as it was a few short years ago when the mills were working at capacity although now many of the stores are boarded over and the cars that fill the narrow main street are headed out of town to the local malls . . . it is the day after the first of the month, that being the day the welfare and the unemployment checks and the food stamps are handed out, and again, for a few days at least,

The Building

the town has a semblance of prosperity . . . as Jack Crawford
pushes out through the heavy counterweighted doors at First City
Bank onto the sidewalk, having wire-transferred three thousand
dollars from a private account of his to a joint account with his
daughter, Marcy, thinking Now I should feel good, right? Now my
good mood should come back but it doesn't, he's in the same funk
as he was when he left the jobsite a few minutes before noon, he
tries to crank up Jack *but either his battery's dead or he's out of*
gas, thinking Bill's got to be crazy coming at me like that, head
up his own asshole, worse, head in the clouds, I'm thinking of
leaving my wife for Pamela, as if it was that easy to leave your
wife, or as if Pamela would have him even if he did, they keep
coming and coming, don't they, but hey, let 'em come, I'm tough,
that's what I'm here for, better me than somebody else who can't
take it as he continues down the sidewalk, absently rubbing the
place on his elbow where the golf ball–size lump had been, the
joints in his ankles and knees tightening up as the day gets in-
creasingly hazy and there's a new chill in the air, the warmth of
spring seemingly a long way off, lifetimes, heading for the Reo
Grill for a couple of horns to ease the pain . . . as Vincent
Nicholson, after trying once again the doors to the Alhambra
Theater where Julian Lyle, Esquire, has his office only to find
them still locked, stands on a street corner above the town, having
climbed up the hill from the main street to work off his frustration
and growing concern, and yes, fear, climbing the narrow angled
brick-paved streets to the very last one before the backyards dis-
solve and become indistinguishable from the woods that cover the
slope farther up the hillside, standing here trying to catch his
breath and still the pounding in his chest that threatens to pop
the buttons of his custom-made shirt and burst the seams of his
blue fitted Armani suit, thinking That's a good way to get a cor-
onary, climbing a hill like that, I know I feel as if my heart might
break but it's only a figure of speech, ha ha, looking down the

stepped streets over the rooftops of the town to the bluff of the valley on the other side of the river, the thinning leaves exposing the dark trunks and branches of the trees webbing the slope as if the skeleton of the hillside were revealed, thinking of how the natural setting must have looked to the first settlers here, remembering the stories he read as a child growing up in this area, stories of the settlers up the river at Fort Pitt who huddled in the battlements listening to the cries of other settlers on the opposite side of the river, other settlers who hadn't made it to the fort in time, listening to the taunts and laughter of the Indians drifting over the water along with the screams of their captives who were being burned at the stake or flayed alive, the Indians sometimes cutting off chunks of flesh and eating them in front of the dying person, thinking I guess every world has its dangers no matter how bland or benign it appears, thinking That's the trouble with living in a valley, it's cozy and safe but your horizons are too close and too high above your head and you spend your life wondering what the hell is going on in the next valley, looking down at the town and thinking all over again how much it reminds him of Donora, the mill town on the other side of Pittsburgh where he grew up and has spent his entire adult life trying to get away from, a connection he's made on some level of his mind before but one that has never seemed so real as it does at this moment, thinking That narrow frame house sitting on that slanting street, it's just like the one Billy Hromyak used to live in, God, I haven't thought of Billy Hromyak in years, we used to play together all the time, we used to build model airplanes together until he stomped one of mine to pieces, what a pig, I wonder what ever happened to Billy Hromyak, he probably grew up to be a grown-up pig, that could have been me if I had let it, if I hadn't worked to make something of myself, thinking Mies said architecture is a language having the discipline of a grammar, and if you are really good you can be a poet, though I know I am no poet, as

The Building

the meister *never hesitated to remind me, the question now being if I am even much of an architect . . . as at the Furnass Grill, as she stands at the shoulder-high pickup window from the kitchen waiting for the numbskull cook to correct her order—who ever heard of a BLT without the L?—Jo Schramm looks down the length of the crowded restaurant and knows that Jack's not coming to see her at lunch today either, while the tall skinny guy with the screwy mustache whose name she learned this morning is Orville is back sitting at the counter grinning at her, and thinks Orville? I'm really going to fuck a guy named Orville? But what's a poor girl to do, especially when she's no longer a girl but a middle-aged woman, thinking as she leans her fleshy upper arm against the edge of the tall window, her weight shifted to one hip, the first chance she's had to rest all morning, Jack Jack Jack, I know what you want, no, I know who it is you want even if you don't, even if you can't admit it to yourself, before her BLT with enough L this time for three sandwiches comes sliding across the stainless-steel windowsill at her and she's off and running again to see who needs what . . . as at the serpentine bar of the Blue Boar in the Colonel Berry Hotel, local businessman Dickie Sutcliff, after sitting here since mid-morning and having several drinks and still is unable to feel what he wants to feel, finding no one worth talking to among the other local businessmen who come in—it is no secret around town that Dickie is not only something of an outcast, a renegade among local businesspeople, but that he doesn't care, finding his own company infinitely more interesting—takes up his ongoing conversation with the man in the mirror behind the bar, his secret sharer: So, how am I doing? he asks the heavy-jawed, pastel-lit face among the bottles of Jack Daniel's and Crown Royal and Beefeater, a jaw meant not for poking through a thing but for rooting around with and for clamping on, and the sharer replies, You're okay, though you still wish there was someone to tell about your good news, and Dickie says,*

*Yeah, but there's some satisfaction knowing that if the other busi-
nessmen in town will raise their collective eyebrows when they
find out I'm a silent partner in Furnass Towers, a limited partner
with nothing to lose incidentally—and the sharer laughs and fin-
ishes the thought—Just wait till they find out you've just become
the sole agent and developer for the new industrial park along the
river and Dickie asks himself, How come I'm so much smarter
than these other guys? and the sharer says, Because you just are,
and Dickie sips his drink, Most people are fools, and the sharer
toasts him, People don't listen to you because they're afraid of
you, because you listen to yourself and not to other people, and
Dickie thinks Some people have it, and the sharer nods, Yes you
have it and you're not some people, and Dickie winks, The world
is for the taking, and the sharer winks back, The world is for
those who will take it, as a flash of sunlight from outside comes
through the entryway and Pamela DiCello dressed in a gray sweat
suit enters the darkness of the room and perches prettily on a
stool at the end of the bar and Dickie says to himself, Speaking
of things for the taking, don't I wish as he picks up his drink and
stalks down the bar toward her and the sharer calls after him,
Wait, wait, there's more I have to tell you . . . as in what was
once the Alhambra Theater and was later the Alhambra Shoppers
Bazaar and is now the office of Julian A. Lyle, Esquire, Attorney-
at-Law, as well as the office of the Furnass Development Corporation, the two being one in the same, Julian Lyle stands in the
center of what is designated as his secretary's office on the days
when she decides to come in, dressed in his work clothes, a buffalo
plaid flannel shirt and army surplus fatigue pants, in his bare feet
with his trouser legs rolled up, ankle deep in water and the soggy
remains of his suspended ceiling, looking up through the runners
and channels and conduits and lighting fixtures and pipes and the
empty squares where the ceiling tiles used to be at the gaping
darkness beyond, thinking Well, there's this about it, what else*

The Building

could possibly go wrong? . . . as Bill van Hayden, after leaving the jobsite as soon as the first noon whistle blew and hurrying around the block to Pamela's apartment, ringing the doorbell for five minutes until he was satisfied, for the time being at least, that she wasn't home, sits in the back end of his pickup truck parked on the main street with the rest of his crew, Bill perched on the toolbox behind the cab with Crazy Levon and Tony sitting against the tailgate facing him, eating their lunches and watching the girls go by, what few girls there are in a town like Furnass, as Bill tries to think of something, anything, other than Pamela but with little success, remembering that before noon he saw Jack heading up the street, which meant that Jack wasn't over at Pamela's in case she just wasn't answering her bell when he rang but thinking maybe that explained where Pamela was, maybe she went to meet Jack someplace else—Stop it!—or maybe she was at her apartment after all and Jack was only pretending to go up the street, Jack was good at disappearing so people didn't know where he was—Stop it!—that was one of the things Bill learned from Jack, keep your secrets secret, that and you make your own party, maybe Jack wanted Bill to see him heading up the street and then doubled back to her apartment and she was over there with Jack now—Stop it! Stop it!—and maybe he should go back to her apartment and try her bell again—Stop it! Stop it! Stop it!—and he shakes his head violently to stop the voices in his head and looks at his chromed hardhat sitting on the box beside him, looking at the warped image of himself and Levon and Tony and the bed of the truck and the facades of the buildings around them, thinking I've got to get hold of myself, I've got a wife and son to consider here, that's it, think of Mary, I love her, I used to love her, she's always so busy now, all I hear about is all that shit at her office— Stop it! Think good things about Mary—and thinks That's it, that's better, I don't need Pamela, I can get along without her, until he happens to look at the traffic along the narrow street and sees coming toward him a white Lincoln Continental, a car that means nothing to him except that as it passes he looks down from his perch on the toolbox in the back of his truck and sees Pamela curled up on the front seat beside some guy in a suit and the world and everything in it goes suddenly irreparably numb . . . as across from him in the bed of the pickup, munching on his sandwich of peanut butter and honey and bean sprouts on whole wheat bread, between sips of papaya juice from his Thermos, Crazy Levon turns over in his mind the problem of what to do about Bill, sick at heart to see his friend make a fool of himself running after Pamela, the same way he made a fool of himself earlier on the project running after Jack, thinking You got to keep your eyes on what's going on around you, on what's in front of your face, that's where salvation is, man, the Buddha says the only sin is unawareness and let me tell you, bud, you're about as unaware as they come right now, you've lost your center, man, you've let yourself be scattered to the four winds and six directions, sitting with his long, lanky legs stretched out with his lineman's boots crossed at the ankles, the band taken from his ponytail so his shoulder-length red hair catches the slight chilling breeze, enjoying the day nonetheless and the gray sunlight on his face as he thinks What do you do? How much do you interfere with somebody else's karma? Everybody should do their own thing, that's righteous, but what is the responsibility then to other people? It's the job of the strong to take care of the weak, and it's the job of us humans to be the keepers of the earth and tend the garden, but we're only responsible for our own journeys to enlightenment even though we're all One, how does any of that work when you watch your friend act like an asshole? by chance watching Bill's face as his friend watches a white car go by and Bill's face appears to collapse in upon itself and the red patches spread like a disease across his cheeks and Levon thinks Oh my God, what is it, Billy, what is it this time? . . . as on the top deck of the building, Gregg

The Building

Przybysz, having missed the manhoist's last trip down before lunchtime because he was too shy to get on the crowded car with the other workmen, stands leaning on the two-by-four guardrail overlooking the street, thinking I don't care, I'm not hungry anyway, bullshit, I'm starved but I'm just going to have to live with it, I'm sure as hell not going to climb down those ladders again, shudders as he remembers the sensation of backing over the edge of the stairwell groping for the ladder with his toe, stands looking at the view spread before him, the winding river at the foot of the town and the hills on the other side of the valley, the spring day having turned wistful, no longer cut up in extremes of light and shadow, and Gregg looks at the landscape with new eyes, the hills no longer with a frosting of green but the trees predominantly black and brown as if a dark underpinning were showing through, thinking I have become a whiner and a complainer, worse, I have become a coward, or showed that I've been one all along, I let Jack and Nicholson dick me around any way they wanted, and all I did was bend over and take it, I'm better than that, maybe not as an inspector, but as me, turns away from the view and wanders back across the empty deck, figuring that as long as he's up here with nobody around to bother him—meaning Jack—he'll take another look at a couple of things, he's got an uneasy feeling, it's almost as if he knows there's something wrong, something he's looked at already but it hasn't registered yet, maybe something to do with the rebar in the columns, something besides the welding, goes to the plan table to have another look at the drawings . . . as the welds on the bottom snap unevenly and the ties and the hairpins and the candy canes break free of the heavy vertical bars, the column beginning to rotate on its axis, the vertical bars fanning out at the bottom, kicking free of the wood form, the column even as it continues its plunge appearing to take a step or two, as if the whole thing might walk at a tilt across the deck . . . but we're getting ahead of our story again, or maybe it insists on coming back through the spirals of time to meet us. . . .

16

"Nurses' station."

"Hi, this is Pamela. Who's this?"

"This is Connie, Pamela. How're you doing?"

"I'm fine. I wanted to find out how—"

"—How Mr. Enright is doing."

"Yeah," Pamela said, and laughed a little. "I'm sorry to be a pest."

"No problem. Let me get Joyce, she's been in there the most this morning."

"Thanks." Through the receiver, Pamela heard the phone on the other end being placed on the counter and the sound of Connie asking one of the nurses' aides to get Joyce. Pamela stood in the hallway of her apartment, around the edge of the doorway from the kitchen, holding the receiver of the wall phone; the curlicues of the cord were stretched almost straight, threatening to snap the phone out of her hand like a taut rubber band. She leaned around the edge of the door frame and bent over far enough to look up through the kitchen window, over the top of her café curtains; on the top deck of the building under construction across the alley, Bill stood near the guardrail fiddling with something on his belt but looking down toward her windows. Pamela ducked back and blended into the shadows of the hallway as she heard through the receiver the squeak of soft-soled shoes coming closer across a heavily waxed floor.

"Hi Pamela, this is Joyce."

"I'm sorry to bother you. . . ."

"No problem. He's asleep right now and seems to be resting comfortably this morning. And Mavis said he had an okay night after you left."

The Building

"Was he asking for more morphine?"

"Mavis didn't say. But Dr. Keller gave him a shot just after I got here."

"That's good. Did Dr. Keller say how long he thinks?"

"You know Keller. That bastard never tells you anything. But I wouldn't think he could make it more than a day or two."

"I know. That's what I was thinking." Pamela bit at the underside of her fingernail, then told herself Don't.

"You're in this evening, aren't you?"

"Yeah. I wasn't supposed to be, but I traded so I could be around for the next couple of days, you know?"

"Yes, I know. Look, I'll tell him you called if he wakes up and seems at all lucid. He was asking for you already this morning, I should be jealous." Joyce laughed.

"Thanks, Joyce. I really appreciate it."

"Got to keep moving. See you at four." And Joyce hung up.

Pamela reached around the door frame with the receiver, groping blindly until she located the wall phone and hung it up. Then she chanced another peek at the window. That nice old man. Face like a pickax but sweet as pie. Coal miner, drove a donkey engine he said, all proud as if I'd know what that was. Spent his whole life under the ground, now he'll. . . . All his funny little jokes trying to make me feel better and he's the one in pain. Bill said You got a thing for this Enright guy? and I said He's a sick man, Bill, you're a sick man if you could think such a thing. That's probably truer than I'd like to think.

Across the alley, Bill had moved away from the edge of the building. Pamela stood in the doorway, her arms folded, resting her head against the frame. The man is nothing but trouble but he certainly does have a nice butt. Well, that's all over now. He said I want to talk to you about something next time, it's time we had a talk about our future and I know what that means too, I know I can't let there be a next time. Mr. Enright took my hand

and said something but I could hardly hear him since he lost his larynx, I bent over him and in what was left of his raspy cancer-smelling voice he wheezed out If I was twenty years younger I'd scoop you up and I squeezed his hand and said If you were twenty years younger I'd let you and he shook his head and wheezed Don't worry, the right one will come along, and I wanted to say He already did but I didn't.

The boom of the truck crane swinging across her field of view called her back from her reverie. She smiled to herself and went down the hall to her bedroom to finish getting ready. Jack used to—no. Think of something else. Robert Kaputo. I wonder whatever happened to Robert Kaputo? Somebody, I'll bet it was Romano, said he was at the class reunion and looked better than ever, Romano would. Said he was an astronomer or something out in his beloved California. Ah Robert. She checked her makeup in the dresser mirror; tucked her keys and wallet into the hand-warmer pocket of her sweat suit; looked around her bedroom to see what she was missing. Robert Robert Robert. My rich boy from the suburbs. The only heavenly body you were interested in in high school was mine, we studied the stars together in the backseat of your mother's convertible out at Berry's Run Park. Did I get you started in your stargazing? Maybe you were what got me started as a nurse. She took one last look at herself, ruffled her hand through her nest of thick black hair, and left her apartment before Bill got the idea to come over. She hadn't decided how or when she was going to tell him that she was breaking it off with him, but she didn't want a scene at her front door.

It had been a mistake with Bill, she knew that now. She had actually known it from the beginning, but she had continued to see him, hoping something might come of it. Hoping it might lead to something else. The thing was, Bill had turned out to be very different from the way he appeared. She had seen him on the construction site across the alley as she looked out her window, as she sat at her kitchen table drinking coffee or putzied around doing dishes, looking down at the hole in the ground when the project first started. He looked like a male model with his chiseled jaw and high cheekbones, the kind of guy you see in advertisements or on posters, strong, a real hunk. When she got to know Jack, she asked about Bill, but only in passing, out of curiosity really, she wasn't that interested in him, she certainly wasn't interested in dating him. But you didn't do things halfway with Jack, as she was learning at the time; you didn't bring up something unless you were ready to follow through with it.

"You're always talking about the guy," Jack said, one afternoon as they were sitting in her kitchen having a beer.

"I am not. I only asked a couple of questions."

"A couple of questions a couple of times. So what's the story, you want to meet him?"

"No, I didn't mean that. . . ," she said, but she hesitated—she was playing with him, trying to be a bit coy, to get him thinking. But you didn't play with Jack, not that way at least; he sensed it and threw it back in her face. She had still been learning.

"It's no big deal," Jack shrugged and took another swallow. "I'll bring him over to meet you sometime. Maybe you'll like him better'n me."

Then he seemed to forget about it. A couple of months went by and he didn't say anything more about Bill, and neither did she. But she was also learning that Jack never forgot anything either. One afternoon out of nowhere Jack brought Bill along when he came to see her. Up close, there was no question that the man was handsome, as handsome as any man she had ever seen in the flesh. That, and almost painfully shy. It was his shyness that actually made him most appealing to her; and when Jack abruptly broke it off with her and Bill asked her out, Pamela started to see him. It wasn't very long however before she realized that what she saw as a chance for a good time, an interlude, Bill saw as serious, the beginnings of a lifetime together. That wasn't what she wanted from Bill at all, not at all.

*

There were a lot of things she had to do today, before she went to work. She had to pick up her Corvette at Smitty's Service. She had to do her weekly grocery shopping at Giant Eagle. She needed to pick up her winter clothes at the cleaner's and get a new band for her wristwatch. She wanted to find someone to join her in a game of racquetball out in suburban Seneca at her health club. She wanted time to do nothing at all, to be by herself for a while and enjoy her own company. A lot of things she had to do, and needed to do, and wanted to do—but as soon as she left her apartment and stepped out into the chilly spring sunlight, instead of heading toward her first stop, Smitty's Service, she walked up the hill at the end of the block and catty-cornered across the block-square park to her parents' house.

It was a small narrow Insulbrick-covered frame house, sitting on the slant of the side street facing the park. On the front porch the swing had been hoisted up for winter, riding high at the top of its chains like a balloon bumping against the ceiling; Scotch-taped to the glass of the front door were several paper cutouts of Easter bunnies and decorated eggs her mother had put up for the grandchildren. Before Pamela went in she stopped and looked back down the hill. Below the park, the top deck of the building under construction floated above the buildings on her street like the top of a stack of cards; the boom of the crane crooked toward the milky blue sky like an accusing finger. The sounds of hammering and electric saws and other machinery reached her over the terraced lawns and leafless trees. Thank God Bill doesn't know where my family lives, it would be like him to try to track me down here. Jack used to say—no. I won't do that, I can't. Robert and I used to sit on the porch here when we were in high school, how many years ago, Daddy pacing back and forth inside the living room peering out the window, quick kisses and cheap feels before he turned around again. Someday he'll come along Mr. Enright said. Robert would run from the porch and jump into his mother's car and peel away at midnight. Back to his comfortable house in Seneca. Pamela went on into the house, bouncing a little as she walked, light-footed in her running shoes, feeling for the briefest instant like a teenage girl again.

In the living room, her father sat stretched out in his Barcalounger beside the door, slung back in his chair like an astronaut lifting through the atmosphere, watching *The Price Is Right*. He didn't look up as Pamela walked in beside him.

"Hi Dad," she said, bending over to kiss him on the bald spot on top of his head. Her father grunted and shied away to keep his view of the screen; without looking at her he took her hand and held it.

"Wait a minute," he said. "They're about to focus in on Holly."

On the screen, the three young women who showed off the prizes were dressed in bikinis to demonstrate a sailboat. "Which one is Holly?" Pamela said.

"The redhead with the pretty knees."

"Men," Pamela said.

"Women," her father said, still watching the screen.

Pamela tried to pull her hand away; her father held on a little tighter, glancing at her and grinning before he let go. The sudden release sent her bounding through the dining room and on into the kitchen.

"You're certainly bright-eyed and bushy-tailed this morning," her mother said.

"I was having a tug-of-war with Dad."

"Your father," Mrs. DiCello said and shook her head. She was a sturdy, compact woman in her mid-sixties, with flawless skin and her black hair laced with white. She was standing at the kitchen table, punching a mound of bread dough in a large wooden bowl loosely covered with a dish towel. Pamela gave her a kiss on the cheek; her mother smelled of yeast.

"The man wants home-made bread, store-bought bread's not good enough. That's all well and good for him, he's in there watching his redhead with the pretty knees." She shook her head again but smiled.

"You don't have to do it, you know," Pamela said, sitting down at the end of the table, one leg folded under her. She reached across the table and pinched off a small bit of dough from beneath the dish towel; her mother swatted at her.

"Of course I have to do it. Why wouldn't I?" Her mother straightened up and looked at her, incredulous. Pamela ate the raw dough, wishing she had chanced a little more.

"So. What are you up to this morning? Or did you remember I was baking today? Go ahead, have some more. I was going to call you and tell you to come over."

Pamela wondered if that was the reason she came over. No, I wish it was. I wish it was that easy. This time she took a good-size lump.

"I was just out running errands. Thought I better drop by. See how you and Dad were doing."

Mrs. DiCello wagged her head and made a face, the visual equivalent of saying *mezza-mezza*—half-and-half, so-so.

"Actually, I thought of something on the way over that I want to look for, up in my room. As long as I'm here."

Mrs. DiCello made the same face as before, only nodding this time, as if she knew something of the sort all along. She dipped her hands in flour and powdered a wooden board on the table; then she removed the mound of dough from under the dish towel, plopped it on the board, and began kneading it.

I hate it when she does that. Like she knew I had some ulterior motive all along. I didn't, did I? Pamela was afraid to say anything more; she was equally afraid of what else she might show without saying anything at all. "I'll be down in a few minutes," she said, bouncing up from the table and heading upstairs.

As glad as she was to see her parents, she was glad to get away from them now that she was here. Am I a terrible daughter? Of course not, I'm sane, that's all. Jack used to say that—no. I remember the way Mom used to coo over Robert every time he came down, Ooo Roberto, she would say and cup his cheeks in her hands, come have some pizza, *mangia, mangia.* Robert would stand there in his layered haircut, blushing, it drove Daddy batty. Oh Robert, you were so young and so suburban and so much out of your element in this Italian household, a cake eater Daddy called you, there was the time we went down to the basement for something, I think it was my turn to do laundry, the whole family overhead watching television and you dropped on your knees and pulled down my shorts and buried your nose in my muff, the ceiling was covered with Daddy's sausages curing, all I could do was laugh, Jack once—no.

The upstairs of the small narrow house smelled of Pine-Sol; muted sunlight from the bedroom windows gloomed across the bare wood floor of the hallway. The first thing her mother had done when each of her children left home was to rid their rooms of any trace of them. I used to think that was hard of her, that she was glad to get rid of us, that maybe she was getting back at us for wanting to leave at all, but I understand now, that wasn't it at all. Rosalie and Marie's room was nearly bare, only the two beds, a dresser, a straight-backed chair, nothing more; there were no pictures on the walls, no clothes in the closets, no personal effects to show that it was ever lived in. Yes, I understand now, perfectly, it wasn't that she was glad to get rid of us at all. Only Billy's room looked lived in, because it was; her younger brother had moved back home after he was laid off from Buchanan Steel and his marriage busted up. A pair of jeans and a T-shirt were draped over the chair; a pair of work boots sat in the corner; several magazines, *Playboy, Rolling Stone, Easyriders,* lay scattered across the bed. It was because she didn't want to be reminded of us, it was the only way to make it tolerable, to make it so she could go on. Pamela continued down the hall to the bedroom at the front of the house.

Her old bedroom was as bare and antiseptic as her sisters'. The bedspread was one she had never seen before; weighing down the doily on top of the dresser was an old bottle of unfamiliar perfume and a china figurine of a child with a toothache her mother had picked up at a garage sale sometime after Pamela was gone. From beneath her feet came the sounds of the television in the living room, the sounds of cheering and music as some contestant won a prize. When I was in high school late at night it would be the applause and theme music for Johnny Carson or maybe the late news, Daddy winding down from his late shift. Winding down after chasing Robert out again. From where she stood beside the bed she could see the park across the street through the window, the clump of bushes where Robert would stand after leaving and then doubling back to make sure she made it to her room safely, to make sure her father didn't say something to her after he was gone. What was he afraid of? That Daddy might hit me? No, only that he'd say something to change my mind about Robert, say something to make me break up with him. Silly boy, he had no idea what love was. I didn't either. Someday the right one will come along. Bill said I want to talk to you about our future and he had the same misty look in his eyes and the same clinging tone of voice that Robert used to have when he said good night, before he stood in the bushes for hours waiting until I turned the light off, before he would leave me alone again. When they need you they never want to leave you alone and they call it love. On the wall was a small plaster head of Christ, something else her mother must have found at a garage sale; a dried palm frond was wedged behind it and several rosaries were draped over it, the tiny crucifixes dangling down. It was the Christ of the Crown of Thorns, blood and sweat trickling down his face; he was screaming but it seemed as much from astonishment as pain. Pamela went over to the closet, took a Kaufmann's suit box from the top shelf, and carried it to the bed.

Inside the box were drawings she had done in grade school; her confirmation certificate; letters Robert had sent her when he first went away; the wallet-size photographs she had traded with friends in high school . . . Never forget the great times we had in Miss McKee's class . . . Best of luck to a swell girl . . . the program from a choral recital; the remains of her prom corsage. She found her yearbooks at the bottom of the stack and opened the 1969 edition of *The Stoker* on her lap. She thought she was looking for Robert's class picture, to try to remember what it had been that attracted her to him, but she barely glanced at it once she found it. Instead she leafed through the pages, picking out her own face from among the cheerleaders, Tri-Hi-Y, Honor Society. God, I looked so trusting, so full of hope. Dumb. Everybody thought I was so wild, but it didn't feel wild. It only felt lonely. That's why I started going with Robert, wasn't it? She turned back to the senior class pictures again and found her own. A nice-looking girl, not pretty, not cute, but attractive, with long straight hair that she ironed flat to be in style.

> Pam's a girl who's loads of fun,
> Always on the go and ready to run.

God, even then I was known as a girl who liked to run around. A girl she recognized but who seemed to have nothing to do with the woman she was now. Hi little girl, whose little girl are you? Nobody's. And that's the way we like it, isn't it? Jack—no.

"Did you find what you were looking for?" her mother called up the steps.

Yes, as a matter of fact I did. "I'll be right down." But that doesn't mean you can keep it, does it? That's what's different between me and this girl in the picture, the girl in the picture hasn't learned that yet. What did he say, Come there with me, we can do it together. She closed the yearbook, put it back in the box with the other mementos, and returned the box to the closet. Before she went back downstairs, she stopped and looked out the window again, leaning down to see under the shade; from this height the bare branches of the trees blocked her view of the building under construction. It's almost noon, I wonder what he's doing now, that's no concern of mine, you're better off not knowing. She touched the plaster forehead of the astonished Christ— it was as cool as the dead—and skipped down the stairs.

Ah Robert, that time you came back after you had been gone a couple of years and we sat on the front porch like we always did during the summers and we could see my dad through the living room window pacing back and forth keeping an eye on us just like he used to, it still bothered you but I put my hand on your hand and told you not to let him worry you just like I always used to when we were in high school though by then you were a college boy from California and I was already in nurse's training up at Mercy. And you told me all about your new life there and then like I already knew you would you kissed me and said, Come there with me, we can do it together, I mean you can get a job or something, and my family would help us, they always liked you and I was already shaking my head, poor Robert. . . .

Her father was standing at the sink in the kitchen having a glass of water, watching her mother work another mound of bread dough.

"It must be time for commercials," Pamela said.

"Yeah. And Holly was just on. They take turns showing the different girls, she won't be back on for a couple more minutes. I got a little time."

"Don't worry," her mother said. "He wouldn't miss his precious Holly."

He was a short, squat man, only a few inches taller than his wife, but built solid; he and Pamela had the same olive skin, her mother was fair.

"Your car still at the shop?" he said to Pamela, holding the empty water glass upside down over the sink to drain the last few drops. "I can take you to pick it up. After Patti Burns and the *Noon News*."

"He wouldn't miss his precious Patti Burns either," her mother said and thumped the bread dough once more for good measure. She straightened up and looked at her husband with one eye closed, as if taking aim. "His days are full up with his pretty TV women."

"I'll walk up to Smitty's this afternoon and pick it up," Pamela said. "I need the exercise. But thanks."

Her father shrugged, suit yourself. "How's Jack?"

"Sando!" her mother said and swatted at him with a flour-covered hand.

"What's wrong with that? I just asked."

Pamela smiled at her father's consternation. "It's okay. He's fine, Dad, as far as I know. I haven't seen him lately. And I doubt if I will. He's busy with other things."

"That Jack," her father said, shaking his head. "I still remember him taking me up on the building that time and showing me around. He's quite a character, that Jack."

"Yes," Pamela said, running her finger along the back of one of the wooden kitchen chairs. "He's quite a character."

"And you're an impossible man, Sando DiCello."

Her father went over and grabbed his wife from behind, his hands on her broad hips. "Your mother, now, there's a lot of life in her yet, you know?"

Her mother giggled and tried to reach around behind her to swat him again but he dodged away, still holding on. Then he released her suddenly. "Oops. There's my music," he said, and chugged out of the kitchen and back to the living room.

"Don't mind him," her mother said, trying to reset a loose strand on her forehead with the back of her wrist so she didn't get flour in her hair. "He's still a vital man, you know?"

"I have no doubt."

"It's not right, they take a vital man's job away from him."

"He took early retirement, Mom."

"They made him take it. A man is not a man without his work." Having said what she wanted to say, her mother abruptly changed gears. Her flour-covered fist rested on her hip as she smiled at her daughter. "Sunday. You can come to dinner Sunday?"

"I'll have to see, Mom."

"Don't pull too far away from your sisters, sweetheart."

Come on, Mom, don't start. "That's not it. I may have to work."

"Even though they don't live the kind of life that you want to live, you should still keep in touch. Someday that'll be important to you." Mrs. DiCello went back to punching the mound of dough.

How do you know what I want? "How do you know I don't want to live like Rosie and Marie?"

Mrs. DiCello stopped punching the dough and looked under her eyebrows at Pamela. "I'm your mother. And it's not a dirty word."

They both laughed. Pamela went over and kissed her on the cheek. "I'll let you know about Sunday, Dirty Word."

The Building

Her mother grunted and looked to the ceiling as if to say Oh sure and continued beating the bread dough under the dish towel. On her way through the house, Pamela said good-bye to her father in the living room but he only raised a hand as she passed; his eyes were fixed on the screen where the redhead with the pretty knees demonstrated a dishwasher. Pamela kissed him again on his bald spot and closed the door behind her.

How does she know what I want? Even if she is my mother. Pamela stuck her hands in the pocket-pouch of her sweat suit and walked down the steps of the front porch and headed across the street to the park. She thinks I don't want to live like Rosie and Marie, to have the kids and the 2.5 husbands and the Sunday dinners with the family and the tidy little house in the suburbs, because she thinks I think it would cramp my style, Pamela the good-time girl, always on the go and ready for fun, and she's accepted that and I love her for it, how could she know there was something else, I never told her, I only told one person and all he did was see it as a threat or a joke, all he saw was that it was what I wanted and not what he wanted. She continued down the hill through the park, angling back toward the main part of town, ignoring the walks and concrete steps, cutting diagonally across the terraced lawns, kicking the dead leaves.

You kissed me and said Come there with me, we can do it together, I mean you can get a job or something, and my family would help us, they always liked you and I was already shaking my head, poor Robert, and you said Why, is it because of him? flicking your head toward my dad inside the house and I couldn't tell you, I couldn't say No it's because of you, because you think that might stop me and then I told you I had a plan of my own, that I wanted to become a doctor and you said Don't be ridiculous, you're only studying to be a nurse and I told you that after I got my RN I was going to try to save enough money to go to college and then put myself through med school and silly me I thought maybe you'd be happy for me because I was planning a life for myself like you were planning a life for yourself but all you said was How could you even think of doing such a thing? How could you do this to me? and I said What does it have to do with you? and you said If that's what you want then we could never be together and I said We're not together now, you're the one who went away to school and started a new life for yourself, I'm just trying to build a life for myself, but you didn't hear me, you only looked like you were about to cry as if I had wounded you in some way and then you ran from the porch and got in your family's car and peeled rubber as you sped away and it was the same dumb scene we had played out so many times before except this time I was glad to see you go because I had seen once and for all who and what you were and were not and my dad came to the screen door and said Is the cake eater gone? and I said Yes, he's gone.

As she neared the corner of the park, there was a commotion in the bare branches of a sycamore tree above her. At the top of the tree, a crow faced a squirrel that it had chased out to the end of a branch. The squirrel ticked petulantly, its tail flicking; the crow didn't say anything, but several of its fellows on nearby branches kept up a steady cawing as if to goad it on. The crow whetted its beak on the side of the branch and took a step forward. The squirrel scolded, then realized it was running out of branch; it turned and jumped down to another branch a few feet below and scampered away. The crows flew off together, cawing raucously.

Farther down the hill, the building under construction hovered above the buildings on her street; the black steel of the columns for the next two floors reached up like fingers clawing at the sky. You were right about that at least, Robert, if nothing else, you never said I didn't have what it would take to become a doctor in so many words but the implication was there, that's what

everyone in town would have thought about the idea if they had
known about it, Pamela DiCello, a doctor? Don't be ridiculous,
she likes to run around too much, besides, well, you know, what
makes a girl like that think she could ever do something like become a doctor? Is the reason I didn't become a doctor because I
liked to run, or did I like to run because I knew I wouldn't become
a doctor? I guess it doesn't matter now. The funny part is I don't
even like to run that much anymore. I got one part of my wish
though: I became more than just a nurse, all right, I became a
nursemaid to men, starting with you, Robert, the first of a string
of weak men who looked strong. And then the one man who is
strong enough to settle me is too strong to admit it. Bill said I
want to talk to you about our future. Someday the right one will
come along. She tossed her head to set her thick black hair and
crossed the street. Like Jack always says Isn't that wonderful?

*

The Blue Boar wasn't her favorite place. She probably liked
Camarrotti's just as much, or Charlie's Top o' the Hill, or even
the Holiday Inn when they had a good band. After work the other
nurses at the hospital often drove to the Riverside Inn, across the
Allehela from Furnass; Pamela probably liked the Riverside Inn
best of all—she and Jack used to go there a lot late at night, it
was almost "their" place—but for the past few months she had
declined the offer to join the others and just went home in the
evenings. The Blue Boar was okay, of course; it was dark and
cozy, the nicest place in town, a favorite haunt of local businessmen, a convenient place for executives of Buchanan Steel to en-
tertain clients and vendors before the mill shut down. But it was
hard for Pamela to work up much enthusiasm for the Boar—it
never felt like she was going out when all she did was walk over
a block or so and down the hill. But today, after stopping by to
see her folks, a drink sounded awfully good. Besides it was noon,
the bells of the Angelus and the other churches were ringing out

over the town, the guys working on the building would be coming down for lunch; after keeping out of sight all morning in her apartment since her shower, she didn't want to run into anybody on the sidewalk now. And the Boar was right here. Singing to herself the song that she and Jack used to sing along with the church bells—Sweet hour of bears, sweet hour of bares, we'll screw ourselves silly and have no cares—she pushed through the sky-blue doors into the darkness of the bar.

Her eyes were slow to adjust after being outdoors but she knew the layout of the place well enough; she settled herself on one of the empty stools at the apex of the horseshoe bar near the door. The restaurant was decorated in the style of an Elizabethan banquet hall, with dark wood-veneer paneling and false-beamed ceilings and light fixtures shaped like torches; a mural depicting cartoonish figures of Henry VIII and his court covered one wall. A few years earlier when the place was busier, the waitresses were required to dress like serving wenches and the bartenders wore doublets, but now things were more casual.

Today the Boar was nearly empty. On the brighter side of the bar toward the restaurant a trio of local businessmen was watching her, making comments among themselves. Let them. Dream on, guys. She smiled at them and nodded and they looked away. She originally thought to have a Bloody Mary; now she was considering having a double shot of Jack Daniel's. Might as well give them something to think about as long as they're doing it anyway. Safer drinking anyway. Always know what you're dealing with, Jack used to say. But she remembered she was going on duty in a few hours and ordered a bottle of Perrier. He said Pay attention and I'll teach you how to drink and I said I already know how to drink and he said No, you just think you do. First of all forget that mixed-drink crap. Don't ever drink anything that has straws or umbrellas or fruit or anything else sticking out of it. You drink the best stuff available and you drink it straight, why drink anything at all if you're not going to taste it, and then you always follow whatever you're having with a glass of water, when you order ask for a water-back. You do what I tell you and you'll have a great time, you'll never get drunk-sick, and you won't have a hangover either. Or if you do I've got a remedy for that too. I said You make a better nurse than I do and he said I just don't like to see people not drinking smart, that's how they get into trouble. I said Why do you always feel responsible for everybody else and he said—no, I'm not going to think about that. As the bartender brought her drink, a figure sitting alone on the dark leg of the horseshoe stood up and carried his glass toward her.

"Pamela the Italian," Dickie Sutcliff said.

"Dickie the WASP," Pamela responded.

Dickie laughed his loud braying laugh and mounted the stool beside her, snuggling in against her, sitting too close as Dickie was wont to do. "What are you doing in here at this time of day, sport? Drinking your lunch?"

"That's Dickie. Always assuming that everybody else shares your vices."

Dickie brayed; the smells of Polo and alcohol wafted about him. He was in his early forties, with a long face and heavy jaw and his ash-brown hair in the same brush cut he had worn in high school and college; his chin appeared long enough to contain a compartment in which he kept wads of food or secrets. He wore an expensive gray glen plaid suit, the double-breasted coat open and hanging loose.

"Actually, I'm having myself a little celebration," Dickie said. "I'm glad you're here, I've been looking for someone to celebrate with. As you can see, there's sure as hell nobody else in this place I'd want to talk to."

"I'm not sure that's a compliment, seeing as how there's hardly anyone here."

"It's a compliment, believe me," Dickie said and took a drink. He was looking at the image of the two of them sitting together in the mirror behind this end of the bar.

"Believe Dickie Sutcliff. Oh sure," Pamela said to him in the mirror.

Dickie flicked his eyebrows at his reflection, sharing the comment with himself.

"So, what occasion are we celebrating?"

"You need to keep this to your pretty little self for a while," Dickie said turning to her, snuggling even closer against her. "But I just signed a deal that will put this town back on its feet."

"I thought the new building they're working on was supposed to do that."

"Furnass Towers?" Dickie said and laughed sarcastically. The three businessmen down the bar glanced at him and continued to make comments among themselves. Dickie lowered his voice when he spoke to her again, as close to her face as if he were going to kiss her. Pamela lowered her head slightly and met his gaze. I'm not budging, Dickie Sutcliff, I know what you're up to, I wouldn't give you the satisfaction of shying away.

"I'll tell you something, as long as you keep it among us girls. That building is finished right where it is now. It's not going any higher, at least under the present owners. They're about to shut it down."

Now Pamela felt herself shrink inside. "Who's going to shut it down?"

Dickie shook his head and checked his reflection in the mirror. "I better not say anything more. But I will tell you this: if you've got any money in Sycamore Savings and Loan, you better get it out of there pronto. I mean today, right now. I'll take you over there myself."

Dickie took her elbow and was ready to leave, but Pamela shook her head.

"No, I don't have any money there. I never liked Sycamore."

"A lowball operation for lowball people. And now the ball is in somebody else's court, you might say."

I wonder if he knows, they're still working today as if there's nothing wrong, as if everything is the same. What would he do after this job, where would he go? When would I—no.

"How do you know all this?"

"It's my job to know. I keep my eyes and ears open. My business, my livelihood depends on it."

"If what you're saying is true, it sounds like more than just the building is in trouble. It sounds like Sycamore is going under."

Dickie checked his image; the Dickie in the mirror wagged his head, noncommittal.

"But that's terrible," Pamela said.

"You're right," Dickie said.

"That's going to hurt a lot of people."

"It's going to hurt the whole town."

"You don't sound real broken up about it, Dickie."

Dickie looked at her sideways; it was a different Dickie, at one and the same time more calculating and more direct. "Don't believe everything you hear about me, Pamela. I might not be quite the hard-hearted bastard everybody thinks I am."

"'Might,'" Pamela said and batted her eyes at him. "I think that's the operative word there."

"Yeah, might." Dickie grinned. "Anyway, yeah, it's too bad about Sycamore, but there's still a viable bank in town, so we'll be okay. Not great, but okay. It's shakedown time for a lot of marginal savings and loans around the country, for a lot of marginal businesses. Owners and managers who think easy money doesn't come with a price, but surprise, there is a price. The trick is to stay afloat while everything else is being flushed down the toilet. It's too bad that the investors in Julian Lyle's project are going to get hurt, but I tried to warn them. And I tried to warn Julian not to do it in the first place."

"Tricky Dickie," Pamela said, not unkindly.

"That's what they say."

"They say you're always trying to screw somebody. And if the building project goes down the tube they'll probably blame you for it some way or other."

"Probably. But I've learned to live with what people think of me." Dickie worked his shoulder against hers and put his hand on her thigh. "And if they say I screw everybody in this town, what's your excuse?"

"I said 'trying,' Dickie," she said, picking up her bottle of Perrier and putting the wet bottom on the back of his hand.

"Hey, that's wet!" Dickie said.

Pamela put the bottle back on the bar and handed him a napkin. "That's the only wet thing you're ever going to get from me."

Dickie brayed. "You're a cold lady."

"Don't you wish."

"Oh, I wish, all right."

"Dickie, you and I both know that the only thing you're interested in is the chase. If you ever had me, it would spoil all your fun. What would you have to look forward to?"

Dickie looked at the Dickie in the mirror, as if confronting a sad truth about an old friend. "You're the only one who ever understands me in this town. Sometimes I think I should leave my wife once and for all and be with you."

"Oh sure, Dickie." Dickie had been trying to go to bed with her for so long that it had become something of a joke between them. Today, however, the joke seemed a little stale, maybe a little sour. How can I find out if he's okay? Does he know about the building shutting down? If he does why are they still working—no. What'll he do?—no. She didn't mind Dickie, not as much as other people in town did; people cut him down a lot, even the girls she knew, most of them married, who slept with him. He was thought of as loud, overbearing, crass, in addition to being a bastard to deal with in business. All of which was probably true; but at least she always knew where she stood with Dickie. Jack's room is right upstairs, did I think of that when I decided to come in here today? Oh Pamela. My God you're lovely he said as we lay on his creaky bed, he traced the line of my breasts and stomach and hips with his fingertip, barely touching my skin, soft as a whisper, then he turned away abruptly. Why stop? You look almost sad and he said You'd be sad too and tried to make a joke out of it and I said You don't have to be sad, you can have me anytime you want, and he said You kids, you think there's all the time in the world and I thought maybe what upset him was that I was so young but that wasn't it, I understand that now, that wasn't it at all. She also knew she didn't have to worry about Dickie; for all his insistence and kidding around, he would never do anything to hurt her.

"So, how're your folks doing?" Dickie said, turning to her again. "I see your dad around town once in a while. He seems to be getting along okay."

"Yeah, they're doing all right. I just stopped by to see them."

"That's good. Real good. You know, when the time comes and they ever think about selling that house, I'll be glad to take care of it for them. I'll make sure they get as much as they can for it."

"That's nice of you, Dickie."

"And that goes for you too, you know. Are you still in that apartment on Eighth Avenue?"

"Still there," Pamela said, looking at herself now in the mirror. She was beginning to wish she had fixed herself up a little better before she came out today, spent more time on her makeup, done something with her hair. Was it the light in here, or was she beginning to look old? Older.

"If you ever think of buying a little place for yourself, I can fix you up. You might want to consider something like one of those new condos out in Seneca."

"Seneca Towne Centre. Which, if I'm not mistaken, is a development of Sutcliff Realty."

"I might have an in," Dickie said wagging his head.

"Tell you the truth, I'm a little disappointed," Pamela said, feeling flirty again and not wanting to stop herself. "I thought maybe you would offer to set me up somewhere. You know, a nice little love nest, help with the payments, some spending money on the side. . . ."

"See that? That's a woman for you. One minute you're turning me off, getting my hand all wet because I put it on your leg, and the next minute you're talking about becoming my mistress. What's a guy to think?"

"You don't have to think. Just go with it."

"Yeah, right," Dickie consoled the Dickie in the mirror.

"You mean to sit there and tell me, Dickie Sutcliff, that you wouldn't like to give me a ride?"

"Why do I have the feeling that you and I define 'ride' differently?"

Pamela tucked in her lower lip and hung her head, pretending to be coy, a little girl caught in the act. "I was just thinking that maybe you'd like to take me out to Seneca to the racquetball club and play a couple of games. You're always telling me how good you are."

"I am good. I'm pretty good at racquetball, too. Even after a couple of drinks."

"And then on the way back into town, you can drop me off at Smitty's so I can pick up my 'Vette."

"Just what's in this for me? What do you think I get out of it?"

"You get the pleasure of my company, and the chance to burn off some of that middle-age spread you're putting on." She patted the small roll of fat above his belt line; but the truth was that he was in good shape.

"You really know how to hurt a guy."

Bill said I want to talk to you about our future. Jack said I'm not going to get old, I'm going to break before I wear out. "And afterward, who knows what will happen?" she said suggestively, running her fingertip into a circle of water on the bar and smearing it around.

"I'll tell you what'll happen afterward. I'll be too pooped to pop, and you'll have to go to work." Dickie nodded good-bye to the Dickie in the mirror and stood up, adjusting the waistband of his pants and buttoning his double-breasted jacket. "But I guess I'll have to take what I can get when it comes to you, won't I?"

"Isn't that what you do anyway?" Pamela said, finishing her Perrier and sliding off the stool. "Take what you can get?"

Dickie acted like he didn't hear her as he left money for their drinks on the bar. "You know, don't you, sport, that any time you need something, whether it's a ride or anything else, all you have to do is call?"

Pamela nodded.

"No strings attached."

She smiled at him affectionately. "Yes. I know that, Dickie."

He nodded and took her arm and escorted her outside. Even though the day was turning overcast, the subdued sunlight hurt her eyes after the darkness of the bar. Dickie's white Lincoln Continental was parked around the corner, down the steep side street in a yellow zone. He held the door open for her.

"Thank you, kind sir."

"You're welcome, fair lady."

The interior smelled of leather and Dickie's cologne. As Dickie walked around the car to the driver's side, Pamela tucked her feet up under her and curled into the luxurious upholstery.

I want to talk to you about our future. I'm not going to get old I'm going to break before I wear out. For that matter, why haven't I ever considered Dickie seriously? You could do a lot worse, little girl. He probably would set me up in a place, a nice place too, maybe help me get a townhouse so I'd have something for the future. Everybody knows he'll never leave his wife and that's okay, I'd have the best of both worlds. I'll never marry now, I've lived alone too long, I've learned to like it too much, I don't want to run anymore but I want my freedom. Funny, I guess I'm more like Jack than I ever realized, I'm not going to get old, I'm going to break before I wear out and I said, What's the matter, Jack, are you afraid of getting older? Or are you just afraid—no. Yes. With Dickie I'd have security and a kind man who throws money around to have a good time and a steady fuck. I'm ready to settle for that, aren't I?

Dickie got in and seated himself behind the wheel.

"Comfortable?"

"Very."

Dickie glanced at the eyes in the rearview mirror and drove up the hill, turning left onto the main street.

"Speaking of banks and such, I've got to swing by First City and give Harvey McMillan some news. This will be perfect, I don't want a lengthy conversation with him. I'll just double-park and run in, then we're on our way."

"You're the driver."

They smiled to each other like an old married couple, or like two friends who had been through a lot though not necessarily together. Pamela looked out the window. Yes. Very comfortable. Is that so bad? As they approached the building under construction, something glinted in the corner of her eye; she glanced up in time to see Bill's chromed hardhat sitting on the toolbox in the back of his pickup, and Bill beside it, looking down at her as they drove by. Then he was gone, behind her, the narrow streets of the town rolling past in precision-machined silence. Damn it. She reached over and adjusted the louvers of the vent on the dashboard so the fan didn't blow in her face. Damn it, damn it. It's never the right one who sees me.

17

"Hello?"

"Hi."

"Hi yourself."

"Whatcha doing, kid?"

"I'm cleaning, if you want to know."

"Of course I want to know. Why do you think I called?"

It came out like a reproach and Vince didn't mean it that way, at least he didn't think he meant it that way. He didn't want to start any trouble with Rita, they'd had too much of that already; that wasn't why he called. Why did I call her? What did I want? What did I think I could get? He went on.

"I'm sitting here in the contractor's trailer at this Furnass job. You should see this office, it's a real crud hole. There's drawings thrown all over the plan table, the desk is piled high with stacks of papers and old Styrofoam coffee cups, and there's a layer of dust over everything. Not a thin layer either. You could make sand paintings in this stuff."

He laughed, waiting for some response from his wife, but the line was silent. Is she still there? Maybe she just wandered off and left the receiver dangling and figured she'd hang it up later after I stopped talking. Oh Rita. Her silence only made him want to talk more, faster. Pile it on.

"I don't know how this superintendent gets anything done with his office like this. I certainly couldn't function this way. I could never find anything. You should see this guy, a real slob. The guy's pants ride so low on his hips that you can see the crack of his ass when he bends over. I've told you about him before: his name's Jack."

"Why does he let it get like that?"

Thank God, she's alive after all; I was afraid she died. "Why does he let what get like that?"

"His office, of course. What else would I be asking about?"

"I didn't know. I thought maybe you were asking about the crack of his ass." He meant it as a joke and waited for a laugh, a chuckle, even the voice intonation of a smile, but there was only silence. Great. Now I've probably offended her. Ass is a dirty word to Rita. Nice work. Vince sighed and ran his hand up his forehead and back over his thinning gray hair. "You'd have to know Jack to understand why he lets his office get like this. It's totally in keeping with his character. You talk about cleaning, this is one place that could certainly use it."

"I've got enough cleaning of my own, thank you. Don't you think I have enough to clean around here?"

The whiny, worried, supplicant tone. He could see her in his mind's eye, standing there at the counter in the kitchen, dressed in her gauzy floral housecoat and matching flat slippers, her beautiful thick auburn hair a tangle of snags, her wide gray-green eyes tearing up in her anxiety, her fear that he was criticizing her, her wide full mouth wrenched to the side with apprehension. As if all he did was criticize her. Do I criticize her too much? As if he only thought bad things of her? What do I think of her now? Do I ever think good things about her now? As if what he thought of her could have any effect on her, could mean anything to her. Just go on, just continue as if she didn't say anything. As if there is nothing wrong. Your whole life.

"I was thinking about that project where you were the secretary when we first met, remember? Your office was in the basement of the building next door, and there was an old boiler right behind your desk, with all the heating and ventilation ducts sprouting everywhere. It was like you were sitting in front of this huge gnarly tree, with the branches shooting off in all directions over your head. People had to duck whenever they came in to talk to you about something. That's what I always think of when I think of you on that job, all those ducts and vents and you sitting there calm as could be in the middle of them."

"Actually, the furnace wasn't in my office at all. It was in Mr. Bradley's office."

"It was? Oh." I could have sworn. Can memory do that? That and a whole lot worse I'm afraid. Now she probably thinks I'm a fool besides whatever else she thinks of me. Or doesn't think of me. But it seemed to be her turn to try to smooth things over, to be careful what was said.

"It was nice of you to think of me though."

"Is it?"

"Is it what?"

"Is it nice of me to think of you anyway?" Why did I say that? Why did I have to ask? Why am I trying to start something when I don't even want to?

"Why did you call, Vince?"

He sat hunched over, the wooden chair turned at a ninety-degree angle to the desk; his feet rested squarely on the floor, flatfooted. On the floor, in swirls around the rubbers that covered his expensive shoes, a thin layer of tracked-in dirt obscured the patterns of the linoleum. Like the swirl of clouds on a satellite weather map. A cold front coming in. Hard weather ahead.

"I was just thinking. I used to call you every morning at ten o'clock. No matter where I was I'd always find a phone. I can remember walking out of meetings on jobsites to call you. Important meetings. I guess being here at this project reminded me."

Is that true? Is that really the reason I'm calling her? I guess it could be.

"It's not ten o'clock."

"No, I guess it isn't." Vince laughed, shuffled his feet; the tracked-in dirt was gritty under his rubber soles. That's Rita. Always so damned literal. "I guess that goes to show how hard it is to keep a thing like that going. We got busy. And there were the kids."

He wondered, the more he thought about it, if he also simply got tired of always trying to find a phone at ten in the morning. And he remembered how frustrated and angry he would get, after going to all the time and trouble to find a phone, after looking forward to talking to her all morning, when she wouldn't have anything to say or would tell him she couldn't talk at the moment or would not even make the effort to be around at ten when he called. He remembered what a relief it had been, finally, not to call her anymore.

"I was just cleaning the kids' rooms."

"They won't be home till summer, Rita. That's several months away."

"Well, I thought I'd start on them now anyway. I want everything to be nice when they're here."

That's the only thing that really makes her happy. Nowadays. The kids. She was happy when we first got married. And I've seen her happy since then with the kids. But she's never happy anymore with just me. That wide-eyed enthusiastic happy excitement she used to have, the kind that brimmed right out of her. The kind she used to have with me. Now her eyes only brim over with tears.

"Would you like that again?" he said.

"What? For the kids to come home? Of course, I can hardly wait. I love it when they come home. And all their stories about school and how grown-up they're getting—"

"No, I mean would you like me to call you?"

"You are calling me. Oh, you mean some other time."

"I mean in the mornings, at ten o'clock, like I used to."

"Well, sure."

Does she mean it? I can't tell. "I'll see what I can do." I wish I hadn't called. I wish I hadn't said anything about it. Why do I always feel so empty now when I talk to her? Emptier when I do talk to her than when I don't? "I have to go."

"Vince."

"Yes?"

"I love you."

"I love you too."

"Thanks for calling. See you at dinner."

"See you, kid."

*

He hung up the phone and sat staring at the swirls of grit at his feet. Not a word about my leaving this morning without saying good-bye. Not a word about her little scene or the things she said about me. She said You can't take responsibility for what you don't see and you don't see if you don't open your eyes and you haven't seen what's going on for so long that you don't see things at all anymore and then dumped the whole pan of French toast into the garbage and left the room and all I did was sit there and watch the end of the weather forecast. Clouds increasing in the afternoon. Winds ten to twenty miles an hour. Barometer falling. This is getting me nowhere. There are serious things to consider here. Like the fact that the contractor on my building apparently hasn't been paid for several months and is talking about walking away from the most important project of my career and nobody told me a thing about it. Yes, offhand, I'd say that was serious enough. Thanks Rita for all your sympathy and concern. Vince shuffled his feet, creating storms in the swirls of grit-clouds, and left the trailer.

It was close to noon. He walked out of the gate and down the street; at his car he stopped and took off his rubbers and left them in the trunk. The more he thought about what Jack had said about the contractor pulling off the project, the more concerned and anxious he became; he needed to see Lyle more than ever and find out what was going on. But when he went back to the Alhambra, the doors to Lyle's and the Development Corporation's office were still locked, the foyer inside the old theater was still dark. He gave one more tug on the handle—Damn it! Damn them all!—and decided to take a walk to try to clear his head.

At the corner he turned up the hill and started climbing the steep streets, setting a pace for himself faster than he meant to but unable to slow down once he got into the swing of it. The noontime bells and whistles called out over the town; Vince climbed on, up through the layers of the town. Beyond the old brick homes and apartment buildings on the street above the main street, the houses became smaller and in worse condition, narrow frame houses covered with Insulbrick or aluminum siding; as he climbed higher, the streets became steeper too, the foundations of the houses seemingly wedged against the slope, as if keeping very still to maintain their toehold. After five or six blocks he turned onto the topmost street and stood panting to catch his breath.

That's a good way to get a coronary, climbing a hill like that, I know I feel as if my heart might break but it's only a figure of speech ha ha. Whooee, slow down heart. The street—it was more like a road, a path—was of broken blacktop and poorly maintained and there was no sidewalk. Above the houses on the upward side of the slope, the steep backyards dissolved into the woods that covered the rest of the hillside. Down the hill, the slope dropped away into the long backyards of the houses fronting the street below, the backs of the houses—because of the slope, he stood level with the second floors—seeming naked and exposed, as if he glimpsed parts of the occupants' lives that should remain private: clotheslines, a child's bright orange plastic hobbyhorse, a broken straight-backed chair, a rusted lawn mower, a stack of wood, old barrels, garbage cans. What was it Mies said? An orderly building can be a powerful force for greater order in the world around it. What he didn't say was that the converse must be true too. These poor people are living the second law of thermodynamics; the heat of their lives is running out and there's no way for them to get it back. Hello entropy. Beyond the houses, the rooftops of the little town riprapped on down the slope to the river; the brownish hills on the other side of the valley sealed off the distance. Vince continued along the street to a vacant lot to get a better look at the town.

He was struck by how much Furnass reminded him of the town where he grew up, fifteen miles or so down the Monongahela on the other side of Pittsburgh; he had been aware of the similarities before, of course, but they had never seemed so real before now. The two towns were cut from the same cloth, interchangeable in many ways, as all the small industrial towns shouldered in among the valleys around Pittsburgh seemed to be. No wonder I hate Furnass. And along the main street his building lifted from the jumble of rooftops like the first stages of a tower to the sky.

A peculiarity of the little valley towns was that over the past decade most of them had put up a high-rise building right in the center of town, subsidized housing for senior citizens or low-income families—a testament to public funding in the '70s and '80s, if not to aesthetics or good city planning. Furnass was behind the times in putting up its tower, and public funding was no longer so easy to get, but that hadn't stopped Julian Lyle—a testament to the unsound lending practices of the early '80s, if not to good common sense. Lyle's idea for Furnass Towers was not subsidized housing—there was no one to subsidize it anyway—but for upscale apartments or offices—he really didn't care which, and hoped for a mixture of both. True, there was no one looking for upscale apartments in Furnass at the moment, and there was more office space available than businesses in town to fill it, but Lyle's theory was that the tower would draw the kind of people and businesses he was looking for. The kind of people and businesses that would bring new life to the town. In Julian Lyle's mind, the savior of Furnass now that the mills were closed would be Furnass Towers—and (by association, Vince supposed) Julian Lyle.

Why had Vince allowed himself to become involved with such a project? Well, he knew the answer to that, too. His firm, Vincent Nicholson & Associates, badly needed the work; the mill closings and the faltering local economy had affected his business along with everyone else's. But during the initial talks with Lyle about Furnass Towers, Vince realized Lyle's ambitions for the project could serve a purpose: he realized that here was his chance to do a building worthy of his own ambitions. There was nothing he could do about where the building would be located or the purpose it was intended to serve, but that didn't mean he couldn't make it a showcase. He had never received a commission for any of Pittsburgh's major projects; he had never had clients who wanted more than buildings of the least common denominator—tilt-up industrial buildings like concrete shoe boxes; glass-and-steel office buildings that were lifeless shells; houses that could have come from a carpenter's pattern book. He decided to give Lyle a building that was beyond his expectations whether Lyle appreciated it or not. Whether he wanted it or not.

Jack said I was building the Vincent J. Nicholson Architectural Memorial Tower and he's probably right, that is what I tried to do. Funny that of all the possible structural elements I could choose to test that young inspector I chose a cantilevered floor, I told him That's the type of slab this little drawing

represents in case you ever need to know. You really have no idea
what you're doing out here, do you? No sir. I should have told
him about the principles I used to design the building, maybe
that would have impressed him, how I based the building on the
design Mies did for a reinforced-concrete office building for the
1922 Novembergruppe show, a landmark design that influenced
practically every office or apartment building that came after it.
A grid of reinforced-concrete columns to carry the floor slabs that
are cantilevered beyond the face of the outside columns and
turned up to form continuous parapets to support the ribbon
windows. Did I really think that I could do it better? Philip John-
son said the terrible thing about Mies's style is that it is too easy
to copy, and he's right and he's wrong, the terrible thing is that
it's easy to think it's easy to copy. Mies said All our buildings
don't have to look alike, there are thousands of seashells and they
don't look alike even though they have the same principle. The
trouble is that most architects try to invent something new every
time. The real thing is a very slow unfolding of form, we have to
refine what is known, and then when a new problem comes along
we'll know how to solve it. Easy for Mies to say, he whose perfect
eye never doubted for one second that he was right. Well, take a
look at Furnass, old man, and tell me what you would have done
with it. Mies the Irascible wanted to impose the factory ideal on
the world, but he never saw this little factory town, he thought
technology was the demiurge of the age extending its own eternal
verities but guess what, old timer, your eternal verities just ran
out, here's the end of the Industrial Revolution in living color
and what do you do with a town whose only future is rust? For
Le Corbusier the absence of columns was a hallmark of the new
architecture, he moved them back from the facade so you couldn't
see what supported the building, but then Mies came along and
moved them forward, he even chromed them in the Barcelona
Pavilion and added extra flutes on the 860 Towers to call

attention to them, he wanted to make sure you didn't miss what he designated to support his structures, he claimed he wanted a faceless architecture rooted in egoless technology but the fact was he hit you over the head with his perfect nameless elements, but then there's me, I took it one step further, I made the entire building like a column sticking up in the middle of main street as if to support the town from collapsing, a "pillar" of the community as it were, ha ha. If only it were funny. I'm probably the only person in the entire area with enough intelligence and training to appreciate how thoroughly I followed the Miesian dictums on this building, everything in perfect symmetry, every element based on multiples of twelve, I even sold Lyle on the idea of ribbon windows to foster the idea of flexibility of function, a universal building that could be used for anything throughout its lifetime, I played on his uncertainty about whether he wanted apartments or offices and showed him how the floors could be adapted to either, he didn't have to decide beforehand exactly what kind of a building he was building, he could change it depending on whatever tenants he could find, he only had to let me alone and let me build it. At the presentation Sutcliff looked at me and said There wouldn't be something you're not telling us, would there Mr. Nicholson? And I'm the only one who knows how far I bastardized Mies's ideals too, his reinforced concrete office building was designed to express its horizontal structure and I made mine a vertical high-rise in relation to the rest of the town around it, nice going Vince. Arthritic Mies hung on his crutches by my drafting table: Your works are all dead until some motive impels you to act. Sutcliff said Take a look at your estimate again, are you sure we can build this building for what you say, and Lyle said What's the matter, Dickie, don't you think the man knows what he's doing? and Sutcliff didn't laugh, he only said I'm afraid he knows too much of what he's doing. Beauty is the splendor of truth, Saint Augustine said and Mies never tired of quoting it, but look how far it got either one of them, they're still dead aren't they, ha ha. Truth is beauty in all its splendor, which could be another way of saying the end justifies the means. Hey, that's pretty good, that could be another subject for an essay on architecture, did you read Nicholson's latest book? Oh Rita, I've got so much to say if only you'd hear me. If only you'd stop sniveling and listen.

He was suddenly ravenously hungry. And aware of how out of place he was here in this section of town. In the old frame house next to the vacant lot, the bedsheet used as a curtain for the front window was pulled back and a black woman in a housedress stood watching him. On the front porch of a house across the street, a large stuffed Easter bunny hung by its ears surrounded by chains made from colored construction paper; at another house, multicolored plastic eggs dangled from the bare branches of a small tree, with a white cross resting against the trunk with the legend HE HAS RISEN. Farther up the block a car with several men inside pulled over and parked though none of them got out. For a few moments an undercurrent of pulsing music came from the car, then everything grew quiet. Too quiet. There was only the chatter of a sparrow in the dead branches of a bush. The distant rumble of a train far below in the valley along the river. The thumping of Vince's blood within his temples. *Crunch!* Vince whirled around. Two ten-year-olds on Huffy bikes pedaled toward him, their wheels slipping in the ruts and loose blacktop. As they passed him, one said, "Look out for the spy!" and hurried on.

Of course, my trench coat. The people up here probably think I'm a cop or something. A narc. This might not be healthy. Prominent architect killed when he strays into wrong section of town. Thanks for saying "prominent." This isn't funny, I better get back to civilization. Such as it is.

Keeping his dignity, and his eyes straight ahead, he walked past the parked car, the faces watching him from the shadows within, and turned down the hill at the next corner, letting the tug of gravity pull him toward the main part of town.

*

Back among the confines of the narrow main street, he was exhausted but curiously elated, as if he had just survived something, a rite of passage or a trial of some sort. Yea, even though I walk through the shadow of the valley, I will fear no weasel. In his mind was a vision of a steak salad; he headed toward the Blue Boar. I'm through chasing that son-of-a-bitch Lyle, I don't care what happens to the damn project at this point. But as he passed the Alhambra—I don't care if everybody walks away from the project and the whole mess falls down—he noticed one of the doors standing open. Of course. Seek and you won't find. Don't ask and you'll trip over it. Cautiously, he crossed the entryway under the marquee and looked in. Stepped inside.

The lights were on now in the foyer but there was no one around. He went on into the main lobby. The Moorish theme of the building continued through the interior; there were tile mosaics on the floor and latticework on the walls, gilded stucco vaults across the ceiling and fluted, many-sided columns. Whenever Vince had been here before, the lights were subdued and the place seemed to have a nostalgic grandeur about it, but today the lights were harsher and the old theater looked seedy; the carpet was faded and threadbare among the arabesques, the lattices were broken, the plaster was chipped and the paint faded. Sometimes it's better to keep things in the dark. Piled on one side of the lobby were a dozen or more large green garbage bags filled with rags and wadded-up paper towels and building materials of some sort. A number of the bags leaked water.

"Hello! Julian Lyle! Anybody here?"

His exhilaration of a short time ago was quickly dissipating. Now what's he up to? What craziness this time? Axiom of business number 1: The client is always right. Axiom of business

• *204* •

number 2: The client is always an asshole. The sum of the squares of the short sides of a right triangle equals the square of the long side. Dirty word: "client." And he had a new sense of foreboding. *Any man who could be talked into financing the building I talked him into is capable of anything. Careful now.* He called again and continued through the main lobby.

There were no lights burning farther on inside the old theater, but Vince could see well enough. The interior was taken up with Lyle's earlier attempt at a redevelopment project, a shoppers bazaar; along a narrow promenade the plywood facades of a variety of little shops, all of them blanked out now, stared back and forth at each other. *It looks like a cheap stage set for a Grade B movie. Worse than Grade B. Who on earth would ever think that working-class people in Western Pennsylvania would go for a thing like this? Julian Lyle, that's who. The same man who thinks Furnass Towers is going to revitalize the economy of this town. Your client, buddy-boy, the same man who's paying your salary.* He didn't call out now, thinking it was better to keep an element of surprise. Not quite tiptoeing, Vince made his way toward a light beyond the arcade.

The light was coming from the open door to Lyle's office. More of the green garbage bags were piled next to the secretary's desk, but there was no one in the reception area. His hands in the pockets of his trench coat, feeling more like a spy than ever— *This is not your normal client-architect relationship*—Vince continued toward the main office.

Someone was in the next room, moving about, humming tunelessly to himself; through the doorway, Vince saw a hunched figure dragging something across the floor. *Body parts. The man's murdered someone and is hacking them up and stuffing them in these bags. Murdered dozens by the looks of it. Don't be ridiculous.* Vince took a couple of steps forward; it felt like he had stepped in mush. *Squish!* What the hell? The carpet was sopping

wet; milky water had splashed up over his shoes, oozed up over
the edges of his soles. My four-hundred-dollar shoes! I survived
visiting the jobsite without a speck on me and have my clothes
ruined in Lyle's office. As he rolled his eyes with exasperation he
realized the suspended ceiling was missing in the office next door.
He squished over to the doorway.

"Welcome to the party," Julian Lyle said. "I hope you brought
a bucket."

18

Lyle was in old clothes, the bottoms of his pants legs rolled; the
milky water partially covered his bare feet, oozing up from the
carpet wherever he stood. He was a tall thin awkward man, with
a disjointed appearance, not so much as if his body didn't fit
comfortably within his clothes but more as if his bones didn't fit
comfortably within his skin. He was scooping soggy debris—
sections of channel stock, broken acoustical tiles, bent wires—
into a green garbage bag with a coal shovel.

"What happened?"

"Pipe broke. I've been bailing out all morning—actually things
are starting to look a lot better now. You should have seen it
earlier. On the other hand, maybe it's a good thing you didn't.
The interesting thing is that there seems to be a tidal effect going
on. And it helps that the floor of this old theater slants toward
the back here. Otherwise we could have had a tsunami rushing
out the front door and down the street, *whoosh!* That would have
surprised the good people of Furnass, don't you think?"

Vince had the distinct impression that nothing Julian Lyle did
would surprise the people of Furnass, good or otherwise. They
must be used to him by now. How does he live knowing everyone
considers him a fool? He must not know. Lyle stood in the middle
of a puddle, a bemused expression on his face as if in wonder at
the mysteries of the world. Worse: maybe the town doesn't think

there's anything strange about him. Maybe to Furnass he's the norm. An exemplary. Scary thought. Vince's patience was wearing thin; he had no more time for silliness; now that he had Lyle cornered, he wanted to find out about this talk of the contractor pulling off the project. He stepped carefully into the room, creating his own puddles around his shoes. My four-hundred-dollar shoes!

"I was just over on the building. How long have you known there's a problem?"

"I didn't know a thing until I came in this morning and found half the ceiling lying on the floor along with several inches of water. Now that I think about it though, I do remember hearing a gurgling last night before I left. . . ."

"No,"—You idiot—"I'm talking about Furnass Towers. Remember? You called me yesterday to tell me there was a payment problem. Only you didn't tell me the problem was a total lack of payments to the contractor."

Lyle laughed at his mistake. "Oh, that problem. There are so many problems around here lately, it's hard to keep them all straight."

"Then it's true? Drake hasn't received payment for several months?"

"'Several months' is a bit misleading—"

"But how can that be? Why didn't you tell me? Do you know that Drake is talking about walking off the project? If the superintendent is to be believed, they're talking about abandoning it altogether."

Lyle swished in the shallow water around his feet, looking for something with his toes. Then, leaning on the handle of the shovel to steady himself, he lifted one foot and rested it against the side of his other leg, standing stork-like. "Yes, I did hear that. I didn't think Drake was serious about abandoning the project when I first learned about it, but now it seems they are."

"But I didn't know about any of this."

"No, I didn't think you did," Lyle said, musing about something.

"Why didn't you tell me?"

"That's why I called you yesterday. To have you come out so I could tell you."

"But I'm the project architect!" Vince exploded, unable to contain his anger any longer. "I'm supposed to know these things. Good God, man, don't you realize we stand to lose this entire project because of your futzing around?"

"I don't think getting angry at me at this point is going to solve anything," Lyle said. He shifted his weight on the shovel handle from one hand to the other, then tilted his head to look at Vince. "What payment problem did you think I wanted to talk to you about?"

Careful, be very careful here. I'm in no position to make a stink—do all my change orders have something to do with why Drake hasn't been paid? Are you sure we can build this building for what you say, Mr. Nicholson? The bastard.

Vince sighed. "That's my point. I didn't know there was a payment problem of any kind. And I'm not angry at you, I'm concerned, that's all. As I would think you would want me to be. It's my responsibility to be aware of these things, the same way it's your responsibility to keep me informed of what's going on. All I knew was that I had approved the invoices for payment as they crossed my desk. I thought that was the end of it. Now I come out here today and find that some rather basic assumptions are blown out of the water."

Lyle nodded sympathetically. "I'm sorry, that was my omission. I was remiss in my duties, I admit it. I just didn't want to bother you with it."

"Bother me," Vince echoed. He puffed a little air up under his nose. Jack said Jeez, what kind of architect are you anyhow, you don't even know what's going on with your own building. Rita said You haven't seen what's going on for so long that you don't see things at all anymore and then dumped the French toast into the garbage. "It's no bother to know what's going on with my project. At the very least, it's what you pay me for."

With his foot resting against the side of his opposite knee, Lyle took the opportunity to examine a callus on the side of his heel. "In my defense, I don't think the picture is quite as bleak as the one you're painting. It's only been the last month that Drake received no payment at all. Well, the month before this one, so I guess that's two. For the two months previous to that they received partial payments. Granted, they were small partial payments, but still, it was something. Given the situation, don't you think Drake is overreacting?"

Contractors are funny that way. He really doesn't see the seriousness of the situation, does he? But if it's been going on this long why didn't Drake contact me? Careful now, this could all turn on you.

"I still don't understand why the payments weren't made after I approved the invoices. I don't have the exact figures, but I don't see how we could have exceeded the construction loan already, even with the number of change orders. . . ."

"It does seem that there have been a lot of change orders."

Julian put his foot back down on the carpet, creating a new puddle, and sloshed over to his desk as if looking for something related to their discussion. There was that look again. What does he know? Maybe he's not as dumb as I thought. Careful, he is an attorney, even if a bad one. His desk was a victim of the deluge along with everything else in the office; the desktop was a mass of soggy papers and crumbled ceiling tiles. Julian picked up a few of the papers by their corners.

"It's a good thing there's nothing of real importance here, isn't it? Just some materials for an essay I was thinking of writing, on the shortfalls of Scottish Presbyterianism as it was transplanted here in the New World. Still, it's a couple years of research turned to pulp." He looked at Vince, shook his head, and dropped the papers back on the sodden pile. "What were we saying? No, the fact that Drake hasn't been paid has nothing to do with the change orders. I guess there's no easy way to say this. Four months ago, Sycamore began to dispute the construction reports, and used it as an excuse to make only partial payments of the loan, claiming there were discrepancies, incomplete data, all sorts of reasons that turned out to be for the most part bogus. At the time I didn't think it was that much out of the ordinary, just some clerical work that needed cleaned up. You look like you might want to sit down."

Vince was indeed feeling suddenly shaky. He looked around but every chair and flat surface in the room was covered with soggy debris. Soggy or not, Vince sat down on one of Lyle's office chairs.

"Good," Lyle said. He pushed a pile of soggy papers aside and rested one hip on the edge of his desk, his foot speckled with mineral fibers from the ceiling tiles dangling above the dirty water. "Best to sit down. It gets worse."

"How could it?"

Lyle wagged his head, as if to say Judge for yourself. "For the last two months, Sycamore continued to make only partial payments, though the one for last month was close to eighty-five percent of the requested amount."

"Well, that's something," Vince said. "It sounds like they're working to solve any internal problems that they have. . . ."

"The problem was that Sycamore simply didn't have the money at that point. They had overextended themselves on a number of fronts, loans of one sort or another. Things came to a head when First City Bank didn't get its payments from the construction loan and the checks I was writing began to bounce. First

The Building

City is okay according to Harvey McMillan, but the reports of maleficence and unsupported checks were enough to send Sycamore into a fatal tailspin. Their own creditors started calling in their loans and the office is experiencing what I described yesterday as a brisk trot and what today can only be called a full-fledged run of customers wanting to close their accounts. I'm told it's very doubtful they'll open their doors on Monday, it's doubtful there will be anything left to open on Monday."

Vince watched a drop of water form at the end of Lyle's big toe, hang there for a moment gathering volume, then drop into the murky water below. Then realized he was staring at Lyle's toe to see if another drop formed. It hadn't. He shook his head to clear it, stood up briskly.

"You have to call Drake. You have to convince them to stay on the project. You have to convince them that the money will be coming, some way or another."

"That's very funny."

"I've never been more serious in my life."

Lyle stood up as well, his foot making a small splash on the sodden carpet. He picked up his coal shovel again, using it as a leaning post. "As my own attorney, I'd advise me strongly against it. When this project ends in interminable lawsuits, which it can't avoid doing now, the last thing I want to do as the owner is to do anything that might indicate collusion, such as that I knew anything about the payments or had any control regarding them, including that I have any control over the payments in the future, which might be construed to indicate such knowledge in the past."

"Then I'll call Drake myself. We can't allow them to abandon this project."

Lyle shrugged. "That's entirely within your discretion. I certainly can't advise you on that. But you might want to consult your own attorney first. You don't want to be in the position

yourself of admitting prior knowledge. Whether you did or
didn't."

"Are you suggesting that I knew anything about this?"

Lyle shrugged again, noncommittal. "I don't think it matters
one way or the other what I think about it. Personally, I doubt
it. But the real issue for you is what an inquiry in that direction—
and the resulting trial by media—would do to your reputation.
Offhand, I'd say the further away you position yourself from it,
the better for you."

Lyle started searching for something again in the shallow water around his toes. He bent over and picked up a metal nail file,
holding it up for Vince to see, delighted. "I thought I felt something under there."

"Holy Christ, man, are you out of your fucking mind? How
can you be worried about a nail file when your entire project is
tumbling down around your ears?"

Julian looked surprised. "I could have cut my foot on it. I get
my tetanus boosters regularly, but still, with this dirty water and
all. . . ."

Vince saw himself grab the coal shovel out of Lyle's hands and
swing it at him, catching Lyle on the side of the head, his skull
bleeding profusely, standing over the fallen man, hitting him with
the shovel again and again—but only for a split second and only
in his mind's eye. He came back to reality when he realized his
shoes were stuck to the soggy carpet; he wrenched a foot free
from the suction with a large *Gulp!* and almost toppled over with
the effort.

"Watch yourself there," Lyle said, offering a hand. "If you fall
over in this stuff, it could suck you right under."

Vince had to get out of there before he did or said something
he'd regret. Lyle was right, he had to be more careful than ever
now. He turned and slogged toward the door, squishing with each
step. Behind him, Lyle said, "I'm sorry about your shoes."

19

A voice laughed from out of the sky. Gregg looked around. A crow came toward him over the deck, no more than a dozen feet above his head. For Gregg it was a kind of vision. The crow looked down at him as it passed, laughed again *Haw! Haw! Haw!* and continued down the sky, over the rest of the town sloped toward the river, until it was only a slowly wavering line in the noon-gray sky, a black dot above the far wall of the valley.

Oh wow, I haven't seen a crow in years, not since I was a kid. We used to have lots of crows back home, they'd sit in the cornfields up on the hill, you could hear them for miles, or down by the highway looking for roadkills, carrion birds. There was a kid from one of the patches, out toward the old MacDougal Mine, who had a tame one, brought it to school a couple of times, had it take a peanut out of his mouth, kiss of a crow. What is the old rhyme? One for sorrow, two for joy. Sorry, Mr. Harbinger, but there's no sorrow here now, nothing but joy, it's Friday, in a few hours this job will be wrapped up and I can get out of here, I'm going to have a great weekend and forget all about things like my job and people like Jack and places like Furnass, it's nothing but good times ahead, bon ton roulet.

He was aware, however, that before he could do any real celebrating, he had to get through the rest of the day first.

He stood at the guardrail on the top deck of the building, grateful for the chance to be alone. After the impromptu meeting about the welding and his conversation with the architect afterward, Gregg had spent the remainder of the morning hiding out near the rear of the deck, pretending to keep an eye on the welding but in truth simply trying to stay out of everyone's way. (While he was in the vicinity he also kept an eye on the windows across the alley, but he didn't catch another glimpse of the girl who danced in the shower.) When the noon whistles started to blow, everyone on the deck dropped what they were doing and ran for the waiting manhoist. Gregg followed, but by the time he got there the cage was packed.

"You going down or are you just going to stand there?" the operator said, ready to close the door. Inside the cage, the men stood jammed together looking at him; there was barely room for him to squeeze aboard.

Gregg waved him on, trying to appear nonchalant. "No, go on ahead. I'll catch you on the next trip."

"Then you're going to wait till after lunch," the operator said and slammed the door closed. One of the men said something and a few of the others laughed as the cage descended below the edge of the slab. Gregg stood at the guardrail as he watched the cage rattle down the side of the building.

I don't care, I'm not hungry anyway. Bullshit, I'm starved but I'm just going to have to live with it, I'm sure as hell not going to climb down those ladders again.

The panorama of the valley and the town lay before him, the jumble of rooftops, the rusted hulls of the empty mills along the river, the first of the buildings being demolished. Overhead was a metallic sun in a sheet metal sky; it seemed chillier now than it was this morning. He wanted it to be Saturday, he wanted to take a walk on Walnut Street, along the boutiques and trendy shops in Shadyside, with the expensive doctors' wives buying their pâté and pastries for the weekend and the young marrieds going to brunch; he wanted to go for a beer at Brandy's or Humphry's, or sit at one of the little sidewalk tables and have some Häagen-Dazs; he wanted to go running in Schenley Park, or bicycling if the weather was good; he wanted to go to a party where he could meet some new friends, maybe meet a nice girl. He wanted to be away from all this noise and dirt and confusion and people yelling at each other, he wanted to have some fun. He wanted to be someplace where he didn't have to worry all the time.

The Building

I have become a whiner and a complainer. Worse, I have become a coward, or showed that I have always been one.

He had decided to get a job, to become a contributing member of society and join the workaday world, because he wanted to better himself. But sometimes it was hard to see if he was making any progress. At Pitt he had worn the same work clothes he did now as part of the university's punk rock scene. That way of life had paled considerably, however, as soon as he graduated. He found he was tired of not having anything. He was tired of always having to bus it, of never having enough money for even coffee and a sweet roll. He was tired of mattresses on the floor, bedsheets for drapes, crates for bookcases. He was tired of girls who looked like waifs or rejects; worse, he was tired of the really pretty girls looking at him as if he were a reject. He was tired of feeling on the outside looking in. There were good things in the world, he decided, nice things, and he wanted some of them for himself. He wanted a real life.

I let Nicholson and Jack screw me around any way they wanted, and all I did was bend over and take it. I'm better than that, maybe not as an inspector, but as me.

But so far, "real life" seemed to consist mostly of getting dirty crawling around construction sites and having to deal with people like Jack. Jack: a trumpeting bull elephant came to mind. I got fucked and didn't even get a kiss, as the ironworkers say. He turned away from the guardrail and wandered about the deck, among the stacks of wood and debris, the stretched-out electrical cords and junction boxes and bundles of reinforcing steel and abandoned tools. Actually the job didn't seem that bad without the other workmen around. Hell is other people says Sartre. To hell with other people says me.

He decided that as long as he was up here on his own, without anyone else to bother him—anyone, meaning Jack—it was a good time to look at some of the things he was supposed to look at.

Nicholson told him to keep his eyes open and ask a lot of questions, but so far Gregg hadn't turned up a thing. The architect seemed to like him—at least Nicholson hadn't run him off when he had the chance—and Gregg wanted to stay on the good side of him. If nothing else maybe you'll learn something about the art of building out of all this.

The rows of rebar columns stood against the gray noontime sky; even though guyed at the top to hold them in place, the tall rebar cages were bent slightly like flower stalks under their own weight, delicate yet massive—black steel bars, each cage a giant's gathering of pickup sticks before the fall. They're like rows of antennae to receive messages from distant worlds, like steel ladders to the sky, Oh for shit's sake, I don't know what they look like. Like work that needs to be done. Gregg was still worried. He didn't feel that he had inspected the rebar in the columns as closely as he should have; he couldn't let go of the idea that there still might be something wrong. The men would be coming back from lunch soon; his chance to really look things over, without Jack or Bill or somebody else breathing down his neck, was almost gone. Chewing the stray hairs of his beard and mustache at the corners of his mouth, beating a quick-march tattoo against his leg with his clipboard, he set about to do something.

Nicholson said Sometimes it's the person who doesn't know the first thing about what he's looking at that sees the most. I certainly qualify for that.

On the plan table he found the wadded-up rebar drawings where Bill had thrown them on his way to lunch. The drawings were blue on light blue; the dimensions and piece numbers were barely legible, the lettering blurred in some places almost beyond recognition, the ink exploded into small bomb craters from drops of water or someone's sweat; the paper was rubbed almost to shreds from being carried, often twisted into a kind of pretzel, in Bill's hip pocket. From what he could make out, these placing drawings looked the same as the architect's drawings Jack had given him earlier: the same size and number of vertical bars, the same size of perimeter ties spaced up the height of each column, with hairpins and candy canes—so named because that's what they looked like, hairpins and candy canes—through the center to tie the configuration together.

In other words, your basic run-of-the-mill square twelve-bar column. Yawn.

At the bottom of the page, in lettering so faint he could barely make it out, was a note that said "Alternate the position of the hooks in placing successive sets of ties"; there was a chart of bending details and a label list and a floor schedule and the date the drawing was made—all standard stuff. Blah blah blah. Nothing out of the ordinary, nothing he hadn't seen before; nothing that an experienced crew of rodbusters hadn't seen hundreds of times. Bill and his crew could build these columns blindfolded, no wonder everybody hates inspectors, these guys spend their lives working with this stuff and then a dumb shit like me comes along asking stupid questions, I'd hate my guts and think I was an asshole too. He wadded up the drawings again and tossed them back on the plan table.

Scaffolds were as much of a problem for Gregg as ladders— more so, because scaffolds were always dirty and rickety and he could never figure out where to put his hands and feet. There was certainly no way he could climb a scaffold and maintain his dignity. I always look like a fool when I try this, everybody can tell I don't know what I'm doing, I was the only kid in the history of the Thirty-Seventh Street Grade School who failed the jungle gym. Remember that school job a couple months ago, five floors of scaffolding straight up, I had to climb the X-braces on the outside of the framework to get up there and when I got to the top there was no place to go, I knew if I bellied up onto the planking I'd never have enough nerve to belly down over the side

again to get back down so I just hung there for a while like a
spider on a web or maybe I was the fly until I was pretty sure
nobody was looking and climbed back down the X-braces and
told them everything was okay, I don't think I even saw the
flashing they sent me up there to look at, so much for my integrity as an inspector. But now with no one around to watch (and
laugh at him), he went over to the nearest column and struggled
up the section of scaffolding to the top, a third of the way up the
three-story column.

There was, of course, no safety railing at the top of the scaffold. There was only a single plank that lifted like a teeter-totter
when he grabbed one end. He stood up slowly on the plank. I
can't believe I'm doing this, standing up here in the empty air,
this thing is swaying back and forth like I'm on a balance board,
I could be a circus act, Ladies and gentlemen, the Great Przybysz
will attempt to keep from falling off and killing himself, come one
come all, see an intelligent human reduced to a quivering mass of
jelly, feats of skill and daring, you won't believe your eyes, let's
have a fine round of applause for the little trooper. At his feet
was the opening at the top of the wooden formwork: the steel
bars for the next two stories rose in front of him like the trunk of
a giant metal tree. He dug his tape measure from the pocket of
his field jacket and, moving gingerly, took a few hasty measure-
ments.

Yes, it's all here, just like on the drawing. Christ, there's
enough steel in these columns to choke a horse, it's a wonder they
can get the concrete down inside the forms at all, but don't think
about that, that's another problem, all I care about at the moment is that the steel looks like the picture, and it does, that's
my job and I'm a happy puppy, now get me the hell off this
scaffold.

He started to climb down; he was on his knees on the plank,
one leg groping over the side for a toehold on the end bracing,

The Building

when it struck him what was wrong, froze him with a kind of horror. The hooks of the candy canes were supposed to alternate, one candy cane with the hook on one side of the column, the next one above it with the hook on the other side, back and forth up the height of the column. And they didn't. The hooks were all on the same side, all facing the same direction, all the way up the column, as neat and tidy—and wrong—as could be. His heart sank, his bowels turned to water.

Maybe I misread the note on the drawing, that has to be it, I can't even remember what it said now, that has to be it, they wouldn't put them in wrong, please don't let them have put them in wrong.

He scrambled down the scaffold, hurried over to the plan table and smoothed out Bill's drawings again. *Alternate the position of the hooks in placing successive sets of ties.* Shit. He hadn't been mistaken. But it seemed like such a small thing—It can't be that important, maybe it isn't important, please don't let it be important—he didn't want to nitpick—Oh please—he was sure he had seen columns on other projects where the hooks didn't alternate. Or had he? Maybe he didn't recognize what he was looking at on those other projects. And the note only says *ties*, it doesn't say what kind of ties, maybe it doesn't apply to the candy canes, or maybe the hooks of the ties are always supposed to alternate and I missed it on all those other projects and I approved them anyway and all the columns on all those other projects are wrong, if the note means just the stirrup ties that would only be the bars around the outside of the column or maybe the note only applies to this project, or maybe when I looked at these columns I only thought the hooks didn't alternate because I was afraid what would happen if they didn't, but if the note means all column ties then it would include the candy canes and hairpins too, I can't believe the ironworkers would put the bars in wrong, the ironworkers are the ones who know what they're doing here,

I don't, how could I see something they missed? It was 12:27. Bill and his crew would be back from lunch any minute. Oh please let the bars be right. He ran back to the column and scrambled up the scaffold and looked at the rebar again, his fear of falling off the scaffold replaced by a fear of another kind. But he already knew. And I know what the note means too. The hooks didn't alternate. It means I'm dead meat.

His next hope was that maybe this column was the only one like it; maybe the hooks alternated in the other columns. He climbed down from the scaffold again, but he didn't have to climb any of the other scaffolds to find the answer. Standing on the deck he could look up and see everything he needed to see. The rows of columns, the patterns of steel bars against the steel-colored sky, were all the same. Wrong.

No, wait a minute. . . .

From below in front of the building came the sound of a generator starting up; a cloud of dark smoke rose from the street like a genie. The boom of the crane slowly came to life, the cables singing in their sheaves; the superstructure of the manhoist quivered as the men on the ground loaded into it. Why am I so worried about this, I'm only doing my job. If a mistake was made, I'm not the one who made it; I'm not the supervisor of these men, I'm not the one who directed the steel to be put in this way, I'm only the inspector. The older inspectors always told him that if he found a major problem, the first thing he should do is to go take a walk or get a cup of coffee or just sit in his car, anything to give himself time to settle down and get his thoughts together. Besides I'm only doing what Nicholson told me to do. He said I want you to question everything, the only wrong questions are the ones you don't ask. But if I do say something, I know what Nicholson will do, he'll throw it back on me like he did the welding, he'll say it's my job to say whether the steel is acceptable or not after leading me to the position he thinks I should take.

Because there's no way he'd want me to reject these columns because if these columns are wrong then every column in the building is wrong so it would be up to me to say they're okay and get everybody off the hook, so to speak, and I'm screwed all over again, the sacrificial lamb. Inspector as scapegoat. What to do? Should I talk to Nicholson first? Or Jack? Call his office? Have the company field supervisor come out? Call the city engineer? Or simply walk away and hope everything is okay the way it is?

He needed time to think. He knew he should get away from here, figure out the best way to handle it. But he was tired of being pushed around and bullied, he was tired of these guys thinking he was an asshole. To leave now would be like running away—and he might decide to just keep going—but he didn't want to run away and hide anymore. And don't you ever let me see you turn your back and try to walk away from a mess you've made again, little brother. As the cage of the manhoist bobbed to the top and the door slid open, Bill and Crazy Levon and Tony came across the slab toward him. Here they come. Wow I'm really going to do this. Gregg stood his ground.

20

Lunchtime over, Jimmy, the operator, lowered the manhoist—he spent the noontimes blissfully alone in the cage with the bell turned off, suspended between the second and third floors—and the men crowded on board for the trip to the upper floors, jostling among themselves, not saying anything, pressed shoulder to shoulder against each other as they got settled within the confines of the cage. When the last man had squeezed aboard, Jimmy closed the platform door and wedged in himself.

"C'mon boys, give me a little room here, ain't none of us going nowhere until I get this thing buttoned up," he said, bumping elbows and backsides out of the way as he slid the cage door shut.

It took him a moment to squeeze over to the controls and get himself situated; the men quietly joggled against each other back and forth in little waves as they tried to give him enough room to work. After a minute or so when the cage still hadn't moved, Levon broke the silence, drawling in a voice loud enough for everyone to hear, "Whoever's got his hand in my pocket, would you mind scratching my left ball too?"

A couple of the men chuckled. Another said, "Shit, I thought that was one of my grapes left over from lunch."

Levon grinned at Bill; they stood next to each other, pressed tight against each other as if joined at the hip. Bill looked away. He could feel the red patches blazing on his cheeks, but not from anything Levon said; they had been burning there for some time, ever since he was sitting in the back of his pickup and saw Pamela go by in a white Continental with another guy. Now he stared at the backs of the heads in front of him, his eyes cold, his jaw set. He looked like a man who, if he had a gun, could have killed them all.

He told himself that it didn't matter now, that he didn't care now, that it made no difference to him now if she was with somebody else; he told himself that it was over between them, that what he had with Pamela had run its course, that he would be leaving this project soon and that they wouldn't be able to see each other as much anyway and that it was time for both of them to move on. He told himself that he was better off without her. He told himself that he had no rights as to whom she saw anyway, now or ever, that he had never had that right. I've got a wife and kid to think about, I've got Mary and Billy, that's who I should be thinking about, not some girl I just picked up on a job. Not some tramp. He told himself that it didn't matter now that she was in that white Continental with another guy, told himself that he didn't care that she was laughing and carrying on and having a good time for herself. That's Pamela, all right, she always has a good time for herself, no matter where she goes or who she's with, and it doesn't matter who she's with, does it? He told himself that he had known from the start that she knew a lot of men, that she had been with a lot of men; when he started to see her he even liked it that she was popular with other men. I used to think it was okay if there were other guys sniffing around her all the time because I thought it meant I must be really special to her. I told myself she wasn't sleeping with anybody else, just me. Just me. Stop it!

The car lurched and began to grind slowly up the side of the building. "Lift-off, we have a lift-off!" someone said in a NASA announcer's voice.

"Fly me to the moon."

"I'll moon ya."

"Moon this."

He barely heard them; he was only vaguely aware that someone was talking. He felt tired, so very tired. It's like her dancing in the window when she takes her shower. I never cared that the other guys could see her because I was proud of her, I was proud that she was my girl, that I was the guy who had won her. Let the others look, I was the one who was fucking her. I was the one she chose over everybody else. But now I don't know. Was I the only guy fucking her? I always thought she didn't know anyone could see her in the window, but maybe that wasn't it at all, maybe she knew all along. Maybe that's why she did it, maybe she danced there in the window so everyone could see her—stop it! His head snapped to the side as he tried to chase the thought away. Levon glanced at him. That Continental came from up the street, it could have come from around the block. Maybe she was home after all when I went over to her apartment before lunch, maybe she was there with that other guy. Maybe that's why she didn't answer her doorbell, because she knew it was me and she didn't want to see me, maybe they were in bed together when I rang the bell and that's what they were laughing at when they drove by, maybe she was fucking other guys the whole time she was with me, maybe I was nothing to her and never was, maybe I was just another guy—no! Stop it!

The cage jolted to a stop on one of the lower floors and a few of the men got off. As the men remaining in the cage adjusted themselves to the additional space, Levon looked again to see what was bothering him. Bill ignored him. The cage shuddered and continued its grinding ascent; the ground continued to sink away from them.

Jack told me the way it is with her, didn't he? He as much as told me she was seeing other guys, that she was fucking other guys, that night at the Triangle Tavern after work, back when I first came on the job when we were still friends.

"Hey look, Bill, personally I don't care who you fuck. You can fuck goats for all I care, that's your business, just as long as you don't hurt the goat," Jack said, reaching for more peanuts, throwing the shells with the others on the floor. "All I'm saying is, you gotta be aware of what you're getting yourself into. That girl's been down a lot of highways. I don't want to see you get hurt if you start going too fast or you run into a lot of bumps."

"Yeah, but the scenery sure is pretty along the way," I said, pretending I was driving a car.

"Sure, it's pretty. As long as you don't start thinking you own the view. Or that you're the only guy on the road."

"Maybe not, but I'm the guy in the driver's seat now, aren't I?"

"All I'm saying is, if you think you're going to be driving her for very long, don't be surprised when she starts shifting her own gears."

"What makes you think you know so much about it?" I asked him finally.

The Building

"Varoom-varooooooom!" Jack puttered like a race car, gripping his bottle of Rolling Rock like a gearshift and slamming the lever home. We collapsed on the bar laughing but why did I think it was funny? Maybe he was telling me something else too. Maybe he was telling me that he fucked her too, no, Jack wouldn't do that, he introduced me to her, Jack is wild but he wouldn't, would he? Stop it! Stop it! Bill's head snapped back and forth as the cage jolted to a stop on the uppermost deck.

Bill pushed his way out of the cage ahead of the others, Levon and Tony close behind. As they headed across the deck, Levon fell in beside Bill. The lanky redhead walked with an extra swing to his step, trying to make the tools dangling from his toolbelt clank as much as possible, trying to get a laugh out of Bill. But Bill was in no mood for laughing. I know what he's doing, he's trying to stay close in case he thinks I need help, sometimes Levon is a real pain. The young inspector was waiting for them at the plan table, a dumb smile on his face. A troublemaker's smile.

"What's the matter, bud? You look like somebody raped your turtle," Levon said, ambling up to Gregg. "What'd you do, stay up here over lunchtime? Billy, I think this boy's sunstroke."

"How can he be sunstroke?" Tony said, missing the joke. "It's a gray day now, nobody gets sunstroke on a gray day. He got a problem? Maybe the band on his hat's too tight."

"Your band's too tight, bud," Levon said. "You heard Tony."

"Bill, I think we got a problem. . . ," Gregg said.

"We got a problem," Levon said. "You got a problem, I got a problem, we all got problems. . . ."

"We all got problems," Tony echoed. "The only problem is what problem you going to pay attention to, you know?"

"What's your problem?" Bill said blankly, motioning with his head for the other two to go on without him. Levon and Tony went over and continued sorting out the bundles of steel delivered that morning, but Levon kept an eye on Bill.

Bill leaned against the opening of the shed over the plan table as Gregg bent inside and unfolded the placing drawings. The young inspector busily pointed things out to him on the drawings, something about the hooks and candy canes, and made sketches on his clipboard. But Bill wasn't listening. He was looking across the deck, across the alley to where he used to be able to see Pamela's apartment building. He thought about the first time he saw her, there in the window of her apartment—not in her shower, in her living room window—back before the building was this tall and you could still see her windows from the deck. Everything was different then, not just his perspective of her.

It was early in the fall, he and his crew had recently been assigned to the project, after the foundations were poured, to place the reinforcing steel for the floors and columns. The weather had been cold and damp, the chilly winds of October blowing down through the valley from the north, the coming winter in the air; at the time they were a couple of floors off the ground so it seemed even colder and windier, the wind above and below them, their feet so cold their toes felt ready to snap off. One morning when it was particularly chilly, after working for an hour or so bent double tying spacer bars, he unfolded himself, stretched, one arm extended above his head as if he were reaching for something, and happened to look up at the apartment building across the alley. There was a young woman in the window; she was dressed in a bathrobe and seemed to be looking back at him. He waved and she waved, but then he realized Jack had come over beside him.

"Nice, huh?" Jack said. Even though everyone on the deck was freezing, Jack had his jacket unzipped. "Her name's Pamela."

"You know her?"

The Building

"Sure," Jack said. "Come on, I'll introduce you, you look like you need a break. Send your guys for coffee."

Bill thought he must be kidding. But Jack walked over to the edge of the deck and started down the ladder, looking at Bill to see why he wasn't coming. Bill told Levon and Tony that he'd be back and hurried across the deck after him.

Jack led the way, deadpan, all business, as if they were on an important errand, out the gate and down the sidewalk, up the steep side street and around the corner to the other side of the block. In his hurry to keep up, Bill jammed his bad ankle; he tried to ignore the pain, and was careful not to let Jack see him limp. At the front door of an orange brick apartment building, Jack rang one of the doorbells three times, then again, perhaps a signal. When the buzzer on the door sounded, Bill followed Jack inside and up the dark stairs to the third floor. The door to the rear apartment was ajar; when she saw who it was, she unfastened the door and opened it all the way. The young woman stood in the doorway, still wearing a long white bathrobe, a pair of tufted mules on her feet. From the moment Bill saw her there he wanted her; he wanted to open her bathrobe and peel it from her like the skin of a fruit.

"And to what do I owe this honor?" she said, tempering her sarcasm with a slight smile.

Jack didn't say anything; he nodded and clomped by her into her apartment. Bill stared at her from the hallway.

"Well, I guess you might as well come in too," she shrugged. "I take it you're a friend of his."

"Yeah, sort of." Bill felt himself blush. Jack walked in there like he owns the place, what am I supposed to do? He took off his hardhat, holding it in his two hands like a steering wheel; he was aware of every patch of dirt and grime on his cold-weather coveralls.

She grinned at his embarrassment; she motioned with her head for him to come on into the apartment and closed the door behind him. As she leaned past him, she smelled powdery and fresh. "We better go see what he's up to," she said confidingly. "You know Jack."

No I don't. I don't know how he has enough nerve to act this way around a pretty girl. I don't know how to act around her at all.

Jack stood in the middle of the living room waiting for them, looking totally out of place in this domestic setting and yet totally at ease with himself being there. His hardhat was cocked to one side and the collar of his shirt inside his jacket was pulled up; he had the same smirk on his face that he had on the job when he was daring someone to try to take him on. With his feet planted wide and his elbows angled out from his jacket pockets, Jack seemed to take up all the available space in the small room.

What's he up to, why is he bullying her this way? If I had a pretty girl like her, I'd never treat her this way, ever. I'd treat her like a queen.

"So, are you going to tell me what this is all about?" Pamela said.

"We came up to have a look at your cracks," Jack said. "This is Bill."

"H'lo Bill," Pamela said, barely glancing at him.

"I told Bill all about your cracks."

"Oh, did you?" As she reached up to comb her fingers through her thick black hair, the robe pulled open and showed her pretty legs. Bill's heart caught.

"Yeah, he really wants to see them. Come on in the bedroom and show him. I told him he hasn't seen cracks until he's seen yours."

What's he doing? I can't believe he's saying these things to her. Is she really going to do it, oh my God will she? She's so pretty. . . .

Jack walked on into the bedroom, looking back at Pamela. I guess that's the way you do it, that's the way you get what you want you just take it. Pamela looked at Jack questioningly, her smile more an expression of doubt than amusement, but she followed him. She's going to do it, she really is. Bill trailed along behind, stopping at the door.

Jack stood on the other side of the bed. He nodded toward the wall behind him for Bill's benefit. "See there? Cracks."

Sure enough, on the wall behind the headboard were several large cracks in the plaster. I always get things turned around, always. I'm an ass.

"Landlord's trying to claim our building caused them. But you can see they've been here a long time. Pamela says they've been here as long as she has."

"But I'm not going to say that to anyone else, because I'd probably lose my apartment if I did."

"You would if I asked you to though, wouldn't you?" Jack said, and for the first time smiled at her, gave her all his little-boy charm, though there was an edge to it.

Pamela didn't smile in return. She was wary, watching Jack closely, her arms folded about herself, as if she were sizing him up, trying to read him.

What's going on here, what am I missing?

Jack reached down and prodded the mattress on the bed, his fingers spread on the chenille cover like a stiff white spider. "For a while, I was even thinking of moving my office over here."

"And I told you what you could do with that idea," Pamela said.

"I could hang around here all day and keep an eye on things out the windows and stay nice and warm. . . ."

"And I'd have all sorts of dirty workmen tramping in and out all day long." She looked at Bill. "No offense, I didn't mean you. You're nice, you can come back anytime you want."

"The best invitation in town," Jack said, his hand retreating into his jacket pocket. "And when she says you can come back, she means it. I'd take her up on it, if I were you."

Pamela stared at Jack. Something else had entered her expression, something that tinged her brown eyes with anger and bitterness and tears.

"Oh, I get it now."

"Get what now?"

Get what now?

"I'm not stupid, Jack."

"Nobody ever said you were."

"You son-of-a-bitch, I know what you're up to. I know what you're doing."

What? What are they talking about?

"I'm not doing a thing. It's taking care of itself."

"Oh sure. And what else do you want me to do?"

"Nothing, Pamela. Nothing at all."

What's going on here? What's going on between them?

"Oh sure. Nothing at all. All right, Jack. I get it. You made your point."

"Did I?"

"You'll see. You'll see."

See what? What?

Gregg stopped talking; he straightened up from under the covered plan table and looked at Bill as if challenging him.

Bill didn't look at him right away. He continued to lean against the side of the shed over the plan table; he pulled a length of tie wire from the coiler on his belt, snipped it off with his wire clippers and folded it double, then absently threw it away. He felt as if he were drifting away inside himself, as if everything in the world were removing itself from him, getting farther and farther out of reach. His arms were so heavy he could barely lift them. Finally he met the younger man's gaze and drawled, "I don't know what the hell you're talking about."

21

"You want another one, Jack?" Red the bartender called from the end of the bar.

"Yeah," Jack said, then added as Red started toward him, "but I'm not going to."

Red flicked his hand in Jack's direction and returned to reading the paper.

"I've got to go back to the job this afternoon and be brilliant," Jack said.

"You're always brilliant, Jack," Red said without looking up from the paper.

"Isn't that wonderful?" Jack said, and sipped his Jack Daniel's.

On the television, Joe Carcione, the Green Grocer, talked about cucumbers.

Yeah, Joe, you tell us about those cukes. Imagine spending your life with nothing else to worry about except vegetables, whether the lettuce was going to come in or not, how the cucumbers are doing. That's right, Joe, you always want a firm cucumber, so do I, Lord that my cucumber never goes soft. Joe looks like a happy man. I spend my time worrying about other kinds of kooks.

Jack wanted more than just another drink; he was in the mood to sit here all afternoon and tie one on. Go on a toot. There was a time when he would have too, but those were the days when he and Mac worked together on projects, when Mac was the superintendent and Jack was the general foreman, when Mac was running the show and Jack could get away with disappearing for an afternoon. In those days when Jack went on a toot, Mac would holler and swear and, after finding out where Jack was drinking, make a big production of going to the bar to bring him back— the only times Jack ever went on a toot were when he was sure everything was caught up, and then he always did it at a bar close by so they could find him in case there was a problem—but after chewing Jack out a bit, during which Jack would sit sideways on his barstool with his head on his hand leaning on the bar, an amused grin on his face, watching the older man rant and rave, Mac would join him and the two of them would end up drinking together on into the night. But things were different now. The fact that things were different now was one of the reasons he was ready to get drunk today.

I don't know how that old bastard used to do it. Put up with all these sons of bitches coming at you all the time. Bill trying to wrap himself around my ankles, You and I used to be buddies when this job started, are you mad at me about something? Jesus, to let yourself sink that low. Why won't you be my friend? Oh boo-hoo. As bad as a woman, for shit's sake. Thank God everybody on the project isn't like that. Damn it, got to remember about Chucky moving his pipes. And Chalmers and his goddamn hose. I'm going to forget that yet. At least the kid, what's his name, Greggory, settled down after Nicholson screwed him over, no more trouble from him. Need to get George to start cleaning up if we're pulling off the building today. . . .

"Did you see this about the mill closings?" Red said, hitting the newspaper with the back of his hand. He read: "'The long-term devastation takes in the loss of plant tax revenues plus the impact the closings will have on the local businesses, which rely on the mills and their employees. It's the trickle-down theory,' a spokesman said. 'There will be less mercantile tax because the businesses have fewer customers and make less money.'"

The Building

Red looked at Jack down the bar. "No shit, Dick Tracy. It took some fat-cat politician to figure that out. He coulda come in here and seen my empty bar at lunchtime. When the mills were going, this place would be packed for lunch. And when the shifts let out, I'd start lining up the shots and beers before the first guy came through the door, and they'd be calling for a second round before I could get all the first round poured. Those were the days."

"Those days are gone," Jack said. "Like all days."

"No shit, Dick Tracy."

The *Noon News* was over, *The Young and the Restless* was starting; it was time to head back to the job but Jack stayed where he was. Just a little while longer. Before the dance starts up again. You'd think they could do without me for a little while without the building falling over. She said Why do you always think everything depends on you? Why do you always think you're responsible for everybody else? And I told her Because that's my job and she said But you're ill, you've been ill. Why can't you let somebody else help you for a change? He lifted his left arm from the bar, worked it around a little; the pain had eased somewhat, the joints in his legs didn't seem quite so stiff. The two double shots were enough, and his mind was still clear. Takes more than that to get me muddled. To get me to forget anything. At least I'm not a cheap drunk. Downright expensive. On the soap opera, a young couple seemed to be having the same argument they were having the last time Jack had seen the opening of the show. Maybe soap operas are more true to life than people think. Just fuck her and be done with it I say. Fuck 'em all. He toasted the screen and finished his drink. Fuck 'em all but six. And remembered the time he had used the expression one night when he was with Pamela.

"What does that mean?" she had said. "I've never heard that one before."

He looked over at her, beside him in the darkness of the cab, and looked back at the road. (He looked beside him now, at the row of empty barstools, at the place where she used to sit beside him when they came here to the Reo Grill, and looked back at the row of bottles behind the bar.) When he didn't offer an explanation, she persisted.

"Why all but six?"

"Because you need six people to carry your coffin at your funeral."

"Is that the way you really think?"

"Sure. Except now that I've lost so much weight, maybe I don't need all six."

He grinned over at her. In the passing headlights, her nurse's uniform glowed, luminescent; her nurse's cap sat halo-like above her black hair. But Pamela wasn't smiling.

"You know what I mean," she said.

Jack thought a moment, cleared his throat. "Yeah, well, I'll tell you something. You're really lucky at the end of your life if you've got six friends. I don't mean people you know, I mean real friends, people you can really count on. You're lucky if you've got enough friends to count on the fingers of one hand."

He held up his hand to her in the darkness to demonstrate. (Sitting at the bar, he held up his hand and gathered it slowly into a fist. Wish it didn't feel so good to hit somebody. But it doesn't really get you anywhere in the long run. For that matter, it doesn't really feel all that good once you start thinking about it either. Shit. He lowered his hand and gripped the shot glass again.)

"And do you have enough friends to count on the fingers of one hand?" Pamela said.

"Nah. I don't have any. I don't need 'em," he laughed. He waited for her to say it, the way every girl he had ever known would, but she surprised him.

"What about Bill?"

"What about him?"

"Isn't he your friend?"

"Nah. My only real friend was Freddy. Freddy was great. He was an electrician, I met him on the first job I ever worked on in construction. Boy, was he funny. Freddy and me had some good times together. Yes sir, old Freddy."

"What happened to Freddy?"

"Died."

"I'm sorry."

"Not as sorry as Freddy." He looked over at her in the darkness, expecting to see her laugh, but she was solemn-faced. He thought awhile as he drove on, before he started to speak again.

"At the funeral home after Freddy died, his wife came up to me in the hall and squeezed something into my hand. I looked and there were Freddy's rings. He always wore a couple rings, he loved shit like that, jewelry and stuff. One ring had a diamond in it, the other was an onyx. 'I want you to have Freddy's rings,' she says to me, all teary-eyed. Can you imagine that? Giving me Freddy's rings? I threw them at her."

"But why?"

"I didn't want those rings. Those were Freddy's rings. What the hell would I want with Freddy's rings?"

"She probably thought you'd like them to remember Freddy by."

"I don't need nothing to remember Freddy by. I already got enough. I got too much. You know what I mean?"

"You must have really loved Freddy."

Jack puttered his lips at her. "Guys don't love guys. At least straight ones don't. Nah, it wasn't that. Freddy was great. Freddy was my buddy."

He kept waiting for her to say it, the way every girl he had ever known would—What about me? Aren't I your friend?—but he should have known her better, that wasn't like Pamela at all. She was too much like himself, independent, to ever say anything like that, to ever push herself on someone that way. Pamela didn't like people getting too close any more than he did. They were alike, he and Pamela, in a lot of ways. Maybe too many ways.

Forget about that. Like the man said, those days are gone. Good riddance. Think of something else. Jo. That time Jo said she wanted to see the building so I took her up late at night after everyone was gone, pitch-dark, had to hot-wire the manhoist and Jimmy the operator never knew a thing about it, took her up under the starlight and the lights of the town all spread up the hill and down toward the river and we started fooling around and I had her lean down over a sawhorse so she wouldn't get her dress dirty and I pumped her doggy-style at midnight and just as I was about to come the lights came on in Pamela's apartment across the alley, she was just getting home from work and I couldn't tell if there was anyone there with her or not and I didn't care, did I? I hoped she was having as much fun as I was and afterward I nailed Jo's panties to the wooden form and in the morning Frank the German found them and said "Vat is dis?" and I said "Dis was one hell of a piece of ass" and we poured them in the concrete as a memorial to every hell of a piece of ass wherever the hell it may be. . . .

"Got to go, Red," Jack said, finishing his drink and getting up abruptly from the stool and heading toward the door.

"Come back when you can stay longer," Red called.

"Cheer up, Red. It's going to get worse. Everything does."

Jack didn't wait for Red's reply; he pushed out through the studded-leather door onto the sidewalk, having no desire to hear what Red might say about anything.

*

The Building

As Jack squeezed between the fender of the ready-mix truck and the gatepost, Bert, the truck driver, stood on the rear fender with the water hose in his hand, idly squeezing off squirts of water at the revolving drum of the mixer, the concrete sliding down the chute, the fence, anything that caught his eye. When he saw Jack, Bert aimed the hose at him. Jack stopped and looked up at him. Go ahead, sucker. Do it. Bert laughed without any jolliness and pointed the hose in the other direction.

"You know I wouldn't squirt you, Jack."

I know I'd be the last one you ever squirted.

He went over to where Sloopy stood beside the pump leaning on his shovel, munching from a bag of Cheez Doodles. "How's everything going?" he yelled above the din of the engines into Sloopy's ear.

"It's going," Sloopy yelled back, chewing his words as well as the Cheez Doodles. Jack started to walk on but Sloopy yelled after him, "That inspector didn't come down for lunch."

Jack went back to him. "What do you mean, he didn't come down?"

Sloopy pumped his shoulders twice. "He didn't come down. He stayed up on the deck."

"Didn't everybody break for lunch?" Every time Jack leaned close to him or Sloopy spoke, Jack got sickening whiffs of decaying food; half the Cheez Doodles appeared stuck to Sloopy's teeth.

"Sure did. But he stayed up there on his lonesome. Maybe nobody told him he was supposed to come down with everybody else. Or maybe he thinks it safer up there where nobody else is. 'Specially if you're not up there with him."

"Wonderful," Jack said. "Now what's the son-of-a-bitch getting himself into?"

Sloopy pumped his shoulders twice again. "I don't know. But I thought you'd want to know. Was I all right, Jack?"

"You were fine, Sloopy." Jack patted him on the shoulder and headed toward the manhoist.

Where in the hell did my good mood go? I'm back here less than two minutes and they're already coming at me. No rest for the wicked. Hey Red, I'm ready for another horn.

The cage was starting up the side of the building, but Jimmy saw Jack coming and brought it back down again. The two block-men inside were complaining about the delay as Jimmy opened the door—"This ain't no goddamn amusement-park ride, I don't care what asshole wants you to . . ."—but when they saw it was Jack, and saw the expression on his face, they shut up. As the cage started up again, the bell rang from the top floor.

"I wonder where else they think I'm going to go?" Jimmy said to Jack out of the side of his mouth.

"Goddamn bells drive you nuts," Jack said. I wonder if her doorbell still works after I fixed it. No way to find out except ask Bill, oh sure. I'm going to fix it, somebody could just walk in and come up the steps, I don't want to take any chances. That's nice, you're looking out for me. Forget about it, she's not your problem now. Her and her front door and the light bulbs she can't reach to change and the windows that need new ropes and counter-weights and the closet door that keeps coming off the track and whether or not she parks in a safe spot at the hospital. None of it. I should never have introduced her to Bill. "Goddamn people drive you nuts."

"Amen," Jimmy said.

On the top deck, Gregg was at the plan table talking to Bill and Levon. Some people just ask for trouble, don't they? They want it more than anything. Before he did anything else, Jack lit up a cigarette—Think I'm going to need this, no sense being in a hurry, trouble has a funny way of waiting for you once it's got your number—then went over to the column where George and the concrete crew were standing on top of the scaffold. The thick

The Building

rubber hose at the end of the boom of the concrete pump snaked along the boards on top of the scaffold; the scaffold jerked with each push of concrete through the system.

"You okay?" Jack shouted up at George.

George, his hands folded underneath the bib of his overalls, nodded. "Except I'm getting seasick," he shouted down, grinning as he swayed back and forth with the movement of the scaffold.

"Don't take any chances with these scaffolds. If you don't think they're safe. . . ."

George shook his head. "Don't you worry. I'm keeping an eye on them."

Jack checked the scaffold for himself, checked to make sure the braces between the scaffold and the form were holding up under the constant throbbing of the pump, checked to make sure the guy wires were holding the tall rebar cages in place. When he was satisfied everything else was taken care of—Guess I'm ready for it, do your damnedest, give me your best shot—he headed across the deck to the plan table to find out if there was a problem. When Gregg and the ironworkers saw him heading toward them, they stopped talking. Bill turned and walked a couple of steps away.

"What's going on?" Jack said, looking in turn at Bill, Levon, Gregg. Come on, somebody tell me something. I know something's going on. "You guys organizing a basketball pool or something?"

Gregg looked at Bill; when Bill only looked away dreamily toward the rear of the deck, Gregg took a deep breath, drew himself up, and faced Jack.

"The hooks in the columns are wrong. The drawings say the hooks on the candy canes are supposed to alternate. But the ones in the columns are all placed facing the same direction."

"Is that right?" Jack asked Bill. Dumb jacking-off sons-of-bitches.

Bill looked at him, nodded, blinked once slowly, and turned away again.

"You sure you're reading the drawings right?" Jack said to Gregg.

"There's a note that spells it out."

"Does it say that on both the placing drawings and the architect's drawings?"

"Yes," Gregg said, unflinching.

"You're sure?" What's the kid trying to do, stand up to me all of a sudden?

"Yes, I'm sure. I checked while I was talking to Bill about it."

Wonderful. "How come?" Jack said to Bill.

"How come what?" Bill said.

"How come you put the candy canes in that way?"

Bill shrugged, still looking off toward the rear of the deck. "That's the way we assembled the cages. That's the way it was easiest while the cages were lying down."

"Didn't you see the note he's talking about on the drawings?"

Bill looked at him lazy-eyed but didn't say anything; he looked away again.

Don't do this to me, sucker, don't play this kind of game. Jack wanted to grab Bill and spin him around and make him pay attention; he wanted to hit him. He jammed his hands in his pockets and felt a seam rip. Just talk to me, goddamn it. Give me something to work with here.

"Hell, Jack," Levon said. "There's too much steel in those columns anyway, you know that, those little hooks aren't going to make any difference. The last job we were on, they *wanted* the hooks on the candy canes to all go the same direction, and that was a frigging twenty-eight-story building."

Jack looked at Gregg to see what he had to say about that.

The Building

"I don't know about any other buildings right now. I only know about this one. And on this building, the drawings say that the hooks of the candy canes are supposed to alternate."

"Wonderful," Jack said. He took one last drag on his cigarette then threw it down on the deck—The most intelligent thing the kid said all day, said it like he meant it too, none of that wishy-washy scared-of-everybody shit, and it could send this project right down the toilet—grinding it to a swirl of shreds and ashes with the toe of his boot. "So now what?"

"The architect said he was going to be here most of the day."

Yeah, old Bouncy-Bouncy. Get him in on this too, I need some more grief in my life.

When Jack didn't say anything, Gregg went on. "I'll go find him and tell him what the problem is and see what he says."

Sure, everybody come, pile on. Make a party out of it. Let's all screw Jack. No, get hold of yourself, stop whining, I'm as bad as Bill. Turn on *Jack*, got to deal with this shit, it's my job. "Are all the candy canes like that?" he said to Bill.

"That's the way I put 'em in."

"I mean on all the other floors too?"

"Yep. Every floor."

Bill turned away again. Jack stared at him a moment—Look at him, he can't take his mind off her for two minutes and he can't even see her windows from here, stop thinking about her, get hold of yourself, be a man. You can't let thinking about some girl take over your life—before addressing Gregg.

"You realize what you're getting yourself into, don't you? What you're getting all of us into? If you bring up the question of the candy canes on this floor, the next question is going to be if they're like that on every floor. It might mean ripping out every column in the building."

"They're not going to make us rip out every column in the building," Levon said. "That'd be crazy."

"I'm saying I don't know what they'll do. But I'm also saying you got to be ready for that eventuality. I've seen stranger things happen."

Gregg stood with his knees locked, clipboard down at his side, and looked Jack straight on. "My job is only to see if the work is according to the drawings and to report what I see. And in this case, the columns aren't according to the drawings. But Nicholson will probably work it like he did this morning with the welding: I'll tell him about the candy canes, he'll ask me if I think they're acceptable the way they are, I'll tell him yes, and that'll be that. We'll all be covered. Bill should probably come along with me in case there are any questions, but I'll take care of it, I'll tell Nicholson I think everything's all right the way it is."

That's the best we can come up with? We're going to send the kid to talk to Bouncy-Bouncy? And Bill just stands there looking into space. I was never that bad about Pamela, was I?

After a moment when no one said anything, Bill turned slowly and looked at Jack, a sly grin on his face. "Isn't that wonderful?"

Jack jammed his fists in his pockets and headed back toward the manhoist. I got to get out of here before I kill somebody.

22

In the mornings, sometimes—as often as he could, as often as he dared, though for several weeks now there had been no opportunity, no invitation for him to do so—after telling Mary, his wife, that he had to go in early to make some last-minute changes on a slab or columns that were going to be poured that day, Bill would leave their house in Plum Borough in the suburbs east of Pittsburgh, at three-thirty or four in the morning (he counted on the fact that Mary was a heavy sleeper, that she never realized just how early he left) and drive through the darkness of the hour, along the empty Parkway, past the blackened office towers of downtown Pittsburgh, continuing along the black rivers and the black empty spaces where the mills used to be, to Furnass, where he would be lying in Pamela's bed as the first light of dawn filtered through her bedroom window; he would look at the softness of her bare skin amid the tangle of sheets and her thick black hair against the pillow—she would be back to sleep already—and get up from the bed thinking This is the second sleeping woman I've left this morning, that's pretty wild, and go out to the living room or into the kitchen and part the curtains as the sky across the valley was beginning to lighten and look down at the job across the alley and watch Levon and Tony as they started in on whatever it was they had to do that day, and he would go back to the bedroom and get dressed and bend down and kiss her naked shoulder and leave her apartment and walk around to the other side of the block and go to work. Those mornings, when she got up at her regular time and took her shower, when he saw her dancing in the window in the spray of water, had special meaning to him, because he knew she was washing his sweat from her skin, washing his kisses from her body, his sperm from her pussy.

He had never known a woman like Pamela before, a woman uninhibited about sex. Sex for Pamela was no different from any other bodily function, no more, no less; she viewed it with a clinical eye, while being open to whatever happened along the way. She was the kind of woman he had dreamed about, especially since Mary had become so involved with her job; sex with Mary had become as planned and compartmentalized and unappetizing as the frozen dinners they ate most evenings. But the truth was he had known very few women in his life, sexually free or otherwise. Despite his movie-star good looks (it didn't help matters that he looked as if he were a ladies' man) he barely knew anything at all about sex—before Pamela.

By the time Bill got out of the army and started work as an ironworker and married his high school sweetheart, he had made love half a dozen times with various girls, enough to feel that he knew how to do it (with Pamela he found that he didn't, it was like starting over, everything was new), enough to know that you were supposed to feel around some before you put it in and that you weren't supposed to just roll right off and go to sleep after you were done and that you were supposed to try to get her to come too. (Although Mary always said she came when he did, the fact that she didn't want to make love much anymore led him to believe that she faked it; there was no doubt, however, when Pamela came, no doubt at all that she thoroughly enjoyed herself; that he could cause such a reaction in her made him feel as if he owned the world.) He had had a few girls since he was married, pickups in bars and such, but nothing at all serious, nothing that could threaten his marriage to Mary, mother of his child. (Because he *did* love Mary, he *did*, didn't he?) But that was before Pamela. Pamela, or perhaps more to the point, sex with Pamela, unhinged his world. He discovered that what had started out as a want (it had been something of a game, something in which he and Jack were involved, a competition he thought as to who would win her) quickly became a need.

Jack was coming toward them across the deck, hands in his pockets, displaying his usual casualness but with an air about him that said he was ready for trouble; his cigarette stuck out between his teeth like a fuse.

Yeah, Jack, you tell us about it. You set it all straight.

"What's going on?" Jack said, looking in turn at Bill, Levon, Gregg. "You guys organizing a basketball pool or something?"

Gregg looked at Bill—Don't look at me, asshole—but Bill turned away, looked across the deck to where he used to be able to see Pamela's windows—She wouldn't even answer the door, she knew it was me and she wouldn't answer, I'll bet she was up there the whole time with that other guy, that fancy son-of-a-bitch in the white Continental—as Gregg told Jack about the problem, yakking on about it like a kid tattling to the teacher.

". . . the hooks in the columns are wrong. I looked and the drawings say . . ."

Choke me she said choke me real hard as if you mean it and I didn't know what she was talking about, I didn't think I could ever feel that way about her, I didn't think I could ever want to hurt her, but she kept insisting, I want to try something she said and took me by the hand and led me up there on the roof.

It was late last fall before it got too cold and she was wearing a pair of gray flannel sweatpants, I used to think sweat suits were baggy and sloppy and even dirty like something you'd wear only to a gym but on her and the way they showed the lines of her thighs and clung to her ass they were as mysterious and sexy as a harem outfit, and a sweatshirt with some Asian characters on it under a circle that was divided by a wave, one half of the circle white, one half black. On the roof was an old mattress and she led me to it and had me stand at one end facing her and took my hands and placed them around her neck. I took her face in my hands and tried to kiss her but she shook my hands away and put my fingers back around her throat.

I mean it she said I want you to try to choke me and I thought What's this, another one of her kinky ways to get off, because I did things with her I only dreamed of doing before, I did things with her I had only heard about before. And when I thought about that, thought about where she must have learned that stuff because she didn't learn it from me, thought about all the other guys she must have been with, I don't know, it seemed to bring something out in me and I got a little carried away because for a moment I felt what it must be like to really choke someone, I could feel her life between my fingers, feel the cords of her neck and the beat of her pulse, her throat taut as she tried to swallow and couldn't, I understood for a moment how someone could be driven to do such a thing, to be angry enough to squeeze the life from someone else, and we looked in each other's eyes and I think she could see it too, I think she knew and I don't know if it scared her but it scared me and I was ready to stop, ready to release my grip, I know I was, I didn't want to hurt her, I never wanted to, when she brought her arms up between my arms with her fists clenched and broke the hold then wheeled about, half turned away from me and snapped her elbow into my chest, sending me flying backwards, gasping for breath onto the mattress where I landed with a thud that shook all the remaining air from me and before I could do anything else she aimed a kick at my groin, her face contorted as she let out a sharp loud scream, the kick stopping mercifully inches from my balls before her foot snapped back to rest close to her knee, ready to strike again if she wanted to. She stood over me on one leg, balanced like a heron.

Wow, she said and grinned happily, it really works. . . .

"How come?" Jack said to him.

"How come what?" Bill said.

"How come you put the candy canes in that way?"

Bill shrugged, still looking off toward the rear of the deck. "That's the way we assembled the cages. That's the way it was easiest while the cages were lying down."

"Didn't you see the note he's talking about on the drawings?"

Bill looked at him lazy-eyed but didn't say anything.

. . . What the hell, I could barely croak, lying there fighting for breath as she clapped her hands and danced around on her toes like a cheerleader. She said It's a move the guy who runs the kung fu studio taught me the other night. I didn't think it would work but he said I should try it sometime and boy does it work.

How do you know him? I said feeling around on my chest for broken ribs and trying to sound normal, men are supposed to be able to take things like that.

Who, Kim? she said as unconcerned as ever, Oh he's a friend of mine.

I looked up at her trying to read her face but I couldn't, it was the standard answer she gave whenever I asked her about some guy she knew, Oh he's a friend of mine. But before I could ask her what kind of friend Kim was, she pulled her sweatshirt up over her head and kicked off her running shoes and wiggled out of her sweatpants and blue panties and stood over me, as cold as it was, naked against the sky.

Somebody'll see you I said but she said No they won't and looked over the low wall that surrounded the roof at the houses farther up the hillside. I sunbathe nude up here all the time in the summer, the only people who could possibly see me are way up there on the hill and I'm sure they have better things to do than watch me.

I can't think of anything I'd rather watch I said looking up at her black muff, the undersides of her breasts, imagining dozens of men standing on their front porches with binoculars getting an eyeful.

That's because you've got a dirty mind she said and I said What happens when the building across the alley gets taller? and she said Then the guys will really have something to watch won't they? and I thought What do they have to watch now? because that was before she started dancing in the shower in the mornings but before I could say or think anything else she plopped down on top of me with her knees on my shoulders pinning me, her breasts dangling over me. Gotcha!

I tickled her foot and we wrestled around a bit, Pamela still on top of me, working her shoulders so she bopped my nose a couple of times with her breasts and she giggled and I gave a lick to a pendant nipple and said Are these some more of the moves you practice with your kung fu friend?

She stopped and looked at me then got up, That's none of your business she said and picked up her clothes and walked naked back inside and down the steps to her apartment, I don't know if anybody saw her that way or not. When I went down and tried her door it was locked and I knocked and she wouldn't answer even though she knew I knew she was in there and I wondered if I would ever see her again. . . .

"Hell, Jack," Levon said. "There's too much steel in those columns anyway, you know that. Those little hooks aren't going to make any difference. . . ."

. . . but the next night when I left the jobsite she was sitting on the front of my truck like a hood ornament but she didn't say anything, she led me back around the block to her apartment and up the stairs and back up on the roof again, positioned me standing on the edge of the mattress again, still without saying anything, put my hands on her throat again and nodded for me to squeeze and I did and she broke the hold again though I was barely touching her this time and she snapped her elbow into my chest again only this time I knew it was coming and was already falling backwards when it hit me and sent me sprawling on my back again and she almost kicked my balls again and stood on one leg like a heron and stripped and plopped down on top of me again. And we made love there one way or another which I guess was what she had in mind the night before before my stupidity of asking too many questions ruined it, lying there together until the sky overhead turned pink then a richer blue than I'd ever seen in the daytime and then black, and she still didn't say anything, and it wasn't the joys of outdoor sex I learned that night, I learned if not not to question her at least not to say it out loud.

". . . all I know is that the drawings say the hooks on the candy canes are supposed to alternate."

"Wonderful," Jack said. "So now what?"

Yeah Jack, tell us about it. Tell us what we're going to do about it now, you always know how to make everything right.

Bill looked away again, across the deck to where Pamela's windows used to be, as if her entire apartment building had sunk into the earth. No, there wasn't always a way to make everything right. How could he make it right about Mary? Did she know he was seeing somebody else? Fucking somebody else? In love with somebody else? How could she not know? There were times in bed, long into the night, when he could feel her beside him, her back turned to him, crying. I woke up, I don't know why, and she wasn't there, so I got up and walked quickly through the house and found her in the living room in her nightgown standing in the dark or rather in the light that came through the picture window from the streetlight at the end of the cul-de-sac, in the dark room her gown almost ghostly in the light from outside, and I went over to her and stood beside her and took her hand. Mary, what is it? her skin as cold as death.

You tell me, Bill, what is it? she said looking past me out the window and for a moment I thought there must be something outside but all there was was the dark empty suburban street, the dark houses all in a row, all looking the same in the darkness as they curved away into the night. She turned to me then and touched my forehead with her fingertips, like she was brushing back a wisp of hair that wasn't there, touched my eyes, my cheek, my mouth as if she were a blind person searching for an identification, something to tell her sightless eyes that it was me, searching my eyes with hers though hers were faraway, looking at something I couldn't name. Then she turned and walked past me and went back to bed. When I asked her about it in the morning she said she didn't remember a thing, I thought she must have been sleepwalking, or maybe she just didn't want to think about it in the light of day. . . .

"Are all the candy canes like that?" Jack said to him.

"That's the way I put 'em in."

"I mean on all the other floors too?"

"Yep. Every floor."

Jack stared at him for a moment—Yeah, Jack, you always have an answer for everything, what's your answer for this one?—then turned to Gregg.

"You know what you're getting yourself into, don't you?"

You knew what you were getting yourself into when you started seeing her you said that night at the Triangle Tavern, turning away from me on your barstool and then turning back again What do you want me to tell you? That it's okay to be screwing the girl? That it's okay to run around on your wife? You got yourself mixed up with a girl who's popular with a lot of guys, you knew that. You want me to tell you she loves you? Or that she's going to love you? I don't know any of that stuff.

And I said to you All I want to know is what you think I should do, but you said I don't know what you should do, Christ I don't even care what you do, or who you do it with. What do you want from me?

What did I want from you, Jack? That's what it all comes down to, doesn't it? What I wanted was to be like you. You make your own party you always say, well, I wanted to learn how to make a party for myself. Your life always seemed more real than mine, you always seemed more alive than I did, you knew how to have fun and enjoy yourself and I wanted that too, I wanted my life to seem real, I wanted to feel part of it, part of the world. I wanted to be you. But all I said to you that night at the Triangle was I thought we were friends. And then you told me how wrong I was about that too. . . .

". . . they're not going to make us rip out every column in the building," Levon said. "That'd be crazy."

"I'm saying I don't know what they'll do," Jack said. "But I'm also saying you got to be ready for that eventuality. I've seen stranger things happen."

Gregg stood with his knees locked, clipboard down at his side, and looked Jack straight on. "My job is only to see if . . ."

Friends? Just because we go out and have a couple drinks once in a while? No way. We're just guys who work together, that's all. We're coworkers, drinking buddies on a job. That's all we are. When this job's over, we'll move on to the next job, and the next set of drinking buddies. Me, I don't have any friends. I don't want 'em.

And I said Why don't you want anybody to be your friend? and you looked at me across your shoulder, Because it's only your friends that will screw you. Your enemies, they never screw you because you never let 'em close enough and I said That's a hard-ass way to be and you stared at your image in the mirror behind the bar, grinning to yourself, and said Yeah, maybe so, but I don't get screwed this way either.

Jack stood there looking from one to another. After a moment, when no one said anything, Bill turned back from where he was looking across the deck—Well Jack, we all get screwed one way or another, whether we want to be or not—and said, "Isn't that wonderful?"

Jack jammed his hands in his pockets and headed toward the manhoist.

What's the matter, Jack, that was supposed to be funny, can't you take a joke?

23

"Hello?"

"Whatcha doing, kid?"

"Twice in one day."

"I told you I thought we should start talking more often during the day."

"It must mean something's wrong."

"Why do you say that?"

"Because I know you, Vince. I can hear it in your voice."

I know you too, Rita, and I can hear it your voice too. The sound of weeping. Of someone who can barely keep from crying. What is the great sorrow of your life, wife o' mine, is it me? Let me tell you my sorrow—I would tell you if I thought you'd listen. If I thought you'd hear me. Lyle said Probably best to sit down, the savings and loan is out of money and the contractor is abandoning the project. Other than that . . . Julian stood there like a one-legged stork with his world crashed down around his ears—my world—and worried about a nail file.

"Vince?"

"I'm here. Just thinking about something. I'm surprised to hear you say that about my voice. I thought I sounded particularly lighthearted and jolly." Considering.

"That's what I mean. You usually only sound like this when there's something really really wrong."

"Well, you're the one who's really really wrong this time, because this time something's really really right." That sounded a little too sarcastic, even for him, and he laughed to soften it. He listened to himself laugh; he sounded jolly enough, didn't he? No, maybe she's right, maybe a little too jolly, things certainly aren't that great. Not great at all as a matter of fact. Maybe she's just in one of her moods. She's always in one of her moods. I'm trying to do a nice thing here, trying to cheer her up.

"Are you going to tell me what it is?"

"What what is?"

"What's really really right."

Now I really really don't want to. What is that about people? We love to see something tumble down after we go to all the trouble to build it up. "I guess it's not all that wonderful. But at least it's something. You know I was telling you this morning that I had to tell a fellow today that he didn't have enough money to finish his project?"

"You mean the building in Furnass?"

"Yes, that's the one—"

"Is that where you're calling from now?"

Just hold your horses, Rita, let me tell the story. "Yes, that's where I am now. Anyway, I had to come out here today to—"

"That's where you called me from earlier. That messy trailer."

What difference does that make? "Rita, you're interrupting." He tried to soften it again with a little laugh.

"I just wanted to know where you're calling from now, that's all."

What's wrong with that? She's interested that's all, don't be so hard on her. "Yes, I'm back here in the messy trailer. Jack's, the jobsite superintendent's, messy trailer."

"I just finished cleaning Christopher's room. And I was getting ready to start on Julie's as soon as I get something to snack on here in the kitchen. I don't know how things get so dirty so quickly."

Vince sighed; he ran his hand up across his forehead and over the top of his wiry, graying hair. "Do you want to hear my story or not?"

"Of course I do. You told me where you are and what you're doing, so I was telling you where I am and what I'm doing. Go on ahead, tell me about what put you in such a good mood."

Amazing, she remembered why I was going to tell her in the first place. Maybe I expect too much of her, so many things are beyond her. But before he could say anything, Rita said, "Oh, before I forget, did you see the key for the French doors?"

Vince looked at the milky blotches on the toes of his shoes. Where did I get those? That's right, Lyle's office. Seems like I'm always stepping in one thing or another. "Which key is that, Rita?"

"You know, the key for the dead bolt on the French doors."

"I didn't have it."

"Well, I certainly didn't. You must have it."

"I'm not sure I follow your logic." Vince, sitting in the chair at Jack's desk, tapped a brief tattoo with his shoes; the floor crunched grittily under the soles. "I know I didn't have it. Why would I have it? I don't even know where you usually keep it."

"That's right. You never know where anything is," she said, her voice trailing off as if she turned away from the phone, as if she turned away in disgust.

"Rita, what's all this about?"

"All I did was ask you if you knew where the key was for the French doors, and you said you didn't have it, and that's that."

"But it's your tone of voice. It's like you're accusing me."

"I'm not accusing. All I was doing was asking."

Stay calm, somebody has to, just explain it to her. "Maybe you didn't mean it that way but your voice sounded like you were accusing me."

"You always make so much out of everything," Rita said, her voice loading up with tears and anger. "It's like last week, I asked you for something, I don't even know what it was now, and you said you didn't have it. And then it turned out that you didn't have it after all, but just the same. . . ."

What the hell is going on here? Menopause? Or cranky genes? Jesus, I can't win. Vince didn't say anything; he stood up and walked the few steps to the door of the trailer and back again, carrying the phone with him. The grit on the floor crackled under his leather soles like the sound of ice breaking up, giving way.

"Why did you call, Vince?"

Lord knows. "I thought we talked about me calling you more often during the day. I thought we decided that would be nice, that I'd try to do it more often." He noticed that his voice sounded world-weary; he also noticed that now he was the one using an accusing tone, the undertones of his voice full of blame. I don't care, she got what she wanted, there's certainly nothing jolly and cheerful about me now. She's brought me down to her level, we'll all be miserable together. Vince sat down again in Jack's chair. "And I was going to tell you about my meeting out here today."

"Oh yes, you started to tell me. I want to hear how it went."

Absolutely amazing. As if nothing happened, as if nothing were wrong. Maybe it is me, maybe I am the one who's crazy. "As it turned out, I didn't have to talk to him about refinancing the construction loan after all. It's a non-issue at this point."

"I know you were pretty concerned about it this morning."

She knew? I didn't think she noticed at all. She said You've always been good at putting a spin on what you say. "I thought I had good reason to be. When Lyle—he's the owner, the fellow I had to talk to—called me yesterday, he said he wanted to discuss a payment problem."

"So there isn't a payment problem after all?"

"Oh yes, there's a problem, all right. It turns out the contractor hasn't been paid for a couple of months." Vince said it as a joke, trying to accent the irony, his good spirits starting to return. Listen to us: we're having a conversation!

"That sounds like a problem to me. It's a wonder the contractor is still on the project."

The worry and concern were coming back into Rita's voice; Vince wanted to stave it off, to keep their conversation light. "That's another thing. The contractor claims this is his last day. In fact they're saying they're going to walk off the project for good."

"Having worked for a contractor, I can't say I blame them," Rita said, a degree of righteous indignation coming into her voice. "The contractor must think they have a strong legal position if they're thinking of walking off the project altogether. Do they have anything else they can base a claim on besides the payment problem?"

Christ, first I can't get her to listen, now I can't get her to leave it alone. Take another look at your estimate, Mr. Nicholson, are you sure we can build this building for what you say? "There have been a lot of change orders—"

"Enough to be a problem?"

"Well, in the contractor's eyes, I suppose. . . ."

"There you have it then. I don't know why you'd be so happy about your meeting with Lyle."

"Not happy, exactly." Not happy at all, in fact. In fact it was devastating. Vince loosened his tie a little. Just leave it, Rita. "It was more of a relief, that's all."

"What could be a relief about the contractor not getting paid and getting ready to walk off your project?"

"It has to do with . . . I thought the reason they might be walking off was because of all the change orders but that wasn't the reason so I was relieved, that's all."

"Are you the one who initiated the change orders?"

"I wrote them, yes." Damn it, Rita.

"Why were there so many change orders? There must have been an awful lot if you were afraid that's the reason the contractor is pulling off."

"There were a number of reasons, if you must know. We felt there were certain changes necessary to the brickwork, and the windows . . . there turned out to be a lot of things. They were all important to the integrity of the final structure."

"I would hope so."

What did she mean by that? Doesn't she think they're important? This is ridiculous, I'm defending myself to my own wife. Why can't she accept what I say and leave it at that? "What I was relieved about was that the problem turned out to be with the savings and loan that holds the loan."

"That made you happy?"

Ignore it. "I didn't mean happy. I meant relieved."

"What's the problem with the savings and loan?"

"It overextended itself and now it's in the process of going belly-up."

"We've seen that on the news, remember?" Rita said. "There are S and Ls failing all over the country, they say it's almost an epidemic. You hear of these things happening, but you never think they'll happen to you, or have any effect on you."

"Well, it's happening to me," Vince said. He stared straight ahead, at the picture on a calendar nailed to the wall, a Vargas-style drawing of a woman in a frilly maid's uniform holding a jackhammer. Yes, it's happening to me, all right. And I don't know how. Jack said You're not real good at paying attention, are you?

"No wonder you're depressed."

"Who said I'm depressed?"

"The way you just sighed. . . ."

"I've got a lot to think about right now, that's all."

"I know. I suppose the first thing you need to find out is if your company has been paid."

Christ, I never thought about that. "Gee, Rita. Do you think so?" he said sarcastically while his mind was racing. Wouldn't the bookkeeper have said something? Probably not, knowing our bookkeeper. "What a novel idea, find out if we've been paid. Just like I run a real architectural firm or something."

"You know what I mean."

"Actually, I was thinking of forgetting the whole payment problem and pretending it doesn't exist. Just let everything go on the way it was."

"Vince . . ."

"You know me, your idiot husband, I've never built a building before."

"Don't talk that way about yourself, Vince. . . ."

"I thought I'd let it slide, you know, like I do everything else. It seems I don't see what's going on and face up to responsibilities anyway anymore—"

"Stop it!"

"I don't know how you ever put up with a fool like me all this time—"

"Stop it! Stop it! Stop it!" she screamed. Then softer. "Stop it, please. Stop all of it. I can't listen to it anymore. I can't stand to hear you talk that way about yourself."

"Okay, okay, Rita," Vince said, shaken. Can't stand it? Maybe she does care. "Take it easy. I didn't mean to upset you."

"No, it's okay. I'm sorry I yelled."

"Look, you take it easy this afternoon, okay? You're probably working too hard, getting the kids' rooms ready and all." Was she crying? She always looks like she's about to cry. Maybe she actually does sometimes. Vince was touched. He never considered that she might care so much about him that she couldn't stand to hear anyone cut him up, even himself. Poor kid. She always was crazy about me. "Take it slow, you've got plenty of time before summer vacation. You clean them too early, the rooms will be dirty again before the kids get home, ha ha."

"You don't think I should be doing them now?"

"No, no, I didn't mean that at all. You do whatever you think best." Careful now, careful, things are going good here. She's loving you, don't blow it. "Tell you what. When I get home we'll call out for pizza so you don't have to fix anything. We haven't done that in years. We'll have our own little party."

"Okay, Vince. Whatever you say."

"That's my big girl."

*

He hung up expecting to feel in a good mood again, but he felt emptier than before. His arms wrapped about himself, clutching himself in his trench coat, he got up from the wooden swivel chair and wandered over to the door. At the very moment Jack came up the steps.

"Hi there," Vince said quickly.

"What's eating you, you stealing something in here?"

"No, why . . . ?"

"You look guilty as hell." Jack brushed by him and went over to his desk, tossing papers left and right as he tried to find something. "Where the hell did Marshall put my keys?" The keys were in his in-basket, slipped down beside a stack of Vince's change orders. Jack put the keys in his jacket pocket and looked around as if to see if there was anything else he'd forgotten, talking to Vince as if he were talking to himself.

"Andy still hasn't finished welding that column we looked at this morning, he seems to have slowed down to a crawl. So it's going to be late before he gets it and the last column welded and we get them all poured. I hate like hell to have to pay overtime when we're not even getting paid for straight time out here. But I don't want to leave any of those columns with only the tack welds holding them if we're going to walk off this project. I told the labor foreman to keep his concrete crew and the pump here all night if he has to to finish up the columns. Mac's going to be thrilled when he hears about that. But it can't be helped."

He looked at Vince as if he suddenly remembered him standing there. "And that kid inspector and the ironworker foreman are looking for you. They'll probably be down here in a couple of minutes."

"Oh, what about?"

Jack looked around the trailer again. Then he stuck his face close to Vince's; he smiled so sarcastically that his eyes went squinty. "I think I'll let them tell you. It's a little surprise they seem to have cooked up between the two of them. Isn't that wonderful? I think that's wonderful."

"What do you mean 'surprise'? "

Jack ignored him. He went over and stood at his desk again. "They got themselves into it without talking to me about it, so to hell with them, let them get themselves out of it."

"If you're this upset about it—"

"Upset?" Jack looked at him and grinned. "Me upset?"

"I just thought . . ."

"Do I look upset? Do I act upset? Hey, *this* is upset."

Jack wheeled around and in the same motion slammed his fist into the partitioned wall behind his desk. The plywood sheeting shattered with a loud *Crack!* leaving a hole with Jack's hand inside. He yanked his hand back out, against the splinters and jagged edges, raking his skin badly; his wrist and the back of his hand looked as if he had been clawed. Jack held up his hand to examine it, looked at Vince, and shook his head. "Dumb, huh?" He left the trailer, brandishing the wounded hand in front of him like a club, and disappeared out the front gate.

24

Outside the open door of the trailer, standing at the foot of the steps, a respectful distance away as Vince made the important call, Gregg and Bill alternately looked at the building, the sky, the gate, their shoes—anywhere to keep from looking at him, anywhere to keep from looking concerned or apprehensive. They're like children, little boys called down to the principal's office, awaiting their fate, it is so easy to bend and mold the working class. In his ear, bright baroque music pumped away as he continued to wait on hold to speak with the structural engineer. Vince got up from Jack's desk and carried the phone over to the plan table, the cord stretched to its limits behind him, out of Gregg and Bill's line of sight. With his half-frame glasses perched midway down the bridge of his nose, his mouth gaping as he worked his head up and down to bring the details into focus, Vince studied the drawings spread before him.

The Building

He felt bad about throwing the young inspector to the wolves
earlier in the day, when Gregg called his attention to the welding
on the column bars. Gregg said Is the welding okay? and I said
Oh no, that's not my job, you're the inspector, it's your job to
tell me if the welding's okay or not. It was unfortunate, but it
was unavoidable; he was certainly not going to get himself in the
position of approving work that wasn't according to code—Jack
said You really waltzed that kid around, he didn't know if he was
coming or going, he didn't have a chance against an old pro like
you—even though he felt reasonably sure that the welding on the
bars, by all practical standards, was more than strong enough for
the design of the columns. What the fuck do you think I should
fucking do, chip out every fucking column on every fucking floor
so you can fucking have a look at them? The inimitable Mr.
Crawford. It was unfortunate, but there was no question he had
taken advantage of a young man who obviously didn't know what
he was doing. Does the rebar go in the top of the slab, the middle
of the slab, or the bottom of the slab? You're wrong, this is a
cantilevered slab, in case you ever need to know. And the young
man certainly did seem to be trying; Vince told Gregg to keep
his eyes open and call attention to any problems he found; and
here he was with another problem, this time with the candy canes
in the columns. Mr. Nicholson? I was looking at the drawings and
I'm afraid some of the bars aren't quite right. Vince supposed
that Gregg was very much like his own son, Christopher, in a
way; they were probably about the same age, and soon Christopher would also be starting out in the workaday world. I said If
you're a history major how did you ever end up a construction
inspector? and he said I answered an ad in the paper and I said
But why did you decide to take such a job and he said What else
is a history major prepared to do in the world? Gregg undoubtedly looked up to Vince because of his position, looked to the
older man for guidance, the way Christopher would be doing soon

Richard Snodgrass

when he started his first job. The way Vince had done when he was a young man starting out. Arthritic Mies hung on his crutches by my drafting table and said Your works are all dead until some motive impels you to act. As always Mr. Nicholson's solution is rather extreme but if we wade through the detritus perhaps we can find a kernel of something useful, and then Mies smiled like a flaw in granite to the rest of the class. Rita was right, he did need to pay more attention to his responsibilities, such as being a good role model for this young man.

On the phone there was the sound of the connection being made and Dillup's voice in the background talking to someone else. Come on, Dillup, quit chitchatting and take your call, this is important. After another minute, Dillup came on the line and Vince explained the problem to him.

"Oh me, oh my," Dillup groaned; it sounded more like a high-pitched whine. In his mind's eye, Vince could see the man rocking back and forth on his drafting stool, holding his head as if his Sikh turban were a bandage. Dillup tended to act out everything, even on the phone, as if that were the only way he could be understood.

"That bad?" Vince said.

"Oh my goodness, Vincent. What kind of people do you have building that building out there?"

"The kind who would put in the candy canes wrong."

Dillup giggled, almost a whinny, which he did at most anything that happened. "Well, very well, very well, let me get my drawings for your project and let me take a look."

Vince directed the engineer to the page and details in question.

"Oh goodness me, goodness goodness."

"As I understand it—I haven't seen them myself—the candy canes are put in with all the hooks facing the same direction in each column. And there's a note on the bottom of the page that says that the hooks are supposed to alternate."

"Goodness, goodness, goodness. How could they do such a thing, Vincent?"

"I think it was pretty easy, Dillup. They just picked up each candy cane from the bundle and put it in the column."

Dillup didn't catch Vince's attempt at a joke. "Well, very well, let me see something a moment." In the background was the whir of an electric calculator. Why does he giggle all the time when I know he's deadly serious, why does he pretend not to take anything seriously and go through all his melodramatics when he's one of the best engineers I've ever worked with? Does being a Sikh in Western Pennsylvania do that to you? Stranger in a strange land. Maybe it's some Eastern mystical thing. Sikh and ye shall find. And I think nobody understands me. Nobody does. Dillup giggled. "Whew boy. Why would they ever do such a thing, Vincent?"

"The ironworkers say they didn't see the note."

"One would have to open one's eyes in order to see it, this is true."

"They claim there's too much steel in the columns anyway."

"Oh yes, there is a lot of steel in there. So why not leave some of it out too, right Vincent?" Dillup giggled. "Oh Vincent, you should see the baby now, she's as big as a little horse and she keeps me up half the night. I am sitting here with my eyelids propped open with pencils, the little demon will not let me sleep."

"That's fine, Dillup. What do you think about these columns?"

"Oh, I think they are a mess, Vincent."

"I mean, do you think—"

"I will tell you what I think, Vincent. It is a question I have often asked myself. The *Manual of Standard Practice* shows that the hooks should alternate for a small column and says that this is typical, but it never shows the same thing for a larger column. Now, what is it typical of, small columns or all columns? It is all very illogical. Myself, I always say that the hooks should alternate, small column or large, that way I am on the safe side. At least I am logical." Dillup giggled. "And I will tell you this too. These columns are overdesigned by quite a lot. I did not do the design on this myself but I noticed it at the time. I think someone here in the office just copied this from some other building, if you want my opinion, but if you ever say I said that I'll deny it the tooth and the nail. I think your ironworkers are absolutely right, there is too much steel in there. I suppose we should have cut it back then but we didn't and there it is and that is the way things are."

"Wait a minute. What is the way things are?" *Now* they tell me the columns are overdesigned, that would run up the cost of the project as well, all that will come out also if people start asking too many questions. "Does that mean you think the columns are okay if the hooks don't alternate?"

"Well, let me tell you, Vincent, I would not like to see it become a principle of construction that the ironworkers don't put in all the steel or don't put it in correctly simply because they don't like what we have on the drawings. But with the columns already overdesigned as they are here, they can probably get away with it this time. Also because I would have no idea how you would fix such a thing now. And I will tell you this, my friend: I would have no idea how to fix them without raising the question of why they are overdesigned in the first place, which would mean a lot of questions from the powers that be in this company and a lot of embarrassing answers from junior engineers. Remember, I am only a poor Sikh who cannot be trusted to actually do the calculations for a building, though I am sufficient to be assigned to field your phone calls, which are always a pleasure."

So somebody else would be on the spot too if too many questions were asked. We spend our lives trying to avoid asking too many questions. It's called mental health. "It still doesn't seem too much to ask that they put the steel in the way it's designed. That's what they get paid to do."

"Ah Vincent, you sound grouchy. What side of the bedroom did you get up on this morning?"

The lonely side. "I'll let you know what happens, Dillup."

"Good luck, Vincent," Dillup giggled. "Give them the hell."

After he hung up Vince continued to lean on the slanting plan table for a while, his chin braced on the strut of his arm, his elbow planted squarely in the center of detail 3/S-3 on the drawings, staring dreamily out the window. Curious. Jack must have known about the problem with the candy canes when we talked here in the trailer. That must have been what he was so upset about, made him angry enough to stick his fist through the wall. Why didn't he tell me about the problem then? I never thought happy-go-lucky Jack would care that much about anything on a project. People certainly do unexpected things at times, don't they? Maybe the reason he didn't tell me about it is that he doesn't think enough of me. To Jack I'm as useless as tits on a bull. Jack said Jeez, what kind of architect are you anyway, you don't even know what goes on on your own building. You're not real good at paying attention, are you? No, that probably wasn't what upset Jack. He was probably pissed off at something else entirely. Or maybe he just wanted to hit something. The basic philosophy of the working class: if something bothers you, yell at it; if that doesn't scare it away, hit it; if that still doesn't settle the matter, kill it. That's the only way they know how to handle the world. The sorry and frightening thing is that more often than not it's enough. Say, that's pretty good, that could be another topic for a chapter of a book. Have you read Nicholson? Nicholson says . . . A cough behind him called him back from his reverie. Gregg and Bill leaned in the doorway of the trailer, expectant looks on their faces. Like children.

"What did the engineer have to say?" Bill said as he came on inside. The reflection of the patch of light from the window slid back and forth across the chrome surface of his hardhat like the bubble in a level. Gregg, grinning hopefully through his bushy beard, stayed in the doorway.

Vince straightened up, adjusted his trench coat about himself; he sighed wearily. "He won't buy it."

"What do you mean?" Bill said.

"The structural engineer says the hooks on those candy canes are critical." Vince shook his head regretfully. What am I doing? "He says the way they are now, with all the hooks facing the same direction, the vertical bars in the columns could buckle under severe load and pop right out of there." Why am I doing this? "It cuts too far into the safety factor, the way they are now. I'm sorry, but they'll have to be corrected."

"Shit," Bill said, turning away. "Well, I guess we can climb up the cages and turn every other candy cane around. . . ."

There's a right way and a wrong way to do everything. I'm tired of all the shoddy workmanship, people not doing what they're supposed to. Your works are dead until you're impelled to act. "You'll also have to figure out some way to correct the columns that have already been poured," Vince said.

Bill turned around and stared at him. Then he laughed, the harlequin patches blazing on his cheeks. "You're kidding."

"I'm very serious, my friend. I don't know how you're going to do it—chip out the whole column, or maybe chip out every other candy cane and weld a hook to the bar or something, I don't know. That's up to your company, how you propose to correct the problem. Your detailer will have to draw something up and submit it for approval."

What am I doing? Why am I doing this? It's like I'm watching somebody else say these things, but I'm into it now, I can't back down now even if I wanted to, and I don't.

"Hey, do you know what we're talking about here?" Bill said, moving closer to him. Gregg stayed where he was in the doorway, dumbfounded, the grin gone from his face.

Vince closed his eyes—I'm tired of people not paying attention to what they're doing—rocked a little on his heels—I'm tired of people not listening to me—his hands in the pockets of his trench coat. "I know we're talking about costing this job a great deal of money."

"No, we're not just talking about this job. We're talking about *my* job. If I go to my company and tell them about this, I won't have a job, I'll be out on my ass."

"I'm very sorry," Vince said calmly, looking at him over the top of his glasses. Ass is a dirty word. Only when it refers to people. He took off his glasses and put them in their case. "But I'm not the one who put the steel in wrong and caused your problem, am I? You did that yourself. And now it's your responsibility to fix it."

For a moment the two men stared at each other. It's like I want him to hit me. I even took off my glasses to give him a clear shot. I must be out of my mind. Vince broke his gaze away from the other's—I must be more desperate than I thought. On Bill's chromed hardhat, his reflection was warped out of proportion like the image in a funhouse mirror. I must be lonelier than I ever imagined. Bill was trembling with rage, the patches on his cheeks as red as if he had been slapped; finally he wheeled around and hurried from the trailer.

Vince turned to Gregg and started to shrug—Touchy, isn't he? but you have to expect that from people when you try to do what's right—but the expression on Gregg's face stopped him: Gregg was looking at him as if Vince had betrayed him all over again. What? What do you want from me? I backed you up this time didn't I? I rejected the work you told me about, I took care of my responsibilities. Vince wanted to say something to him but Gregg left too.

25

It was a set piece Levon did sometimes for friends at night, a kind of rap as they sat around getting drunk or stoned at his or someone else's place, to explain to those who didn't work in construction, who had never built anything in their lives, what it was like to work on a building. He would sit on the floor in the lotus position, his long red hair released from the ponytail and flowing down his shoulders, eyes half-closed behind his horn-rimmed glasses, his hands upturned on his thighs with thumb and forefinger together as if each hand held the end of an unimaginably thin piece of thread, and intone in a deep sepulchral voice:

"It's the first principle of building a building, man, it's the first principle in building anything, maybe it's the only principle in the universe: the tighter two things are held together, the harder it is to break them apart. That's the key, you know? How you hold things together. Put two pieces of metal together with a rivet, and the connection will be able to stand a certain amount of stress. In case you don't know, my children, *stress* is the force acting upon something, and *strain* is the change that that something goes through because of the stress. When your car won't start in the morning, that's *stress*; when you get a headache because of it, that's *strain*. To continue: put two pieces of metal together with a high strength bolt instead of a rivet—a bolt that's strong enough that you can torque the two faces of metal closer together than you can with a rivet—and the connection will stand even more stress. Weld the two pieces of metal together—heat the two surfaces so that the molecules of metal flow together along with some new filler metal—and the two pieces of metal become one, the connection is actually stronger than either of the separate pieces of metal. The tighter things are held together, the more stress they can stand. Or to put it another way, if something has to stand up under a lot of stress, the tighter it has to be bonded to the other things around it. The world is in the binding together. . . ."

About which time someone would usually put in through the haze of an altered state of consciousness, "Speaking of being held together, Levon, your own wrapping ain't exactly what I'd call secure."

Levon was aware that his work as a rodbuster didn't involve anything very binding or conclusive per se; his job was only to make sure the reinforcing bars were held in position until the concrete could be placed around them. True, when the concrete hardened around the steel bars, the two separate materials became in effect one, but Levon's efforts had nothing to do with the actual binding. By the same token, Levon was aware that his best work was always covered over in the final structure; looking at the completed building, no one could see what he had done. But that was okay with Levon, he knew it was there; and somehow it made his work seem more spiritual to him, a kind of spiritual exercise or meditation.

"What the fock you talking about?" Tony Serrabella, the old man of the crew, said to him one day when Levon happened to mention the idea.

"He means the exercise we're doing is only spiritual, not physical," Bill said, straightening up from where he was tying bars for a floor slab.

"I'm not saying it's *only* spiritual. . . ," Levon said.

"How the fock can exercise be spiritual?" Tony said. "You exercise, you use your muscles. That's physical."

"Maybe he means your muscles don't really hurt, it's only in your head," Bill said.

"Thanks a lot, partner," Levon said.

Bill smirked. "Hey, I don't know what you're talking about either."

Tony was already ranting. "What the fock you mean my muscles don't really hurt? I go home at night I can hardly move—"

"Tying bars is sort of like chanting a mantra," Levon tried to explain. "You know, doing the same thing over and over again until it frees your mind and takes you to a higher consciousness. And this steel mat, it's like we're making a great iron mandala and we're at the center receiving positive energy from the universe. . . ."

"You're focking crazy, you focking sonamabitch," Tony said.

Nor was his work as a rodbuster as glamorous as that of the ironworkers who worked on the high steel, the men who performed more or less as aerialists to make connections on the structural steel framework of a high-rise. Levon's job was more subtle, a craft involved with making knots as delicate as a weaver's with sixteen-gauge tie wire. There were times when he was placing the steel for a wall, as he climbed up a hatchwork two or three stories tall of crisscrossing bars, that he felt as if he were a marker in an infinite game of tic-tac-toe; other times, strapped on with his safety rope to free his hands so he could lean back as he worked, the heels of his tall lineman's boots hooked onto the bars he'd already secured below him, he felt as if he were a spider, pulling silk in the form of tie wire from the coiler on his belt, weaving a metal web. He never told anyone about these ideas, however; the guys he worked with thought he was crazy enough as it was.

He had a dream once that he never told anyone about either: he was on a job somewhere, he and Bill and Tony, the three of them working away, not saying anything to one another, bent over at the waist, humping along like coolies tending a rice paddy, tying every third or fourth intersection of the bars for a mat in a foundation slab, stepping in the open squares between the bars, their feet placed like pieces on a giant chess- or checkerboard, performing the work more or less by rote, Levon's mind on what he called automatic pilot, when suddenly the wire from his coiler started to come out by itself, started to unwind on its own; at first he thought it was funny, the wire stuck out beside him and poked the other guys if they got too close—"Hey, come on, Levon, watch that thing, will you? You're crazy"—the wire seemingly with a life of its own; he controlled it for a while by snipping off the end every so often, but then the wire started to come faster and faster and it was endless, it was as if a metal thread from inside him were unwinding, as if he himself were somehow unraveling, he couldn't keep ahead of it, snipping it off, and he couldn't stop it and he couldn't push it back inside the coiler; he grabbed at the wire and tried to hold on to it, hold it back, but he cut his hands and the wire just kept coming, tangling around his feet and tripping him up until he fell and the wire started to wind itself around him and he found himself wrapped in a metal cocoon and couldn't breathe, the wire draining the life from him and squeezing the life out of him at the same time, though that didn't seem to bother him, if that's the way it was going to be, then let it be, what terrified him was that the wire started to wrap itself around Bill and Tony too and Levon couldn't do anything to stop it, he couldn't get his arms free, he could only lie there wrapped up in himself and watch his friends struggle and he woke up screaming, drenched in sweat, the girl beside him whom he'd picked up in a bar screaming too and he rolled over on top of her and drilled her until they both thought they would pass out. Crazy dream. He promised himself never to have that particular combination of hash, coke, and Southern Comfort again.

At the heart of his craft was the tie. It took him about three seconds to make a snap or single tie, from the time he pulled an arm's length of wire from the coiler, hooked the end around the bars to be tied, grabbed the end with the nose of his pliers, pulled it taut, twisted the end around the wire, snipped the wire from the coiler, and gave a couple of quick twists with the blunt nose of his pliers to tighten the knot. Sometimes when he completed a tie he gave the barb a hard whack with the closed jaws of his pliers, so the loose ends wouldn't snag clothes or stick out from the surface of the concrete, or simply for the sheer joy of hitting something, but that was optional. Besides the single tie, there were other ties as well, used for other situations, such as the wrap-and-snap tie, and the saddle tie, and the wrap-and-saddle tie, and the figure eight tie, and the nailhead tie. . . .

Making the ties, and making them quickly, was the craft involved in being a rodbuster; everything else required physical exertion or brute strength. There were the hours spent bent double, knees locked, ass to the wind, tying the bars in place for a floor slab or setting the small cement dobies or spacer blocks under the mats of steel so the bars stayed in place when the concrete crew tramped on them; there were the hours of hefting the steel bars, using his body, aware of the workings of his body and the sensations upon it of heat or rain or cold, and afterward the clean, exhausted feeling at the end of the day; there were the hours spent sorting bundles with red tags from bundles with blue tags or green tags, and following the instructions written on the drawings, such as *#6's @ 12" on center longitudinal and #4's @ 8" on center transverse with all openings trimmed with #4's x 24" top and bottom*—Levon loved it all, it was all part of what made being an ironworker, and in particular, a rodbuster, special.

At times, the work of a rodbuster on a project seemed like a giant puzzle: there was this much steel; and that much space to put it in; and there was a set of instructions to explain how it all was to fit together. Of course, it was more Bill's puzzle than Levon's, because Bill was the foreman; it was Bill's responsibility to take the drawings and figure out what was required, then lay out the chalk marks or scribble instructions on the wooden formwork for the rest of the crew to follow. Bill used his folding rule and a piece of keel to write with as much as he did his blunt-nosed pliers. But Levon often helped Bill with the drawings. He knew that Bill hated puzzles and mysteries, that he had no patience in figuring things out. Levon, on the other hand, loved puzzles, he was always trying to figure out how things fit together in the world.

Bill was more than Levon's buddy; they were partners. They paired off for the difficult and dangerous jobs because they trusted each other, knew each other's rhythms. When an iron-worker found a partner, he stuck with him, traveled with him from job to job; if one got hired, he'd say, "I've got a partner," and whoever was doing the hiring knew he was getting two men or none at all. Partners looked out for each other. That was why, when Bill left the top deck with the inspector and went down in the manhoist to talk to the architect about the candy canes, Levon stayed close to the guardrail trying to see what was going on in the trailer. And that was why, when Bill finally came out of the trailer and headed back toward the manhoist, Levon was waiting by the door when the cage returned to the top.

"So what'd the architect say?" Levon said as Bill walked past him. But Levon already knew it was bad from the look on Bill's face. The almost haunted look in his eyes, the red patches on his cheeks. What is it, Billy, what is it this time? What am I supposed to do?

Bill continued on across the deck. Levon caught up to him and put his hand on Bill's arm but Bill shook him off.

"What'd he say?" Levon said. Come on, bud. Don't give me none of that shit. Tell me what we're dealing with here. Act right.

Bill glared at him, as if Levon were responsible for it all. "He's not buying it."

"You're kidding." Okay, okay, we can take care of this.

Bill's voice was low, quiet. "He said the candy canes have to be in there the way they're detailed, even if we have to chip out every goddamn column in this goddamn building." He looked away, across the deck, toward the alley.

"Jesus," Levon said. Okay, okay, that's rough, that's crazy, but we can handle this, we can find some way to take care of it, we've been in tough spots before. . . . "So, what are we going to do? Maybe when Jack gets back he can—"

"Fuck Jack," Bill said, without looking at him, staring at some distant point as he started to walk away. "Fuck that architect, fuck this job, fuck the world."

Not the world, bud, it's all we have. "That ain't no way to talk, Billy—"

"Get away from me, asshole," Bill said without looking back. "Fuck you too."

Aw Bill, if you were anybody else I'd kick your ass, but I don't think I'm going to have to, I think the world's going to take care of that on its own. And the way I'm feeling right now, I'd say it's good enough for you.

26

What's everybody looking at me for? Haven't they ever seen somebody act stupid before? Or maybe they're thinking Here comes Bill, the dumb shit who put the candy canes in wrong. Everybody loves it when somebody else fucks up, the bullet that gets the next guy in line. Why don't they turn around and mind their own business? Please.

Behind him came the steady clank of the tools on Levon's tool belt, constant as a bell cow, the sound of his friend following him. Even after Bill told him to fuck himself. Why take it out on Levon? It wasn't Levon's fault. Blowing off at his friend a minute ago had taken the fight out of him; more than that, it seemed to have cleared the air for him. The whole business—first the kid inspector making a big deal out of finding the problem with the candy canes; then Jack for once not having a ready answer to the problem and stalking off after Bill's attempt at a joke; and now the architect threatening to have all the columns chipped out— was too much for him. I give up. What's the use of getting angry about it? What good did that do? The more he thought about it, the more it all seemed ridiculous to him, almost laughable, not worth the trouble; in fact, he felt a sense of release, as if a weight he had been straining against suddenly went slack. Let 'em chip out the columns if they want to, let 'em take down the whole building for that matter, who cares, what difference does it make now? Everything in my life I guess will be divided into time before I met Pamela and time after. He wanted to turn around and apologize to Levon but he was afraid of appearing foolish. More foolish. He might make it worse than it already was. Levon understood, they were friends.

Friends? We're not friends, we're coworkers, that's all we are. What's the matter, Jack, you too good to drink with me now? Why did I chase after Jack all those months, wanting his friendship? He already told me what he thought of me, that night at the Triangle. And yet I continued to chase after him. Like a puppy. Like me, please like me. What an ass. No wonder he tries to stay away from me now.

He continued down between the rows of columns toward the rear of the deck, past the other work going on, carpenters building forms and electricians pulling wires and the concrete crew finishing up pouring one of the columns and plumbers checking a floor drain. All of it seemed pointless to him, a lot of fuss and bother over nothing. Everybody taking themselves so seriously, everybody looking out for number one; and yet somehow the building got built. Almost in spite of their efforts, or so it seemed at times. He was through worrying about it, through with knocking himself out trying to do a good job. It wasn't worth it. What did it get him? From now on he was just going to go with it, go with the flow, float along like everybody else.

What's the use of trying to do a good job? What's the use of trying anything? It just gets screwed up anyway. The world does with you what it wants to. For a while when I first started seeing Pamela I thought my life had changed, I thought things were really going to be better, but surprise: same old shit. S.O.S. Same old me.

As he got closer to the end of the deck, he could look down across the alley at Pamela's windows. The windows where he had often stood, looking to where he looked from now. His anger at her was gone too. All he felt was a sense of loss, that she was gone, irretrievably, out of his life. He had torn himself apart on account of her, worrying that she might be seeing somebody else. I've been afraid she didn't love me. What kind of love is that? No kind of love at all. I guess I've known it all along but just didn't want to face it. By the same measure, I wonder if I ever really loved her. Seeing her with the guy in the white Continental, supposing that the two of them had been in her apartment when he went to see her, had been the final blow. It confirmed what he had long suspected on some level of his mind, but it had nothing to do with the guy in the white Continental, or anyone else for that matter. He understood now what had been going on all along. None of them was important to her. Not the guy in the white Continental, not the guy from the kung fu studio, not the guys from work or the guys she talked to at bars or the guys she called her friends—none of them. He wasn't either. Only Jack.

Andy Yurick stood up from where he was working on the last column in the row, stretched, and leaned on top of the plywood barricade around the base of the column, his welding hood up and sticking straight out from his forehead.

"All through here, William." Andy took a long drag on a cigarette.

Bill stopped beside the next-to-the-last column in the row. All the work we put into these goddamn columns, and they're all wrong. What a joke. Think of how badly we could have screwed 'em up if we had really tried to. He unhooked his gloves from the clasp on his toolbelt.

"Doesn't make any difference now," Bill said, gazing up at the cage of steel bars rising above the section of scaffolding. Levon came and stood beside him.

"Maybe it doesn't make any difference to you," Andy said, "but it sure as hell makes a difference to me. I've only got one more to go."

Bill wasn't paying attention; he pulled on his gloves, slammed the webs of his thumbs together several times, and started to climb the scaffold.

"What are you doing, Billy?" Crazy Levon said.

"They said we have to fix the candy canes, didn't they?" He wanted to do something, anything; he wanted to keep busy. He wanted to keep from thinking too much. He scrambled up the section of scaffolding, hoisted himself onto the plank across the top, and stood up.

Levon cocked his head to look up at him. "Don't you think we better wait and see what they want us to do about them first? Maybe they'll change their minds or something." Levon looked at Andy to enlist the other man's help.

"What's this about a problem with the candy canes?" Andy Yurick said.

"Hey, what do I know?" Bill said, looking down at Levon and trying to give a clownish shrug, then looking back up at the column again. "They said fix the candy canes, so I'll fix the candy canes. Go with the flow."

On top of the scaffold, he stood at the level where the next floor would be; the cage of reinforcing steel for the second and third lifts of the column towered above him. He took handholds on two of the column ties, the half-inch-diameter bars that enclosed the heavy vertical bars, placed his foot on one of the lower ties, using it as if it were the first rung of a ladder, and started to climb.

"Hey Bill. . . ," Levon said.

"I suppose you know what you're doing," Andy called up to him.

"Hell no, I'm only the foreman, what the hell does the foreman know about anything?" Bill called down, still climbing. "I've only been working rebar now for fifteen, eighteen years, I've only been a foreman for a dozen years, what the hell would I know about reading drawings or placing rebar or what these bars need to hold them in place?" He talked over the rest of what Andy said so he didn't really hear it, something about I wouldn't go climbing on that column if I were you.

You wouldn't do a lot of things I do, Andy, if you were me. You wouldn't be the foreman of a crew of dumbass ironworkers for one thing. You wouldn't let yourself worry about a chickenshit building like this one. You wouldn't let yourself get messed up with a girl you knew from the start was no good for you. . . .

Bill continued to climb, straddling the corner of the column because the footholds were easier, pulling his sleeves and pants legs free when they snagged on the barbs of tie wire. Below, Levon was starting to climb the scaffolding on the other side of the column, scrambling after him, but Bill ignored him.

"Hey, Billy, hold on a minute. Bill."

It's not only that I shouldn't have gotten mixed up with Pamela, the thing that seems so clear to me now and yet so bewildering is that I didn't really want to get mixed up with her in the first place. Part of me didn't. And yet I went on ahead and did it anyway. Why? What was I looking for? What did I think I'd find? Nice, huh? Jack said as I looked at her standing in her window across the alley looking down at us on the deck. You want to meet her, come on, I'll introduce you. This is Bill, I brought him over to look at your cracks.

The Building

Bill was close to the top of the column, thirty feet above the deck; he was barely paying attention to what he was doing, he was only vaguely concerned about where to put his hands and feet, letting his body take care of itself; he certainly wasn't expecting any obstacles over his head when he banged his chromed hardhat into one of the guy wires, slanting down from the top of the column to the deck below.

Son-of-a-bitch!

Holding on to the cage with one hand, Bill took off his hardhat to check the damage. The wire had scraped across the top, the chrome was scratched, he'd have to try polishing it at home tonight to see if that would take off the mark. Damn it to hell. Just my luck. He put the hat back on and looked around. From this height he could see beyond the roof of Pamela's apartment building to the buildings on the next street, and farther up the hill, the streets stacked up the slope of the valley, the cramped little houses with their spiky roofs and staring windows all piled up on top of one another, fighting for space as if to keep from sliding off; he felt as if he were hovering over the jobsite, released somehow from his body, as if he floated above the town on a level with the top of the valley's hills.

She looked at Jack standing on the other side of the bed and said Oh I get it now and he said Get what now? and she said You son-of-a-bitch Jack, I know what you're up to, I know what you're doing and he said I'm not doing anything, it's taking care of itself and she said And what else do you want me to do? And I didn't know what they were talking about then but I do now all right. She might as well have said And what else do you want me to do Jack, fuck him too? And what would you have said Jack, what would you have said?

On the next block in front of Holy Innocents, a car turned the corner, its blinker flashing impatiently as it waited for an old man in the crossing who walked a small black dog; several blocks away on a side street, a little girl carrying a satchel ran up the sidewalk, on her way home from school; an old woman swept her porch, a man in a backyard bent over to look at the foundation of his house. The life of the little town was going on far below him, and no one was aware that he was up here, that he was watching what they were doing. It made him feel secretive and godlike and slightly giddy.

All that time and I didn't see what she was doing, didn't recognize it. She was just using me to get back at Jack for something. For what? Because he didn't love her? Because he brought me over to replace him? Because that's what he did, I can see that now too, he was using me as well to try to get her off his back or take her mind off him or whatever. Whatever, because it doesn't matter now, it didn't matter ever, because I was using the two of them, I was using them to try to make my life different or better, I was trying to live through them instead of living through my own life, I was trying to fill my life with theirs.

On the roof of Pamela's building was the spot where she put the mattress to sunbathe whenever it was warm enough, the mattress on which they made love that day and evening late last fall; it seemed ages ago now, the sun warm on their bodies, afraid the whole time, or at least he was, that someone farther up the hill could see them. Afraid. Always afraid of something with her. From where he dangled on the steel column, her apartment windows below appeared blank. Empty. At least for me. How much time he had spent—Wasted time—watching those windows—I've been such a fool—keeping an eye on them—Weak—checking them every minute or so that he was on the deck. Sad. What had he been looking for? Pathetic. What had he hoped to see? Dumb. But he knew the answer to that now too.

All those times I kept looking at her windows, I wasn't looking for a sign of her, I didn't want to see her, I was looking for a sign that she was looking at me, I wanted to know if she was watching me. They were using me because they were in love, I was just caught in the middle, and it doesn't matter because we were all using each other, I'm not mad at her now because what she did was no worse than what I did to her, I forgive her and I guess I forgive Jack too and I wish I could forgive myself for ever hurting Mary or at least hurting my ability to love her.

His leg was aching, from his weight resting on it as he clung to the column. He was getting cold too, there was a breeze, a chill wind on a spring day; the heavy sky looked as though it could snow if it got much colder. Funny how things change, this morning it was warm, even sunny for a while, you never know. He started to climb higher, to reach the candy canes at the very top of the cage, tried to work his way around the guy wire, but the slanting wire crowded him, there was no easy path around it. You're in my way, wire. Useless with the column welded anyway, unnecessary. Like me, I guess, hah. You're gone, you're outta here, you're history. Holding on again with one hand, Bill took his clippers from his holster and cut the guy wire beside him, wrenching the clippers back and forth to cut through the heavy wire, then reached around the column and cut one of the wires on the other side as well. The wires fell limp, the second one brushing past Levon who stood on top of the scaffold, looking up at Bill, waiting to see what he was going to do.

"Headache!" Bill said as Levon ducked, the joke being that the warning was too late.

Below on the deck, Andy Yurick looked up, horror-struck, as the wire hit the concrete slab. "Oh Jesus, Bill!"

This column isn't welded. Shit.

The column started to lean slowly in Bill's direction, his weight at the top pulling it that direction, as if the column would keep coming and topple over with Bill underneath it, would fall on him—No, stop, don't, don't let this happen, no!—but as the cage of reinforcing steel leaned farther, Levon was already climbing as fast as he could up the opposite side of the column, anticipating the pull of the column and leaning back against it, trying to counterbalance Bill's weight on the other side, trying to pull the column back toward himself and away from Bill. And for a moment it seemed to work. The column stopped leaning and slowly straightened up again, stood upright, paused a second or two, then slowly kept on going, this time leaning toward Levon's side, leaning farther in that direction, far enough to finally come to rest against the top of the wood form for the concrete.

"Whoa!" Bill said, riding on the top side now. He looked down around at Levon on the underside and managed to grin. "Wow, for a minute I thought we were goners." Jesus H. Christ!

"Get your ass down from there!" Levon called to him. "If this thing starts to tip back again, I don't know if I can stop it!"

But the small tack welds at the base of the column of reinforcing steel were never intended to hold the weight of the heavy bars under stress, and the scaffold around the lower third of the column wasn't braced separately from the column itself, there were only a couple stubby two-by-fours inside the scaffold wedged against the wood form for the concrete, with only small inch-and-a-half cement dobies inside the form to keep the cage of reinforcing steel from resting against the wood; and after the column continued to lean against the top of the wood form for another second or two, before the two men clinging to the cage, one at the top and the other halfway up the opposite side, could do anything to prevent what was happening or climb down to safety, the dobies inside the form cracked and crumbled and the two-by-four braces snapped and the square of scaffolding began to tip and the wood form splintered and broke open as the column kept on going in the direction it had started, only faster now, the tons of top-heavy steel leaning farther and farther until there was no question now that it was going to fall on the concrete deck, that nothing could stop it now, Bill riding it down from on top, Levon slung from the underbelly, the column set to fall on him when it hit, the two men silent though there were shouts from the other men on the deck who looked up and saw what was happening and couldn't do a thing about it except try to get out of the way, the descent of the column at one and the same time irrevocably fast and immeasurably slow, like the felling of a tall stately steel tree, Levon, his face full of terrible intent, busily trying to swing himself around to the side of the column so he would be out from under it until, as the welds on the bottom snapped unevenly and the ties and the hairpins and the candy canes broke free of the heavy vertical bars, the column began to rotate on its axis, the vertical bars fanning out at the bottom, kicking free of the wood form, the column even as it continued its plunge appearing to take a step or two, as if the whole thing might walk at a tilt across the deck, the twisting mass of metal bars just beginning to look as if it would throw Bill clear as it fell, before it collapsed finally, splayed out like giant jackstraws, and then the noise.

27

Pamela told him once that on days like this when she was younger, gray spring days when there was a chill in the air and the sky was heavy, when the leaves from the previous fall were still on the ground even as the shoots of crocuses and daffodils and hellebores broke through, she would put on her favorite jacket—it was called a barracuda; he remembered she told him that when she was in high school she loved that jacket even more than her Furnass Stokers cheerleader jacket—and go to the park. Yeah, that's what it was called, a barracuda. Hell of a thing to call a jacket. Would putting it on make her a man-eater? Is a barracuda a kind of shark? Another thing I'm probably supposed to know and don't. So sue me. Add it to the list. It was a large park, a block or so square, up the hill from the main street, built on terraces with a lot of steps because it was on the slope of the hill. In the center was a statue of a Civil War soldier; people in town, if they noticed the statue at all at this point, knew it as a Yankee cavalryman, but Pamela had her own idea, she told Jack she thought it was a Confederate spy dressed up as a Yankee. That's Pamela. Never take anything at face value. Don't go along with it just because everybody else does. Crazy kid. A lot like me. Forget about it. Stop thinking about her. She's no concern of yours now. There would be a lot of other kids in the park after school, playing football or throwing Frisbees or just hanging out around the statue. A lot of kids went to the park to do drugs. Hate to think of her exposed to drugs at that age. I mean I guess I've tried about everything at one time or another, uppers, downers, sideways, backwards, but that was different. She was lucky. No, she was Pamela, she'd have her own thinks on that too. She told me I smoked reefer a couple of times and giggled a lot but I decided I liked the world too much to be away from it for even that long. Pamela. I wonder if Marcy did drugs at that age. Another thing I should have protected her from and couldn't, add it to the list. A different list. But even though the park was close to the center of town, with houses facing it on all sides, there were areas that seemed totally isolated, small groves of trees and bushes where she wasn't aware of anything else around her, where she would go for walks as the dark day grew darker, not really kicking the soggy leaves but listening—she said when she described it to him—to the *swish swish swish* of her footsteps, listening to the sounds of herself passing by. It was an image Jack often thought of, whenever he thought of Pamela.

I can see her at dusk walking across the grass through the leaves with her hands in her pockets, the pockets of her barracuda, there's the smell of old leaves in the air and down the hill are all the lights along the main street, the mills were working then, the main street was crowded with cars from the changing shifts and farther down the hill the blast furnaces glowed along the dark river, clouds of smoke billowing up into the night sky, but in the park it's quiet, there's only the sound of her footsteps swishing through the dead leaves and in the distance behind her the sound of other kids calling to each other in the darkness as she passes through the circle of light from a streetlight and leaves the park, crosses the brick street and heads home alone along the empty sidewalks through the shadows of the bare trees—I got to cut this out before I drive myself crazy. It's bad enough I'm driving to see my wife.

In his pickup on I-79, Jack headed north toward Franklin and the mountains in the upper part of the state. Trying not to think about Pamela. Without much success. It was one of the things that made Pamela different from other women he had known; he could remember all sorts of little things about her, remember the times they had been together, her touch—not only remember things but couldn't forget them. That's sad. The only things I can ever remember about Ellie are all the fights we've had, all the arguments and hassles and all her moaning all the time, oh boo-hoo. The rest of the time she's just there. Like a hemorrhoid. Like breathing. He could remember the imprint of Pamela's body against him when she tucked herself up under his arm, and the softness of her hand in his when they sat on her couch watching a football game or spooky movie, and the curve of her buttocks against his crotch and thighs when he came into her from behind—Ah for shit's sake stop it! He slammed the side of his fist against the steering wheel; the rim vibrated violently, giving off a low hum, the scratches on the back of his hand burned.

She's the first girl, the first woman, I ever let get to me this way. No, I didn't have anything to do with it, it just happened. She's the first one I don't like being away from. The first one ever. Shit, if I didn't know better I'd say I missed her. Ha. Me. I never missed anyone in my life. No, I miss her, all right. Think of that. I miss her. Pamela.

Dumb, to ever let himself start thinking this way. What did he think was going to happen—what did he think *could* happen— if they had continued to see each other? Play touchy-feely all their lives? Besides everything else, he wasn't going to be around that much longer anyway. He would certainly die before she did, it wasn't right to cut off her chances to meet someone closer to her own age; it wasn't fair to saddle her with someone as old as himself.

No, he had been right to break it off with her when he did. Even to introduce her to Bill. He thought the two of them could have some laughs together, he thought Bill could help Pamela forget about him. How did he know that Bill would mess himself up so badly on account of her? At the time he hadn't had much choice either, it got to the point that he had to do something. She had started coming at him, just like everybody else, after they had been seeing each other for a while. Why couldn't she leave well enough alone? Why did she have to start picking at him, pushing him, why did she have to go and spoil everything? She turned out to be like every other female after all, always wanting more. Why couldn't she be content with what he gave her?

All I said was there's a really great specialist up in Pittsburgh who can maybe help you with your arthritis. What's so wrong about that?

I don't need any specialist up in Pittsburgh. I don't need anybody sticking their nose into my business about my health. How'd you find out about it anyhow?

About your arthritis? About the fact that you get crippled up so badly sometimes that you can hardly move?

Yeah, what business is it of yours?

I looked up your records at the hospital, if you must know.

What records?

The Building

The time you came in for a cortisone shot. It must have been right after you started working on the building because it was before I knew you. I was thinking about you one evening and just for the hell of it I looked you up on the computer and there you were.

Are you happy now?

No I'm not happy. I'm concerned about you. Jack, I'm a nurse. It's my nature to be concerned about people. Especially people I love. I want to know what's wrong with you.

So I told her about the time I had trouble a year or so ago with all the knots on my arms and legs and my joints started to freeze up but I made a funny story out of it, I told her about how I had a laborer push me around in a wheelchair and I still surprised Mac by bringing the building in ahead of schedule, I expected her to laugh but she just sat across from me here in the truck with a blank look on her face until I was finished and then she said Why do you always think everything depends on you? Why do you always think you're responsible for everybody else?

Because that's my job.

But you're ill, you've been ill.

I'm not *ill*, as you call it. I'm not even sick.

What are you ashamed of? Don't you think people ever get sick?

I told you, I'm not sick. Maybe I was sick then but I'm not sick now.

Why can't you let somebody help you?

Why would I need help?

Because everybody needs help at some time or other. If for no other reason, people get older and can't do as much.

I'm not going to get old. I'm going to break before I wear out.

What's the matter, Jack? Are you afraid of getting old? Or are you just afraid?

Me? Afraid? What the hell would I be afraid of?

Maybe you're afraid you'll find out you really care about me instead of just wanting to fuck me—he veered sharply, the turnoff already past, bouncing across the berm and gravel, down through a drainage ditch and across a small embankment, the pickup fishtailing on the grass, cars in all directions honking at him, up onto the pavement of the off-ramp and around a bend toward the golden arches of a McDonald's. He parked in the lot and, ignoring the stares of the people who had seen him leaving the interstate— What's the matter, haven't you ever seen a crazy man before?— went inside to look for a phone.

*

"How you doing?" he said gruffly into the receiver, before she even said hello.

"I'm okay. Where are you calling from?"

"Some pay phone. There's a lot of noise."

"Sounds like you're in the middle of a tunnel."

"Yeah. Marcy there?"

"You want to speak to her?"

"No, I was just wondering if she was there, that's all."

"She hasn't moved out yet, if that's what you're wondering. It isn't as if she's going to throw her things in a suitcase and leave overnight."

"I know that. I was just wondering."

"So, why are you calling, Jack?"

"I was worried about you."

"Of course you were," she laughed a little.

"Don't start it, Ellie."

"I'm not starting anything."

"I was worried about you, I wanted to know how you were doing after you called this morning. That's why the sound's bad, I'm right off the interstate."

"What were you doing on the interstate?"

"I'm on my way up to see you."

"Of course you are, Jack."

"Well, it's the truth. I left the job early. Bunch of bullshit anyway. I finished everything that had to be done, just about everything. Mac tells me we're going to walk off the project so I figured to hell with it. I thought I'd come up and see you. I know you're worried about Marcy."

"That's a load of crap, Jack Crawford. A load of crap."

"You trying to tell me you're not worried about Marcy? And Little Jack?"

"No, of course I'm worried about them. But there's nothing new in that. It's a load of crap that you were coming to see me."

"I am. I'm already at Mars. That's where I'm calling from."

"If you were coming to see me, you would just come, Jack. You wouldn't stop and call me and tell about it. Remember, this is your wife you're talking to. Not one of your girlfriends. You would just come."

That stopped him. She's right. As usual. I would have just showed up on the doorstep. My doorstep. Ours. If that's where I was going. The more surprise the better. Hey I'm home. What do you mean, what am I doing here? I own this place, don't I? I pay for you to sit around here all day and watch soap operas, why shouldn't I come to my own home? Now how about getting me something to eat, and get dressed, we're going honky-tonking to-night, don't give me no back talk. He leaned against the partition beside the phone, the toe of one work boot resting on the toe of the other.

"What's the matter, Jack?" she said after a minute or so.

"I'm thinking, that's all."

"I mean, what's the matter? That you're calling?"

"Nothing's the matter. If I was any better I'd have to charge admission."

"I don't believe that either. Because this isn't like you. Something's got to be really bothering you. For you to call me like this."

"You don't think I'm concerned about my own family?"

"I know you can be, Jack. I know that if you thought I was really in trouble or if I was really upset about something, you'd be here in a flash."

"Yeah, I would." You're damn right I would.

"Yes, you would. But about Marcy moving out, you're the one who's most upset about it, not me. I was perfectly content before she moved back home, as much as I love her and Little Jack, and I'll be perfectly fine after they leave. We all know you're the one who won't be able to handle seeing her and the boy go. That's why Marcy plans to be gone before next weekend, when you'd normally come up."

"If we walk off this job, I'll be up there sooner."

"Maybe, and maybe not. But it won't be because of me, and it won't be because of Marcy. You could no more stand to see that girl and Little Jack get into a car and drive off than you could fly. So why are you calling now, Jack?"

I don't have to listen to this crap. "See ya later."

"Jack's all-purpose 'See ya later.' You always were good at leaving."

"It's a good thing I left the project when I did today. I was afraid I was going to lose it and pop some guy."

"But you didn't, did you?"

"No. I told you, I left instead."

"So it sounds like you weren't close to losing it at all. The Jack Crawford I know usually goes on ahead and hits somebody if he's going to. You were enough in control of yourself to get out of there. That's what I mean. You never have any trouble leaving someplace where you don't want to be. Me, I was always good at staying put."

"A mismatched couple."

"No, I'd say made for each other. It worked out for our mutual advantage. For you, you've got me right where you want me. Up here in the mountains, tucked away all nice and neat so you can come and visit whenever it suits your fancy, and then leave again as soon as you get tired of being here."

"You don't sound like you're suffering."

"No, that's what I mean. It's what we both want, isn't it? I was never the physical sort, we both know that. Oh, I liked what we used to do in bed and all, it was nice, but I never liked it all that much, not the way you did. I used to feel guilty about not liking it more, but then I realized that wasn't what you want from me anyway. You want me just to be here, not because you want to be with me or because you want to touch me. You want me to be around, preferably in the background, but close enough that you can get to in case you want to talk to somebody, or when you have to let go for a while. When I first realized it I was hurt, but I also realized there's nobody else like me in your life. Because you can get the sex you want anywhere, but not every-body's going to be content to be your ice queen up here in the mountains—"

"Don't talk like that about yourself, Ellie." She's right, isn't she?

"It's okay, I know I'm not one of the warm people of the world. Right now we have the perfect arrangement because most of the time all I am to you is a voice on the telephone. That's what you need me to be. The beauty of it is, I don't want anything more from you. I like to be alone, I don't want other people around me—not my husband, not my daughter, not even my grandson. All of you: come visit me once in a while, then leave me alone again. Leave me in peace."

She said our sex was *nice*? "Ellie . . ."

"Go on, Jack. Don't worry about me. Have fun with your girl-friends. Of course if you ever need to come up here, that's a different story. I want you to come in that case. Otherwise, I'll see you next weekend, that'll be soon enough. For both of us."

As he tried to think of what to say—Need to go see her? What kind of a wimp does she think I am? What the hell am I doing out here on the interstate? I got a job that needs looking after—she said, "Jack?"

"Yeah?"

"Take care of yourself, okay?"

"You know me."

"Yes, I know you. That's why I said it. Take care of yourself."

"You too. See ya later."

"See ya later."

*

. . . and I still haven't told Chucky to move his pipes and I still have to get Chalmers his new goddamn hose, but if we're not going to be on the project after today I guess none of that matters anyway. But that's no way to take care of things, to let them slide, Mac would never do that, but Mac had me to take care of them for him. That's what I need, a Jack Crawford to keep me straight, oh sure, next time I run across one I'll snag him. The first thing I've got to do is find Nicholson and find out what he said about those candy canes in the columns. How come every-thing has to come apart so easily? If everybody would just do their goddamn jobs. And what got into the kid inspector this afternoon anyway, trying to stand up to me like that all of a sudden? Way to go Greggory, fine time to decide you're going to be a man. Bet everyone's going to be surprised to see me, proba-bly figured I was gone for the weekend, probably find them all sitting around with their thumbs up their asses. . . .

As he crossed the viaduct on Ohio River Boulevard, over the mouth of the valley on his way back to the job, he caught a glimpse of some flashing red lights somewhere in the town below, somewhere along the main street, near his building as a matter of fact, but he didn't think anything about it; there were a lot of elderly people in Furnass, which meant there were always ambulances charging up and down the main street, emergency lights flashing, on their way to or from the hospital, another old woman who fell and broke her hip or an old guy with a heart attack. What's the matter Jack, you afraid of getting old? You're damn right but she didn't have to know that. As he came down the off-ramp into the lower end of town and the beginnings of the main drag, past the Triangle Tavern across some empty lots, he heard the sirens from farther uptown, but he didn't think anything of that either, only that there must be a fire someplace, or that maybe the police finally decided to do something about the low-lifes and drug pushers who haunted a couple of the alleys. It's about time. As he headed up the hill from the lower end, he could see his building, towering over the rest of the town, but he still couldn't tell that anything was out of the ordinary—then as he passed through the crook in the main street, he could see that something was wrong. Very wrong. The street in front of the building was blocked with fire trucks and ambulances and police cars; a policeman stood in the intersection at Twelfth Street directing cars away, down the hill to the backstreets; on the top deck of the building men were running back and forth along the guardrail and the boom of the crane was swinging over to make a pick . . . and there was something else too . . . something that wasn't right—

Holy Christ, one of the columns is gone, what happened to the column?

The cars in front of him had slowed almost to a crawl, the drivers wondering which way they were supposed to go and rubbernecking to see what was going on. With nothing coming toward him in the other lane, Jack swung out around the line of cars in front of him and sped past them, laying on the horn. The cop at the intersection saw him coming and blew his whistle, gesturing wildly for Jack to stop, but Jack drove on past him, into the next block. When he couldn't go any farther because of the fire trucks and ambulances blocking the street, he angled his truck into the opposite curb and ran on, leaving the motor running and the door standing open, his jacket flapping about him, pushing bystanders out of the way, past the police and firemen standing around outside the gate and on inside, past the other workmen watching the cage of the manhoist climb up the side of the building. Jack bellowed for the cage to stop and come back and get him but it kept on going. He whirled around and grabbed Sloopy.

"What happened? What happened?"

"It fell, Jack," Sloopy stammered, trying to hold his hardhat on his head as Jack shook him. "Something fell."

Jack let him go and ran over to the manhoist and rang the page bell repeatedly, then picked up a piece of angle iron and beat on the framework of the hoist, the sound clanging up the height of the metal tubes, but the cage, at the top of the building now, stayed where it was. When he stepped back he saw Marshall looking down over the guardrail.

"Bring that fucking cage down here and take me up!" Jack shouted.

At his elbow, Sloopy said, "It can't, Jack, it can't. It's bringing the hurt men down." Sloopy looked as if he was going to cry.

Jack looked around wildly as Gregg came through the gate and ran over to him.

"What happened?" Gregg said. "What fell?"

"Jesus Christ, get the hell out of here!" Jack said.

"But I—"

"I said get the hell out of here! Now!" When Gregg continued to stand there, Jack made a move toward him, the piece of angle iron still in his hand. Gregg stumbled backwards and hurried out the gate through the crowd.

When Jack was sure Gregg was gone, he said to Sloopy, "You let me know if he comes back."

"Yes sir, Jack," Sloopy said. "This ain't no place for no inspector now, is it? This is just for us, isn't it? The working people."

Yeah, Sloopy, just for us. Just for us.

The cage at the top of the building bobbed up and down as it was being loaded. In a few minutes it began its slow rattly descent. Jack had the door on the docking platform open and ready as the manhoist came to the bottom but he was pushed out of the way by the medics and firemen who came out of the cage and by those who came forward to help. Inside were two stretchers standing at an angle. Levon was strapped onto the first stretcher they brought out the door. His face and the front of his jacket were covered with blood; his arm was bent unnaturally and he appeared unconscious, or worse. When they unloaded the second stretcher there were too many people clustered around for Jack to see who was on it.

"Who is it? Who is it?" Jack yelled as he ran after them. As the medics pushed through the crowd gathered outside the gate, he caught a glimpse of Bill's crushed face.

Damn it damn it damn it damn it. . . .

The crowd in the street had grown to a hundred or more; the police were having trouble getting people out of the way. In a blind rage, before he knew what he was doing, Jack picked up a four-by-eight sheet of plywood from a stack inside the gate and hurled it at them, bellowing, "Get away from here, everybody get the hell away from here!" The plywood wavered through the air, landed on its corner and danced a few feet, then fell with a *Whoosh!* sending up a cloud of dust as it barely missed several bystanders. For a moment the crowd was stunned, then they scrambled to get back out of the way. Jack picked up another sheet of plywood and heaved it after the first.

"Everybody get away from this building! Goddamn people, haven't you seen somebody hurt before? Goddamn people. . . ."

Two policemen started in the gate to stop him but before they could reach him Jack picked up another sheet and hurled it at them as well, scattering the men. As the policemen started toward him again Jack picked up a two-by-four and wielded it as a club, standing there with his shirt hanging out and his pants legs bunched up around the top of his boots and his hardhat cockeyed on his head, ready for them—Yeah, come on, come on, what are you going to do about it?—when George the labor foreman stepped in front of him.

"Leave it, Jack. Put it down now and come on."

"You tell me one goddamn reason why."

"Because this isn't going to help anything. Because we need you here, not sitting in jail."

Jack felt the air go out of him. He lowered the two-by-four and sat down on the edge of the stack of plywood, suddenly overwhelmingly tired. The elderly labor foreman turned to the policemen and motioned with his head.

"Go on now, leave him alone. Those are friends of his, they work together, you know how it is. Everything's under control now."

The policemen looked relieved not to have to deal with the crazy construction worker and went back outside the gate. Beyond the fence came the sound of the ambulance pulling away, the scream of the siren against the storefronts along the narrow street. Overhead, pigeons wheeled frantically against the leaden sky. George came over and stood beside Jack.

"I should have been here, George," Jack said, staring at the ground in front of him. I'll never forgive myself.

George unfolded his hands from beneath the bib of his overalls and touched him on the shoulder. "You're here now. That's all that counts now. Come on, we've got things to take care of."

PART FOUR

The Building

. . . and the afternoon wears on in the valley, and the river continues to wear away its channel between the hills, as it has since the last finger of a glacier scraped the valley from the landscape before retreating again, the farthest reaches of the Ice Age . . . the river flows on as darkness gradually settles over the town, the days growing longer here in early spring though the evenings still come too soon for most people, those who, after the dark days of winter, anticipate the longer warmer days toward summer . . . the sky turns from dirty gray to dirty black, a starless night because of the layer of clouds that fits like a lid over the valley's hills, though above the ridgeline across the river there is a touch of red, a slight glow, from the lights of Pittsburgh ten miles or so to the south, and to the west a flickering orange from a mill still in operation at Wyandot or somewhere farther down the Ohio River . . . the streets of the town are empty, only an occasional car passing along the main drag where earlier this afternoon the street was choked with emergency vehicles because of the accident on the building under construction . . . the events of the day, at the time so momentous, so life-changing, having flowed on, wearing their way into the channels of consciousness of those who live in the town . . . in their homes people are settling down now to eat and watch the evening news, watching for pictures of the accident to find out more of what happened and if anyone was hurt and perhaps catch a glimpse of someplace or someone they know, "Oh look! Look! There's what's-his-name" . . . the story of what happened in town today being told and retold, lived and relived, in the minds of those whose lives are one with the life of the town, the story changing as it goes, wearing the course of its channel deeper and wider depending upon who is doing the telling and living, the story-now and the story-then and the story-to-be like the lights of the town reflecting on the river, skeins of silver that spread and unravel and drift away and form again into new shapes on the black surface of the water as the river continues on

Richard Snodgrass

. . . as the consequences of what happened today on the construction site continue on as well, setting up their own ripples in the lives of those the accident affects, either directly or indirectly, in some cases the effect of an effect of an effect, impacting their lives nonetheless, the effects discernible but not necessarily predictable beforehand, the event-then considered to cause the event-to-be, unless the unthinkable is somehow possible, that because of the wrinkles of time or the nature of consciousness the event-to-be was somehow already included in the event-then, time-then and time-to-be actually one and the same, the apparent chain of events not linear at all, the possibility that the event-to-be could occur even before the event-then, as if the events-to-come of our story happened prior to the events-that-happened, as if the river never flowed on at all but was always the same river, the All not Many but One . . . as in his office long after everyone else has gone home, Dickie Sutcliff looks over the documents establishing his limited partnership with Julian Lyle for the Furnass Towers office and apartment building, searching for any possible evidence of liability on his part, and satisfied that he had in fact covered himself sufficiently as the silent partner and is free and clear no matter what happens to the building now, thinks about the accident today—he wasn't in his office at the time, he was out at Seneca Towne Centre, his townhouse and shopping-plaza development in the hills beyond Furnass, playing racquetball with Pamela DiCello, but his employees filled him in about what happened when he got back to town—shakes his head and thinks that the accident is the coup de grâce for the project, finishing off what the failure of Sycamore Savings and Loan started, that it's apparently impossible for Julian to have good fortune with a project, says out loud, "Maybe it's in the Lyle genes, the poor dumb fuck," wonders momentarily why he allowed himself to get involved in such a business deal with Julian in the first place, wonders if he suffered an uncharacteristic twinge of generosity toward a guy he *grew up with on Orchard Hill, wonders if he felt sorry for him, a scary thought for a businessman with a reputation like Dickie Sutcliff's, but smiles to himself—No, he tells himself, looking at himself in the dark glass of his office window, you don't have to worry, you're not getting sentimental on us—remembers that there was history involved, precedent as it were: after Julian's father led the family business, the Keystone Steam Works, into failure and bankruptcy, it was Dickie's father, Harry Sutcliff, in an effort to jump-start his realty business, who brokered the deal to sell the buildings and property to Buchanan Steel, the deal that made Sutcliff Realty, gave Dickie's father the resources to start his housing developments for the workers flooding into town to work in the mills during World War II, Dickie being aware, almost guiltily so, or as much as Dickie would ever allow himself to feel such a thing, that Julian's father was always grateful to Dickie's father for coming up with the idea for the deal and working it in such a way that the Lyles got some income from it, unaware that Dickie's father actually made a killing out of it, says to his secret sharer in the dark glass, "It must be genetic, there are those born to be kicked, and there are those born to do the kicking," as he winks to his reflection, "And today I'm happy to be alive and kicking," aware that even as he signed on to become part of the Furnass Towers development he was banking on the prospect that Julian would fail as he had with every other thing he had ever attempted, feeling on account of it not guilt but despite himself some compunction to take care of Julian, as one might feel, he thinks after kicking a dog in the middle of the night that you knew was there but ended up kicking regardless, thinking "The poor dumb bastard," and, Dickie being Dickie, already thinking of how he can take advantage of the failure of Furnass Towers for his own purposes, saying to the sharer in the glass, "It's almost like it's a family tradition" . . . as earlier this evening in another Sutcliff Realty development in Seneca, this one a gated*

*community called Seneca Pines, John Bagley, founder and pres-
ident of Sycamore Savings and Loan, walks his wife Monica and
eleven-year-old daughter Jessica through the kitchen and out the
entryway to the garage, saying, "No, you two go on ahead, I'm
not in the mood tonight, there's just too much going on at work,"
and Monica says, "Come on, John, it would do you good," and
Jessica says, "Please, Daddy, please," and Monica says, "It'll
help take your mind off what all's going on, you know you always
loved the story of the Wizard of Oz and they say this musical
version is wonderful," and Jessica says, "Please, Daddy, we're
not in Kansas anymore," and John cups the girl's head and
smiles, "No, Dorothy, we're certainly not in Kansas anymore,"
and then to both of them, "But not this time, you'll have more
fun without me, and I've got some things to do here, now you
have to get going or you'll never make the curtain, parking in
downtown Pittsburgh can be tricky," and Monica looks at him
one more time and kisses his cheek and his wife and daughter get
in the car and John stands and watches as they back out, calling
to them, "Be careful, have a good time!" watches as the car turns
and starts down the drive, the taillights and the darkness cut off
from view by the lowering garage door, goes back in the house
and, after getting what he'll need from the linen closet, goes
through the house and out the patio doors to the swimming pool,
which stands empty now, drained for winter, climbs down the
ladder and sits himself beside the drain at what would be the deep
end of the pool, thinking at least this will be easier to clean up,
wraps his head in a bath towel to help contain the splatter, takes
the .45-caliber automatic he bought as protection from the death
threats he began to receive a few weeks ago from angry depositors
when it was evident the direction that things were going to go and
puts it to his head thinking I have to do this fast—thinking in a
split second, Shit I was going to make a sign to warn Monica to
keep Jess away from the pool, I even screwed that up—as he pulls*

The Building

the trigger . . . *as in the cavernous First City Bank on the corner of Eleventh Street in Furnass, arguably the center of the little town, after locking the door behind the last teller to leave after the Friday evening hours, tonight an especially busy time, Harvey McMillan, manager of First City, sits in his glass-walled office on the platform, going over the initial reports of today's activities, checking among other things to make sure that the shortfalls from Sycamore Savings and Loan won't have a crippling effect on his bank's resources, making sure he hasn't missed something during the last six times he's checked since he became aware of the depth of Sycamore's problems, but no, his previous assessments are correct, it's unfortunate of course that it seems inevitable that Sycamore will go under but the sorry truth is that his bank is profiting from it, things never looked rosier, folks are taking their money from what's left of Sycamore and walking down the street and putting it in First City, the bank has gained more than fifty new depositors in the last two days, and there will undoubtedly be more if Sycamore dares to open its doors come Monday, closes the ledgers and locks the reports in the center drawer of his desk and turns out the light, leaves his office and walks through the dark empty bank, the tall two-story center lobby, past the marble columns under the vaulted ceiling, the ornate brass teller windows and the inlaid marble floor, the building built as a temple to commerce during the days when money flowed from the activities of the mills along the river, peeks out the ornate grillwork on the front doors to make sure no one is waiting to jump him when he steps outside, then sets the final alarm and hurries out the doors, locks them behind him and heads to his car parked at the curb, glancing up the dark sidewalk toward the construction site for Furnass Towers in the next block, thinks about the accident today and the rumor he heard that it had something to do with code violations and will require major repairs, thinks that now that Sycamore is down the tubes any refinancing will more than likely*

• *305* •

be done through First City, starts the car and backs out of the space and heads down the empty street, thinking Wow, even that's working in my favor at the moment, when Lady Fortune smiles on you . . . knowing the bank will never reach the level of its glory days when the mills were working and paydays made the bank the social hub of the town but as the only financial institution in Furnass now First City is going to do okay for itself, at least until he reaches his retirement which is foremost in his mind regardless, circles the block and heads toward Eleventh Street Hill which will take him out of the valley to his home in Furnass Heights, the older, at one time exclusive suburb along the crest of the valley's rim, the grand stone house on six acres of land that once belonged to the president of Buchanan Steel and now belongs to him, remembering in his own fashion the line from Joseph Campbell that he read in college and never understood until he got older, Everything you do is evil to somebody, wishing the world wasn't such that his good fortune was coming from the bad fortune of others, but unable to stop grinning . . . as in his study at the rectory of Graystone Church in the Pittsburgh suburb of Drumlins, only five miles or so away from Furnass as the crow flies but worlds apart from the struggling mill town, the Reverend Bryce Orr sits at his desk with Satan The Cat on his lap, humming along with Charlie Parker's "Now's The Time" from the original Savoy recording of the 1940s, with Dizzy on trumpet and Max Roach on drums, tapping time on Satan's head—the cat would prefer to be scratched between its ears but it'll take whatever it can get—as he thinks about the story of the accident on the building under construction in Furnass that he saw on the news tonight, thinking it must be Julian Lyle's project, the one Julian told him about a year or so ago the last time they saw each other, a chance meeting at a funeral, Julian his best friend growing up on Orchard Hill or at least his closest one, their houses side by side near the college, and thinks Julian, Julian, Julian, thinks of himself making a pastoral visit to his hometown, sees himself in his mind's eye walking through the musty foyer and across the deserted grand lobby of the Alhambra Theater, up the anything-but-grand staircase to the top of the balcony and then down the steep steps to where Julian sits by himself in the second row, looking out over the patchwork ceilings of his failed Shoppers Bazaar at the blank screen of the old theater, takes a seat in the row behind him, "I thought I'd find you here," and Julian says without turning around to look at him, "It wouldn't take much detective work to figure that out," and Bryce says, "The TV said there was a report that they were working on the columns, including the one that fell, even though the contractor was going to walk off the project," and Julian says, "I wasn't given official notification from the contractor that they were abandoning the project, but yes, I had heard that was their intention," and Bryce says, "And the only reason why I can think of that a contractor would simply walk off a project would have to do with not getting paid," and Julian doesn't say anything, he only shrugs, looks back across the expanse of the auditorium at the screen glowing softly in the darkness as Bryce continues, "And you told me way back over a year ago that you were having trouble securing the money to complete the project," and Julian looks back at him and says, "It doesn't help when the primary lender is itself going belly-up," and Bryce settles back in his seat, feeling secure that he has sufficiently loaded his moral gun, "So you went ahead and let the contractor keep working on the building today, even though you knew the project was going to come to a screeching halt because of your money problems," and Julian says, "I didn't stop them from what they were going to do, if that's what you mean," and Bryce says, "And as a result a man got killed and another severely injured," and Julian sighs and says, "I'm told the second man's injuries aren't critical," and Bryce says, "But they're bad enough," and Julian says, "Yes, of

*course, they're bad enough, any injuries at all, or deaths . . . ,"
and Bryce says, "You know, don't you, that by just about any
philosophical, ethical, or moral standard you can think of, you're
as responsible for what happened to those men as if you pushed
that column over?" and Julian says, "It wouldn't take much of a
philosopher, ethicist, or moralist to figure that out either," and
Bryce says, "So what do you have to say for yourself?" and Julian
sighs again, looking out again over the dark shell of the old theater, and says, "We do what we can in this world, we do what we
do, who would ever presume to say why?" and Bryce says, "I'm
surprised you think that's a good enough answer," and Julian
says, "Why did you come here, Bryce?" and Bryce says, "Because it's my job to comfort the bereaved, even if they're not,"
but thinks No, that isn't it either; wonders again for the ump-
teenth time what in fact he would say to Julian if he had gone to
see him this evening; he'd probably say in so many words I told
you so; and what would he expect from Julian in response, that
he'd break down and admit that he was sorry—but sorry to
whom?—say that he was wrong and Bryce was right and that he
would change his life?; but Bryce, if he's honest with himself, isn't
sure that's what he wants from Julian either, he has chided and
criticized and moralized at Julian for so long, ever since they
were kids growing up on Orchard Hill, that he can't imagine feeling any other way about Julian; not sure, if he's honest with
himself, that he'd want it any other way, or would know what to
do and how to act if it were any other way . . . as Julian sits in
the balcony of the old theater as he is wont to do of an evening
thinking over the events of the day (sitting in the same seats he
and his friends from Orchard Hill used to sit in when they came
to the theater as teenagers to see* Peyton Place, Pal Joey, Witness
for the Prosecution, *a habit of Julian's now and a trait of character so much in keeping with what Bryce knows about his once-
upon-a-time neighbor that Bryce could guess where Julian would*

*be even if he had never been told) and hears in the audio equiva-
lent to his mind's eye footsteps come down the steps and someone
slide into the row behind him and without bothering to turn
around says, "I figured you'd probably come," and Bryce says,
"Why did you figure that?" and Julian says, "Because I figured
you'd probably come to say I told you so," and Bryce says, "Well,
I did, you know," and Julian sighs and Bryce goes on, "Maybe
not in so many words this time but," and Julian says, "Yes, I
know, you didn't have to know whatever the particulars," and
Bryce says, "Do you also know that by any philosophical, ethical,
or moral standard you can think of you're as guilty of killing that
construction worker as if you pushed the column over on top of
him?" and Julian says, "I know that all too well, but I can't think
about that," and Bryce says, "Can't, or won't?" and Julian says,
"It doesn't make any difference," and Bryce says, "It makes all
the difference in the world," and Julian says, "It doesn't matter,
because if I dwell upon what happened I can't go on," and Bryce
says, "Julian, Julian, Julian, that was always like you," and Julian says, "Why did you come here tonight, Bryce?" and Bryce
says, "Because it's my job to counsel the stricken, to comfort the
bereaved, even if they're not" but only in Julian's thoughts, he
sits alone in the balcony of the dark theater, looking across the
abandoned auditorium at the blank screen luminous in the ghost
light, the single bulb on the floor stand left on the stage, and
addresses the absent Bryce, "Funny, tonight I would have settled
for a friend" . . . as along the bank by the old lock, a raccoon
drags a loaf of bread that it found in a dumpster behind the
Onagona Bakery down to the edge of the water, tears open the
bag and, knowing to do only what it has always done, watches
bewildered as it tries to wash the bread and the bread dissolves in
its paws . . . as in a front yard on Seventh Street a young rabbit
on its first foray hunting for food on its own comes across a
cardboard cutout of an Easter bunny surrounded by a border of*

fake grass and can't make hide nor hair of it, knocks it over in its attempt to determine more about it and scares a cat on a nearby fence which only sees that something moved that shouldn't . . . as on Third Avenue, which is now the first avenue in town after the mills expanded and absorbed First and Second Avenues in the early twentieth century—First Avenue then known as the Avenue of the Seven Oaks before the dust and smoke and grit killed all the trees—a field mouse scurries in the darkness across a bare field close to the river, the lights of the town climbing the slope of the hillside as distant from it as the galaxies of stars are from the residents of the town, the animal unaware that a short time ago this field was the site of Buchanan Steel's pickling shop, hurries on to a hole in the brick wall that once housed the Keystone Steam Works but more recently warehoused two-ton coils of steel wire produced in Buchanan's wire mill, the mouse unaware that in a short time this building too will be demolished and leveled and become a brownfield site, for the time being content in its unknowing as it climbs up the framework of an abandoned generator and finds its path among the fuel lines and carburetors to a vent pipe and makes its way through a series of man-made tunnels to its nest near the fan motor . . . as farther up the river in the woods beside the race of what was once the iron furnace that gave birth to the town a bear recently out of hibernation digs at an opening in the wall of the dry ravine and uncovers an old Indian shrine, sniffs at the artifacts inside, and decides it's no place for a bear . . . and a few miles farther up the river, on the island in midstream known as Crow Island in what was known to the Indians for centuries before the white settlers came as the Valley of the Crows, where for hundreds of years hundreds of the birds have traveled hundreds of miles each evening to roost here during the cold winter months, a solitary crow left here after the others have returned to their usual nests cries out in its sleep

The Building

from a dream of hawks and wakes to find it is alone and takes comfort only in the fact that it is awake now and watching. . . .

28

After Bill and Gregg left Jack's office trailer—after Vince told them that the candy canes in the columns were unacceptable, that they would all have to be corrected, even those in the columns that were already poured—Vince sat at Jack's desk for a while, his hand on the phone; he was in a funk and wanted to call someone.

His first thought was to call Rita; but after the way their earlier phone conversations had gone today he didn't dare. If I need pain in my life that badly, why don't I just step on my foot? He was also past due to call his office to check in with his secretary; the trouble with that idea was that there might actually be some problems that needed attending to, and Vince had had enough problems for one day. I could always call the recorded weather forecast, at least I know that would be a friendly voice, ha ha. Finally he gave up the idea—It's pretty bad when a businessman can't think of anyone to call—and got up to stand in the doorway, his trench coat open and swept back so he could stick his hands in his pants pockets, looking out at the narrow lot in front of the building.

All Cretans lie, said the Cretan. All cretins think they know what's right too. Are you sure there isn't something you're not telling us, Mr. Nicholson? Are you sure we can build the building for what you say? Bill said Hey we're not just talking about this job, we're talking about *my* job, if I go to my company and tell them about these columns I won't have a job, I'll be out on my ass. Too bad, so sad. But it is too bad too, it was his responsibility and he blew it and now he has to pay the price. He's a sacrificial victim to the Vincent J. Nicholson Architectural Memorial Tower. There's an old Italian superstition that says a builder should always throw a stone in the shadow of the first passerby after a building is complete, because the building needs a sacrifice to make it solid. But what kind of worthy sacrifice is a shadow? Maybe the same idea applies to modern buildings with those stories you always hear about of a workman who supposedly falls into the fresh concrete for a bridge pier or building foundation and can't be pulled out in time and drowns and they decide to leave the body in there. As if the spent spirit of a man could somehow make it all worthwhile. Maybe Bill is the spent spirit in this case. Well, welcome to the club, I'm another one. I'm liable to lose my entire company because Julian Lyle was too chummy with the savings and loan. Is that a worthy sacrifice?

Beside the concrete pump in front of the building, the operator in his cowboy hat was washing out a section of the six-inch-diameter hose used to pump the concrete to the upper deck. The operator squirted water into the section of hose, then lifted the end above his head and passed it along hand over hand, being careful not to knock off his hat in the process; the hose arched above him like a giant inchworm as he walked the length of it, chasing the muddy water out the other end. When he was finished, he looked at Vince standing in the doorway of the trailer and grinned.

Why did I reject all the columns when I know the candy canes are probably all right the way they are? Was I out of my mind? Temporary insanity, Your Honor. Well, why not, everybody else seems hell-bent on seeing my building go down the tubes, why shouldn't I save them the trouble? Jack puts his hands through walls, I throw away my life's work. Dumb, huh? But I know nothing will come of my rejecting the columns anyway, except to throw a scare into the ironworkers and maybe teach them a lesson to be more careful next time, all the companies involved will send out their bigwigs and we'll have endless meetings about the problem and eventually I'll appear to reconsider and be convinced by

their assurances and end up accepting the columns after all, I'll
come out of it looking like both a hard-ass and a good guy, a win-
win for me. Take that, Mies, you old cripple, somebody thinks
I'm capable after all. You certainly never did. The Vincent J.
Nicholson Architectural Memorial Tower. No, the fact is this
building was dedicated to you, old man. Jack said After all the
contracts for this building were let you came out with change
orders for twelve different special shapes of brick, most of them
that have to be shaped and finished by hand, you can't tell me
you can't build this building with standard-shape brick like
everybody else, and I said Of course you can but then you end
up with a building that looks like everybody else's. I ordered those
bricks because I wanted the building to have surface and texture
and ornamentation, to get away from the modernists' severity, I
wanted it to be everything that Mies's work was not. Because the
fact is I was never any good at severity, I was never any good at
the Miesian ideals. I was never any good. Arthritic Mies hung on
the cross of his crutches and said If your works are to have life
God must move you from within, from the depths of your soul,
that is where your work and your life are, and it is only there
that you are truly alive. And I went to him afterward, followed
him down the hallway to his office, a room as brooding and as
spare as a monk's cell where he had collapsed into a chair, not
even one of his Barcelona chairs but a plain leather one, panting
from the exertion and the pain, though still able to keep his cigar
lit, the late afternoon Chicago sunlight through the venetian
blinds dividing his body into Miesian segments each precisely one
inch wide, and he looked up at me under his heavy black eyebrows, that granite-chiseled face, and said to me before I could
even say anything to him, Ah Mr. Nicholson, you've come for a
private audience, you've come because you think I pick on you
and that I don't see the value of your work and in your heart you
want to know why I don't like you. And the fact is whether I like

you or don't like you has nothing to do with it, I am here as your teacher and though I'm sure it doesn't appear that way to you I am only trying to help you. I am trying to help you by hurting you, I am trying to save you from yourself, I am trying to save you a lot of agony later on in your life, and I said But I want to be an architect and the old man wheezed, I know you do and perhaps someday you can become one, but what I am trying to tell you is that you are not one now and I don't know that you can become one ever and perhaps you should reconsider before you spend your life flagellating yourself for something that may be beyond you. If you think I am causing you pain now, it will be nothing compared to the pain you will inflict upon yourself if you try and you find you cannot do it. That is all I have been trying to do, Mr. Nicholson, despite what you may think of me. Now I must ask you to leave, I need my rest.

As if any of it mattered now, my ridiculous fantasy of saving the day by reconciling the problem with the columns, my futile attempt to best an old man who is now dead and buried now and wouldn't care even if he were still alive—the contractor is walking off the building, there's no money to finish the project, I'll be lucky now if I'm not drawn into a lengthy and expensive legal battle just to keep my name clean. All of it for what? At the thought of the depth, the hopelessness of the situation, his breath caught, like a sudden drop from a great height. It's like my heart is breaking. Me. Is that deep enough for you, old man? He turned and looked around Jack's office again, looked once more at the phone on the desk—I'll call Rita, no—and left the trailer. As Vince crossed the front lot along the fence, Cowboy, standing on the back of the pump, said, "Bye"; it was then Vince realized that yes, he was in fact leaving the project for the day. Outside the gate, he waited for a few cars to pass, then crossed and headed down the opposite side of the street toward his car. He wanted away from there; he had had enough pain for one day, enough pain to last a lifetime.

He stopped at the trunk of his car and opened it, trying to find a rag to wipe off his shoes. Then he looked at the building back down the street. The building seemed to have nothing to do with him now; the fact was it was Jack's building, and Cowboy's, and Marshall's and Bill's and the rest of the workmen's. They were the people who built it, who lived with it day after day. His building was a dream, a series of drawings on paper, an idea; truth be told, this building of brick and concrete and steel rising above the little town meant no more to him than any other building. He felt as if all his life he had been concerned only with dream stuff.

From this angle, half a block down the street, he could see the columns on the top deck along the front and near side of the building. And as Vince watched, Bill and then a second iron-worker began to climb one of the columns at the rear of the deck. What are they doing? Which column is that? Isn't that the—No. For a moment it didn't register what was happening; then when it did register, it was too late. Isn't that one of the—No—columns we looked at? The column that isn't finished? No. Even when Vince knew for certain that the ironworkers were in danger, that they were making a mistake, he was too far away to be heard if he tried to call out. No, Bill wouldn't do that, why would he do that? He could only watch as Bill climbed to the top of the column, silhouetted against the gray afternoon sky, the column already swaying with his weight, and reached up and cut the guy wires—No. He wouldn't. Why?—he could only watch with a growing sense of dread and disbelief and horror as the top of the column leaned slowly first in one direction and then the other— It's like watching a squirrel that's climbed too far up the top of a tree—the column hesitating momentarily then continuing on, the bars of reinforcing steel splintering and twisting apart as they

fell, Bill and the other ironworker holding on for dear life—
There's one slung underneath its belly like a nursing animal—the
sounds of the crash and the cries of the men and the shudder
along the street coming to him a surprisingly long time (half a
second? a tenth?) after the column dropped from sight onto the
deck.

Who told Bill it was okay to cut the guy wires? For a minute
or so, through the deep dead stillness that immediately followed
the crash, and then the rush of activity afterward, Vince continued to stand there, unable to move. What were they doing up
there anyway? Who told them to climb up there? He came to his
senses when he realized that he shouldn't be seen at a time like
this, that now it was imperative to get away from here. Who told
them that column was safe enough to climb on? Was anyone
hurt? A construction site after an accident is no place for the
architect of record—Those columns have so much steel in them
no wonder it fell over—especially if there are questions about
design criteria: the architect approved putting in the column steel
three floors at a time but shouldn't that be the structural engineer's determination?—or if somebody brings up the fact that
just before the accident he and Bill had had a heated discussion
about the columns. Who told them the welding on that column
was finished? Is everyone okay? Insurance investigators would
soon be swarming over the place, tempers would be hot, things
might be said that could give the wrong idea. He needed to see
what caused the accident—I didn't tell him that—there were
bound to be lawsuits and the telltale evidence would still be
undisturbed—I didn't tell him he had to fix the candy canes right
that minute—but it was best to let things settle down for a day
or two, it was best for him to get away from here. I didn't tell
him anything of the sort. It wasn't my fault.

He closed the trunk and went around to the door and got in
behind the wheel. From the building came the frantic shouts of

workmen on the deck and on the ground calling to each other; traffic was at a standstill in the narrow street, people were running along the sidewalks and between the cars toward the building, crowds were forming. A great honking fire whistle sounded a block or so away, in the distance there were sirens. Vince tried to put the key in the ignition but found his hands were shaking violently. I can't just drive away, I know those men, I don't even know what happened to them, what kind of person am I? He adjusted his sideview mirror to see what was going on, afraid to be spotted from the building. On the top deck, Marshall was directing the boom of the crane, apparently to pick up some of the debris. Now the street was full of emergency vehicles, ambulances and police cars and fire trucks, red lights flashing; traffic was completely tied up, he couldn't move his car if he wanted to. Jack appeared from somewhere down the street, running, shoving people out of his way as he hurried inside the gate.

Please let everyone be all right. Please.

After what seemed an interminable length of time the cage of the manhoist came down from the top deck and medics loaded two stretchers into a waiting ambulance. Please let them be okay. Please don't let anybody die. Oh please Lord. As the sirens screamed again through the narrow streets, there was a new commotion from inside the fence. A sheet of plywood came dancing on edge out of the gate, followed by another and another. Two policemen started inside then retreated just as quickly though Vince couldn't see why. Then a fire truck was moved directly beside Vince's car and boxed him in; all he could see were stacks of hoses and gleaming valves.

Vince slouched against the wheel, his forehead resting against his arms circled on top of the rim. He closed his eyes, only to rest them for a moment, to give himself a moment's respite and try to clear his head. He woke with a start a couple of hours later as the fire truck beside his car revved its engine and pulled away.

What's happened? Oh my God, I wasn't dreaming. He felt exposed, as if a curtain had suddenly been pulled back. He was also so stiff and sore he could barely move; his neck ached, his arms were tingly. Around him, the street was back to normal again. There was no one in front of the building, the front gate was closed, the floors stood silent and empty; traffic was moving again. There was nothing to indicate that the accident had ever happened. That anything had changed.

What have I done what have I done?

It had grown dark while he was asleep; the edge of the sky along the hills was smudged with gray but the valley was sinking into darkness, the streetlights had come on and the lights in the store windows glowed along the narrow main street. He rubbed his neck and shoulders, trying to work out the cricks as he got his bearings. When he was sure no one was watching, he started the car and drove slowly up the street, being careful not to do anything that would call attention to himself. At the upper end of the main street, he pulled into a service station to ask directions to the nearest hospital.

*

Onagona Memorial was up a long hill from the main part of town, in the section known as Orchard Hill; it was a six-story brick complex at the end of some residential streets, tucked back into a recess of the valley wall. In the growing darkness, the building was ablaze with lights against the black hillside behind it. Vince drove to the emergency entrance, left his car in a parking lot marked DOCTORS ONLY, and went inside. There was a small waiting area occupied at the moment by a middle-aged black woman with a wide-eyed four-year-old boy stretched across her lap. Behind a sliding glass window, a nurse with prematurely gray hair typed on a typewriter while she said to another nurse, "He didn't fix it at all. I don't know why he said he fixed it when he didn't fix it at all." When she noticed Vince, she slid open the window and gave him a professional smile. "Can I help you?"

"I believe some injured men were brought in here earlier. From an accident on a construction site."

"Yes." Her hair wasn't prematurely gray after all, she was older than she first appeared, at least his own age and maybe more, though she was still very attractive, a lean, straight-backed woman. At another time Vince would have flirted with her.

"I'd like to find out how they are."

"Are you a relative?"

"No. Actually, I'm not even sure who they brought in." He tried to smile but was afraid he appeared grisly. She's looking at me suspiciously, I can't blame her. "I was hoping you could tell me their names too."

"I'm afraid if you're not a relative, we can't release that information to you. Was there anything else?"

"No, but—"

"Then if you'll excuse me."

She smiled perfunctorily and reached up to close the window but Vince stopped her, reached out and held the window open, touching her hand without meaning to. She quickly pulled her hand away. She thinks I'm a pervert.

"I'm afraid you don't understand, this is very important business. I'm the architect of the building they were working on. If some men were injured I should have the right to know their names and their conditions."

"And I'm responsible for the privacy of the patients who come here," she said stonily. In her pale blue eyes all Vince saw was You are nothing to me. "Until you can prove to me that you have some legitimate right to know the conditions of patients in this section, I'm afraid I can't help you."

Jack said What kind of architect are you anyhow, you don't even know what's going on on your own building. "But I told you, I'm the architect!" Vince said, ready to explode.

"Ginny, let me take care of this," said the nurse who was standing inside at the counter. She came out the door and over to Vince.

"Are you the supervisor? Do you know about the injured men?" Vince said. Her name tag said PAMELA DICELLO but he couldn't read her title.

"Why don't we go to the lounge where we can talk?"

Across the room the woman and the child stretched across her lap were watching him; the child's head hung upside down, his eyes bulging as if they were ready to roll out of their sockets. It doesn't matter what any of these people think of me, I've got to find out. His trench coat weighing on him like a lead cloak, the bounce in his step more like he suffered foot drop, Vince followed the nurse down the hall to a small lounge. There were half a dozen empty tables and chairs, with a row of vending machines along the wall.

"Would you like some coffee?" she asked, taking a seat at one of the metal tables.

"No, I'm fine," he said. Why did I say that? I'd love a cup of coffee, I'm about ready to drop, and hungry too, God I'm so hungry, but I'd look like a fool if I changed my mind now. Vince took a seat across the table from her.

"I wasn't working the emergency room when they brought them in," she said, looking momentarily at her hands on the tabletop, one hand resting on the other, then looked at him. "But I know something about the men."

"How many were there? I saw them put two stretchers into an ambulance. I was afraid there might be more."

She adjusted the powder-blue sweater draped about her shoulders. She was young, he thought in her mid-thirties, with black-brown eyes that made him uneasy with their directness, the intensity with which she focused on him when she addressed him. I'm an architect, I hold a position of authority, I don't have to be intimidated by her, God they have Ritz peanut butter crackers in the vending machine. . . .

"There were only two. The one, Levon Simmons, has a badly sprained wrist and a couple of broken ribs, as far as we know. We were afraid there might be some internal injuries and we were going to keep him overnight for observation and some tests, but he seems to have gotten himself dressed a while ago when no one was around and walked out. We don't know where he went. That's why I was down here in the ER when you came in, we're trying to find him to make sure he's all right."

Wise potato chips. Frito-Lay. Planters peanuts. What's a Little Debbie? "And the other one?"

She paused a moment. "A man named Bill van Hayden. He died shortly after he was brought in."

Vince felt something give way inside him. Pamela reached over and touched his arm. "Are you all right? Are you sure I can't get you something?"

"No, no, I'm okay." You can get me a new life, I've ruined this one. "It's a bit of a shock, that's all. I was talking to him only a short time before." Careful what you say here, you don't know what you're dealing with yet. "He seemed like a nice guy."

"Then you were there when the accident happened."

"No, I mean, well"—Careful!—"I wasn't on the deck when the column fell. If I had been I would have stopped them before they did something that stupid, of course. I was down on the sidewalk at the time, across the street, but I saw the thing go over with them. It was too bad. There was just nothing I could do." There was nothing I could do. It wasn't my fault.

"What do you mean they did something stupid?"

"By climbing on the column in the first place. If a column is properly welded it should be able to withstand a fair amount of lateral stress. But a column like that isn't meant to be climbed on when the only thing that's holding it are a few tack welds. Then, to make matters worse, one of the men, Bill, the one you say died, cut the guy wires that were supporting the column at the top. I watched him do it, from down on the street, I mean"— Careful!— "he just reached up and cut them: snip, snip. It was all over then."

"Did somebody tell him to cut the guy wires?"

Why would she want to know that? "I don't know. I know I didn't tell him to. Like I said, I was down on the street."

"What about the superintendent?"

What does she know about jobsite superintendents? What business is it of hers? "You mean, did the superintendent tell Bill to cut them? He could have, I suppose, but if he did, it was sometime earlier. When the accident happened the superintendent wasn't on the jobsite, he was out gallivanting around somewhere. It's the question everyone is going to be asking about the accident and what went wrong up there: did somebody tell Bill to cut the wires, or did he misunderstand what somebody told him? Or was he simply careless?" Here's your chance. Careful. Easy. "I was wondering if the injured men said anything to the medics or anybody else when they were being brought in."

"I didn't hear if they did." Pamela seemed to be thinking about something else; she sat with her arms wrapped about herself, looking past Vince at something far away, glancing at him only occasionally. "I'd be interested to know that myself."

"You would?"

"Of course. I'd like to know why he cut those wires. Not that it makes any difference now, I suppose."

"It might make a lot of difference."

"The man's dead. Nothing can change that. Or bring him back."

Nothing can change any of it. Are you sure there isn't something you're not telling us, Mr. Nicholson? We are all responsible for what we do, it was his responsibility and he blew it and he paid the price. "It's important in terms of who is responsible."

"Responsible." She thought about something, then smiled wryly to herself. "Of course. That would be important to you."

"It all comes down to a matter of responsibility, doesn't it?" All human conduct comes down to personal responsibility, doesn't it? Funny I should know that, and don't really know it at all.

"You said you're the architect of the building."

"That's right."

"So that explains what you're doing here and why you're asking these questions, doesn't it? You're gathering evidence."

"Evidence?" She's looking at me like she's looking for a disease. Like the way she looks at a patient for symptoms. "Well, there are certainly going to be inquiries but. . . ." But that's not all of it.

"You're trying to find out who's to blame for the accident."

Suddenly I'm the enemy to this woman. What did I do to her? "Look, nurse, I came here because I want to know what happened—"

"Oh sure. I'll bet you do," she said, getting up quickly and starting toward the door. "This was a mistake."

But that's not the only reason. There's more to it. More to me.

At the doorway she stopped and stared down the corridor for a moment as she struggled to regain her composure. She wrapped the blue sweater a little tighter about herself, then turned back to Vince.

"I'm sorry," she said. "I shouldn't have spoken to you that way. You have every right to want to know what happened."

"There's nothing for you to be sorry for." I wish I could say the same for me. "I should have known better than to come here tonight. But I couldn't stay away. After the accident everything seemed so . . . I don't know. Unresolved."

"A lot of things in this world are, it seems."

"Are *you* all right?"

She thought a moment. "I guess I'm not sure."

"I didn't mean to upset you." Why is she so concerned with all of this? It's like she's personally involved, almost like she's trying to protect someone. But who? Hot-blooded Italians, they're passionate people. I've let so much of the world go by me.

"It's not your fault. I shouldn't let these things get to me. We see a lot of death here, you'd think I'd. . . ." She shook her head as if to clear the thought away. She stood for a moment considering something.

No, that's not it at all. She feels the kind of compassion for the death of a stranger that I should feel having known the man. But I don't. I want to but I don't seem to know how, it's like that part of me is missing, it got left out.

After a moment a little smile tucked itself into the corner of her mouth. "It's funny: I'm not used to somebody asking me if I'm all right. I'm usually the one who does the asking. Thank you." Then she turned around and left.

For a few moments Vince sat where he was. Snickers. Three Musketeers. Hershey's Kisses. I haven't had a Clark Bar in years. I could even eat a Little Debbie and I don't know what it is. She said I'm not used to somebody asking me if I'm all right. And I meant it too, I was really concerned for her, it wasn't just because she was a pretty girl. I'm not a bad person, I can do good things. I guess I know what I should do now too. Feeling a little better about himself, he left the lounge and followed the signs through the maze of corridors to the main lobby where he found a public telephone.

*

Rita answered after the first ring. "I was so worried about you. I saw the accident on the news. Are you all right?"

"I'm okay. I knew you'd be worried because it's getting late. I wanted to let you know everything is all right."

"Come home, Vince. Right away, okay?"

The intensity in her voice almost made him blush. Like she really means it. "I'll be there as soon as I can."

As he made his way back through the corridors, he thought about all the things he wanted to tell Rita when he got home. The truth is I lied to Lyle from the beginning, I never told him what the actual cost of the building would be. I falsified the numbers at the presentation so he thought the building would cost several million dollars less than it actually would.

How could he not know how much it would cost?

He really didn't know what he was doing or what he was looking at, and I knew it. I thought his partner in the deal, Sutcliff, saw through me and knew that I was up to something. But Lyle apparently convinced him to go along with it.

They sit together at the counter in the kitchen, across from each other, the box of half-eaten pizza and their dirty plates and beer glasses between them, under the circle of light from the bell-shaped fixture overhead. Rita lifts her thick auburn hair touched with gray away from her ear and leans forward on her elbow, closer into the circle of light, as if she doesn't want to miss a single word.

But why would you do such a thing, Vince? That's not like you.

Because I thought that was the only way I could get the building that I wanted to build. I was afraid Lyle wouldn't build it otherwise. I was afraid he wouldn't go through with it if he knew what the actual cost would be. He would tell her about why he wrote all the change orders, to make up all the elements of the building that he had kept hidden in the bid documents; he would tell her that he knew all along that Lyle wasn't going to have enough money to complete the project and would have to refinance the construction loan; he would tell her that his only surprise when Lyle called to tell him there was a payment problem was that apparently Lyle had realized the shortfall this early.

If you were able to convince him to build the building from the figures you presented to him, then Lyle must have wanted to be convinced. You were only telling him what he wanted to hear.

Maybe. But that doesn't change the fact that I should never have presented it to him that way in the first place. Oh Rita, I've done some very bad things. When Bill was on that column and it started to fall, he must have known for one glaring moment that he had made a terrible terrible mistake, and that there was no way to take it back. And when I saw him fall I felt a part of myself fall with him. I wanted too much from this building, I was willing to sacrifice anything or anybody to get the kind of building I wanted. I wanted to show the world once and for all that I could do something worthwhile. I wanted to show Mies, I wanted to show you. I wanted to show myself.

You're not falling, Vince.

But it feels like it sometimes.

She reaches across the counter, her hand moving from the shadows into the circle of light as she takes his hand, her eyes brimming over with affection. I'm right here, Vince. I've got you. I'm not going to let you fall.

He wanted to tell her all the things that had been weighing on him for so long. I was afraid if I told you you wouldn't listen.

I wouldn't listen because you never said anything. You only talked for the sake of talking. You only talked to avoid what you really wanted to say. Now that you're saying what is really in your heart, I'm listening. I hear you.

Dusk had turned to dark. Before he stepped outside, he pulled up the collar of his trench coat against the chill spring evening, buttoned all his buttons, knotted the belt around his waist. There were only a few cars left in the doctors' area where he'd left his car. A slight breeze sent a dried sycamore leaf scuttling en pointe across the blacktop.

He headed back through the dark residential streets, passed the lights of the houses burning against the darkness; in the windows were glimpses of families sitting down to eat, figures watching television, visions of ordinary life going on, going on as if nothing had happened. As if no one knew or cared that a man died in the town today.

Another topic for a book of essays. Life is enhanced by the presence of death, in the same way that the presence of darkness is enhanced by light. Or is it the other way around? Whichever: it may be true but it sounds mawkish. Yuck, as the kids would say. So there are some things better left unsaid. But how to know which ones? No easy answers. Ah Vince, you never found the key, did you? But you keep trying. Good for you, old friend.

As he descended the long hill back toward the center of town, he could see the lights of the boulevard that would take him home, the lights of the tall concrete viaduct across the end of the valley. When he had his talk with Rita later this evening, would she listen now when she hadn't in the past? Would he be able to express all the things that were in his heart? Would their life together really change? He didn't know; he knew the odds were against it. If change did come, it would be gradual and over a long period of time, with a lot of work from both of them. He didn't know if they could span their differences after all this time; but he wanted to try. He opened his window to feel the chill night air whistling in. I'm alive. Bill died today. But I'm still here.

Thank you. He set his sights through the dark streets on the distant bridge.

29

On the brightly lit front porch of the J. Howard Griffith Funeral Home, Levon tried one of the large double oak doors, then the other—Good thing one of these suckers is open, now I don't have to beat them down, why have two doors if you don't open both of them? Why do they always have to make things so hard?—and let himself inside.

There was a foyer with a coat closet, and a large central hallway, but nobody seemed to be around. Dead, man, the place is real dead. They must want it this way to keep in the spirit of things. Bastards. The plush cream-colored carpet was spongy under his feet; it led off in all directions, down a corridor and into rooms that opened off to either side. The walls were covered with grass cloth; the woodwork was painted white. A large chandelier, tear-shaped crystals arranged in a tear shape, hung directly over his head—from reflex he stepped out from under it. A sign propped on an easel said MATTHEWS; another easel stood empty. They got room for you, man. A reservation for Billy. He was already light-headed from the medication they gave him at the hospital; and the sticky-sweet smell of flowers that permeated the air made him queasy. It's enough to gag a maggot. And I like flowers too. They ruin everything in a place like this, even death. He stuck his head into one of the rooms but there were only a lot of empty chairs; the room across the hall was empty too. Well shit, there's got to be somebody around here. Living or dead. The stacked heels of his boots dragged across the cloud-like carpet as he made his way to the end of the corridor. A door marked OFFICE opened to a set of stairs leading to a lower level. Levon ducked through the doorway and, splaying his feet to fit on the narrow treads, clumped down the steps.

The Building

He was still in his work clothes, the clothes he was wearing when they took him to the hospital—red plaid flannel shirt, dirty Levi's, lineman's boots. His long red hair was loose around his shoulders; a nurse undid his ponytail when they were working on him in the emergency room and he couldn't fix it again with only one hand. His jacket wasn't with the rest of his clothes when he got dressed and left the hospital—when he got fed up with lying there in bed, when it became clear to him what he had to do— but he figured he couldn't have worn it anyway, it would never fit over the cast on his left forearm. As it was he had to tear the sleeve of his shirt to get it on; he carried the cast upraised in front of him like a lobster carrying his claw. When he walked he jingled slightly, from the ring of keys hanging on his belt.

At the bottom of the steps was a large oil painting taking up most of the wall, lit from above by a small lamp clipped to the top of the gilded frame—the picture of a dark and roiling sea under massive thunderheads, though it wasn't storming yet, only threatening, the white combers breaking up along a deserted beach. What the hell do they have a picture like that here for? I thought this was supposed to be a peaceful place, a painting like that could scare some people to death. Shoulders rolled, walking slightly hunched over, his head at an angle, Levon followed another corridor, this one smaller and narrower; the ceiling here was low, there were only several inches between it and the lanky ironworker if he stood upright, low enough that he was conscious he was in the basement of a building. That he was underground. Like walking in a crypt. Maze of passageways inside a pyramid. The mummy walks. They probably make it this way on purpose, to keep people like me from ever seeing what goes on down here. Bastards. Where are you, Billy? Hang on, I'm coming. He turned a corner and was almost run into by a bustling young man.

The young man, who came up to Levon's chest, was wearing an official-looking pea-green blazer; his blond hair appeared to be both flaxen and lacquered in place. He stared wide-eyed at Levon, at first as if he had seen a ghost, and then as if he were offended by Levon's work clothes.

"Van Hayden," Levon said, expressionless.

The young man looked dumbfounded, as if Levon had asked him a riddle. Then it dawned on him.

"Oh. Van Hayden. Yes. William. They brought him in a little while ago. Mrs. van Hayden is in there now with Mr. Griffith. But I don't know if you should. . . ."

Levon looked down at him through his horn-rimmed glasses. Bud, what exactly do you think you're going to do to stop me? He nodded thanks, and slouched on past him, in the direction the young man indicated, down another long carpeted corridor and up a few carpeted steps and into a room whose ceiling seemed even lower than the hallway's.

There were no windows; the room was illuminated by a border of indirect lights running around the perimeter a foot or so below the ceiling; the lights aimed upward so that the top of the room seemed to hover, like a lid about to close. A few lamps sat around on end tables but they seemed more for effect than for illumination. Plush sofas and straight-backed chairs circled the room on three sides, facing a small spindly-legged desk and chair. Behind the desk was another large threatening-sky-and-roiling-sea painting, this one featuring the skeleton of a lifeboat rotting on a beach.

Must've got these paintings on discount. Christ, the shit people buy.

Seated at the desk was an oversized man with a long face like the man in the quarter moon. He wore a pea-green blazer similar to that of the young man in the hall, except that J. Howard Griffith managed to look rumpled in his; he sat sideways at the spindly desk, his legs too long to fit beneath it. When he saw Levon, he smiled comfortingly.

The Building

I won't let 'em take advantage of you, Billy, I won't let the bastards do you wrong, my man.

"May I help you?" Griffith said.

No.

Mary was sitting in the middle of the sofa directly across from the desk. When Levon went over to her, it took her a second or two to register who he was. Then she smiled tight-lipped and reached up and took hold of his hand.

"I came as soon as I could," Levon said. "As soon as I could get away from the hospital. I heard them say you were bringing Billy over here."

"I'm glad you came," Mary said, still holding on to his hand, the one without the cast. What I am supposed to do, why is she holding on to me? Billy would know. He had a wild idea to kiss her hand but was afraid it wasn't proper. But Billy's gone.

"I take it you were a friend of Bill's," Griffith said.

Levon studied him a moment through his glasses, as if sighting him down a gun barrel. Bill's? What gives you the right to talk about Billy as if you knew him? "He was my partner."

"In business?"

"On jobs. Buildings."

"Oh, I see."

No you don't. "He was my buddy. We always worked together. Sometimes it was like we were almost married—" Shit. He turned to Mary. "Gee, I'm sorry. . . ."

"No, that's okay, Levon. What you say is true. Sometimes I used to think he was closer to you than he was to me." She smiled wanly.

Why is she smiling? Why isn't she sad about that? That's one of the things I want to ask her about.

Griffith coughed once into his hand. "We were just going over Bill's announcement for the paper. Is there anything you can think of that we should say about him?"

Levon thought a moment. I loved him. "He was an ironworker. The best ironworker I ever knew."

Griffith nodded and wrote something down.

Don't patronize me motherfucker I'll rip your lungs out.

Mary pulled him gently but firmly down on the sofa beside her, keeping his hand in hers on her lap. Levon sank into the low, plush cushions until he felt as if he peered at the room over the tops of his knees.

"Bill and I never talked about what we'd do if . . . the other one died," Mary said. "So I decided to just have the funeral here in Furnass. It's close to the hospital, I didn't feel like I should take him very far. And he grew up in Ambridge so I'll have the burial there. This will be convenient for any of the old friends he grew up with, and I hope it's convenient for the guys he worked with too. He didn't have any friends, really, out in Plum Borough where we live—oh, he was friendly and all to the neighbors over the fence, but there was nobody like you or Tony or the other guys on the jobs. I guess the only friends we have out there are people I work with, and they were always more my friends than his." She thought a moment. "I guess that says a lot about us as a married couple, doesn't it?"

Why are you telling me about this? What do you want me to say? I know I'll never have a friend like Bill again.

She was a short, squared-off woman though nonetheless attractive, with a broad Slavic nose and pale skin whose touch of color seemed below the surface. Her dark hair was wild despite a curly-perm's attempts to organize it; her gray business suit, tailored but not expensive, was stretched at the seams.

Griffith was smiling at them, trying to get their attention without being intrusive.

They're meant to be undertakers, what's the word? Morticians, they're always white and pasty, bloated as slugs, it must be from being around dead people all the time.

"We still have some important decisions to make," Griffith said. "Let's move to the selection room, shall we?"

Mary let go of his hand and stood up. To get himself out of the low couch, Levon had to rock back and forth a couple times to gain momentum and use the heavy cast on his arm as a counterweight. Griffith waited for him at the door, smiling sympathetically, then led them both down the corridor, farther under the house, through a pair of swinging double doors, and into a large temperature-controlled room. There were caskets stacked around the room three tiers high, each bearing a printed sign listing its features; the lids of those on the top row were open and tilted forward to display their interiors. In the center of the room were a number of special models, mounted on gurneys and artfully arranged at angles to one another. Griffith was unable to conceal his quiet pride.

"I'm pleased to be able to offer you one of the finest selections of colors, fabrics, and appointments in this part of the country. And if you don't see anything you like here, we probably have it back in our storeroom."

With the exposed fingers of his cast, Levon touched carefully the raised molding and filigree on a platinum-colored model in front of him. They're prettier than Billy's pickup, if Billy could see this he'd laugh himself silly. But Billy's gone.

"If you have any questions. . . ," Griffith said.

Mary methodically read the list of features for each model. "I don't know. . . ."

"Of course," Griffith said, "we offer several insulated vaults, to protect against seepage and insect damage and deterioration in general, depending upon the degree of permanence you think appropriate."

"You mean you also buy a vault, to stick the casket in?" Levon said.

"Of course," Griffith said.

Don't take that tone with me sucker, I don't know how this shit works.

Griffith tried to explain. "You see, when you make an investment in a fine coffin, you certainly wouldn't want to just place it in the ground."

"I thought that was the whole idea." Investment? What kind of return does he think somebody's going to get?

Mary patted Levon's arm reassuringly. They followed Griffith to another part of the room.

"For a man such as your husband, I would suggest something strong and masculine. And color-coordinated with the suit you'd like him to wear. That is, if you want him to wear a suit, anything you choose would be fine. Or even a sport coat, we only need a jacket, the rest is covered by the blanket. . . ."

In his mind's eye, Levon pictured Bill standing before the throne of God without his pants. You see, Lord, it was like this. That would be Billy, always trying to explain everything. Levon snorted. Mary and Griffith looked at him. What? What did I do? This whole thing is crazy, Bill's dead, that's the only important thing, we should all go out and get stoned in his honor and listen to some music and then stick him up in a tree somewhere to feed the crows, that'd be righteous, man. As Griffith went on to talk about prices, Levon tuned out completely. He was feeling woozier as time went on and his arm was starting to ache; he was beginning to wonder if leaving the hospital had been such a good idea after all. He propped the cast on top of one of the caskets and tried to think of something else. *Om mani padme hum, om mani padme hum, om . . .* When Griffith left the room to check on something and Mary came over to him, it took Levon a moment to realize she was speaking to him.

"What?"

"I said, I didn't ask you about your arm. I'm sorry."

The Building

Levon blinked, trying to focus back on the room; at the end of the cast his fingers waved at him as if they and the cast had just appeared. "No, that's okay, I mean it's okay, it'll be all right." He lifted it up and down a couple times to demonstrate.

She smiled but it was obvious she was thinking of something else. "I'd like to know what happened, if you could tell me. I mean about the accident. I've heard a lot of different stories in the last few hours."

"I don't know much of what happened myself." I won't tell you what I know. "We were up on this column and it started to tip over. I called to him but he kept climbing anyway. I thought we were both going to be able to ride it down okay, but then it started to rotate and the cage came apart and it caught Bill underneath." I watched him and I called to him but I waited too long to stop him, no, I can't be thinking that.

"I heard he was busted up pretty bad. They didn't want me to see him at the hospital."

"'Busted up.' Bill always said you were a matter-of-fact lady."

"I guess I have to be. I don't know any other way to get through this. But I do want to know what happened to him. The rest of it, if you'll tell me."

"I'm afraid he fell on some stuff on the way down." I won't tell you that he fell on a #6 rebar dowel sticking up out of the slab and it went right through his chest, that he was impaled on it and Andy Yurick had to burn it off so they could take it and Bill to the hospital, I won't tell you that. "Otherwise I think he still might have made it."

She looked away as she thought of something, her lips turned in upon themselves, before she remembered Levon again. "I'm glad at least that you're okay. It was very good of you to come. You should be home, you've had a terrible shock."

I won't tell you how in the ambulance he was still alive and he looked over at me and saw me on the stretcher beside him and grinned a little, managed to point weakly to the shaft of rebar still sticking out of him and said real soft, only mouthed the word, "Indians," trying to make one of his dumb jokes like he always used to and I laughed out loud even though it hurt so much and I saw him laughing with his eyes and then he closed his eyes and I never saw them open again, I'm not going to tell you that because that was just between him and me.

"I wanted to make sure you didn't need anything. Or Billy."

"That's the terrible thing, you know? When you say good-bye to somebody in the morning to go to work, you don't think about that you might be saying good-bye to them forever." She laughed, a puff of air that came out like a small growl. "It's so dumb, but all I can think about is that I didn't know he was going to die today, somebody should have told me."

"I don't know if Billy knew he was going to die today or not." Sometimes I wonder if he wanted to die. The way he was acting lately, he sure didn't seem to care if he lived. "Least he didn't say anything to me about it."

She looked at Levon peculiarly, but before she could say anything Griffith came back into the room.

"I'm happy to report that we do have that model in a good masculine brown. I was pretty sure we had one in stock. It will be perfect for Bill."

"Good old masculine-brown-Bill," Levon said under his breath.

"What?" Griffith said, smiling, looking from one to the other.

Levon shook his head, feeling the split-second lags in the movement of his long red hair.

"If that's been decided, then," Griffith said, "let's go back and we can take care of the final details."

Levon slouched behind them, out the door and down the hall, back to the room where they started. He felt flushed and sweaty—What the hell's wrong with me? You'd think a column fell on me today or something—as if he were embarrassed about something; he felt as if he inhabited someone else's body—Gots to hold it together for a little while yet, there's things to be taken care of here—and he couldn't make this stranger's body do what he wanted it to. As Griffith went to his office to complete the paperwork, Levon sat again with Mary on the sofa. She worked a small handkerchief in and out between her fingers.

"It was especially good of you to come this evening," she said finally, not looking at him, "considering what you must think of me. I can imagine some of the things Bill must have told you about me. About us."

You're Billy's wife. That's enough. I don't care about none of that other stuff. No one would ever believe how much I don't care.

She went on. "We were childhood sweethearts, you know. We grew up together and dated all through high school and got married right after he got back from the army. I don't know why I'm telling you all this."

I don't either. I don't know why Bill already had himself an okay lady and couldn't stop thinking about that girl Pamela. I don't know why he'd spend his whole day looking for ways to work on that end of the deck so he could be closer to Pamela's windows. I don't know why sometimes he'd leave you and come to work in the mornings and be so gloomy I couldn't talk to him, and why sometimes he'd be up on the deck and he'd see Pamela down on the sidewalk or at her window and she'd give a little wave to him and he'd be walking on air the rest of the day. I don't know why, when he already had me as a friend, he chased after Jack.

When Levon didn't say anything, Mary continued. "I guess I want you to understand that Bill and I were still very close. Even though we had grown apart in some ways too. Couples go through a lot of changes over the years, but that doesn't mean that the couple itself goes away. He was like my best friend."

He was my best friend. "You shouldn't blame yourself for anything."

"I know, but I still should have put a stop to it. Or tried to talk to him about it."

There was the time we were on that hanging scaffold twelve stories up and one of the motors let go and one end of the platform started to drop, I don't even remember now whose end started to go, whether it was his end or my end but it didn't matter because for a few seconds there it looked like the whole show was going into the well and the first thing we both did was reach for the other, it was a total reflex, I reached to make sure Billy was okay before I even thought about worrying for myself and afterward he said he did the same thing too, I'll never forget that feeling, of caring that much about somebody without even trying to, you don't find friendship like that very often in this world, that's why we were partners. Jack wouldn't have reached across a curb to help Billy. Why couldn't Billy see that?

"I don't know what good it would've done." Levon thought of the look on Bill's face as they sat in the back of his pickup truck at lunch and saw Pamela go past in the big white car, when Bill saw Pamela with somebody else. He thought of the way Bill copied Jack's walk, retold Jack's stories.

"I should never have started going out with him in the first place."

What? Never started going out with Bill? What is she talking about? I wish I had all this medication in me sometime when I could enjoy it, now it's just giving me the whips and jingles.

Mary studied the handkerchief wound around her fingers, not looking at him. "It was just lunches at the beginning. They seemed harmless enough, and I always had such a good time.

Then it was drinks and dinner after work and it all sort of grew from there."

"I'm not sure I'm getting this. . . ."

"Then he asked me on those business trips. . . ."

"I don't think we're talking about the same thing. . . ."

Mary looked at him. "Bill didn't tell you I was seeing somebody else?"

"No, I never heard anything about it. I doubt if Billy knew— if he did, I'm sure he would have said something. Bill wasn't the kind to keep something like that bottled up. He would have talked about bashing the guy's head in."

"But he must have known. I assumed he knew all along."

Levon shrugged. "Did you ever tell him?"

"How could he not know? How could he not see a thing like that?"

The same way I don't understand how he couldn't see that Jack didn't want to be his friend, or that Pamela didn't love him. We spend our lives wandering through the world never knowing where any of it connects.

"You must think I'm awful," Mary said, her eyes starting to tear up, turning away.

"I don't think anything like that at all. Honest. I just think you're human, like everybody else."

"There's so much I should have done differently—"

"No, I meant what I said, you can't blame yourself," Levon said. Oh wow, here's my chance to explain this to somebody. "I was thinking about this a lot when I was in the hospital and all the way over here. Because as soon as the accident happened I started blaming myself too, I started thinking about all the things I maybe should have done differently. I mean, maybe I should have done more to stop him from climbing on that column, or maybe I should have paid more attention when he started to cut the guy wires. But it wasn't up to me to try to stop him, that's the whole point. It wasn't up to anybody else to stop him from doing anything. I was confused on this for a while but I got it straightened out now. It's the same about his running after Jack or Pamela too."

"Who?"

"I mean, you and I have something in common, if you think about it. We're both the leave-behinds. We were both sort of betrayed by Billy, me on account of him running after Jack, and you on account of him running after Pamela. But none of that really matters if you think about the universal—"

"I don't know who you're talking about."

"You know, Jack, the superintendent on the job, and Pamela—"

"What are you talking about?" Mary said, a look of growing concern on her face. "I've never heard of somebody named Pamela. What did she have to do with Bill?"

She didn't know about Pamela? Oops. "But that's what I mean, even though Billy was seeing a girl like her doesn't mean that it had anything to do with you. I mean it wasn't because you lacked anything or anything like that. Whatever Bill did, he was only working through the things he had to work through. We're not responsible for anybody else's karma, we're just here to look out for our own—"

"You're crazy. You're out of your mind."

"It all works out, that's what I'm trying to say. It all comes around, you know? We're all one, everything is part of everything else. That's what I was always trying to tell Billy, you got to stop and look around, because we're all around us. And Billy was a good man, even though he did bring this all on himself. We'll probably run into him again somewhere as a patch of grass or a tree or a crow—"

Mary's face was wrenched with horror and grief; tears coursed down her cheeks as she screamed at him, flailed at him, trying to scratch out his eyes. "You crazy hippie, I want my husband! I want him back! I want Bill!"

Levon rolled on his side to escape her blows. What the hell, lady! I want him back too! He pushed himself up from the sofa and hurried to the door just as Griffith returned.

"What happened?"

"I don't know," Levon said. "All of a sudden she flipped out." What did I do? What did I do wrong? Across the room Mary lay on the sofa where Levon had been sitting, holding one of the pillows, crying.

"Maybe you'd better go," Griffith said kindly, his voice hushed as if he shared a confidence. "It'll be good for her to get this out of her system." When Levon continued to stand there helpless, Griffith gently but firmly took Levon's elbow and guided him toward the door.

Get your fucking hand off my . . . oh, okay.

As soon as they were in the corridor and Griffith had closed the door, Levon said, "I was only trying to help."

"I know you were, but sometimes it's hard to know what's the best thing to do."

Levon started down the hallway then turned back—Wait, I've got to set this right—but before he could say anything Griffith put his hand on Levon's chest and stopped him cold.

"It's obvious that you find everything about a funeral home and what we do here distasteful, and I think I can understand why. But you must also try to understand that we provide comfort for most people, however inadequate that comfort seems to you. That's our job here, and we try to do it the best we can. I'm sure Bill would be very glad you came, but now you must let us do what we're paid to do. And the first order of business is to see that Mrs. van Hayden is all right. If you'll excuse me. . . ."

Griffith shook his hand and went back inside the room. For a moment Levon stood in the narrow corridor looking at the closed

door. Finally he turned away and continued back the way he'd
come, looking for the steps. That's our job here, we try to do it
the best we can. Yucca. I'd sure hate to have a job like his, no
way, bud. I'll just keep on humping rebar. God I'm lucky to be
alive. He thought what a great story everything that happened
here would make to tell Bill. But Billy's gone.

30

"Yeah, you'll take care of it. You'll talk to Nicholson about the
columns and make sure we're all covered. You took care of it, all
right."

Bill's face was inflamed, the red patch on each cheek aligned
with the other as if his face had been gripped in a vise; he spoke
to Gregg under his breath, then brushed past him in disgust and
went on down the steps of the trailer and headed toward the
manhoist. Gregg looked in the open door at Nicholson. The architect stood at the plan table holding his half-frame glasses;
without the glasses, his face seemed pale and exposed like something found under dead leaves. He looked at Gregg, a kind of self-
satisfied smile on his face, and shrugged as if to say Who cares?
Gregg turned and hurried from the trailer.

Who cares? I do. Bill was right, I said I would take care of it
and I didn't, I never thought Nicholson would reject the columns.
I should have stood up to him, I should have told him I thought
the rebar was acceptable, I'm sure I've seen the hooks that way
on other projects. I was only doing what he told me to do in the
first place, ask questions, I never would have said anything if I
thought he would act like that. I should have stood up to him
and I didn't.

He left the jobsite and headed down the street, not sure where
he was going. When he saw the Furnass Grill on the corner of
the next block, he remembered he hadn't eaten. Anyplace. Just
get me away from this job. At mid-afternoon the restaurant was

busy but not crowded; he took a seat at the counter. In a few minutes a waitress whose name tag said JO sidled along the counter toward him holding a coffeepot, exaggerating the movement of her hips as she walked as if doing a parody of a sexy waitress.

"Coffee?"

"Looks like a whole pot of it," Gregg said, giving from reflex the kind of smartass answer he always gave waitresses when he was in college.

Jo hung her head to the side and gave him a look as if to say Give me a break.

"Sorry, I couldn't resist. Yes, I'd like some coffee."

"Why be sorry? I'm just mad because I couldn't think of a snappy comeback."

"I'm sure you've heard just about every line in the book by now."

She screened her face with a menu and peered over the top at him, her eyes provocative. "I've been kissed before too, and a whole lot more, but that doesn't mean I wouldn't like it all to happen again sometime." She handed him the menu as she laughed wildly, looking down the counter as if offstage.

This is going too fast, what's she flirting with me for? I'm not really up to this right now. Gregg studied the menu.

Jo leaned one elbow on the counter, studying him sideways. "Let me guess. Clipboard. Hardhat. Work clothes. I'll bet you work on the building they're building down the street."

Hamburger $3.95, cheeseburger $4.50, fries or slaw . . . "What? Oh yeah, right."

"But I don't remember seeing you before."

"No, this is my first time here." And probably my last. That bastard Nicholson, he fucked me over again, didn't he?

"What do you do on it?"

Maybe I should get chicken or fish, something healthy. Nah, I want grease. Christ, I think she *is* flirting with me.

"I said, what do you do on the building?"

"Oh. I'm the inspector." Not much of one either.

Jo hunkered down on both elbows and leaned closer to him, her head canted to one side so she looked at him out of the corners of her eyes. "And what do you inspect?"

If she were younger I'd say Anything I can. She's old enough to be my mother. Still . . . "Concrete, rebar, welding. Stuff like that."

"'Stuff like that.' You know a guy named Jack?"

"Oh yeah. Everybody knows Jack," Gregg said, unable to keep looking at her. Nicholson fucked me over again, only this time he did it the opposite way. Still she is pretty. . . .

Jo fingered the lapel of her uniform, as if she were trying to keep it closed but in fact opening it more. Gregg hazarded a quick look down her blouse, at her ample breasts ready to spill out of her bra, and quickly looked away again. Christ.

There was a shudder, the entire restaurant quivered for a second, the stacks of glasses and coffee cups behind the counter tinkled. They both looked toward the large front windows but didn't see anything out of the ordinary, traffic moved normally along the narrow street; they couldn't hear anything unusual from outside above the sounds of the restaurant, the fans and the noise from the kitchen and the canned music. Everything seemed as it was. Jo went down the counter a ways for several minutes, checking on her other customers while Gregg studied the menu, then sidled back to him.

"Do you happen to know where he went this afternoon?"

"Who?"

"Jack."

"I didn't know he went anywhere." And all I did was bend over again and take it.

Jo played with the strings of the little flowered bow at the V of her blouse. "Yeah. I saw him drive off a little while ago. I know he sometimes goes up to the mountains for the weekend. I was wondering if he was getting an early start or something."

Gregg shrugged. She's asking a hell of a lot of questions about Jack if she's flirting with me. But maybe she thinks Jack and me are friends. "Nope. He didn't say anything to me about taking off early."

Jo straightened up and looked at the front windows again; there seemed to be some commotion outside. "He probably just went down to the Triangle Tavern for a couple horns. That seems to be his favorite getaway place these days. . . ."

"Yeah, the good old Triangle." That's the place I saw this morning. I'd get drunk out of my mind if I had to live here too. I'll bet she could show me a whole lot, tricks of an older woman, take me, mama, and make me a man. . . . He was watching her as she stood there, making an inventory of her, her short auburn hair dark at the roots, her large soft body, her pretty features, imagining what it would be like to go to bed with her, when he realized traffic along the street outside had come to a standstill and sirens were starting to wail and people were hurrying down the sidewalk toward the next block, toward the building.

He stood, trying to see where everyone in the restaurant was looking—What is it?—edged down the aisle a little way for a better look over the people crowding the windows—What's happening? What's happened?—moving slowly at first, then faster, heading toward the front door—What's going on?—pushing his way through the gawkers at the front counter and out among the clusters of people standing along the sidewalk.

"Something fell on the building."

"It was one of those columns. I saw the whole thing."

"Terrible. Just terrible."

A policeman had appeared in the middle of the intersection, directing traffic, trying to keep the street clear for the fire engines and ambulances that were arriving. Gregg couldn't move, he didn't know what he should do. In a few minutes a pickup truck came speeding down the wrong side of the street, passing the line of stopped cars; the policeman waved his arms and blew his whistle frantically but Jack sailed past him, heading into the next block, going as far as he could until he had to abandon his truck then got out and ran the rest of the way to the fence and inside the gate. Gregg heard someone behind him; Jo stood in the doorway of the restaurant, a napkin held to her mouth as she watched, her eyes fearful, murmuring, "Oh no, Jack, oh no. . . ."

Gregg started running then, across the intersection and down the street, past Jack's truck nosed to the curb with the door left standing open, past the medics readying a gurney from an ambulance and workers coming out of the gate craning their necks to see what was happening on the top deck. Inside the fence, workers were trying to clear the area to make room for the stretchers when they brought them down. Jack stood beside the framework of the manhoist beating on one of the metal uprights with a section of pipe to get the operator's attention.

"Bring that fucking cage down here and take me up!" Jack hollered to Marshall looking over the top railing.

"It can't, Jack, it can't," Sloopy said, looking as if he were about to cry. "It's bringing the hurt men down."

"What happened?" Gregg said. "What fell?"

Jack wheeled on him, wild-eyed. "Jesus Christ, get the hell out of here!"

"But I—"

"I said get the hell out of here! Now!"

When Gregg only stood there Jack made a move toward him, the section of metal pipe cocked on his shoulder. He's going to hit me! Run! Gregg stumbled backwards and retreated out the gate, making his way blindly through the jumble of emergency vehicles and the growing crowds of spectators as he hurried to his car. He backed down the street until he was in the clear and made a U-turn at the end of the block, heading back through the town toward the boulevard that would take him to Pittsburgh.

He didn't go back to the office; he didn't stop at a pay phone and call Emory the dispatcher and let his company know what had happened; he didn't do any of the things he knew he should after an incident of this kind. Instead, he went home. For one thing, he still didn't know what actually happened; he only knew what he had pieced together from what he heard others say, that a column on the top deck fell, that some men were hurt. What could I tell Emory? That I was talking to the rebar foreman a few minutes before one of the columns fell over? That the column that fell was one of the ones I inspected? That the reason I don't know more about what happened is because I was down the street in the coffee shop when it fell because I didn't have lunch at the same time as everybody else because I was too afraid to get on a crowded manhoist? Yeah, right, I'll tell him that. But more important, he didn't know how to explain why he wasn't still on the project. Explain it to Emory, explain it to himself. He ran me off. He saw me and said, Get the hell out of here. As if I had no right to be there. He looked like he was going to hit me with that pipe. And I ran. Ran away again. I let him chase me away. Like some dumb kid. I haven't learned a thing. I'm no better now than I ever was.

When he got to his apartment, he thought he might cry, his emotions were welling up inside him and his eyes were heavy, narrowed to slits, but the tears never came; it turned out that he was feeling something quite different. His apartment was in a singles complex in the North Hills suburbs off McKnight Road. Without the energy to remove his field coat or change his clothes, he sat on the sofa—he had picked it out himself at Sears and used his first paycheck as an inspector to make the down payment— in the otherwise empty living room. As it grew later in the day he could hear his neighbors arriving home from work. Pumping up through the floor from the apartment of the bank clerk underneath him came Led Zeppelin's "Stairway to Heaven," over and over again; overhead were the footsteps of the stewardess upstairs crossing and crisscrossing her apartment. Gradually the grayness of the early spring afternoon turned to darkness around him.

From force of habit he had carried his hardhat in from the car; he sat with it on his lap, his hands cradling it as he would a fallen shield, a sleeping cat. It was an American Bridge hat, considered one of the safest and most prized among workmen who cared about such things, a fiberglass connector's hat for which he had traded two baggies of marijuana and then spray-painted it white over Ambridge's brown. White: the color traditionally on jobsites of big shots and officials, the color generally used to designate architects and engineers and inspectors: the color of the good guys. By the color of their hardhats ye shall know them, he had thought once upon a time when he was learning his way around construction sites. The color for visitors, too. It had always been a kick to wear the hat away from the jobsites, into restaurants and stores, back and forth between his car and his apartment, his badge of honor, something that set him apart; if he could have justified it to himself, he would have worn the hat when he went out in the evenings and on weekends. "Guess I better go move the hat around," he would say on a project, repeating what he had heard an older inspector say, though it seemed at times that the hat wore him rather than he wore the hat; "I'm going incognito," he would say if he went somewhere during the day without the hat, a comment he made up on his own, though it always felt as if he left behind more than just the hat. But all that seemed far beyond him now, something that had happened a long time ago in a different country, a different time. Something that happened to someone else.

The Building

At six o'clock he turned on the news and watched pretty Patti Burns on KDKA as she showed the pictures of an accident on a construction site in Furnass and said that a workman named Bill van Hayden had been killed and another, Levon Simmons, seriously injured. Gregg turned off the television again and sat awhile longer in the dark, listening to life going on around him through the walls, through the ceiling and the floor, people fixing dinner and listening to the news broadcast he had just turned off, people talking as they passed along the balustrade, laughter and voices from distant rooms.

Bastards. Of course I'm not crying now. Crying has nothing to do with it now, it's something very different. I've taken shit from people for the last time. Goddamn bastards. Nicholson, Jack, Bill, the whole bunch of them. I deserve to be treated better than that. Look, my hands are trembling. Adrenaline rush. I feel stronger now than I ever have in my life. Bastards. I could tear somebody apart. I'd like to see somebody try to push me around now. Jack says Get the hell out of here and comes at me with the pipe and I grab it out of his hands and hit him backhanded with it across the face, the blow knocking him to his knees and his hardhat goes tumbling across the ground and Jack looks up at me as if he can't believe I did that and I hit him again with the pipe only this time on his skull and I hear it crack under the blow and it only makes me want to hit him again and again and again until his head is nothing but pulp. Bastards. Bastards. Bastards.

Leaving his hardhat on the sofa, he went to the kitchen and splashed cold water on his face. Then he left the apartment and got in his car and drove back to Furnass.

*

He didn't have a plan, really; he only had a vague idea that Jack might still be at the jobsite, or that someone might be around who knew where Gregg could find him, or that if worse came to worst he would scale the fence and break into the trailer to find

• 349 •

Jack's address. But as he drove through the lower end of the town, he spotted what he thought was Jack's pickup in the lot beside the Triangle Tavern. Gregg circled through the lot to make sure the truck was Jack's, then parked down the street and walked back through the darkness.

It was an old wood building that had once housed a feed mill— the Purina checkerboard showed dimly through the paint on one wall—wedged in at the intersections of several sharply angled streets, one side curved to follow a railroad siding that headed back toward some dark factory buildings; with its front door at the point of the street corner, the building did indeed appear triangular until you started to count up sides. It was damp this close to the river; Gregg pulled up the collar of his field coat against the chill, then from reflex started to put it down again— I don't want to look like I'm tough—then left it up. Nobody's going to mess with me tonight. Not the way I'm feeling. I hope they try. The street was quiet. The only sound was the buzz of the neon sign sticking out over the door; most of its letters were burned out so that it spelled

angl

ern

and cast a flickering red glow along the sidewalk. He went inside.

The place was high-ceilinged and plain and, it seemed to Gregg, too brightly lit for a tavern. On one side of the long, oddly shaped room was a lunch counter that, after a few stools, became a bar; on the other side was a scattering of mismatched tables and chairs, all of them empty. Farther back the room, which opened up from its apex at the door, darkened amid a stack of crates and beer cases and a couple of video poker games, and disappeared completely into the gloom at the rear of the building. There were half a dozen men sitting toward the front of the bar, ranging in age from a teenager to a gap-mouthed old man, all of them in work clothes; they turned as one to look at Gregg when he came in the door—Turn around assholes, what the hell you looking at?—then turned back to the television behind the bar. On the screen, a police car chased a van through an industrial district that looked a lot like the lower end of Furnass. Jack sat by himself at the rear of the bar, talking to the bartender in a voice loud enough, despite the gunshots and squealing tires and music on the television, to be heard over half the room.

". . . So I put the waterbed out there in the cabin behind the house and fixed the place up for myself, because that's where she tells me she wants me to sleep. Which is fine with me. Hey, I go up there on weekends to get some rest, the one thing I don't need is her flopping around beside me all night. . . ."

The bartender, a spindly man with clamped-down hair and a nosy face, stood with one foot up on the edge of the sink below the bar, leaning forward as if to catch every word. As Gregg approached, Jack glanced at him and turned back to the bartender and then looked at Gregg again; without pausing in his narration, he pulled his Rolling Rock bottle closer to him and nodded for Gregg to sit down.

". . . I mean, that's the way she wants it, and that's fine with me, and I'll tell you something else, one thing I don't need is her getting any lovey-dovey ideas, you know what I mean? Me and her, we did that enough when we were younger, it's time for us to give that a rest, you know? When I go to bed nowadays, all I'm looking for is a good night's sleep. We're comfortable the way things are, especially with me down here most of the time and her up there in the woods." Jack drained the rest of the beer from his glass, pushed the wad of bills in front of him toward the bartender, and said without looking at Gregg, "What do you want to drink?"

"Iron City," Gregg said before he thought about it. Shit, I don't even like Iron City, never did. Pump an Iron, millworkers' beer, be a man. Going to change that too.

Jack didn't wait for the bartender to return with Gregg's beer before he continued with his story.

"So everything's okay the way it is between me and the old lady, right? Everything's copacetic. And I'm really looking forward to some good sleep on the weekends. Let me tell you, a waterbed is great for your back. This girl I knew up in Pittsburgh had one and she thought it was great for screwing, but that's a lot of bullshit. When you're screwing a girl, you don't want anything moving under you that's got a rhythm of its own, whether it's the girl or the bed or anything else. I kept going back to see her because of the bed, all right, but only because I slept so well on it afterward. Anyway, this night I'm up in the mountains and I'm sound asleep out there in the cabin, floating along just as happy as can be on my waterbed, and the next thing I know I'm bouncing up and down like I'm in a tidal wave and I don't know what the hell is going on. I wake up and here's the old lady, I can just make her out in the dark, she's in her frilly little nightgown and she's crawling up the waterbed toward me, except that she's got it sloshing around so much she can hardly stay up on her hands and knees. She finally makes it up to where I am and she plops down and grabs hold of me like she thinks I'm a life preserver or something and she says all sweet and sugary, 'Ja-ack, Ja-ack, wouldn't you like to make waves with me?'" He twisted up his face as if he had just bitten into something distasteful and puttered his lips, "Bthwr-r-r-r-p!"

The bartender laughed silently, his mouth open.

"On the other hand, what could I do? I hate to leave a lady disappointed, even if she is my wife." He laughed a little, but his heart didn't seem to be in it.

The Building

Gregg picked at the label on his beer bottle. Waterbeds don't bounce around like that, why is he exaggerating? Forget it, it's not worth it.

"So, Greggory," Jack said after the bartender moved away, "what are you doing in this neck of the woods? You don't live around here, do you?"

"No, I live up in Pittsburgh."

"That's a long way to come, just for a beer."

Jack sat with his elbows on the bar, his fingertips resting against the base of his beer glass as if he were ready to catch it in case it started to tip over; he looked across his shoulder at Gregg, then straight ahead again. When Gregg spoke to him, he addressed the image of the two of them in the mirror behind the bar.

"Did you hear how Levon's doing?"

"What about Levon?"

"You know, the accident. I heard on the news—"

"I don't know nothing about either one of them," Jack said, reaching for a handful of peanuts. "Somebody said Bill died. I didn't ask any questions."

"I thought maybe you went to see them in the hospital."

"Me? I wouldn't go to see them if they were friends of mine, I wouldn't go see them if they were my own family." The bartender came back, rested his foot on the edge of the sink, and hunkered over his upraised knee again; Jack directed the story at him. "I can't stand having anybody around me when I'm sick, you know? So I leave people alone when they're sick. If somebody's sick, that's their business, what am I going to do, stand around and watch them? I mean, who the hell wants to be around a sick person? Blah. I only went to see one guy in the hospital my whole life, and that was my buddy, Freddy. He was an electrician I worked with. They had him stuck full of needles and there were tubes coming out of him and a sack of his piss hanging over the side of the bed and he was attached to this big machine with a monitor over his head to tell him whether he was still alive or not. I didn't recognize him, he was all wasted away, the cancer ate him inside out. Screw that, I don't go to hospitals anymore to see anybody."

Jack lifted his empty beer glass and the bartender got him another bottle of Rolling Rock and a clean glass and poured him another double shot of Jack Daniel's. He also brought a second Iron City though Gregg was only halfway through the first one.

"Hey, bring him a clean glass too," Jack said.

"I thought that was just for you, Jack."

"That's okay," Gregg said. "This one's okay—"

Jack silenced him with a wave of his hand. "Don't let them do that to you. Always get yourself a fresh glass. If you're drinking drafts, order the next one before you're finished with the last one; if you're drinking bottles, don't be afraid to speak up and ask for it. And get them to rinse out the glass with cold water before they bring it to you, you need a clean glass for the flavor."

The bartender rinsed out another glass and put it in front of Gregg; he took a swipe at the counter with his rag and walked away. The trail of the wet rag streaked the countertop.

Jack says Don't let them do that to you? Christ, he's the one who keeps pushing me around. Gregg made a mental note to not use the clean glass when he started the second beer.

"Okay, enough of this shit." Jack turned on his stool so he could look at him, his fist propped into his side. "I'm sure you didn't just happen to find this place. Why'd you come looking for me?"

Gregg picked some more at the label with his thumbnail. A strip of the label accordioned together; he tried to smooth out the pleats so the label looked the same as it did before, then pushed the bottle away. Just say it, idiot, that's what you came for. "Why did you run me off the project after the accident?"

Jack nodded, as if he could have guessed as much, and turned back to his beer. "There was a lot going on, I didn't need anybody else in the way."

"Somebody might have been looking for the inspector."

"Yeah, that's what I was afraid of."

"It was my responsibility to be there," Gregg snapped. "It was my job."

Jack looked over at him, a half smile on his face. "Maybe the real question is what are you so pissed off about, Greggory?"

"It's Gregg, I told you. With two *g*'s. It's not short for anything."

With a sweep of his hand Jack cleaned the peanut shells from the bar in front of him onto the floor. He took a sip of Jack Daniel's and chased it with a swallow of beer, then turned on the stool to face him again. "Okay, Gregg. I'll ask you again. What the hell pulled you all the way back here to Furnass?"

"I told you. Because you ran me off the project this afternoon."

"And I told you why I did."

He's patronizing me. "That's not good enough. You had no business doing that. I was the inspector, I should have been there."

Jack twisted his mouth to one side, working at something with the tip of his tongue against the inside of his cheek. "We'll forget for the time being what you don't think is good enough about what I told you. Or what it is you think you would do about it anyway." He turned his head and spit the offending particle on the floor. "I'll tell you why I ran you off: there were going to be a lot of people around asking a lot of questions. I didn't think you knew what you were getting yourself into."

"That wasn't the first project I've ever been on, you know. I can handle myself."

"Maybe so. But a lot of those questions were going to be aimed directly at you. And the people asking them weren't going to be the friendly type."

"Why would they be aimed at me? I didn't have anything to do with it." They think I had something to do with causing the accident?

"There's talk that somebody told Bill the columns were finished. There's talk that somebody told him it was okay to cut the guy wires."

"Is that what happened? He cut the guy wires?"

Jack nodded. He took another sip of whiskey, then drained the jigger and followed it with more beer.

I didn't tell Bill anything like that, did I? Think, think! "Why would I tell him that column was finished?"

"Like you keep telling me: because you were the inspector."

No, I know I didn't tell him that. Don't doubt yourself. "I didn't tell him anything of the sort. Why would somebody try to blame me?"

"Like I said: because you were the inspector."

"Well, if that's what they want to think, let 'em. I know what I did and didn't do. And I can stand up for myself."

Jack studied him a moment. "You're into this standing-up-for-yourself shit all of a sudden, aren't you? This is a different Greggory—excuse me: Gregg, with two *g*'s—that spent most of today trying to make himself as small as possible around the jobsite."

"It's not shit," Gregg said, meeting his eyes. "I've got nothing to be afraid of."

"Just like that?"

"Just like that."

Jack shrugged. "Maybe so. You're right about one thing: being afraid can get to be a habit. You can change it."

"What do you know about being afraid?" Gregg said.

"Not much," Jack said, and reached for his beer.

That's weird. He said that like somebody who's actually afraid of something after all. Wonder what it could be?

"One person I should have stood up to is Nicholson," Gregg went on. "If I had, maybe this wouldn't have happened."

"What about Nicholson?" Jack said with new interest.

"That bastard. I did what he told me to do: I called his attention to the problem with the candy canes when I found it. I was sure he'd let it go, I was sure he'd handle it like he did the welding this morning. He told me I was supposed to make determinations like that, and then he turned around and rejected all the rebar in the columns."

"Did Bill know that?"

"Yeah, Bill went down with me to the trailer."

"And then he went back up to the top?"

"Yeah, I guess he started to change the candy canes. I should have told Nicholson I thought the rebar was okay, even if it wasn't the way it was detailed."

"That wasn't your job."

"Bill thought it was. He was pissed at me before he went back on the building."

"Bill was a cry baby," Jack said, turning again to the bar. He stuck his fingertip into a ring of water left on the counter from his beer bottle, chasing a miniature wave around the circle, then smeared it away. "He always blamed somebody else for anything that happened to him. He always wanted somebody else to get him off the hook, instead of taking care of things himself. He was always pissed at somebody too. That was the only way he knew how to handle things."

"Well, I still should have stood up to Nicholson—"

"Christ, quit trying to take the world on your shoulders. Give it a rest. If we need a savior, I'll give you a call."

Jack finished his beer and gathered up his loose change, getting ready to go. Gregg reached for his own wallet, but as Jack stood up he put his hand on Gregg's arm to stop him.

"Your money's no good here," Jack said, nodding to the pile of fives and ones he had left on the bar. "Good night, Sully. Take it easy, you guys."

The bartender waved and said, "See you tomorrow, Jack." The other men along the bar nodded as he passed like corks bobbing in his wake.

"See ya, Jack."

"Take it easy, Jack."

"Thanks for the drink, Jack."

Gregg hurried to finish his beer and followed him. No, I'm not going to give it a rest. God I hate his guts. If we need a savior I'll call you. Bastard. He can't get rid of me that easily. Is he trying to get away from me? Wonder what made him uneasy back there, is there something he is afraid of?

Outside, Jack looked around the dark empty street and zipped up his jacket. "Getting a little chilly."

"What about you?" Gregg said. "Are people trying to blame the accident on you?"

"Why would they blame it on me?"

"I don't know. Maybe because you were away from the jobsite when it happened."

Jack shook his head and looked around.

"But doesn't it bother you that you weren't there when it happened?"

"Nope," Jack said and pushed out his lips like a duck.

"But you're the superintendent on the job. It was your responsibility."

"You make your own party. If Bill did it to himself, it was his responsibility. I'm glad more guys weren't hurt because of his stupidity, that's all." Jack nodded once and moved off down the sidewalk.

"What's the matter?" Gregg said after him. "Don't you want to talk about this?"

"Nothing to talk about," Jack said without turning around.

Bothers you, huh? "Maybe you're afraid you didn't take care of your responsibilities after all."

Jack shrugged as he kept on walking.

You son-of-a-bitch. I know how to get you. "What's the matter, Jack?" he called. "Am I running *you* off this time? Afraid I'll say something you don't want to hear?"

Jack stopped as he was about to turn into the parking lot. For a moment he stood there, his back to Gregg, his hands in his jacket pockets. The only sound was the buzz of the electric sign overhead, a distant train along the river. Then Jack turned slowly and came back down the sidewalk, coming toward him out of the darkness. He stood in front of Gregg, loomed over him, close enough for Gregg to smell the alcohol and cigarettes on his breath, the dark smell of his clothes. His pudgy face flickered and danced in the reddish glow.

"You did a good job today, and I'm glad for you that you found out what it is to stand up to people. But don't ever forget there's always some son-of-a-bitch in the woods who can rip you a new asshole. There's always somebody. And in your case, it's me. Sometimes there's a good reason to be afraid."

I'm not running, I'm not running away.

Jack looked at him a moment longer, then grinned, a little deadly, and clapped him on the shoulder. "You'll be okay, little brother. Don't you worry about it."

I didn't run. I'm still here. Me.

Jack breathed deeply and looked around, up at the starless sky scummed with clouds, the blacked-out factories and warehouses along the dark street. "Isn't this wonderful? I think it's all wonderful." His hands in his pockets, he headed again toward the parking lot. He didn't look back. "Bye, Greggory. See ya later."

31

As he pulled out of the Triangle Tavern parking lot and headed down the street, Jack checked in his rearview mirror to see if Gregg was trying to follow him. He turned down a dark side street then switched off his lights and made a quick U-turn, bouncing up over the curb and across the dirt sidewalk, and parked beside the loading dock of an abandoned warehouse. In a few moments Gregg's foreign car went past the end of the street; Jack watched as the headlights climbed up the on-ramp to the viaduct. He puffed a little air between his teeth, the sound like a hissing valve; he rested for a moment, his arms draped over the top of the steering wheel.

Dumb son-of-a-bitch. He'll never know. I wanted to pop him so bad. Tell me I didn't take care of my responsibilities. Afraid I'll say something you don't want to hear? He'll never know how close he came. Tonight I could kill someone if I had the chance. Why not, I already killed one today, didn't I?

He waited until his body started to settle down again, until he stopped shaking from the adrenaline pumping through him. Hey God, if you're going to send me somebody looking for a fight, at least send me somebody who'd be worth the effort, not some wimpy kid. In a way he felt sorry for Gregg: Jack was sure Gregg didn't realize what was in store for him because of the accident, the shit that would come down on him in the coming months— the questionings, depositions, maybe even a trial—because a death was involved. But that was Gregg's problem now, there was nothing Jack could do about it.

Poor dumb jacking-off son-of-a-bitch. Sloopy said This ain't no place for no inspector now, is it, Jack? This is just for us, the

working people. Yeah, Sloopy, just for us. Just for us. The terrible
bed we make for ourselves to lie in. To get ourselves fucked on.

He thumped the rim of the steering wheel a couple times with
the side of his fist, turned his headlights back on, and made another U-turn, heading now toward the river. He drove slowly for
several blocks through the deserted streets of the lower end, past
the dark and abandoned factory buildings, then turned along
Front Street near the old lock. Through the branches of the bare
trees and bushes along the river, the few lights in this part of
town shattered over the black surface of the water. In the sweep
of his headlights, two small orange eyes glared at him from the
top of the bank; a raccoon hissed at him as he passed, then slunk
down the slope further into the darkness.

Who am I kidding? I'm so worn-out tonight even Greggory
could probably take me. Gregg. Good thing he didn't push it.
Better be careful, old-timer, one day some kid is going to come
along and clean your clock. I'm not going to get old, I'm going to
break before I wear out. Don't I wish.

As soon as he had time after the accident, Jack called the
company's main office; a secretary told him Mac was out in his
truck somewhere, but she'd try to raise him on the radio and let
him know what happened. When Jack came off the building at
the end of the day, after taking one last look around the deck and
the scene of the accident—it was late, almost dark, he had sent
everyone else home, even Jimmy the manhoist operator, which
meant Jack had to climb up and down the ladders to get anywhere; he realized more than ever that he was getting too old to
be climbing around much anymore; the joints in his legs ached,
his shins felt as if they were about to burn through his skin, and
he was exhausted, puffing like a horse—Mac was in the trailer
waiting for him. Neither one said anything in greeting. They
looked at each other and Jack went over and sat at his desk; he

took off his hardhat and mopped his forehead with his handkerchief as he waited for his heart to stop racing.

Mac leaned with both arms on the plan table, staring out the window at the darkness. As soon as Jack caught his breath, he told Mac about the accident and what had gone on afterward. When Jack was finished, Mac continued to stare out the blank window for a few minutes as he thought about something. The pouches of the old man's face seemed heavier than usual, the many lines etched deeper into his skin. Finally Mac pushed his old tin hardhat up onto the back of his head and turned to Jack.

"What about the inspector? That kid?"

Jack sighed. "Nobody heard him say anything about that particular column. I asked around. But earlier in the afternoon he found some problem with the candy canes in the columns, and he and Bill talked to Nicholson the architect about it—Nicholson was out here today too."

"Is that where that came from?" Mac said, nodding to the hole in the partition behind Jack.

"It's been quite a party today," Jack said matter-of-factly. "Anyway, my guess is that Nicholson said something to Bill and that's why he was up there on the column."

"You don't know what the architect told him?"

"I was gone for a while," Jack said, meeting Mac's eyes. "I had some business to take care of."

"I can guess what kind of business."

"For once it wasn't what you think. And what if it was? I can't be around every minute to hold these guys' hands."

"Can anybody make trouble about it? About you not being on the job?"

"I don't see how. I doubt if anybody knew for certain I was gone. I learned how to disappear from an expert."

Mac smiled faintly before he looked out the window again. "Then that's how we'll have to go with it. No matter what we say, the architect will have himself covered. Nicholson's not smart but he's shrewd. So our position will have to be that the reason Bill was up there on that column was to make the corrections that the inspector wanted. It'll be our word against the kid's, and Bill's not around to clarify the fine points."

"We don't have a written report from the inspector saying anything about the columns."

"Even better. We'll say Bill didn't have anything from the inspector to tell him which columns weren't finished with the welding, so he didn't know which columns weren't safe to climb on."

"It's too bad the kid has to be left swinging in the breeze that way. But he asked for it, he wouldn't listen."

"It's too bad about Bill," Mac said, still looking out at the darkness in front of the building. "I liked that boy, even if you didn't."

"He was another one who wouldn't listen," Jack said. He took his cigarettes from his pocket, then thought better of it because of Mac and put them away again. "He wouldn't do what he was supposed to."

"I know something about that problem myself." Mac turned slowly and looked at Jack over his shoulder. His eyes were rheumy and sad, and with a coldness Jack had never seen aimed at him before. "I know the trouble you can get into when one of your men won't do what he's told."

He had slowed the truck almost to a crawl as he continued along the river. Overhead on the viaduct, rising two hundred feet in front of him in the darkness, cars sang across the mouth of the valley like incoming shells; framed in its narrow arches, the mill across the Ohio River at Wyandot flickered orange and yellow as if it were on fire. He passed through the arch under the boulevard and turned slowly into Bridge Street.

Bill. Wonder what he thought about as he went down. What a way to go. Plenty of time to think about things. Plenty of time for regrets. Wish I hadn't. Bill stood there in the doorway looking helpless as Pamela and I faced each other across the bed and she said You son-of-a-bitch Jack, I know what you're doing, and I said I'm not doing a thing, it's taking care of itself, and she said Oh sure, and what else do you want me to do? and I said I don't care what you do now, Pamela, that's your business, and she said All right Jack I get it, you made your point, you'll see, and Bill looked at us back and forth like he was following a tennis match, and he said Did I walk into the middle of something here? and I said No, you walked into the end of it, and Pamela went over and took his arm and said Don't let anything we say scare you off, it doesn't mean a thing, not one thing and then she kissed him lightly on the cheek and walked out and Bill blushed crimson with those crazy patches on his cheeks and beamed from ear to ear as if he thought he had just won something but the truth was he had just started to lose it.

The row of houses was pressed up against the steep wooded hillside; one of the piers for the viaduct rose behind them out of the rock farther up the slope. The houses were basically the same, a dozen narrow frame structures, each with two stories and an attic, built at the same time by the same builder from the same set of drawings, remnants of company housing put up after the turn of the century. Over the years the houses had acquired characteristics of their own: some had porches, some didn't; some were covered with imitation brick or aluminum siding, most could use some paint. Jo's house was near the middle of the row; the lights were on. Her car was sitting in the vacant lot across the street, where she always left it when she had company. Parked in front of her house was a late-model two-door, with fuzzy dice hanging from the rearview mirror and zebra-striped upholstery.

The Building

Jo, old girl, I wonder how long your taste has been going downhill. I wonder if I was before or part of the decline. The lady likes company, no doubt about that. I wonder how she likes surprises.

*

He gave the steering wheel a thump for good measure and slowly got out of the truck. His joints were starting to stiffen up again and everything ached. He had hoped a few horns would help ease his aches and pains, as well as put his thoughts into a comfortable haze; but the joints in his knees and ankles and elbows hurt worse than ever, maybe it was the change of weather, and rather than become fuzzy, his mind seemed to grow clearer as the night went on. He climbed her wooden front steps flat-footed, using the railing—Like a goddamn old man, but as long as nobody's watching—and rang her bell.

She opened the door a crack, saw who it was, and closed it again; in a moment she stepped out onto the porch with a rain-coat draped around her shoulders, her arms folded in front of her to keep it closed. She was in her bare feet; Jack couldn't tell if she had anything on underneath the raincoat or not.

"Are you okay?" she asked.

"Sure, why wouldn't I be? I came by to see if you're okay."

"I'm okay, I guess. I heard about Bill on the television."

"Tough break."

"Have you heard anything about Levon?"

Jack shook his head, stuck his hands in his jacket pockets, and walked over to the railing. This was a mistake to come here. What did I think I was going to get from Jo?

"I saw you drive off before the accident," Jo said behind him, "and then I saw when you came back. I waited at the Grill until late in case you came in, and then I came on home. . . ."

He turned to look at her. "We got started on the clean up right away. . . ."

"I didn't know if you'd need anything or not. . . ."

"Nah. What I need is to be able to turn back the clock half a day so I could do some things different. Maybe turn it back a few years while I'm at it." He grinned a little. Always leave 'em laughing.

"Jack—"

"Look, I got to get going. I just stopped by to see how you were doing. . . ." I can't resist it. He jerked his head toward the house. "And it looks like you're doing okay."

"When you didn't come in to see me today, I figured you must have something else going on for yourself."

"Hey, that's okay. That's the way the cookie crumbles." That's the way the column falls. What did I think was going to happen, that she was going to run the other guy out? Yeah, I did think that. Dumb.

She watched him from the shadows near the door, her arms still hugging herself to keep the raincoat closed; the light from a streetlight coming through the branches of a tree wickered across her face.

"I have feelings too, you know," she said finally.

"Yeah, sure, we all got feelings. I'm glad you're taking care of yourself, I mean it." He nodded once and turned to go. "I'll see ya later."

"Jack, go see her."

He stopped halfway down the steps but didn't turn around. "I don't know what you're talking about."

"She's going to need to see you now. She's going to want to know you're okay."

"She was Bill's girl."

"I doubt if even Bill thought that was true at the end. I know in your heart you never did."

"Then you know more about me than I know about me."

The Building

When she didn't say anything, he turned to look at her. But Jo was already starting back into the house.

*

Me? Afraid? What the hell would I be afraid of?

Maybe you're afraid you'll find out you really care about me instead of just wanting to fuck me.

Don't kid yourself, honey britches. You know I care about you.

Honey britches. Why don't you just call me cunt and be done with it? But you're right about one thing: yes I do know you care about me. That's not the problem at all. The problem is you're afraid maybe I don't really care about you. You're afraid you might have to admit you need somebody, and that that somebody might not be there. You're afraid you might finally want somebody, and find out you can't have her.

The main street was quiet at this hour; the traffic signals on the corners flashed only to themselves; the stores along the street were dark except for the windows of the Five Animals Kung Fu Studio, the Furnass Grill, and the bars. He stopped across the street from the jobsite. Most nights he left the lights burning in the stairwell at the rear of the building, the string of bare bulbs illuminating the lower floors when he drove by periodically to make sure everything was all right. But tonight he must have forgotten to turn them on; the building loomed dark and empty, black floor stacked upon black floor, up out of sight from his truck window. On any other night he would have climbed out of his truck and unlocked the gate and turned on the lights, but not tonight. He sat for several minutes staring at the dark project, the Easter paintings on the fence, childish visions of cartoon characters delivering parti-colored eggs, without really seeing anything at all.

I know the trouble you can get into when one of your men won't do what he's told.

You trying to say something, Mac?

• *367* •

What I'm saying is there's liable to be a lot of trouble when Drake finds out you went on ahead and poured those columns today. After the front office decided not to. They're going to link the accident with the rest of the work going on.

I told you why I went on ahead and poured them. It was my idea to run those columns in three-floor lifts. If we were walking off this project, I didn't want to leave them sticking up in the air without being tied into the rest of the building.

As long as they were welded, they would have been safe enough.

Maybe so. But I didn't want to take that chance. Besides, like I said, I already had the men and equipment here by the time you told me to cancel the pour. It was going to cost Drake anyway. I thought they should at least get something for their money. They should be thanking me for looking out for their interests.

Drake isn't like other companies we've worked for. They prefer to take the loss and write it off.

That's crazy. That's no way to build something.

That's the way it is. These things are decided now by accountants and spreadsheets and pie charts.

Then to hell with them. Let's go work for a company that builds buildings, not starts them and walks away from them.

It's not that easy anymore, son.

What are you talking about? We can go anywhere in this area and get a job. You've got the best reputation in the business. I know because I'm responsible for it.

Mac managed a brief smile but his eyes remained sad. And cold. I'm an old man, Jack. I don't know how much longer I can do this.

You'll go till you drop. And you'll outlive me.

The Building

No, I won't. But I'll live long enough that I'll need some security. And jobs nowadays aren't that easy to find. I know, I've looked. It's a different world.

What are you telling me, Mac?

I'm telling you that I need to hold on to this job because there aren't many out there for an old man. And I'm telling you that Drake isn't going to like it that I told one of my superintendents not to make a pour and he went on ahead and did it anyway. They're not going to like having to pay for it. And they're not going to like that a fatal accident happened while that other work was going on. I'm telling you that I may not be able to protect you this time.

Are you getting ready to fire me, old man?

I won't know what I'll have to do until everything gets sorted out. But if it comes to that, yes, I'll have to fire you. At my age I can't let you take me down with you. You understand, don't you, son?

"Yeah, I understand, all right," Jack murmured out loud.

Something moved along the sidewalk. Scuttling down the other side of the street was a figure dressed in layers of overcoats with dozens of scapulars around his neck. Mr. Mole. The mole-man of Furnass. Poor dumb jacking-off son-of-a-bitch. The figure hurried along, bent double, picking up cigarette butts and scraps of paper and carrying them fastidiously to the nearest trash can. Wonderful. I'm in good company tonight. Maybe I should try to get him back to the community house where he belongs, he's out later than he should be. No, I tried that once, he bellowed like a stuck pig, like I was the one who was scary. Better to leave things alone. Jack was chilled; his chest felt as if his insides were made of ice. He pulled away slowly and turned at the corner, up the steep side street, the back end of his pickup skitterish on the bumps and dips of the paving bricks, past the awning for the Owls Club and around the block to the parking lot behind the hotel.

He turned off the engine and listened to the truck tick cool around him; he wanted a cigarette but still wouldn't smoke in the truck since the time he gave it up so the smell in the cab wouldn't bother Pamela. The only light came from the street-lights along the street and one across the alley, a bare bulb over the service entrance to the hotel; the empty municipal lot stretched away from him into the night. He thought about going for a drink at the Steel City Tavern, or the Reo Grill, or the Blue Boar at the hotel, or even the D&G. But it would be the same wherever he went; everyone would want to know about the accident, everyone would want to know about the guy who got killed. It was cold, the windows of the truck were beginning to fog up; but he couldn't stand the thought of going back to his hotel room. He thought of calling Ellie; she might have heard something about the accident on the news. But she wouldn't expect to hear from him unless he was hurt, or someone else had to notify her. By this time she would have figured out that he was all right. He didn't want to bother her. He looked at his watch; it was after eleven.

Ellie said You want me just to be here, not because you want to be with me or because you want to touch me, you just want me around in case you want to talk to somebody or when you have to let go for a while, I'm just a voice on the telephone. She's right in a way but she's wrong too, because there was a time . . . I remember it was on a Sunday afternoon when we were living in that place on the South Side, the Steelers were on the radio but I didn't care that much, I was going to turn it off because I hadn't been home for a while because of the job I had been on, but she said No, go ahead and listen to your game, and I said I thought maybe we could do something together, thinking maybe we could go upstairs and fool around because Marcy was out of the house playing somewhere, but she said No, there's nothing special I want to do, and I looked at her sitting in her chair in the living room reading a magazine with her arms folded about herself and her hands even at rest clasped into tight little fists with the thumbs peeping out and I knew she was right more than she ever knew, there was nothing special she wanted to do with me ever, and that was okay in a way, I told myself it was the best of all possible worlds, I was both married and free to do anything I wanted to, but that still didn't fill the hole where somebody special was supposed to fit, and worse than that, and maybe what she knew all along and what I was only finding out then, that it could never be Ellie to fill that hole in me no matter how comfortable we were with each other and how much we cared about each other in our own way, no matter how much I wanted to feel different. . . .

There was something in the darkness, a shape he didn't recognize through the fogged window beside him. Now what? Is the mole-man following me? A deer was walking through the dark parking lot. At least he thought it was a deer. He tried to wipe the moisture from the window but it didn't help; through the smeared glass the deer seemed all the more ghostly and unreal. He wanted to roll down the window but he was afraid he would scare it away; he was equally afraid that he would roll down the window and find there was nothing there at all. The doe stood for a moment beside his truck, a few feet away, ears flicking. Its coat blended into the darkness as if transparent; for a moment Jack thought he could see through the animal, see the surface of the dark concrete beyond it, the dim markings on the pavement. When the deer turned to look at him, its eye was a black hole, an empty space in the night, reflecting nothing. Jack felt dizzy and closed his eyes. He opened them again and the deer was gone; he thought he might have heard hooves clicking on the cement, caught a glimpse of a white-tailed rump disappearing in the shadows between the buildings, but he wasn't sure. With his fingertips he touched his forehead, rubbing gently as if he thought his head could break.

Son, I'm starting to worry about you.

He looked at his watch again and left the truck, moving stiffly until he worked the cold from his joints; he crossed the parking lot and the street and headed down the dark alley into the next block. In the middle of the block, across the alley from the blacked-out jobsite, the lights were on in Pamela's apartment.

32

She buzzed him in almost as soon as he rang the front doorbell, almost as if she were expecting him. Goddamn it, how many times did I tell her about that, how many times did I warn her about letting people in without knowing who they are? It could be any kind of weirdo down here. As he came up the last flight of stairs, she was standing in her doorway, watching him; she was still in her nurse's uniform from work, a blue sweater draped around her shoulders. She left the door open for him and went back into her apartment. Jack waited at the top of the stairs for a moment until he caught his breath. I suppose she knew I'd be huffing and puffing too, that I'd need time to rest. He left the door open as he followed her inside; then he thought better of it and went back and closed it.

She was in the living room, curled up in the overstuffed chair, her feet in blue fuzzy slippers tucked under her; she watched him, neither smiling nor not-smiling, as he stood in the doorway. He felt hesitant to go farther into the room.

"I think I just saw a spirit deer."

"What's that?"

"I'm not sure. It looked like a deer but it didn't seem real. Don't Indians have spirit deer and things like that? It was over in the parking lot behind the hotel."

The Building

"What would a deer be doing over there?"

"That's what I mean. Maybe it was a spirit deer."

She didn't say anything. That was a dumb thing to say to her, what the hell does she care about a goddamn deer in a parking lot after everything else that happened today? He crossed the room quickly and went to the window; her collection of china bells on the mantel tinkled faintly with his heavy footsteps. That's something to do, make like I want to look at the job from her window, like I used to. He parted the curtains but the building was only a black looming shape silhouetted against the glow from the main street; all he saw was the reflection of himself pulling back the curtain and a slice of the room behind him—the floor lamp and the lamp on the end table, their white pleated shades throwing crescents of light up and down the walls, the black-haired girl sitting in the chair watching him. Better crank up *Jack*. Pedal to the metal, full bore, leave 'em laughing. No, it's not the time for that either. He dropped the curtain back into place and went over to the couch, letting himself down slowly across from her. He tried sticking his hands in his jacket pockets but he felt like a kid in the principal's office; he rested his hands between his thighs, curled like mirror images of each other.

"I saw your lights on."

"I just got home a little while ago."

Jack nodded. "I was thinking you might be there when they brought him in. It's too bad you had to see him like that. Or maybe not."

She studied him a moment, as if trying to read what he meant by the remark. "I was only there a short time when they brought him and Levon in—the accident must have happened right after I left my apartment. By the time I heard about it and got down to the ER, Bill was dead. They said he never regained consciousness after he reached the hospital."

"I was going to go to the hospital, but there were a lot of things I had to take care of on the job. By the time I could shake loose, I heard he was dead so I didn't bother. I wasn't going to do him any good then."

"I looked for you. Just in case. Later on there was another man there who said he was from the building but I didn't know him. He said he was the architect."

"Must have been Nicholson. Probably asking a lot of questions."

Pamela nodded, thinking about something.

"Mac said Nicholson would make sure his ass was covered."

"What did Mac say about the accident?"

"He said he might fire me."

"Really? I can't believe he'd do that after all you two have been through together."

"Believe it. It seems there are still some surprises left in the world."

Pamela's hands rested one atop the other on her thigh; with one finger she traced the line of an unseen thread on her crisp white skirt. "The architect said Bill was climbing on the column and cut the guy wires."

Jack told her what he knew of what happened, what he had pieced together of Bill's actions and motives.

After she thought about it for a moment, Pamela said, "So, as far as anyone knows, nobody told him to climb up on the column?"

"As far as anyone knows."

"It was all his own doing."

"Yeah. One of the few things he did all day."

"Well, that should free you of any blame."

"Why? Did you think I told him to climb up there?"

"I didn't know. You are the superintendent. And you said Mac might fire you."

"Mac might fire me because I poured some columns after the front office said not to. No, I'm to blame for what happened to Bill because I wasn't on the jobsite when the accident happened. If I had been, I could have stopped him."

"Who said that?"

"I said that." Gregg said What's the matter, Jack, afraid I'll say something you don't want to hear? "It was my job to be there and stop things like that from happening, and I blew it."

"It would be like you to feel that way—you always think you're responsible for everybody to begin with. And then for something like this to happen. . . ."

Why do you think everything depends on you? Why do you always feel responsible for everybody else? "Don't start that responsibility crap again. I know what I know." Little brother was right. I didn't take care of my responsibilities and somebody died. Bill died.

She sat curled in the large chair studying her hands resting on her leg. In the glow of the lamp beside her, the sheen of her black hair caught swirls of light. He had forgotten how pretty she was. Forgotten how much he loved to be with her. After a moment she said, "Do you think it's possible that he cut those wires knowing what would happen?"

"I don't get what you mean."

"I mean do you think he could have done it on purpose? Do you think he could have cut the guy wires knowing that the column would fall and probably kill him?"

"You mean like a kind of suicide?"

Pamela pursed her mouth, as if she tasted the word and found it bitter; she looked at him and nodded.

"Nah. Bill was in his own world a lot of the time, but why would he do a thing like that?"

She thought a moment. "I was breaking it off with Bill. Our relationship, if you want to call it that, was over. I hadn't told him yet, but I'm sure he knew it was coming. And knowing Bill, I'm sure he would take it pretty hard."

I've got this all screwed up, this isn't what I thought she was talking about at all. She's afraid he did it because of her.

"Listen to me," he said, leaning forward. "Whatever happened had nothing to do with you. For one thing, I don't think Bill had the guts to kill himself, for you or for anybody else. Bill did it to himself, all right, but he did it because he wasn't paying attention to his work. It was his job to know which columns were welded and which ones weren't. Whatever happened was his own doing, his own responsibility."

She leaned forward as if to meet him in some middle ground. "And the same goes for you too. Bill did it to himself. It had nothing to do with you. It was his doing. His responsibility." She leaned back again and smiled slightly. "Your words."

Like she thinks she just won something. What is there to win here? Everybody lost this war as far as I can see.

He wanted to get up and go back to the window; he wanted a drink of water, he wanted a drink. In the shadows of the room, small eyes seemed to be watching him: a china cocker spaniel on an end table, a ballerina curtsying on a shelf. A crucifix hanging on the wall. He unzipped his jacket to give himself more room; he stretched his arm out across the back of the couch to ease the ache in his elbow.

Pamela folded her hands as if in an act of prayer; she seemed to have been considering something and made her decision.

"I feel sorry for Bill. I'm sorry he had to die that way. Or in any way. I'm sorry he wasn't happier in his life. I suppose I always did feel sorry for him, that's probably why I got involved with him in the first place. After you steered him in my direction." She glanced at him to see if there was any reaction to what she said, then added, "He was very naive in many ways."

"Bill didn't have a lot of experience with women. I'm pretty sure you were his first girlfriend, besides his wife."

"Is that why you gave me to him? Because I did have a lot of experience?"

"Pamela—"

"No, you don't have to say anything. That's all in the past now, I shouldn't have said anything about it. We were talking about responsibility; well, there was nothing that said I had to go on seeing him, no matter how he found his way over here." She thought a moment, looking a little wistful. "And he certainly was a very attractive man."

"I've regretted a lot of things. . . ."

She cocked her head. "You? I never thought I'd hear you say that. I thought Jack Crawford made it point to live without regrets."

"There haven't been very many," he grinned, trying to regain some position in the conversation. But the words rang hollow even to him. *Maybe that isn't true either. I don't know. God, how do you know what you really think? What you really want?*

She appeared to weigh carefully exactly what she was going to say. "Bill would tell me that he didn't want anything from me. He would talk about his obligations to his wife and how he couldn't make a commitment to me, he would talk about how he wanted an arrangement where we were both free to come and go. But the fact was he wanted a commitment from me as binding as any marriage that ever was. He wanted a guarantee that I would always be here. He couldn't accept that I might be content with the way things were. He couldn't believe that I wouldn't be looking for something more from somebody else. That it was enough for me to see him whenever he could work some time."

"That's one of those things that sounds real good when you first say it. But it's a different story when you're alone too many nights or too many weekends. Or when another Christmas or

Thanksgiving or your birthday rolls around and you're sitting here all by yourself again."

"Bill never understood who I am. Sure, there might be times when I'd be heartsick because I couldn't be with . . . the other person. Because somebody else was with that person and I wasn't. But even if I was lonesome for a while, I'd know it was better than never being with that other person at all. And if I did feel empty for a while, I'd never let that other person know it. If anybody doubts that, then you don't know me very well."

"I think I know you." Do I?

"Do you? Sometimes I wonder if anybody does. No one seems to understand that I've got a life of my own. I'm not looking for a marriage, I doubt if I ever will. There's a lot of things in this world I want to do, places I want to go. Maybe it is too late for me to become a doctor now, but I want to go back to school and take some graduate work. I'm real good at waiting, Jack. I've spent most of my life waiting to find out what I want. And when I know what I want, I fight for it with everything I have."

"Bill was a lucky guy," he said morosely.

She leveled her brown eyes at him. "You and I both know we're not talking about Bill here. That's why I'll always feel bad about him. Bill was right to feel that there would always be somebody else in my life. He got caught in the middle between you and me. But I'm strong enough to live with that too."

No, we're not talking about Bill here. I guess I got this wrong too. I guess I was the one who wanted a commitment, I was the one looking for guarantees. What I wanted her to be was another Ellie. I preferred knowing I'd already lost her to Bill than run the risk of losing her to somebody else later on. Run the risk of love running out.

He shifted his weight on the couch, trying to get comfortable. "I told you once that we're too much alike to be together."

"You told me that when you were looking for some excuse to stop seeing me. You meant that we both like to run. And yes, you were right, we do both like to run. Or at least I did. Now I'm perfectly content to sit."

"Yeah. That's why you took down the curtain in your shower and danced for the guys every morning."

She was watching him warily, as if to see from which direction he would come at her next. You just can't leave it alone, can you? You've got to try to hurt her as much as you can, don't you? When she didn't say anything, he went on.

"He never told you that everybody could see you on the building, did he?"

"No, he never did."

"So he failed his test."

"Yes, he failed his test." She looked at her hands and then back at him. "But I wasn't doing it for him anyway."

"I know that."

"I was trying to remind you of what you were missing."

You didn't have to. I already knew. "I guess I failed my test then too, didn't I?"

She unfolded her legs and got up from the chair and came over to the couch; she sat away from him at first, watching him, then lay down and curled up on the cushions, her cheek resting on his leg. When she spoke, he thought he could feel her breath through his pants leg.

"Let's try not to hurt each other anymore, okay?"

For a moment he didn't know what to do with his hand; finally, he rested it on her shoulder. She reached up and brought it down beside her; she noticed the deep scratches on the back of his wrist and started to say something, then caught herself. She kissed his knuckles and nestled his hand under her chin.

"I'm tired, Pamela. Really tired."

After a moment she said, "You can stay here tonight. If you'd like."

"That's not the kind of tired I mean."

"I know. That's why I offered."

This is probably your last chance. Ever. You got the guts to try it? "Yeah. I'd like that."

"I'd like that too." She lay there, curled around his fist, then twisted her head around to look at him. "You'll have to put the curtain back up in the window, if you want to take a shower in the morning."

"Yeah, I'll put the curtain back up. We don't want to scare people, do we?"

She smiled and put her head back down.

He could feel the weight of her against him, her warmth. I'm home. This is where I belong, with this woman. I don't know how long it will last and it doesn't matter. It's lasting now. He sat there a long time, at peace, feeling his calm and strength slowly beginning to return. And thought about the building. Reminded himself that Mac hadn't fired him yet. There was still a lot of cleanup to take care of from the accident; the Old Man hadn't said anything more about walking off the project either, so he might as well go ahead and start forming up the next pour. He'd have to get the new ironworker foreman to order the steel to replace the column that fell. And he still had to tell Chucky to move his pipes, and he still had to get Chalmers a new hose. Drake might want to get rid of me, but I'm sure as hell not going to go easy. They'll have to beat me off with a stick. It's still my building. Even if they do shut it down, there's still a lot of work has to be done.

Acknowledgements

There are four people—friends, actually; dream catchers—without whom I could never have brought these books to publication:

Barbara Clark
Kim Francis
Dave Meek
Jack Ritchie

I also thank Eileen Chetti for struggling through my quirks of punctuation; Aimee Downing for her patience with all my questions about self-publishing; and Bob Gelston, who is always around to answer questions and take on anything else that's needed. And then, of course, there's my wife Marty. . . .

*

Richard Snodgrass lives in Pittsburgh, PA with his wife Marty and two indomitable female tuxedo cats, raised from feral kittens, named Frankie and Becca.

*

To read more about the Furnass series, the town of Furnass, and special features for *The Building*—including a Reader's Study Guide, author interviews, and omitted scenes—go to www.RichardSnodgrass.com.

Made in the USA
Coppell, TX
06 December 2021

67295013R00226